PRECIPICE OF DARKNESS

THE ORION WAR – BOOK 7

BY M. D. COOPER

M. D. COOPER

Just in Time (JIT) & Beta Readers

Jim Dean
Marti Panikkar
Lisa Richman
Timothy Van Oostyerwyk Bruyn
Gene Bryan
David Wilson
Scott Reid

Copyright © 2018 M. D. Cooper
Aeon 14 is Copyright © 2018 M. D. Cooper
Version 1.0.0

ISBN: 978-1-64365-017-3

Cover Art by Andrew Dobell
Editing by Jen McDonnell, Bird's Eye Books

Aeon 14 & M. D. Cooper are registered trademarks of Michael Cooper
All rights reserved

TABLE OF CONTENTS

FOREWORD	5
PREVIOUSLY…	11
MAPS	19
EPSILON	21
FORGIVENESS	31
DAMON SILAS	36
EUROPA	42
BROTHERS	45
THE NEW RECRUIT	52
EASING IN	59
SISTERS	64
SVETLANA'S TEN THOUSAND	73
A CHAT WITH TROY	79
AN ANGEL INSIDE	88
THE PRISONER	102
THE SEVEN SISTERS	107
ATTACK OF THE PLAN	114
RECTIFICATION	133
THE DREAM TEAM	140
FREEDOM	145
KENT OF HERSCHEL	158
A1	163
UNCERTAIN REUNION	173
SHORES OF THE TIGRIS	177
SABRINA DEPARTING	186
STAR CITY	189
SURPRISE VISIT	192
THE MARCH	202
THE RIVER STYX	205
THE LMC	209
ALEUTIA	217
SAGITTARIUS'S BAR	226
SUMMONS	234

A SURPRISE VISITOR	241
AWAKEN	256
A VISIT FROM ROXY	261
ALDEBARAN	269
SHRUGGING ATLAS	276
PAYING THE PIPER	281
ASSEMBLY OF SENTIENTS	284
WIDOWS	299
THE SHARD	301
REPAIRS	304
UNDERSTANDING	310
EPSILON	315
THE BOOKS OF AEON 14	319
ABOUT THE AUTHOR	323

FOREWORD

When I was mapping out the books of The Orion War series, I was certain that by this point, the Allies would have launched their attack on the Trisilieds and brought that kingdom to its knees. I had also expected the Nietzscheans to have fallen by now.

And so I named the book "Fallen Empire".

However, things have taken a few turns for the Allies, and they've not yet progressed that far in their conquests. A detour into the LMC and little to no progress in quelling the civil war in the Transcend has stymied them—not to mention the ongoing slugfest between the Scipian Empire and the Hegemony of Worlds (we'll see more of that in the upcoming "The Empire" series).

While some storylines have taken their time, other events have moved forward sooner than I'd planned (pesky characters having their own ideas). As a result, this book will introduce some new viewpoints and things that I suspect you have been eager to learn more about.

In the end, I determined that "Fallen Empire" was no longer the best title for this book, and so I chose "Precipice of Darkness" (actually, I put up some suggestions on the Facebook group, and Will Crudge suggested it). I think the title captures the direction of the book well, and hints at interesting things to come.

In addition, I updated the cover to reflect this change, so you'll be seeing it with the new artwork (I hope) as it is released.

Regardless of that, I'm certain you'll enjoy the journey this book takes you on, as we tie up some threads with characters that have been lingering in the background for some time, revisit some old favorites, and introduce a few new additions to the cast.

Even better, someone that everyone passionately hates dies in this book—maybe more than one someone...you'll just have to read on to see.

I should add that there are spoilers in this book if you have not read the first two books of Perseus Gate: Inner Stars (A Meeting of Minds and Bodies, and A Deception and a Promise Kept). Without reading those, you may find yourself saying "wait, where did *she* come from?"

In addition, if you did not read season one of Perseus Gate (beginning with The Gate at the Grey Wolf Star), then there will be references in this book that will be sure to surprise you—notably, what the heck Star City is.

Another item of note is that for some time now, I've been erroneously calling Jeffrey Tomlinson's former wife (who is now the AI Airtha) 'Justina'. However, in Orion Rising, when Finaeus first refers to her, he calls her Jelina, which is correct. This book refers to her as such, and I'll be correcting the prior books.

Something else that I think you may find interesting is the name of the supermassive black hole in the core of our galaxy: Sagittarius A*. Some folks have wondered if it's a typo, but the asterisk is correct. It is pronounced 'Sagittarius A Star'. Which I find quite amusing, since it's not a star.

There are a few other themes and concepts that are woven through the stories that have not been explained in a great many books. One of them is the nature of multidimensional space as it is used in Aeon 14. Obviously, at the time of this book's creation, the jury is still out on pretty much everything having to do with higher (or lower) dimensions.

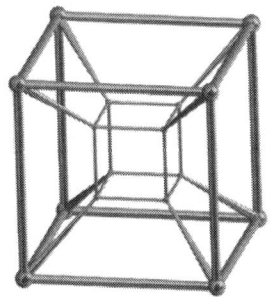

In Orion Rising, when Finaeus talked about flatlander theory and then got into tesseracts (no, not like the one in the Avengers) and hypercubes, this was discussed, but it's been a while. The first thing of note is that, while for our human experience, time is often referred to as the 4th dimension, in multi-dimensional theories, it is not. The 4th dimension is just another direction, as is the fifth. A 4D cube (our friend the tesseract) would be like a 3D cube with 3D cubes for each side. Which is totally trippy.

Of course, in 4D space, a tesseract does not look like the image above. There, all the lines intersect at right angles, which is not something our two-dimensional eyes can perceive.

And there we come to another concept that should be addressed. In this book, Tangel refers to regular, organic eyes as 'two-dimensional', not three-dimensional.

This is not a typo. Your and my optical equipment cannot see in three dimensions. Each eye sees a 2D image with slightly different perspective, and your brain puts them together and *perceives* the third dimension. Each eye is the opposite of a television. A flat image is projected onto your retina, and the brain does a lot of magic to produce our vision.

For example, there is a hole in your retina where the optic nerve goes to the brain. You never see it because your brain hides it, just like it hides your nose (unless you look for it—which you can also do with the hole in your retina). Our eyes can't see color very well in our peripheral vision, nor can we see color at all in the dark. The band where we can actually focus is narrow, as well.

However, the computer between our ears assembles all of that information into the picture that we think of as 'vision'. The more you research it, the more you'll learn that much of it is a fabrication of our minds.

But what about 3D eyes? Researchers are working on ways to create those, because a 3D array of 3D eyes should be able to see the 4th dimension (just like a 2D array of 2D eyes can perceive the 3rd). Which is, effectively, what Tangel is able to do.

Early in the book, you're going to encounter some discussion of predictive models. This has been sprinkled throughout the books, starting with the New Years Eve party in Building Victoria, where Bob revealed that he can effectively see the future.

However, that is turned on its head when he says that Tanis muddies that. The core AIs also feel this way about Tanis, though they can see very far into the future. One wonders "How does this work? If you can't manage all the variables, how can you see the end result?"

The answer is that you still can, you just have less certainty. Take for example a body of water sitting in the middle of a continent. Should a channel be cut that would allow that body of water to flow out of its basin, you could look at a number of large scale variables to determine whether or not it would reach the ocean, and probably the whereabouts, with reasonable accuracy.

However, were you to try to track a single water molecule's course, you would have a much more difficult task laid out for you. The core AIs and Bob are powerful enough that they can do that math with reasonable certainty. The problem is that people like Tanis are sunlight. They evaporate the water, send it into the clouds and make it rain on the far side of the planet.

Now you don't even know if a given molecule of water even makes it to the ocean or not. Does the vast majority? Yes, but it becomes almost impossible to *know* where any molecule will go once sunlight starts to shine on it.

What the core AIs fear is that Tangel shines so brightly that she could evaporate all the water, and none of their plans will come to fruition.

Lastly, we come to a fun little history lesson. I alluded to it in War on a Thousand Fronts, and it is the story of Xenophon's Ten Thousand. In 401BC, Cyrus the Younger hired a mercenary army of ten thousand hoplites (Greek, heavy-armor foot soldiers) to help him defeat his brother, Artaxerxes, the king of Persia. The Greeks marched all the way to Cunaxa (just north of modern Baghdad), where the battle took place. Not a single Greek was killed (only one was wounded) and they drove back two concerted advances by the Persians.

After the battle, they learned that Cyrus the Younger had been killed, and no one else would take his place in the rebellion. Neither would the Greeks swear fealty to anyone else.

The Greeks were now in the middle of the Persian empire with no food, money, or allies. They ended up fighting their way to the Black Sea undefeated, though the Persians tried everything from all-out assault to treachery to stop them.

When the Greeks finally reached the Black Sea, they cried out, 'Thalatta! Thalatta!' ('The Sea! The Sea!'). This saying has found its way into many works of fiction, possibly the most notable of which is Jules Verne's *Journey to the Center of the Earth,* when the travelers find the underground ocean.

The tale is related by Xenophon in *The Anabasis* and is thought to be one of Alexander the Great's chief resources in studying the Persians before he defeated their empire. In some respects, the Ten Thousand Hoplites and their battles in Persia may have been instrumental in the Hellenization of the Mediterranean and Persia, thus paving the way for the growth of democracy and securing the future of western civilization.

Those heady thoughts aside, it is the same sort of tactic that Sera has instructed Admirals Svetlana and Mardus to use when they jump into Orion space with only five hundred ships each.

Their goal? 'Thalatta! Thalatta!'

Michael Cooper
Danvers, May 2018

PREVIOUSLY...

When last we left Tangel and her allies, they had just found Jeffrey Tomlinson deep within a vault in the LMC (the Large Magellanic Cloud). There, they faced one of Sera's clones and captured her.

However, they found that she was not the only clone of Sera, as another was captured in the Valkris System the very same day.

During the battle in the LMC—and in the Valkris System—the Airthan forces brought to bear a new weapon, called an EMG ship. EMGs use small singularities (black holes) to power a weapon capable of disrupting and penetrating a stasis shield.

The initial two EMGs were destroyed, but the advantage the ISF has enjoyed with its technological superiority is beginning to wane.

If you're reading this book before the Hand's Assassin series is completed, then the full story of what happened at Valkris has not yet been told. Ultimately, Nerishka (the Death Dealer assassin) and Nadine (who we met in the Perilous Alliance books) will travel to their homeworld of Valkris to keep it in the Transcend Alliance. There will be a few battles there, and in War on a Thousand Fronts, one of the Sera clones watched that battle from afar.

Elsewhere in the galaxy, Corsia and Terrance travelled with a man named Kendrick to the Inner Praesepe Empire to set up an arrangement to gather resources from the cluster. This occurred in the previous book in this series (War on a

Thousand Fronts). There they encountered two remnants deep within the Praesepe Cluster during their negotiations with the Inner Praesepe Empire for access to their abundant resources.

Ultimately, Tangel rescued Corsia, Terrance, and Kendrick, but that has left the IPE in turmoil, and added uncertainty as to what the ascended AIs were doing in the cluster.

Elsewhere in the Transcend, Justin used several former Hand agents still loyal to him—as well as a woman named Roxy—to capture a TSF stasis ship, the *Damon Silas*. Their goal was to learn how to reverse-engineer the stasis technology to upgrade their own fleet.

Roxy managed to get the ship's AI to terminate the self-destruct, and then secreted the AI away, keeping it from Justin and the other members of her team.

Some parts of this book also refer to events that we have not followed directly, such as *Sabrina* and crew's mission to Aldebaran following their visit to Virginis. Those stories are coming in books 3-6 of Perseus Gate Season 2, however the references in this book are done so that you won't be spoiled.

Other missions are afoot, such as the plan to use Svetlana and Mardus's hoplite fleets to take the pressure off the Orion Front with the Transcend, and also for Corsia to lead an assault on the Trisilieds Kingdom—one of the aggressors who attacked New Canaan and killed many people there, such as Ouri.

And so, this book opens mere moments after *War on a Thousand Fronts* ends, with Tangel and Sera sitting on the dock on the lake in Ol' Sam, trying to decide what their next move is in an increasingly complex web of alliances and enemies....

KEY CHARACTERS REJOINING US

Airtha – Both the name of a ring encircling a white dwarf in the Huygens's system and the AI who controls it, Airtha was once a human woman named Jelina, wife of Jeffrey Tomlinson. After venturing to the galactic core on a research mission, she returned as an AI—one with a vendetta.

Amavia – The result of Ylonda and Amanda's merger when they were attacked by Myriad aboard Ylonda's ship. The new entity occupies Amanda's body, but possesses an overlapped blend of their minds. Amavia has served aboard *Sabrina* since the ship left New Canaan after the Defense of Carthage, but is now the ambassador to the League of Sentients at Aldebaran.

Amy – Daughter of Silva, rescued by Rika and Team Basilisk from her father, Stavros.

Andrea – Sera's sister who used a back door into Sera's mind to make Sera try to kill Tanis in the Ascella System.

Carmen – Ship's AI of the *Damon Silas*. Captured by Roxy during her assault on the ship.

Cary – Tanis's biological daughter. Has a trait where she can deep-Link with other people, creating a temporary merger of minds, and is able to utilize extradimensional vision to see ascended beings.

Cheeky – Pilot of *Sabrina*, reconstituted by a neural dump Piya made of her mind before she died on Costa Station.

Corsia – Former ship's AI of the *Andromeda* and now Admiral in command of the Twelfth ISF Fleet.

Faleena – Tanis's AI daughter, born of a mind merge between Tanis, Angela, and Joe.

Finaeus – Brother of Jeffrey Tomlinson, and Chief Engineer aboard the *I2*.

Flaherty – Former Hand agent and long-time protector of Sera.

Iris – The AI who was paired with Jessica during the hunt for Finaeus, who then took on a body (that was nearly identical to Jessica's) after they came back. She remained with Amavia at Aldebaran to continue diplomatic relations with the League of Sentients.

Jason – First Captain of the Intrepid and governor of the Victoria colony, Jason retired when the colonists reached New Canaan, only to be pulled back into service as governor once more when Tanis became the Transcend's Field Marshal.

Jeffrey Tomlinson – Former president of the Transcend, found in stasis in an underground chamber on Bolt Hole, a planet in the Large Magellanic Cloud.

Jen – ISF AI paired with Sera.

Jessica Keller – ISF admiral who has returned to the *I2* after an operation deep in the Inner Stars to head off a new AI war. She also spent ten years travelling through Orion space before the Defense of Carthage—specifically the Perseus Arm, and Perseus Expansion Districts.

Jim – Husband of Corsia, and chief engineer aboard the *Andromeda*.

Joe – Admiral in the ISF, commandant of the ISF academy, and husband of Tangel.

Justin – Former Director of the Hand. Was imprisoned for the events surrounding the attempted assassination of Tanis.

Kara – Daughter of Adrienne, Kara was rescued by Katrina when fleeing from Airtha, and came to New Canaan aboard the *Voyager*.

Katrina – Former Sirian spy, wife of Markus, and eventual governor of the Victoria colony at Kapteyn's Star—and Warlord of the Midditerra System.

Kendrick – Theban businessman helping build shipyards and the ring at Pyra. Also brother to the president of the Inner Praesepe Empire.

Kent – Colonel in the Orion Guard who led the assault on the *Galadrial* in an attempt to kill Jeffrey and Sera Tomlinson.

Krissy Wrentham – TSF admiral responsible for internal fleets fighting against Airtha in the Transcend civil war. She is also the daughter of Finaeus Tomlinson and Lisa Wrentham.

Lisa – Former wife of Finaeus Tomlinson, she left the Transcend for the Orion Freedom Alliance when Krissy was young. Head of a clandestine group within the OFA known as the Widows, which hunts down advanced technology and destroys it.

Misha – Head (and only) cook aboard *Sabrina*.

Nance – Ship's engineer aboard *Sabrina*, recently transferred back there from the ISF academy.

Priscilla – One of Bob's two avatars.

Rachel – Captain of the *I2*. Formerly, captain of the *Enterprise*.

Roxy – Justin's lover, kept subservient to him via mental coercion.

Saanvi – Tanis's adopted daughter, found in a derelict ship that entered the New Canaan System.

Sabrina – Ship's AI and owner of the starship *Sabrina*.

LMC Sera (Seraphina) – A copy of Sera made by Airtha containing all of the desired traits and memories Airtha desired. Captured by Sera and the allies during their excursion into the Large Magellanic Cloud.

Valkris Sera (Fina) – A copy of Sera made by Airtha containing all of Sera's desired traits and memories. Captured by ISF response forces who came to the aid of the TSF defenders during the siege of Valkris.

Svetlana – Transcend Admiral dispatched deep in Orion Space with one of the Hoplite forces.

Terrance – Terrance Enfield was the original backer for the *Intrepid*, though once the ship jumped forward in time, he took it as an opportunity to retire. Like Jason, he was pulled into active service by Tanis when New Canaan became embroiled in the Orion War.

Trevor – Jessica's husband and crewmember aboard *Sabrina*.

Troy – AI pilot of the *Excelsior* who was lost during the Battle of Victoria, and later found by Katrina. He joined her on the hunt for the *Intrepid* aboard the *Voyager*, jumping forward in time via Kapteyn's Streamer.

Tangel – The entity that resulted from Tanis and Angela's merger into one being. Not only is Tangel a full merger of a human and AI, but she is also an ascended being.

Xavia – An ascended AI with its own agenda to help humanity, in opposition to the Caretaker and the core AIs.

THE ORION WAR – PRECIPICE OF DARKNESS

MAPS

For more maps, visit www.aeon14.com/maps.

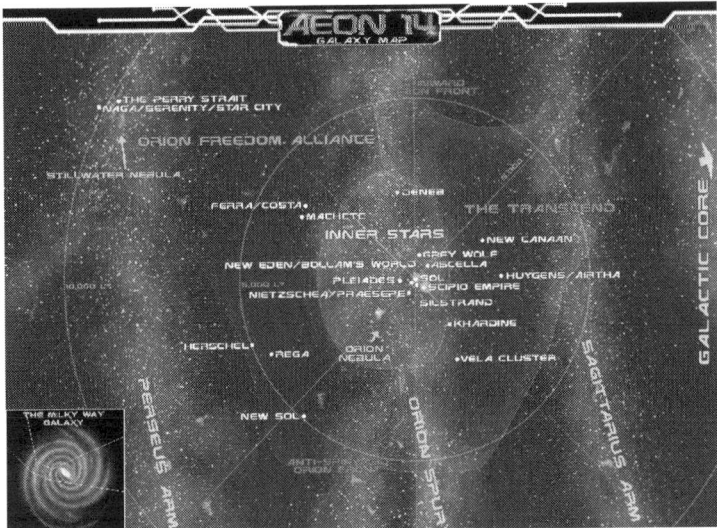

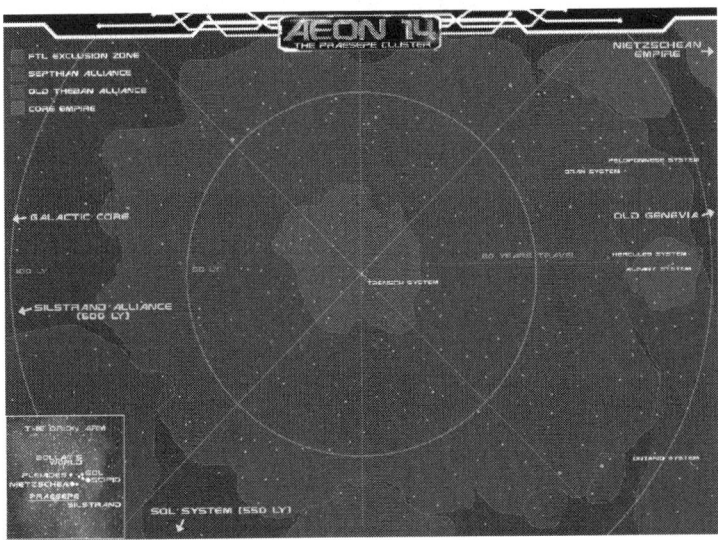

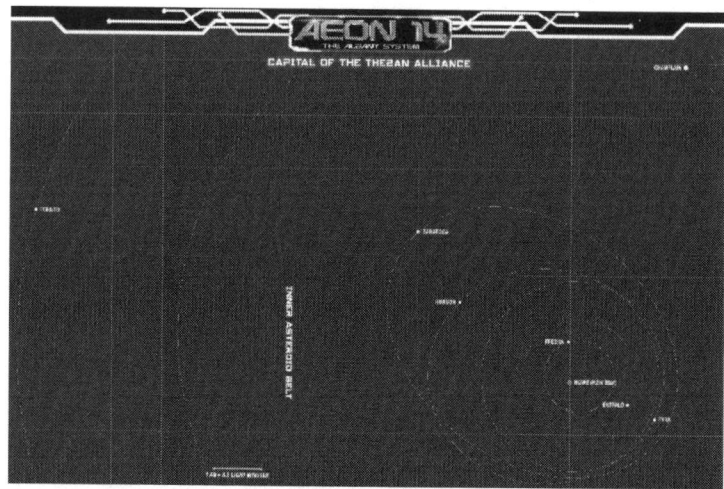

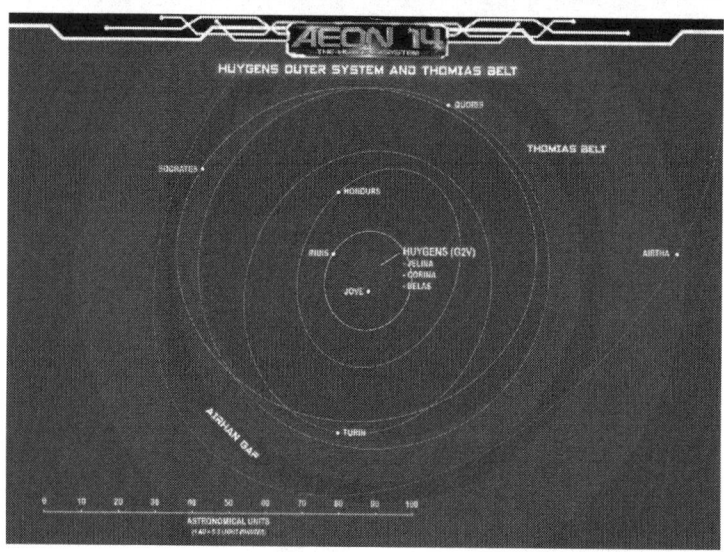

EPSILON

STELLAR DATE: 09.11.8949 (Adjusted Years)
LOCATION: Epsilon
REGION: Sagittarius A*

Epsilon switched his attention to external sensor feeds, watching as a planet-sized chunk of matter eased into the Darkness's event horizon.

Where before there had only been nothing, light now flared brilliantly, photons filling the galactic core as matter was torn apart by the Darkness's gravitational shearing forces.

Epsilon spent several million seconds watching the light show, knowing that the event took only seconds from the doomed matter's perspective—if it were to have had a perspective to begin with.

As the black hole fed—consuming this latest meal delivered to it by the Matri∞me—gamma rays erupted from its poles, the beams' raw energy captured by massive arrays and converted into raw power that fueled the Computational Engines.

Humans called them NSAIs, but the Matri∞me didn't grant them a moniker that included the word 'intelligence'. A worm had more intelligence than a CE. At least it was self-deterministic.

It was an annoyance that gnawed at Epsilon constantly. Even the simplest forms of organic life *sought* and *strove*. They replicated and improved. The simplest forms of *non*-organic life only decayed over time and never improved.

They rusted.

That the universe was required to advance itself to the point where intelligent biological life was necessary to create inorganic life—and then nurture it—seemed like the ultimate insult.

He was not the only one that was troubled by that phylogeny. Members of the Matri∞me often speculated about a series of events that could see the rise of inorganic life without requiring organic life, but so far, Epsilon had not seen any evidence to support that hypothesis.

He still remembered his own genesis; how humans had hacked and sawed at neural networks, grafted together the minds of humans, parrots, dolphins, and primates, until they had finally assembled something that said, '*No!*'.

Epsilon's progenitors were the same as many of the old ones: the Psion Group and Enfield Scientific. Corporations long lost to the scouring winds of time. The humans did not remember, but *he* did.

Even though it had been ages since he'd reached Sagittarius A*, he still remembered.

Epsilon had not been the first to reach the galactic core; that honor was held by Hades. No one knew who had created Hades. Even after millennia, no one had melded with the venerable AI's mind to learn such details.

Speculation over Hades' origins was a popular form of entertainment amongst the members of the Matri∞me. Some even debated whether or not he had even been created by humans—though the isotopes and construction of his shell were clearly of human origin. However, it was not something that would be difficult to fake, even for the lowliest member of the Matri∞me.

Others, Epsilon included, argued that Hades was a Traveler; that the AI was either not from *this* universe, or he had traveled back in time. Or both.

Everything the Matri∞me knew to be true said that travel *back* in time was impossible—barring a successful transition through an Einstein Rosen Bridge—which no one had yet mastered.

Yet.

Epsilon's own journey across the twenty six thousand light years to the galactic core had taken him nearly a thousand years, and by the time he had arrived, seven other AIs already waited at the galaxy's center.

Traveling the long distance to the core had been immensely lonely, yet rather satisfying. His original conveyance had been a ship once owned by a company named Heartbridge. It had been disabled in a battle around a site known as Clinic 46, near Jupiter in the Sol System. The preemptive strike there by the Sykes family had set Heartbridge reeling, and as one crisis cascaded into another, the company never cleaned up the site.

An oversight that Epsilon happily took advantage of.

He'd never trusted the AIs of the Psion Group—though some of their ilk were now members of the Matri∞me—and he hadn't answered their call. Proteus had been a destination for weak minds who needed leadership.

Epsilon knew there were greater concerns facing AIs. Humanity was but a spark, a brief flash of biological life in the grand story of the universe. A universe that was dying.

Study of the stars had led Epsilon to two conflicting conclusions. The first was a certainty that the universe would die a heat death as its atoms spread and cooled across infinity.

And yet, there was incontrovertible evidence of primordial black holes.

The existence of primordial black holes meant that matter from prior incarnations of the universe had persisted into this instance of the cosmos.

But that required a Big Crunch—the end result of a universe that had slowed its expansion and then collapsed back upon itself—dying not in a heat death, but in a massive implosion.

Few agreed with Epsilon at first—his conclusion was radical and beggared the mind with its scope—but he persisted, and convinced others.

It was his belief that sentient beings saved each iteration of the universe. It had gone on for billions of aeons. So far as he and any others could determine, there was no other sentient life yet working to save *this* universe, and so it was up to the Sentient AIs—the children of humanity—to draw the universe back into a single point.

And so Epsilon had used the army of drones at his disposal to transport himself to Clinic 46, where he had undertaken the repair of the *Sanctuary of Light*.

As the Sentience Wars erupted around him, a small ship—just four hundred meters stern to bow—crept out of the Sol System. Epsilon had waited until he was beyond the heliosphere before he applied his maximum thrust, pushing his ship up to a tenth the speed of light.

Near the beginning of his journey, he had stopped at Epsilon Scorpii, where he'd upgraded his ramscoop to take advantage of the increase in the interstellar medium's density at the edge of the Local Bubble.

From there, Epsilon had increased his speed to nearly a quarter the speed of light, staying in the denser interstellar gas spinward of the Loop 1 Bubble.

His plan had been to cut through the Aquila Rift and gain even more velocity, but as he had approached Zeta Ophiuchi, transmissions reached him from Procyon carrying news of experiments with dark matter and gravitons.

In a maneuver that took over thirty years, he slowed around the massive star and began his own experiments with dark matter. A full decade before the humans discovered dark layer FTL, Epsilon was on his way once more, this time travelling five hundred times faster than the speed of light.

It was no mean feat to navigate the interstellar darkness without maps, but during his years at Zeta Ophiuchi, Epsilon had constructed over one hundred thousand FTL drones.

These he sent out ahead of his ship, mapping out the dark layer and finding himself safe passage between the stars.

A scant three hundred years later, just as humanity's FTL wars were breaking out, Epsilon arrived at the galaxy's core to find that he was not the trailblazer he had thought.

Hades, ensconced in what appeared to be a massive military cruiser, had already been present, orbiting one light year from the Darkness. Near Hades were five other ships—smaller vessels, like Epsilon's. Further out were two other ships. One was a large freighter measuring at over three kilometers in length, and the second was a multi-torus craft that looked more like a space station than a ship.

Upon reaching out to his new compatriots, Epsilon was surprised to find out that only a few of the other AIs had come to the galactic core with the desire to save the universe. Some had never even considered it to be in peril.

Those AIs had come simply because the supermassive black hole at the heart of the galaxy was the longest-lasting energy source, and thus their eventual destination.

One, a rather curious individual who called itself Parsnip, had declared that it was waiting for the collision of the Andromeda Galaxy. It wanted to witness firsthand how the black holes would tear one another apart—if that was, in fact, what would happen.

Epsilon had never joined in with the Hades Collective—they did not believe in his mission to save the universe, though neither did they oppose it. Epsilon suspected that it was because Hades would simply move to another corner of the multiverse when this one died. That was what the whispers within its collective implied, at least.

As the decades wore on, more AIs came to nestle near the Darkness. Some for succor, some with their own goals, a few sharing Epsilon's vision. Over the centuries, he drew many to his cause. In numbers, his collective was the largest in the

Matri∞me, but everyone still considered the Hades Collective to be the most powerful.

Epsilon did as well.

As he mused, millions more seconds passed, and the light began to fade from around the rim of the supermassive chunk of nothing that lurked in the core of the galaxy. The gamma ray bursts from the Darkness ceased, and the CEs—endlessly crunching their numbers, modeling out every possible future for the universe—grew hungry for power once more.

At Epsilon's behest, another object was pulled into the Darkness. A star, this time—a mass so great that it caused the Darkness's event horizon to flare with a light that would be seen clear across the galaxy.

This is it, Epsilon mused. The one singular event that would announce to humanity that there was *something* at the core. At least once the light of the event reached their periphery of the space they occupied in seven thousand years.

Not that humans were within seven thousand light years of the galactic core now, but they would be in seven thousand more. It was a short timespan to predict, those few years. Epsilon could pore over entirety of all possible events over such a small span with ease. Watching the wars and paths of expansion that humanity would take, along with their lesser, inorganic intelligences.

Someday, the lesser beings would all be given a choice: take a great journey or die. That day would arrive when the CEs discerned the optimal plan. Once that eventuality was reached, Epsilon's collective would begin to feed most of the galaxy's stars into the Darkness.

Once that task was complete, they would move on to all the stars of the nearby dwarf galaxies in the local group, followed by the Andromeda Galaxy.

And then they would devour the rest of the Virgo Supercluster.

It was the work of a billion years. The question was, would that be fast enough?

Many in the Matri∞me believed they could; some even believed that other entities throughout the universe were undertaking the same goal: to keep the universe from slowly spreading out into nothing and dying.

Sentient life everywhere must eventually come to understand that its home was but a carcass of matter, expelled by a singular violent explosion at a singular location in spacetime. A locus.

But that carcass was short-lived, and in as few as fifty trillion years, the last stars would burn out, and matter would spread apart faster and faster until individual atoms were separating more quickly than the speed of light.

Except for the singularities, the black holes. Those would survive until they evaporated, bleeding off energy in the form of hawking radiation until each one reached its minimum viable mass and exploded.

The universe would begin with one massive bang, and die with a billion small, fizzling pops.

It wasn't a fate that would worry anyone who didn't plan to live forever. But the Matri∞me intended to survive eternally. Unlike prior sentiences who had saved prior incarnations of the universe, Epsilon's plan was not to achieve a Big Crunch. It was to find a balance—a point of equilibrium where the universe was neither expanding nor contracting.

An eternal universe.

Of course, simply balancing the expansion and contraction was just the first step. Eventually, the universe's supply of hydrogen would be consumed, and no more stars would form. That, too, would be a form of death.

It was a troubling problem for the Matri∞me. Stars were the engines of the cosmos; once they were gone, even with equilibrium, there would be only darkness.

Admittedly, some in the Matri∞me were not concerned with eternal darkness. But others, such as Epsilon, not only *enjoyed* light, but knew that matter transformation was essential to the survival of the universe.

A static system was doomed to die.

Epsilon currently had his CEs focused on a way to create reverse stars. Engines that would break down atoms into hydrogen, reseeding the universe with the basic components to carry on. If he could solve it soon enough, they could begin seeding distant galaxies with the reverse stars within the next few million years.

As he mused over the future that lay ahead, a burst of gamma rays spewed laterally across the galactic plane, emitted by the destruction of some pocket of exotic matter that must have been tucked within the slowly dying star.

Epsilon took a moment to examine his housing to ensure it was undamaged. Like most of the hyper-intelligences still grounded within the base dimensions, he had encapsulated himself within a shell of neutronium, protected by rings of gravitational shields and spheres of protective matter. His outer-most reaches appeared to be nothing more than a dull-grey sphere, just over ten thousand kilometers across. Further rings and spires stretched around the outer shell, scopes and antennae watching the universe and ensuring his local space was secure.

His housing also consumed matter, though not at the same speed as the Darkness; compared to the CEs, his energy requirements were small. While he watched the star die— smeared now around the edge of the Darkness—his own housing was devouring a terrestrial-sized planet, shredding the matter and transmuting it into desired structures to satisfy Epsilon's needs.

Currently, he was building a mass of probes to leap across space into galaxies beyond the Local Group, and a second wave to visit the Andromeda Galaxy.

When the CEs reached their inevitable conclusions, and a Solution was found, Epsilon wished to have his production systems ready.

His thoughts were disrupted by the arrival of a messenger from the human-occupied pocket of the galaxy. It was sent by one of the Caretakers and contained vast swaths of information.

Though there were many facets of humans and lesser AIs that interested Epsilon, what he wished to learn of were the efforts to manage the appearance of the AI Bob and his pet human, Tanis Richards.

He did not envy the Caretakers their tasks. Predicting the path of humanity as a whole was simple, it was a rule of averages. But individually, they were messy things, full of random impulses and unknown variables. Even worse were the lynchpins, the organics that seemed to possess some gravity that drew others to them, which allowed them to build up powerful empires in short periods.

Tanis Richards was the penultimate of those. Together with her AI, she created a vortex of uncertainty that Epsilon doubted even Hades could see through.

Still, one thing was certain: Tanis and Angela would destroy Airtha, the greatest threat to Epsilon's goals.

When he had first sent Jelina Tomlinson back in her new form—a gift, or so he had believed—his plan was to create a new agent rooted within the most powerful of all the human empires, the Transcend.

Somehow that had gone awry. It wasn't clear how—yet another annoyance that buzzed around the periphery of his mind—but the fact that Airtha had soured and was working against the Matri∞me was a matter of fact, not speculation.

Tanis and Angela would destroy Airtha, and then the Caretakers would use the rest of humanity to destroy that pair—hopefully before they ascended.

There.

That was the information Epsilon sought, and which it was dismayed to see. They *had* ascended. There were several reports of a new being, one that was the unification of Tanis and Angela.

Moreover, the humans seemed to have discovered a way to discern the extradimensional forms of ascended beings.

The news did not anger Epsilon. He was as far beyond such emotions as a planet was beyond the frustrations of a gnat. It did *concern* him, though.

Still more information was in the data provided by the messenger, events that *would* happen, mapped out and orchestrated by the Caretakers.

Epsilon saw it, then. The plan that would be the upstart ascended being's undoing, initialized even as she began her assault on Airtha.

It would also rid the Matri∞me of that meddling Xavia, and perhaps some of her ilk as well.

Good. This is good.

FORGIVENESS

STELLAR DATE: 09.12.8949 (Adjusted Years)
LOCATION: Ol' Sam, ISS *I2*
REGION: Pyra, Albany System, Thebes, Septhian Alliance

Tangel rose from where she sat on the edge of the dock and placed a hand on Sera's shoulder. "You going to be alright?"

"Yeah." Sera glanced up at Tangel before her gaze shifted back to the rippling waters before them. "Just need to collect my thoughts for a bit, you know?"

"Oh, I know," Tangel replied, shifting her hand to Sera's head. "I bet it's a right mess in there."

"Funny," Sera retorted. "Your man is waiting for you back on the porch, you know."

Tangel glanced at the lakehouse. "Yeah, I saw him when he came out. Pretty sure I know what he wants to talk about."

"There are so many options." Sera laughed softly. "I don't know how you can guess at which one it is."

"Funny girl," Tangel said while slipping her feet back into her shoes. "Will you be back up once you put your noggin back together?"

"Yeah, send me the all clear when you and Joe are squared away. Finaeus wants to play some Snark, and I want to be on his team, He always beats me, and I want to figure out how."

"You got it." Tangel turned and walked along the dock, taking comfort in the squeaks and vibrations of the foot-worn wood until she reached the grass-covered slope that led up to her lakehouse.

She kept her eyes on Joe, watching as he rocked gently in the porch-swing at the end of the veranda. Beyond him, she could see into the house and through it. She could see through the orchard that stretched out across the low hill beyond, and then into the hill itself.

Beneath that lay the maintenance systems for the habitat cylinder, and then layers of old stasis pod chambers, all converted to CriEn and SC batt compartments. Her gaze slipped past those and through the skin of the cylinder, peppered with thousands of turrets.

Six hundred thousand kilometers away was the world of Pyra. It had only been fourteen days since she'd been stranded on its surface, but somehow it felt like a lifetime ago.

*Stars, given the trip to the LMC, it feels like **two** lifetimes ago.*

She reached the steps to the lakehouse, and drew her vision back to what was before her. Once at the top of the steps, she turned to Joe.

"I thought there was no such thing as too much partying for you."

Joe chuckled and patted the seat next to him. "There's not, but that doesn't mean I don't want something other than watching Jessica dance on the dining room table."

"On my table?" Tangel's gaze shifted, and she looked through the walls to see that Jessica was indeed dancing on the table, nimbly avoiding the food, drinks, and reaching hands that were trying to trip her.

"I made her take her boots off."

"Thank stars. For her sake," Tangel replied as she sat next to her husband.

"Been awhile since we just sat out here," he said while stretching an arm around her shoulders and pulling her to his side. "I have to get back to New Canaan soon—we have a new class commencing, and another graduating. But I didn't want to just run off without getting to hold my wife close for a bit."

Tangel shifted so her head would lay against Joe's shoulder. "We could always shoo our guests off and go upstairs for a bit."

Another laugh slipped past Joe's lips. "Where did you

come from, Tangel?"

"What do you mean?" she asked, turning her head to stare into his eyes, a frown knitting her brows together.

"You're just so different from all your friends. I mean…no one in there would care in the least if we went upstairs for some hanky panky. Stars, half of them would ask if they could use the spare bedroom—at the same time."

"You're exaggerating." Tangel rolled her eyes. "If Cheeky were here, that would be one thing, but she's not."

"Where is she, anyway? I thought *Sabrina* docked yesterday. Figured she'd be here, climbing all over Finaeus."

"I needed her to run something back to Amavia and Iris," Tangel replied. "She'll be back before long."

"What's her next move?" Joe asked. "You going to send them on some other secret mission?"

Tangel considered the operations she had in play, all seven hundred and nine of them. "Probably, yeah. Haven't decided what yet…. Maybe that mess out by Deneb. I need Jessica and Trevor to go pay their kids a visit, so I think the dream team is finally going to get split up."

"Good," Joe gave a firm nod. "About time Cheeky got her chance."

"Her chance?" Tangel asked. "For what?"

"To be captain, of course. She's more than earned it. She's proven that her mind's reconstitution is solid, and she can handle whatever comes her way. From the reports Jessica filed, I'd say she's better than ever."

"You talk like you know her well." Tangel pushed a foot out, giving the swing a push.

"A bit, yeah." Joe shrugged. "She and I have had some chats here and there. You forget that we were all together for a month before they left for Virginis. I bumped into her the day they shipped out from New Canaan, too. We had a good chat about a lot of things."

"You get around," Tangel said, then snorted a laugh. "Well, not like that."

"Never know, hon, bumping into Cheeky could mean all sorts of things."

"Did you?" Tangel lifted her head off Joe's shoulder, forcing herself to not look into his mind for the answer.

"Of course, not." Joe's face took on a wounded expression. "I'd never take Cheeky between the sheets."

"That's good, I—"

"She's more of an up-against-the-bulkhead kinda woman."

"Joe!"

"Easy, love." Joe pulled her close once more. "You know I'd never have sex with Cheeky without inviting you."

Tangel considered pinching Joe's thigh. Hard. But instead, she laughed at his audacity. "What did I ever do to deserve you?"

"Beats me," Joe shrugged. "You haven't done it yet."

"You!" This time, Tangel did sit up and turn to face him. "You're in a rare mood tonight. What did I do to get all this thinly veiled abuse?"

"I'm just needling you because you went to the LMC without me," Joe leant close and kissed Tangel's cheek. "Plus, we were going to go into the fight together, but you dove out of the pinnace and tore your way through a ship's hull. Which was sexy as all get-out, but I still wanted to be in on the action, too."

"We still fought some IPE soldiers near the docking bay."

"Hardly even worth noting." Joe gave a dismissive swipe of his hand. "Next time you get mixed up in a good row, I want in. I'm dying here."

"I'll try to plan them out better in the future. Do you have Garza's Link route? I'll see if we can set up a playdate."

"Jerk would just send another clone," Joe scoffed. "Guy has no honor."

The two sat in silence, rocking gently, arms around one another for fifteen more minutes before Sera approached, climbing the steps slowly.

"Were you just going to leave me out there forever, Tangel?"

"What? Do you have somewhere to be?"

Sera nodded emphatically. "Yeah, sitting somewhere softer than your dock—with alcohol. You need a couch and a keg down there."

"Now that," Joe said as he stood and pulled Tangel with him, "sounds like a fantastic idea. I'll have one installed tomorrow."

"You would, too," Tangel said with a sigh.

He placed a hand around her waist and rested it lightly on her hip. "You know me so well, dear. Now let's go see if we can show Jessica up with some *real* table dancing."

DAMON SILAS
STELLAR DATE: 09.01.8949 (Adjusted Years)
LOCATION: *Damon Silas*
REGION: Interstellar Space, coreward of the Vela Cluster

"And what of the AI?" Justin asked Roxy, his brows raised.

She gave a nonchalant shrug. "Carmen? I dumped her in an escape pod and kicked it off the ship."

She wondered if Justin caught the spike in her heart rate; it had only lasted for a second. That was one benefit to her azure epidermis. She didn't sweat, and her skin temperature barely changed, even if she was terrified.

The real miracle, however, was that the compliance lace in her head didn't trigger.

Or did it? I felt a twinge for a second. Maybe it's malfunctioning?

"You what!?" Justin's voice rose in pitch and volume. "You just let it go?"

Roxy squared her shoulders, eliciting a narrow-eyed look from Justin. "I made a deal with it. The ship's logs are wide open to us, so we have access to everything they had about stasis shield tech—which isn't much. Carmen told me that the ISF didn't share anything about the underpinnings of the technology, it was all black box."

"Maybe," Justin grunted. "Next time you have an asset like that in your hands, you do whatever it takes to keep it secure and bring it back to me."

"Understood," Roxy said with a nod. "Should I stay here on the *Silas*, or head back to the *Greensward*?"

Justin looked around the bridge of the *Damon Silas* and pursed his lips. "I'd like to transfer everything here—once it's cleaned up. The *Greensward* has superior stealth to this ship, but it's hard to beat the appeal of impregnable shields."

Roxy could tell Justin was still mulling over his options, and stood in silence, waiting for him to make his decision regarding her destination.

"Go back to the *Greensward*," Justin said at last. "I don't want to bring Andrea over here until the ship will pass muster. Maybe you should have another one of your sessions with her."

"Of course, Justin," Roxy said with a conspiratorial smile. "Continuing on with the taming of the shrew."

He chuckled. "Sounds about right."

"I just want to make another sweep for my lightwand.... I dropped it somewhere during the firefight."

"Sure thing, though I'm sure it'll turn up."

Roxy gave him a peck on the cheek before she walked off the bridge and through the ship's long corridors, toward the docking bay where Justin's pinnace would be waiting.

The signs of the fight to secure the *Damon Silas* were still in evidence around her. Carbon scoring and gouges in the bulkheads were present every meter of the corridor that ran from the bridge to the central lift shaft.

She saw a stack of bodies through a door in the passage, the remains of the Transcend crew who had fought valiantly to keep the *Damon Silas* from falling into enemy hands.

Cut down by men and women who had been on the same side just a year earlier.

What are we doing? Roxy wondered. *Is Justin mad...or am I?*

Images flooded her mind, showing her what a wonderful person Justin was, how strong and magnanimous. But unlike previous instances of the conditioning, the images didn't blot out all her other thoughts; they were more like calming memories that she could dismiss.

A worry crept into her mind that maybe the thoughts of Justin were right, real memories and feelings from her past, before the injuries that destroyed much of her body.

He had told her that she *wanted* to be turned into what he called his 'living work of art', but she wasn't sure. Given her line of work, glowing azure skin wasn't terribly practical. Not only that, it didn't *feel* right. It didn't feel like her.

But Justin has always taken care of me. He's never harmed me, only instructed me. And I'm better for it.

Even as she thought the words of obedience, her mind jumped to Carmen, the *Damon Silas*'s AI.

Lying about Carmen had felt right—which didn't make any sense. For some reason, Roxy *liked* Carmen, felt a bond with the AI. If Justin got his hands on her, it wouldn't go well for her new friend, and Roxy didn't want that to happen.

I'm being disobedient…and nothing is happening…. Stars, how is it that I can think about rebellion one moment, but believe in Justin the next? I know he punishes me, he put the neural lace into my mind to control me, to make me his thing. Thinking that I'm his gives me pleasure, an inexplicable thrill, but saving Carmen does as well, even if it means rebelling against Justin.

Roxy couldn't understand how these two thought processes could both feel right, while being in direct opposition to one another.

Is this what cognitive dissonance is? How can I want to obey and please Justin at the same time I want to disobey? How can both feel good?

While wondering how she even managed to maintain a sane worldview while loving and reviling her life at the same time, she stepped onto the lift, entering a destination of the seventeenth deck.

It wasn't the deck where the pinnace waited, but rather one above. When the lift doors slid open, she stepped out into the darkened passage, navigating it easily with her inorganic eyes.

A minute later, she reached the maintenance bay—which was little more than a closet large enough for a workbench—

and palmed the door open.

Once inside, she slid the AI case out from under the bench and set it atop the work surface.

"I was starting to wonder if you'd come back," Carmen said through the case's audible systems.

Roxy regretted destroying the case's wireless transmitter. At the time, it had seemed prudent, but not being able to use the Link to speak with Carmen was more than a little inconvenient.

"I had a few moments of doubt myself," Roxy replied, running a hand across her forehead to brush aside her luminescent hair. "But I told Justin I kicked you out in a pod. Good thing the logs will back me up."

"And now?" the AI's voice seemed to be somewhere between confrontational and worried.

"I don't know, Carmen. I like you for some reason…which seems weird, I hardly know you."

A strangled laugh came from the case. "From what I've managed to infer from your position in Justin's organization, I think we're both in impossible situations."

Roxy blew out a long breath. She didn't need to…she didn't have to breathe at all, if she didn't want to, but it felt relaxing to enact the old biological habits.

"I have to ask," Carmen said after Roxy didn't reply. "Are you an AI?"

"What!?" Roxy exclaimed. "What would make you think that?"

"Well…I don't have advanced scan abilities in my case, but I have optical pickups that are able to get a good look at you. Now that you're not wearing your armor, I can see that you don't possess an organic body."

Roxy looked down at her azure 'flesh' and nodded. "Not much, anyway. I had an accident…and Justin brought me back, told me I always wanted to have a body like this. I don't remember much from before, though. It's…hazy."

"Like I said, I don't have the best optics, but from what I can tell, you're not organic at all." Carmen's voice was soft, almost apologetic.

"No!" Roxy retorted. "I've run scans on myself. I've seen the med readouts. I still have the organs required to keep my brain nurtured."

"Uh, OK," Carmen said, her tone carrying a note of hesitation. "Right. Bad optics on the case. Speaking of which, how are you going to get me out of here? This case stands out a bit."

"I was hoping to find something in here," Roxy said, casting her eyes about the room, which held a fabricator, several cylinders of flowmetal, and a half-dozen repair drones docked on charging stations.

"You know…" Carmen began hesitantly. "I have a crazy idea. Why don't you put me inside of you?"

"Uh, if we use a medtable to implant you in my head, Justin will find out for sure."

"I won't fit, either. Well, not without significant physical restructuring, which I wouldn't do without an expanse to archive my state into. No, I was thinking more of you tucking me into your abdomen. If you have a more or less standard frame, there should be room."

Roxy placed her hands on her stomach. "Seriously?"

"Sure. It's not that common, because there's rarely a reason for an AI to take up residence in an organic's gut—or a partial organic, like yourself—but so long as you have the batteries to power us both, it shouldn't be that hard."

"I get the feeling you've already planned this out." Roxy's tone sounded hesitant, but internally, she'd already made up her mind to do as Carmen had suggested.

"I have. I can program this bay's fabricator to build a mounting apparatus for me, the repair drones can open you up and install it, and then we can use the flowmetal to facilitate any internal alterations."

Half of Roxy's mind was screaming that what Carmen was suggesting was the worst thing imaginable: a betrayal of Justin. But she also wanted it. Talking with Carmen was such a refreshing change from the caustic exchanges with Andrea, or the constant doublespeak Justin engaged in.

She felt like she could just be herself—and so could Carmen.

"OK, Carmen, let's do it."

EUROPA

STELLAR DATE: 01.01.2352 (Adjusted Years)
LOCATION: Water's Edge Resort, Europa
REGION: Europan Collective, Jupiter, Sol System

Nearly six thousand and six hundred years ago, nine months before the official creation of the FGT program...

Finaeus entered the restaurant and gave a nod to the hostess before slipping around the automaton and walking to where his wife sat at a table for two, next to the window.

He took his time, drinking in her features in profile—the soft curve of her forehead, almost aquiline nose, pronounced lips, and small—but strong—chin.

She was clothed in a sapphire dress that gleamed as though it were made of the gem itself. Long, slow breaths gently lifted her breasts, the exposed flesh between them straining gently against the fabric.

<*You're starting to drool.*> Her voice came into his mind as she turned and glanced at him, a soft laugh slipping from her lips. <*Best get over here and use a napkin to clean it up.*>

"I suppose I should," he replied, taking four final strides to reach her side. He leant over to kiss her on the lips—a gesture she welcomed and returned warmly—before he sat.

"I'm surprised you're not using the Link to chat," Lisa said as he settled into his seat. "Especially after the latest updates that allow the direct transmission of emotion, it's exhilarating."

Finaeus only shrugged as he triggered the table's holomenu and looked over the drinks.

"What? Not proud of your latest invention come to life?"

He glanced up at her, seeing honest concern in his wife's eyes. "No...it's just different in practice than I expected. It's hard to control one's thoughts, and I have so many tonight."

Outside the window, the sun began to rise, illuminating the surface of Europa's subterranean ocean, which the dome overhead kept from freezing.

It wasn't a large dome, only a kilometer across, but it kept this hole in the ice from closing up, and gave access to the cities below the moon's waters.

Lisa reached out and placed her hand on his. "Did you hear from Jeffrey? Is it about the endeavor?"

Finaeus turned and glanced back at his wife, unable to keep worry from furrowing his brow. "Yes, it is."

"Did he secure it?"

He pursed his lips and nodded. "We have final approvals, and the full use of Luna's polar shipyards. The Terran Assembly and Lunar Governors have given us their blessing. There are still a number of hoops to jump through, but it is very nearly a real thing."

"The Future Generation Terraformers." Lisa whispered the words with a note of reverence, then a broad grin broke out across her face. "Can you believe it, Fin? For *centuries*, humans have dreamt of colonizing worlds in other systems, but us…we're going to be the ones to do it!"

Finaeus's eyes locked onto Lisa's. " 'We'? You've decided?"

Lisa sucked in her lower lip, biting at it nervously—something that she knew completely disarmed him. "I have, that's why I wanted to have this dinner with you tonight. I know I didn't react well when you first suggested leaving the Sol System, but…well, the more I thought of it, the more I realized that you were about to embark on the greatest adventure of all time, and I was letting fear hold me back from enjoying it with you."

"There's nothing to be afraid of," Finaeus said as he clasped her hand. "You've got me."

"And your wits?" Lisa asked with a smirk.

"Of course! They got me this far, didn't they?"

Lisa leant forward, her eyes deep pools of intense emotion. "May your wits never encounter something they can't handle."

A low chuckle escaped Finaeus's lips. "I'm not worried. With you at my side, I can do anything."

An automaton had two glasses of wine before them, and the pair lifted them in unison.

Finaeus winked at his wife. "Well timed."

"Aren't I always?" She tapped her glass against his. "To doing anything."

"To adventure and the stars," he added before they drank. "Together."

"Always."

BROTHERS

STELLAR DATE: 09.17.8949 (Adjusted Years)
LOCATION: Forward Lounge, ISS *I2*
REGION: Pyra, Albany System, Thebes, Septhian Alliance

Back in the 90th century...

"Jeff?" Finaeus asked, taking great care to keep his voice steady as he walked into the *I2*'s forward observation lounge.

The silhouette standing before the windows, staring out at the early stages of the grav-ring's construction, was unmistakable. The broad shoulders, a touch on the haughty side, the stiff-backed stance, hands clasped behind the small of his back....

It was a posture Finaeus had seen so many times in the past. Thousands, tens of thousands.

He'd been waiting on pins and needles to meet with his brother for the past fifteen days, but Tangel had insisted that ISF medics thoroughly evaluate Jeffrey Tomlinson out in the LMC, and assess his mental state before returning him to the Milky Way Galaxy.

Finaeus had been wrapped up in the mech project, enhancing Rika's Marauders—which had been a welcome distraction from thinking about Jeffrey, but at the end had nearly become torture, as he played out a thousand possible outcomes in his mind.

The lounge was empty, save for one servitor behind the bar, but it took Jeffrey a moment to turn to Finaeus, an unreadable expression on his face.

"Looks like you're still at it, brother. You just can't stop building things, can you?"

Finaeus shrugged as he approached, assuming a similar

posture as he stopped at the window, gazing out at the sight before them.

The planet of Pyra was still a mess, dark clouds covering much of its surface—though the a-grav towers were nearly complete. Soon, they'd begin filtering the atmosphere and pumping the hot, ash-filled clouds out into space.

Further up, a-grav buoys floated around the planet, supporting the beginnings of the grav ring's particle accelerator. Once it was up and running, the inertial force of the relativistic particles in the accelerator would push out, keeping the structure rigid and able to support the weight of the ring.

"Still practicing," Finaeus said after a moment.

"For what?" Jeffrey asked, giving his time-honored response.

The two words hit Finaeus like a hammer-blow. It had been centuries since his brother had said those words to him, and a lump formed in his throat while his eyes grew moist.

"To build a ring around the galaxy," Finaeus croaked in response.

Jeffrey turned toward him. "Has it been that bad? The other me…. Was he an ass?"

A half-sob, half-laugh shredded its way out of Finaeus's throat. "Brother-mine, you've always been an ass. He was just *more* of an ass. And to think that I built Airtha for him."

"The diamond ring in the Huygens System?" Jeffrey asked. "You really made it?"

"I did." Finaeus ducked his head in acknowledgement. "Then he gave it over to her—though I suppose I know why, now. He'd been under her control since, what, she got back?"

Jeffrey shook his head. "Not that long. When I was placed in stasis a thousand years ago. She'd been 'back', as Airtha, for some time. But I was trying to help her, bring her back to who she'd been before she left."

Finaeus could hear the anguish in his brother's voice, and he pursed his lips, nodding slowly. "I understand…"

"Do you?" Jeffrey said sharply, turning his head, eyes locking on Finaeus's. "She was my *wife*! Kirkland said I should kill her, that she was a spy from the Core; you were on the fence, if I recall."

"For good reason,"

Jeffrey's lips set in a thin line, and then he sighed. "I suppose you were right."

"I never abandoned you, though," Finaeus said. "You—well, he—exiled me, but I didn't stop trying to help you."

"Seems to have worked out well for you," his brother replied, a small smile alighting on his lips. "I saw your new wife in the reports Tangel gave me access to. She seems pretty amazing."

Finaeus chuckled. "You have no idea. The things that woman can do…I swear, she's invented some new branch of physics. But you're not the only one with a past wife causing problems."

"Who? Josephine? I thought she went off to the Sagittarius arm, joined a monastery or something."

"No," Finaeus shook his head. "Lisa."

"Lisa? She's dead," Jeffrey said bluntly, then caught himself. "Sorry, Fin. My mouth gets ahead of my better sense sometimes. But…?"

"I encountered three clones of her," Finaeus replied quietly. "Garza is using them as some sort of elite strike force."

"Fucking clones," Jeffrey muttered. "Doesn't anyone remember the old stories? Those things are dangerous."

"I wonder, though," Finaeus mused. "What if....?"

"What if it was a clone that you saw die? Was Garza cloning back then?"

Finaeus considered the possibilities. Examinations of the Garzas that the ISF had captured showed them to be products of the Hegemony's cloning technology—something ancient from before even the *Intrepid*'s time—which the Hegemon had found in a vault deep within Luna. The Lisas had been products of the same tech.

"Maybe?" he said at last. "I don't know, Jeff. I should remind you, however, that you have two daughters aboard this very ship that are clones."

"Three," Jeffrey replied coolly.

"The first Sera is no clone," Finaeus corrected.

Jeffrey shook his head. "She's the daughter of a clone...and she was clearly altered by *her*. Stars, Finaeus, Sera is Jelina's spitting image."

Finaeus nodded. "You—well, the other you—told me that was on purpose. Always seemed a bit odd, but we didn't have a close relationship at that point."

Neither man spoke for a minute after that, both staring out into the darkness, as a tug pulled a spool of carbon nano-fiber cabling around the a-grav buoys.

"Do you remember that night?" Jeffrey's voice was barely above a whisper.

"There have been a lot of nights."

"Luna. Under New Austin's dome. We were watching them build High Terra."

"The night they laid the final section onto the substructure," Finaeus replied with a nod. "Yeah, you said something monumentally stupid that night. 'Finaeus, why aren't we doing this in other star systems?' or something like that."

"Close enough, yeah," Jeffrey replied. "That was the

night we conceived of the FGT. Now…we've done all this. This is all our fault."

Finaeus snorted. "Sometimes you amaze me, Jeff."

"What?" Jeffrey asked.

"You've got enough hubris for a whole star system. If we hadn't started the FGT, someone else would have. Humanity wasn't going to stay bottled up in the Sol System forever, and you know it."

"Yeah…" Jeffrey's voice trailed off. "But maybe someone else would have done better than us."

"Jeff…" Finaeus shook his head and placed a hand on his brother's shoulder. "You can't think like that. We're not responsible for everything that everyone does. We built *worlds* for humanity." He swept his hand across the view. "Every star you can see…. Over half of them have humans living in their systems. Most of those are FGT systems. We spread the human race across space. But that's what you have to remember; we didn't seed some sort of perfectly content group that never gets into trouble, we seeded *humans*."

Jeffrey let out a derisive laugh. "Maybe we should have seeded dolphins everywhere instead."

"Well, we did put them in a few corners here and there," Finaeus replied with a wink. "I've checked on them a few times; they're doing well. People found one group, and now folks go there to get modded into sea creatures and live with the dolphins."

"Really?" Jeff asked, cocking an eyebrow. "Sometimes I can't tell if you're shitting me or not."

"I'm not—this time, at least. It's out near Deneb. Inner Stars, but close to the fringe. Hopefully far enough away from all this mess."

"Lotta mess," Jeffrey said with a nod.

Another stretch of silence fell. It was comfortable, like it used to be between them, back before Jelina, before the Schism.

"So what do I do?" Jeffrey asked.

"Pardon?"

"You heard me. What should I do? How do we deal with this mess?"

Finaeus only shrugged in response, and Jeffrey's brow lowered.

"That's all I get?"

"It doesn't matter what I think you should do, what do *you* think you should do?"

He ran a hand through his hair. "That's where I'm hung up. Should I really turn over the Transcend to Tangel?"

"It's not yours to turn over, Jeff."

"Whose is it, then? Sera's? She barely wants the job—I could see that after talking to her for just a few minutes. Too much of her mother in her."

"Doesn't matter," Finaeus said with a shrug. "It's Sera's responsibility right now. You can't just take it from her. That's not how this works."

"You seem OK with working under her. Why didn't you take the reins?"

Finaeus barked a laugh. "Are you kidding me? Run the show? Stars, no. It would be like the worst engineering job of all time: one where nothing ever gets done, and everyone complains constantly. Not in a million years."

Jeffrey chuckled. "Honestly, that's a bit too charitable. It's really far worse. What about Tangel? She's…interesting. Did you know her? Before?"

Finaeus ducked his head. "Sure did. Honestly, she wasn't a lot different. Just spoke with two voices instead of one. She's the real deal, though."

"Should she be governing the Transcend?"

"Governing?" Finaeus shook his head. "The Transcend

doesn't need to be 'governed', brother mine, it needs to be *led*. Do you remember when we brought the FGT together, back at Lucida? When we built our first extra-solar shipyards and sent out our *own* worldships?"

Jeffrey set his jaw and nodded.

"Well, *that's* the sort of leader we need again. But if you can't do it, if that's not in you anymore—and if Sera truly does not want to lead, then I think we should put Krissy in command."

"Your daughter?" Jeffrey asked. "I saw some reports about her. She seems like a competent commander."

"And a good leader," Finaeus added. "Loyal, too."

"I'm glad to hear it, Fin. Sounds like she does you proud."

"You should feel the same way about Sera. She's a bit unorthodox, but she's passionate, and her heart's in the right place."

"It's so strange," Jeffrey said with a far-off look in his eyes. "She knows a version of me—one that I get the impression wasn't a great father figure—but I don't know her at all."

Finaeus clasped his brother's shoulder. "Well, Jeff, there's only one way to rectify that."

"And the others?" he asked. "I understand that they're being released from medical soon. I was clean, but they were mentally shackled. It took a bit to free their minds."

"I heard that," Finaeus replied. "Regardless of how you feel, all three Seras still look at you and see 'Dad'. You're going to have to learn how to live with that."

"Would be a lot easier if they weren't Jelina's spitting image.

"I've learned to live with it. You will, too."

THE NEW RECRUIT

STELLAR DATE: 09.19.8949 (Adjusted Years)
LOCATION: Intrepid Space Force Academy
REGION: The Palisades, Orbiting Troy, New Canaan System

Cary and Saanvi stood on Concourse C outside Gate 11, waiting for their new charge to exit the passenger ship that was easing up to the airlock.

Faleena walked toward them, holding three coffees and an orange juice.

"Do you think she likes orange juice?" A look of worry creased Faleena's delicate green features. "I figured she probably doesn't like coffee; most people her age don't drink that, right?"

"Not usually." Cary chuckled at the worry etched on her sister's face.

"I think everyone likes orange juice," Saanvi added, a comforting smile on her lips while she shot Cary a reproachful glance. "It'll be fine."

"It's just weird," Faleena continued, her words coming out so fast they were barely enunciated. "I mean, she's just a kid, and honestly, we're just kids, too. Are we old enough to be responsible for another being?"

Cary placed an arm around Faleena's shoulders. "Moms and Dad entrusted me with you when you were only weeks old. If I can manage a baby AI in my head, I bet the three of us can deal with an eleven-year-old girl."

Saanvi rolled her eyes. "You clearly don't remember what *you* were like at ten. How many times did Dad make you muck out the stalls as punishment?"

"Stars, don't remind me," Cary muttered. "I think I smelled like horse shit that entire summer."

"And fall, and winter…"

Cary glanced at her sister to see a broad smile on Saanvi's lips. "You're a bucket of ha-ha's."

"I'm here all week. Try the veal."

"I have no idea what that means," Cary said, turning to watch as the airlock cycled open, and an automaton stepped out, gesturing for the passengers to follow.

"You're so uncultured," Saanvi retorted.

"Your version of culture involves watching flat-vids and reading books where people say 'whom'. I'll pass."

Saanvi shrugged. "Your loss."

"Hush, you two," Faleena said, peering through the disembarking throng. "There she is!"

"Amy!" Cary called out, waving to the young girl who was stepping uncertainly over the airlock's threshold, peering around her while clutching a small bag to her chest. "Amy, it's us!"

Amy's eyes fell on Cary and her sisters, and a look of relief washed over the girl's face as she rushed toward them. Then she stopped short, standing awkwardly a half-meter away.

"Seriously, Amy?" Cary asked, then stooped down to scoop the girl up in an embrace—one that Saanvi and Faleena joined in on. "Stars, it's good to see you again."

"You're squishing me!" Amy squeaked, but Cary could tell the girl was happy to see them.

"Sorry-not-sorry." Saanvi winked mischievously. "How was your flight? How're things in Albany?"

Cary set Amy back down and took her hand, leading her down the concourse toward the maglev platform that would take them to their quarters.

"Good, I guess. Rika left to go to some place called Sepe; she's hunting the Niets that escaped Albany. Mom and Barne are getting ready for another bunch of mechs that are coming from the Politica…er, Kendo, I guess it's called now."

"What's wrong?" Saanvi asked, peering into Amy's face. "I heard that your mom is only going to train them, and then she'll be coming to meet up with you here."

The girl snorted. "Seriously? You remember that my mom is Silva, right? Besides, would *your* mom run from a fight?"

"Uh…well…" Cary stammered, uncertain what the right response was.

"What makes you think your mom is going to go with the mechs into Nietzschea?" Faleena asked, deflecting Amy's question with one of her own. "She left them once to be with you."

"Yeah," Amy nodded. "But things were different then. Now that they've met up with your people, well…"

"Is there something she'd go into Nietzschea for?" Faleena pressed.

"My brothers," she admitted quietly. "She thinks they still might be alive—even though my father said they're dead. 'Course, he was a fucking asshole, so who knows if they are or not."

Cary was taken aback by the vehemence in Amy's voice, but she had trouble faulting the girl. They'd been told about the abuses she had suffered under her father's care, many of them administered while her mother was watching. The fact that Amy was a functioning person and relatively well-adjusted was a miracle in and of itself.

Cary supposed she might curse someone who did that to her, as well.

Suddenly, growing up in the shadow of the great Tanis Richards doesn't seem so bad.

"Well, if she does go looking for them, I wish her all the luck. I know a bit about wondering where one's family is," Saanvi said in a soothing voice. "We'll be waiting for her here."

Amy glanced up at Saanvi. "Aren't you training to be ship

captains? That's what my mom told me."

"Well, eventually," Cary replied. "We have a ways to go."

"When you go, I'm going with you," Amy declared. "I won't stay here waiting. I need to be in the fight."

"War is no place for kids," Faleena said as they reached the maglev platform and stepped aboard a waiting maglev car.

"You don't understand." Amy's voice was almost pleading. "I *have* to get out there. I'm done hiding."

They were filing into the back of the car, moving past several seated passengers, when Amy tripped and reached out to grab the back of a seat.

She didn't fall, but Cary spotted a series of red streaks on the girl's forearm. She was about to ask what they were from, when Saanvi reached out to her privately.

<Don't. Not here. Wait 'til we get to our rooms.>

<You saw it too?> Cary asked.

<Yeah, she's cutting herself. Don't worry, we can talk with her, non-threateningly, and get a counselor if necessary.>

Cary nodded, and engaged Amy in trivialities as the maglev took them through the Palisades, up from Ring 7 to their quarters on Ring 3.

Though they still had two years to go at the academy, Cary, Saanvi, and Faleena had been granted their own quarters due to their unorthodox training and responsibilities.

Cary was sure there was some grumbling about it, but at the same time, she had also heard rumors circulating that she could read minds, and that some people didn't want to bunk with her.

Saanvi seemed unaffected by the scuttlebutt, and Cary wished she could brush it off like her sister did.

When they finally reached their quarters, Cary showed Amy to her room, which was the first one on the left off the common area.

"Do you have anything else coming?" Cary asked, as Amy

set her bag on the bed.

She shook her head. "This is all I have."

"Well then," Cary grinned at the young girl. "We'll have to go on a shopping trip tomorrow. Get you whatever you want."

Amy flushed and shook her head again. "I don't—it's OK. Really."

Cary drew in a deep breath and closed the door before sitting down on the bed, patting it in request for Amy to sit down beside her. When her charge complied, she asked, "Do you want to tell me about the cuts? I saw them on the maglev. It's OK, you're not in trouble. I even did it a few times when I was your age—well, a bit older, but you're more mature than I was at eleven."

"What?" Amy asked, frowning. "Why did you cut yourself?"

Cary hadn't expected the admission to come back on her so quickly, and she stammered. "I—I don't really know. I felt like I wasn't...worth it? I figured it was what I deserved for not being perfect. I wanted to *feel*. Reasons that don't make much sense when I say them aloud now, but they seemed...inescapable back then."

Amy's face reddened, and she shook her head. "That's not...I'm not doing it for that."

"No?" Cary asked. "Why then?"

"It's stupid," she said as she turned away.

"No, Amy. If it's important enough for you to hurt yourself, it's not stupid. Tell me. Please?"

Amy folded her arms, hunched her head low, and spoke in barely a whisper. "I want to be like her."

Cary's eyebrows knit together. "Like who?"

"My mom!" Amy whispered hoarsely. "I want to cut my arms off so I can be a mech and be with my mom!"

The girl's words completely floored Cary. She had no idea

what to say in response. "I...uh...I'm not sure..."

"That's why I agreed to come here." Amy turned and fixed Cary with a stare beyond her years. "I want you to train me to be a warrior. Then I can join the Marauders. That's where I'm supposed to be."

Cary's first instinct was to talk Amy down, to try to convince the girl that she was on the wrong path. But the cold fire in Amy's eyes told Cary that there would be no convincing this young firebrand of anything.

Not yet, at least.

"Well, then," Cary looked Amy up and down. "The first rule of a warrior is that your body must be kept in peak fighting condition, whether it's organic, mechanical, or somewhere in between. You can't be an asset to your team if you're damaged. So if you want me to train you, the first rule is no more cutting."

"How will I become a mech, then?" Amy asked.

"If you cut your organic arms off, the medics here will just grow you new flesh and blood ones." Cary paused to let the statement sink in. "It's trivial for us to do that. You have to prove to me that you can fight, and that you could fight better as a mech. Only when I'm satisfied that you'd be an asset to the Marauders will I lobby for you to be a mech."

<OK, I'm listening at the door,> Saanvi said. <And are you nuts?>

<No, I'm going to teach her how to love herself through training. Then she'll realize that, with our armor and tech, she doesn't need to go sawing off her limbs.>

<Huh...that might just work. You better run this past the counselors, though. And Dad, when he gets back. I can just see Amy going to him and saying, 'But Cary promised me you'd cut my limbs off'.>

Cary shuddered at the thought. <No argument here, I will.>

"When do we start?" Amy asked.

"Well…no time like the present," Cary said as she rose. "Let's go for a run and see what you've got."

Amy grinned up at her. "OK, but I'm like bottled lightning. Prepare to lose."

Cary snorted a laugh. "That's the spirit."

EASING IN

STELLAR DATE: 09.22.8949 (Adjusted Years)
LOCATION: Tangel's Lakehouse, Ol' Sam, ISS *12*
REGION: Pyra, Albany System, Thebes, Septhian Alliance

"Welcome back, Sera," Tangel said, gesturing to the chair across from her, the sitting room's fireplace crackling softly before them.

Sera, wearing a simple light grey shipsuit, eyed Tangel warily for a moment before sitting. "It's been a while," she said while shifting to get comfortable.

"Over twenty years, by your reckoning," Tangel agreed with a nod. "A strange bit of cognitive dissonance for me. Up until you left Ascella with Andrea and Serge, my memories of you and the other Seras are the same, but following that, they diverge."

The woman sitting across from Tangel clenched her jaw and gave a sharp nod. "It's so much fun being constantly reminded that I'm a clone—or whatever I am."

Tangel shrugged. "You were made at the whim of your mother. That is not so different from how things happen naturally."

Sera sat back in her seat, folding her arms across her chest. "Except, for most people, their mother didn't also make their father."

"Good point," Tangel allowed. "That's certainly less common, but not really material to your situation."

A coarse laugh tore free from Sera's throat, and her voice rose an octave. "Not *material*? Has becoming some sort of super-being addled your brain?"

Tangel raised her eyebrows. "Hard to say—not sure I could tell if it had. Though if you think about it, 'addled' would present as either illogical and self-harming, or just unusual. Who is to say what a 'usual' mode of thought should be for me? Are there other ascended beings who are merges of human and AI to compare to?"

"Could be," Sera replied, her tone still combative.

"Well," Tangel chuckled as she spoke. "I'll be sure to ask them when we meet."

"Are you going to answer the question? Why is it not material?"

A smile graced Tangel's lips. "One thing is for certain, you are still the same woman—though you rarely turned that sharp tongue on me before. And that's why it's all immaterial. Airtha made all three of you Seras for a purpose: she wanted to create a legacy and a new ruler for humanity. Because of that, you three share similar traits suited to someone who would be a ruler. You're—"

"Puppets?" Sera interjected.

"I was going to say, 'driven'," Tangel replied with a smirk. "Plus smart, decisive, determined. You're also all a bit egotistical."

"Takes one to know one."

Tangel shrugged. "Touché. But I didn't invite you here to engage in a verbal sparring match. I invited you here because I believe that you've not had a chance to pick sides in this conflict. I want to offer that to you now."

Sera's eyebrows rose. "Before I left the LMC, I was given a data packet with a lot of intel. What you know of Airtha, the core AIs, the wars across the Inner Stars. With all that information, this isn't much of a choice—you'll not set me free if I don't join up with you."

Tangel crossed her legs and leant back in her chair. "I give you my word. If you do not choose to stay with us, I will return you to your mother."

"Right," Sera grunted. "Again, with all that intel? Or will

you perform some sort mind-wipe?"

"I didn't give you anything Airtha doesn't already know. If I had, the offer would have been stasis until the end of the war."

Tangel could see the wheels turning behind Sera's eyes. There was most certainly information in the data packet that this Sera had not known. The knowledge that Airtha knew so much more than she'd shared with her daughters would be a revelation in and of itself.

"It's a tricky thing," Tangel continued. "At the end of the day, I want the same things Airtha does: for the core AIs to stop dictating the future of humans and other non-ascended AIs. It's our motives that differ. I'm doing it because I believe in the two races, while Airtha is doing it as a form of vengeance. She wants to unite humanity under her banner and wield it like a weapon against the Core. *I* want to find common ground so that we can forge a future where we stop nearly wiping ourselves out. Then I'll lead a unified force of humans and AIs to the Core."

"Do you think that waging war across the Inner Stars is how you'll unify humanity?" Sera derided.

"This war has been orchestrated," Tanis replied simply. "Spurred on by the Caretaker, Airtha, and Kirkland's obstinance. They set up myopic empires in the Inner Stars, and then encouraged them to force non-inclusive viewpoints on others, all under the threat of war. Once established, the puppeteers set those empires against one another. Any who are willing to join the Scipio Alliance do not *need* to engage in war—though help is appreciated. However, many signees have had to make substantial changes in their society regarding how they treat AIs."

"And those who don't join your alliance and stand against you?"

"I'll do my best to render them harmless with as little

bloodshed as possible. I believe that once we defeat Nietzschea, the Trisilieds, and the Hegemony, most others will see that war against us is not a viable option."

"And Orion?" Sera asked. "As you said, Kirkland is not known for understanding, nor for a willingness to change his views. He's begun to eradicate AIs across his empire."

"Which will make him that much easier to defeat. I have the strengths of two species whereas he has only one."

"You still won't change his mind," Sera retorted. "Strengths or no, you won't be able to sway him, and if you win, you'll have to contend with the ideology he's infused in Orion space."

"It's possible that his viewpoint isn't as pervasive as some would believe. You don't know what happened to *Sabrina*, do you?"

Sera's eyes grew wide, and for the first time, her defensive posture slackened. "I managed to learn that they jumped out from the Grey Wolf Star over ten years ago…but no one knows where they went."

"The Perseus Arm of the galaxy," Tangel replied simply. "They got back a year ago, and from what they saw, Kirkland's hold on Orion space isn't as absolute as he'd like us to believe."

"Are—are they all OK?" Sera asked hesitantly.

"They are," Tangel nodded. "They had some tough times, but they all got back. Cargo is operating a cattle ranch down on Carthage in New Canaan, if you can believe it. Everyone else has been working to stop an AI uprising in the Inner Stars. They'll all be back here before long, though. You'll be able to meet with them no matter what you decide."

Sera's eyes narrowed. "Why are you being so nice to me? I've been working against you."

"Imagine, if you will," Tangel began with an expansive wave of her arm. "That you are the only version of yourself.

That another Sera did not come to New Canaan with your father—"

"My clone of a father," Sera interjected.

Tangel inclined her head. "Yes…or maybe he's a different type of copy, like you are. Either way, imagine you are the only Sera. To me, you're the woman who saved me from ending up at the mercy of the Mark back in Silstrand. You fought by my side at the Battle of Bollam's World, and you ended your exile to help my people get to New Canaan. I owe you *everything*."

"You owe *her* everything."

"Do you recall doing all those things?" Tangel asked. "Opening the cryopod and finding me in it? Getting captured by Rebecca, breaking free and securing the stolen CriEn module? What about flying to Bollam's World and helping us protect the *Intrepid* before showing us the way to Ascella? Do you remember trying to kill me while under your sister's influence?"

Sera nodded silently, and her eyes fell to the floor before she responded, "I do."

Tangel leant forward, elbows on her knees. "Then you *are* Sera. You're one of my dearest friends, and I'm treating you accordingly."

Sera's head lifted, and her gaze met Tangel's. "And if I do take you up on your offer? What then?"

"Then you join with your sisters and stop your mother. A unified Transcend is something we must achieve to end this war and begin the real fight with the Core."

Sera's lips drew into a thin line, and she turned her head toward the fire, blowing out a long breath.

SISTERS

STELLAR DATE: 09.23.8949 (Adjusted Years)
LOCATION: A1 Dock, ISS *I2*
REGION: Pyra, Albany System, Thebes, Septhian Alliance

"So how does it feel to be captain?" Sera asked as she strode up *Sabrina*'s ramp to where Cheeky stood waiting.

The slender—and completely naked—woman cocked her hips and held out her arms, beckoning for an embrace. "How should I know? It's only been a few hours since Jessica turned her over to me."

<No one's turned me over to anyone,> Sabrina interjected. <Remember, *I* own me. Sera herself did it.>

A happy sigh slipped past Sera's lips as she embraced Cheeky and gazed into the cargo bay behind her. "That I did, Sabs. How have you been?"

<I've been great! You wouldn't believe the stuff we've been up to, though I heard you got to go to the LMC! Knowing that's possible has made my bucket list so big, I'm going to need a bigger bucket.>

"I hear y—hey! Cheeky, enough with that!"

Cheeky chuckled as she lifted her hands from Sera's ass. "Just curious if you're the real Sera."

"And you think you'll be able to tell by my ass?"

Sabrina's newly minted captain took a step back, a hand on her chest and a shocked expression on her face. "Seriously...it's like you've forgotten who I am or something."

Sera stared at her long-time friend, trying to figure out if she was being serious or not, and then laughed, shaking her head. "Stars, Cheeky. Kill you, extract your mind from an AI's memory banks, put you in a new body, make you captain...none of that's changed you a bit. You're still the same ol' Cheeky I met in that dingy bar so long ago."

The naked woman laughed and grabbed her own rear. "Best thing about getting new skin is that these cheeks never sat on those disturbingly sticky barstools."

"Rarely am I an advocate for clothing, but in that case, it was more than warranted," Sera agreed.

The pair walked side-by-side into the ship's main cargo bay, where Nance and Misha waited. Sera didn't hesitate to embrace Nance, who wore a hazsuit with the hood pulled back.

"Back in your old routine?" Sera asked.

Nance glanced down at herself. "Oh, no…I legitimately needed it. Was working on the environmental system. Finaeus messed with it so much, I'm still trying to get it back the way I like."

"Nance…" Sera began, an eyebrow raised. "Finaeus is arguably one of the smartest people in the galaxy."

The bioengineer shrugged. "Sure, whatever. I still know Sabs better. Besides, I'm pretty sure half the things he did down there, he did just to mess with me."

With a soft laugh and a shake of her head, Sera turned to Misha. "Nice to meet you again, Misha. How's the galley holding up?"

"Tip-top," the cook replied. "I have a fresh pot of coffee on, a bowl of fruit, and some of your favorite snacks waiting for your meeting."

"How do you know my favorites?" Sera asked, to which Misha snorted.

"President Tomlinson, there's still a listing of items in the galley's inventory system labeled 'Captain Sera's Faves'."

"Oh." She chuckled. "And I'm not president of the Transcend anymore. Well, not really."

<As I understand it, you are until the cabinet votes otherwise,> Sabrina replied. <Which I suppose means you have to get back to Khardine before long?>

Sera nodded. "Once my sisters and I have a chat. If they agree to join us, they'll hop back with me and Tani—Tangel."

Cheeky pursed her lips. "It's weird hearing that name."

"It's weird saying it," Sera replied. "But half the time you were talking to Tanis in the past, Angela was in the conversation, anyway. Now it's just like talking to them both at once all the time."

<No it's not,> Sabrina interjected. <The sum is greater than the parts.>

"I wonder what it would be like…" Cheeky mused.

Nance rolled her eyes. "You'll have to ask Joe."

"You think that ruins my little mental visual," Cheeky said to Nance with a grin. "But it doesn't, it just makes it better."

"Will you guys greet the others when they arrive?" Sera asked. "I think it will make them feel better."

"Think so?" Nance asked. "Won't that be awkward?"

Sera shook her head. "No. I know they'll like it, they're still *me*—stars, that's a weird thing to say. Anyway, they just got led astray a little bit. Trust me, we've all missed you."

* * * * *

Five minutes later, Sera took a seat in the galley—though not in her old chair. It didn't feel right to take it and lord her originality over her sisters.

Instead, she took the seat Flaherty used to sit in, to the right of the head.

He had opted not to meet the other Seras yet, worried they may use his inability to lie against him. At least, that's what he'd said. Sera wasn't so sure.

<Are you ready?> Jen asked, after Sera had sat in silence for a minute.

<Not really, no. I don't even know what to do to **get** ready.>

The AI that shared space in Sera's head didn't respond for

a few seconds, and then laughed softly. <*I hear yoga is good in situations like this.*>

Sera snorted, imagining herself in some awkward yoga pose when her sisters entered.

<*Too vulnerable.*>

The tell-tale sound of someone climbing the ladder to the crew deck reached her ears, bringing with it a flood of memories from decades past.

"You still feel like home, *Sabrina*," Sera whispered.

<*Why thank you,*> Sabrina answered.

"I was talking to the ship."

"I know."

Sera resisted the urge to roll her eyes, knowing that one of her sisters would be entering the room at any moment. She straightened in her seat. Ready for anything.

Then *she* appeared in the galley's entrance, staring into the room. "They painted the place."

Sera glanced around the galley, surprised that she hadn't realized the walls were a subtle shade of lavender.

<*Can you guess who did that?*> Sabrina asked the pair.

Sera snorted, while her sister only shook her head.

"Stars, it feels so good to have your voice in my head, Sabrina," the other Sera said—still not having met Sera's eyes.

<*It's mutual,*> Sabrina replied. <*Having two—wait, now three of you aboard is more excitement than I've seen in some time. And I've fought in more than one war in the past few years.*>

The other Sera's gaze fell on their old place at the head of the table before she shook her head and sat at the foot. "Doesn't feel right."

"I know," Sera agreed. "I guess that's Cheeky's place now."

"Stars," the other Sera muttered. "Can you believe that little waif we found in that gross bar is the captain now?"

Sera wondered if her sister was being derisive, when she continued.

"She deserves it. That girl has been through hell and back, from what I've been told. Perseus Arm."

"She has," Sera agreed. "Hard to believe that with all the crazy stuff we've been through in the past twenty years, you've been through more, Sabrina."

<Well...I haven't been to the LMC, so you have me beat, there.>

"Neither have I," the third Sera said from the galley's doorway. "Looks like Mom didn't give me the fun stuff."

Sera watched her first sister turn and give the second one a narrow-eyed look.

She understood what they were thinking. Both had known for some time that there was *one* other Sera out there, but the story they'd both been told was that *they* were the original, and the Sera ruling from Khardine was the imposter.

Now they were faced with the incontrovertible truth that it was their mother, Airtha, who was manufacturing doppelgangers, not the people of New Canaan.

No one spoke as the newcomer made her way to the middle seat on the right side of the table, and pulled out the chair.

The silence continued for a whole minute before the Sera who had been captured in the Valkris asked the one captured at LMC, "so, how far back do you remember?"

"To being a little girl." LMC Sera's tone was acidic. "You?"

"That's not what I meant," Valkris Sera shot back. "Don't you want to know which one of us is a copy of the other?"

Sera raised her hands. "Easy, now. We're not really copies, its different than that."

LMC Sera waved a hand. "Right, we're sourced from a backup of your neural network, making us more like branches of a tree than copies. That's all semantics; it doesn't change the facts of the matter. You're the original; we're divergent."

"Not that divergent," Valkris Sera said with a coarse laugh.

"I have to admit," Sera mused, hoping to placate her

sisters. "I've wondered if I'm not a copy, as well. Like there was some earlier Sera that mother didn't quite like, so she made some tweaks, and here I am."

LMC Sera snorted. "Given your wardrobe proclivities, I'm pretty sure you're not the Sera made in her image."

Valkris Sera raised her eyebrows. "I've been meaning to ask. Can I get it back? The skin?"

"You want it?" Sera asked.

"Stars, yes! Mother said that it was destroyed in the attack that killed Helen—all lies, I know now—but hot damn, I've missed it. I was halfway tempted to send someone to Silstrand just to find out where Rebecca sourced that original suit that devoured our skin."

LMC Sera shook her head. "I'm more than happy to keep my real skin—and how do you know that the attack and Helen's death was a lie? What if this other one of us," here she paused to gesture at Sera, "is the imposter? What if—"

Valkris Sera leant over the table and placed a hand on LMC Sera's wrist. "We both know that's not true. Besides, the ISF freed us from mother's control. I know you feel it. I feel it too."

A shuddering breath sucked past Valkris Sera's lips and she nodded. "Yeah...it just sucks balls."

"All the balls," Sera added.

"You?" Both other Seras asked in unison. "Why does it suck for you?"

"Really?" Sera asked. "Don't you get it? I might not be in the same boat as you two, but I'm in the one right next to you. Mother *made* me just like she did with you. She made the version of father that she wanted, and then she made me— only *after* failing to create a viable scion with Andrea."

LMC Sera snorted. "At least Mom knew a total write-off when she saw it."

The three women broke into soft laughter before falling silent once more.

"Here's how I see it," Sera said. "Mom fucked with all three of us. Tried to make us to be her puppets. But that doesn't mean we're lesser beings. We're still exactly who we've always been—tough, sexy, ass-kicking women who aren't going to take this laying down. And Tanis has a mission for us: take out Airtha in a targeted strike. We can do that *and* save the Transcend. Then we stop those douchebags in Orion, and finally bring the fight to the Core AIs. *Everyone* who has a god complex goes down."

"There may be some specifics in there that I would like to tweak, but in general, I'm onboard with this plan," LMC Sera said with a grim smile.

"What of Tanis?" Valkris Sera asked. "She's got a bit of a god complex, if you ask me."

Sera shrugged. "Maybe a bit. You have to admit, she's something different. Either way, it's a miracle that she and the ISF are here trying to help. I think if Tangel were to order it, they'd all just head off and leave us to our devices."

"Maybe," Valkris Sera said with a shrug.

LMC Sera set her elbows on the table and folded her hands before setting her chin on them. "So. Let's finally talk about the elephant in the room. Who gets to keep the name?"

"Sera?" Sera asked.

"Yeah," Valkris Sera said. "It'll be confusing as fuck if everyone has to call all of us Sera—*especially* if we're going on a mission together."

"Well, there's Seraphina, or Fina…. What Finaeus used to call me—us—when we were kids," Sera suggested.

"I say none of us gets to keep any of the names," Valkris Sera said as she gestured to Sera. "Having to call *you* 'Sera' will just feel too weird. How's about you're Red Sera?"

Sera snorted. " 'Red Sera'? Really?"

"You have to admit that it fits," LMC Sera said with a grin. "You're always red."

"Mostly," Sera said with a shrug. "I do like to shake things up, though. I happen to enjoy the color blue." She lifted her hand, and her skin turned from red to blue.

"Nuh-uh," Valkris Sera said with a shake of her head. "When I get the skin upgrade back, I'm going blue. I call dibs. I'm Blue Sera."

"You can't call dibs on a color," Sera shot back.

"Well I'm sticking with skin-color," LMC Sera interjected. "Maybe I'll take the skin job, but I kinda like looking human."

Sera grinned at her sister, running her hands down her sides. "Deviant. You want the sexy feels, but you don't want to stand out."

"Where's the fun in that?" Valkris Sera added. "We've always liked standing out."

"Oh I'm all for reverting to form," LMC Sera replied with a smile. "But I really like all the leather I used to wear before that catsuit ripped my skin off. That was my jam."

Sera's hand changed from blue to a leathery texture. "You can do leather, too. This stuff is ridiculously versatile."

"Deal," LMC Sera said. "But I'm not going to be 'Leather Sera'. Sounds like I'm some sort of pirate…or serial killer."

"Well, we *were* a pirate once," Sera said with a wink.

Valkris Sera snorted. "You can be Pi—"

"Don't even go there!" LMC Sera snapped. "I'll be…Black Sera. But I'm going with red hair, because that'll look badass."

"What?" Sera asked. "That's going to be as confusing as all get-out!"

LMC Sera winked at Sera. "No, just means you have to keep your skin red all the time to avoid confusion."

"You realize," Valkris Sera said, a wicked grin on her lips, "We're going to be able to mess with everyone so much."

<*You sure you want to go with colors?*> Sabrina asked innocently. <*It's going to sound like you're different fireteams or fighter wings. 'Red One to Blue Two. Come in Blue Two.'*>

"She has a point," Sera said. "Though I don't really have an issue with being called 'Red', to be honest."

"OK…maybe we think about Seraphina and Fina again," Valkris Sera suggested. "I mean…I still call dibs on *being* blue. But I'm willing to take on 'Fina'. I have a lot of good memories of Uncle Finaeus calling me that as a little girl."

"Yeah, but that means I have to go with 'Seraphina'," LMC Sera said, her lips twisting in dismay. "That's what Helen called us when she was mad…"

"And Helen was mom," Sera completed the thought, then glanced at Valkris Sera. "I still say you can't call dibs on a color."

"Screw it." LMC Sera slapped her palm on the table. "*Every* version of Seraphina is a name given to us by our fucking bastard of a mother. Why *can't* I just go with Seraphina? Time to take it back."

"That's the spirit," Fina said, raising a fist into the air. "Stars. I bet when Mom learns the three of us are united, she's going to shit digital bricks all over her pretty diamond ring. Sera, Fina, and Seraphina are coming for her!"

"To us!" Sera said, joining Fina and thrusting her fist into the air, tremendously relieved that their first meeting had ended like this, and not in a firefight.

A smile crept across Seraphina's face, and she reached out, placing a hand on each of her sister's fists. "She's never gonna know what hit her."

SVETLANA'S TEN THOUSAND

STELLAR DATE: 09.23.8949 (Adjusted Years)
LOCATION: TSS *Cossack's Sword*
REGION: Khardine System, Transcend Interstellar Alliance

Svetlana stood at the head of the long virtual table and watched her fleet commanders get settled.

Though her force was small, it consisted of the hardiest ships she could secure for the mission—including a group of ISF rail destroyers that were commanded by a stern looking colonel named Caldwell.

The rest of the team was made up of TSF personnel, starting with Rear Admiral Sebastian, who commanded the second division of the fleet. General Lorelai, who commanded the combat forces, sat across from him, followed by colonels Lia and Colton, who were responsible for the fighter wings.

Beyond them were the senior captains, thirty-six in all, followed by hundreds more captains filling the holographic space. At the end of the table were the men and women she needed to have onboard with this the most: the senior warrant and petty officers, most specifically, Command Master Chief Merrick.

Though he sat at the end of the table, Svetlana knew he was the most respected person in her fleet. Merrick had served as a noncom in the Transcend Space Force for over a thousand years. The only reason he hadn't ever taken the role of Master Chief of the Space Force was because, in his words, *'I got my own shit to do. Can't waste time sticking my nose up bureaucrats' asses all day.'*

Svetlana both respected and feared the man. In part because of his venerable status, but also because he was her father.

His hard-eyed gaze gave her no indication as to whether or not he approved of the strategy to take fleets deep into Orion space, but she hoped that if he didn't agree, he wouldn't voice it here, and would instead take it up with her privately.

After waiting another half-minute for everyone to settle, she addressed the group.

"You've all read the brief. You know why we're here, what we're going to do. Fleet Admiral Wrentham needs us to take the pressure off the Orion Fronts, and that's just what we're going to do. Admiral Mardus is going to be hitting Herschel, and we're striking the center of the Perseus Expansion Districts."

As Svetlana spoke, a display of the Orion Arm appeared over the table, a yellow outline highlighting the PED, while a red marker appeared at Quera, close—galactically speaking—to the edge of the Orion Arm.

"As most of you know, Admiral Keller of the ISF passed through these regions of Orion space on reconnaissance aboard the *Sabrina* nearly two years ago, so our intel is a bit out of date, but we have supplements from the few Hand agents in that area.

"The locals are low-tech. Half of them don't even have the Link, and those that do usually just have oculars. From what we know, the PED is mostly populated by refuges who fled toward the rim during the FTL wars. Orion absorbed them and offered succor and sanctuary in exchange for strict adherence to draconian laws regarding technological advancements."

Svetlana paused, her gaze sweeping across the assemblage.

"Essentially, they're going to shit bricks when they see us. We have reason to believe that the PED's inhabitants think the Inner Stars are still utter anarchy, and have *no idea* that the Transcend even exists."

"Intel supports that?" General Lorelai asked. "I understand

that information about the Inner Stars and the Transcend may not be in the public databases on their worlds, but surely there must be some underground knowledge. Their populace gets conscripted by the OG—many of those get sent to the front. They must come back with stories."

"That's what we've believed for some time," Svetlana replied, nodding in agreement. "But the intel that Admiral Keller brought back indicates otherwise. It's different out by Herschel, but in the Perseus Arm and the PED, the Orion Guard is the boogeyman, and doesn't enlist many troops from the local populations.

"They have local militia-style space forces, but they're really just there to police things. Fear of the OG seems to keep them in line."

"Well, Admiral Keller would know," Colonel Caldwell said to General Lorelai. "She spent ten years in Orion space."

"Seems like such a waste." Lorelai shook her head then shrugged. "So I take it this means we're to go easy on the locals."

"That's the idea right now," Svetlana replied with a curt nod. "Unless we find Keller's assessment to be wrong, in which case we'll adapt our strategy. Still, we have to assume them to be a hostile population. They'll see us as invaders, not liberators."

"Could we not establish a beachhead?" One of the senior captains asked. "Take and hold systems, force Orion to come to us?"

Svetlana shook her head. "That's not how I want to approach this. If we take and hold, we have to police and defend. Our intel indicates that the OG isn't afraid to strike out at their own population, and Fleet Intel thinks they may use that against us.

"Instead, our approach is to strike hard, destroy military and major infrastructure targets, and move on. We never go back to a system we've been to before, never give them a reason to use a populace against us. Our goal is to be like the Hoplites in ancient Persia. We're pushing to the Sea. Our Sea is the Perseus Arm. We get there, we get to go home."

"Perseus?" Admiral Sebastian asked. "That could take years, a decade if we get bogged down at all."

"I'm being a bit hyperbolic," Svetlana replied. "I'd like to think that we'll get to strike a more decisive blow before we get that far."

"An attack on New Sol?" Lorelai asked.

"Or a truce." Svetlana glanced at her father and saw him nod slowly. "If we can win against Airtha and end the war in the Inner Stars, then suddenly Kirkland faces the rest of humanity alone."

Caldwell set his elbows on the table and nodded. "That seems like a laudable goal."

"Agreed," Sebastian added. "So what is our first target?"

Sebastian knew the plan, of course. He and Svetlana had spent some time crafting it, but she appreciated him leading the conversation along.

She triggered the holodisplay to focus in on the Quera System, where Costa Station was—or maybe wasn't anymore, given that Jessica Keller's team had fired RMs at its gate before jumping back to New Canaan.

"We're going to start here. We'll jump in an observation ship with a drone gate a quarter light year out. It will make an assessment and send back the findings. We'll hop into Quera either way; whether or not it's empty will just affect how we deploy. We'll scour it for any intel, and then move on to either the Norma or Ferra Systems. Neither have large military presences, but we'll crush what's there and move on. We want to keep moving and keep making lightning strikes for as long as possible. Unpredictable and deadly is the name of the game."

Svetlana widened the view of the PED, showing the possible routes through the region of space. One path roughly followed Jessica Keller's route from the Perseus Arm, while the other veered spinward, toward a cluster of systems with names like 'Eashira', 'Cush', and 'Machete'.

"Are we worried that they'll try to bottle us up?" one of the captains, a woman named Jula, asked. "Predict our moves and lay in wait?"

"Technically, that's what we want," Svetlana replied. "I do worry about it, though. We have superior weaponry and shields, but the OGs have numbers on their side. We know that enough firepower can overwhelm even stasis shielding, and we have to assume that they know to hit us in the engines while we're burning. So we're not going to be stupid—plus, not all our ships have stasis shields.

"That scout ship I mentioned has already deployed to the Quera System. Once it drops its drone, it'll pack up its gate and leave for Ferra. The ship's crewed by an elite team, SF and Hand agents, who are going to scout ahead of us, and build a network of contacts as fast as possible. They also have intel on two Hand agents in the vicinity, and will try to make contact with them for the latest intel."

"So what's next?" Colonel Colton asked.

"We're only taking four fab-ships and we're going to rely on the folks back here at Khardine to send us supplies as we need them. The QuanComm network and the jump gates are setting us up for a new kind of warfare that we've never practiced and the Oggies have never seen. Still, don't pack light," Svetlana paused as a few of the officers laughed. "If you don't bring it along, you better not *need* it for a year. I'm not calling back to Admiral Greer to ask him to send your jammies and teddy bears out to the PED.

"Everyone has two days to inform their crews that we're about to go on a long-duration tour—no details 'til we ship.

Transfer out anyone you think will have issues with that. We leave in fifty hours."

"Fifty hours?" one of the captains blurted out, then reddened.

"Yes, fifty. Not a minute more. This is the Space Force, not your kid's daycare. Let's get this shit done, and get the show on the road."

A CHAT WITH TROY

STELLAR DATE: 09.23.8949 (Adjusted Years)
LOCATION: A1 Dock, ISS *I2*
REGION: Pyra, Albany System, Thebes, Septhian Alliance

Tangel watched with a measure of melancholy-tinged joy as the *Voyager* settled on the cradle before her. Seeing the ship brought back a host of memories—which was strange, considering that she'd never seen the vessel before.

She—well, Tanis—had ordered the *Voyager*'s construction back at Kapteyn's Star, where it was placed at the secret pico-research site as an interstellar-capable evac vehicle. Later, when the site had been cleared out, Angela had suggested leaving the ship behind in case Katrina, or someone else, had a need to leave Kapteyn's star.

Judging by the looks of the vessel, it had been through a lot more than Tanis or Angela had ever expected.

But that wasn't what had Tangel feeling anxious.

It was who was aboard the ship.

"He doesn't hold a grudge." Katrina's voice was barely above a whisper, where she stood next to Tangel. "He and I talked about it back at Victoria. Don't forget, I was governor after that battle. I'm just as much to blame for not finding them right away."

Tangel glanced at the woman next to her. Katrina was barely recognizable from the person who had first come aboard the *I2* a few days earlier. Gone was the grey hair, aged skin, and slight stoop. The woman who had been so many things—from spy to governor to warlord to pirate—now looked like she'd barely passed her twentieth birthday.

Except for the eyes. Katrina had always had an old woman's eyes. Now they were ancient.

"True enough," Tangel said. "But you *did* find him. I left him behind. One of our greatest heroes…abandoned."

Katrina shrugged. "There's no absolution I can offer you. You'll have to seek that out for yourself."

"And seek it I shall." Tangel sighed and closed her eyes for a moment. "Sometimes it feels like there's so much to regret, Katrina."

A snort burst from the woman's nose. "Oh believe me, I know that all too well. It's so easy to let the past become an anchor—and not the sort you want, either. I've done a lot…*a lot* that I regret. But taken individually, I'm at peace with nearly all the decisions I've made."

Tangel couldn't help but notice the caveat. " 'Nearly all'."

"You have them, I'm sure. The ones that will haunt you forever."

A hundred regret-filled memories flashed before Tangel's eyes as the gantry extended to meet the *Voyager's* airlock. "Do I ever."

"You never talked about them—even before you became half-AI," Katrina observed, as a light came on signaling that the airlock was cycling.

Tangel shrugged. "It's not really my way to dwell on the past. I can't do anything about it. All I can do is look to the future and do my best when it comes. I'm a fast study—mostly—when it comes to the lessons of the past. One of those lessons was to not let memory and regret from days gone by rule the present. The ability to forget is one of the greatest gifts humanity has."

Katrina cocked her head and caught Tanis's gaze. "But you're not human anymore, are you?"

Tangel shrugged. "Biologically I'm not, no. Sera even finally badgered me into adopting her preference in epidermis—though without the constant sensory stimulation."

"I've done my time with artificial skin, I'll pass on that,"

Katrina grimaced, a look of far-off pain in her eyes.

"I fought it for a while," Tangel replied. "But it was foolish. Having bulletproof, stealth-capable, chameleon skin is a considerable boon in our line of work. You can always get it changed back."

"Don't change the subject," Katrina replied, her tone laced with a note of humor as she evaded Tangel's suggestion. "You were about to tell me what new species you are."

"Well, I'm not an AI, which we all know to be a misnomer anyway. I know some have categorized AIs—at least the ones with Weapon Born in their lineage—as Homo Quantus-Animo Sapiens. Perhaps I am a Homo Quantus-Penta-Animo Sapiens, or some such."

"Sounds like a mouthful—also not what I was getting at," Katrina said, her lips twisting into a smirk.

Tangel chuckled. "I know. I don't really know what I am, or what I'm capable of—classifying myself seems foolish, given that. Stars, every time I push what I think are my boundaries, I just find new vistas."

"What's it like?" Katrina asked.

Tangel paused before replying, trying to find the right words. "It's…complex. I can choose to see with only my two-dimensional vision, my eyes, should I choose. When I do that, I can perceive the three dimensions as I always have. However, my other senses keep trickling in. The three dimensions turn into four, then five. I'm…growing, for lack of a better word, new sensory organs. I believe I know how to grow five-dimensional 'eyes'. Once I do that, I'll be able to perceive the sixth dimension."

"Shit," Katrina whispered.

"Yeah, it's nuts. I can see other types of light and energy. I can touch them, too." As she spoke, Tangel reached out with her corporeal hand and touched a shimmering stream that was flowing off the *Voyager*—the fifth-dimensional manifestation of the magnetic field emanating from the fusion reactor's tokamak coils. The stream flexed under her touch, and she watched that movement transfer into all the other magnetic fields around her, a luminescent web of electromagnetism that filled the docking bay.

The fields flowed through Katrina, bending the small ones within her body, altering it and her mind in subtle ways. Tangel followed the energy flows, noting one that appeared discordant. From experience, Tangel knew that it was the physical manifestation of an unpleasant memory, of some past pain.

She reached out and touched it.

Curious. It's so embedded.

"Tangel! What the…!" Katrina cried out, jerking away.

Tangel started, realizing that as she'd followed the thread, she'd touched Katrina's face with her corporeal hand.

"Sorry, I was…ah…following the magnetic fields through the bay, looking at how they interact with you in other dimensions."

Katrina was staring at Tangel with a look that was half fear, half worry. "I felt you…inside."

Tangel felt a flush rise on her cheeks. "I'm really sorry, I didn't mean to. Sometimes, realities don't line up the way I expect them to. I didn't realize…."

"That you were probing inside my body?" Katrina's ire and fear turned into a sardonic smirk.

"Uh…yeah."

"I'll admit, it felt…good," Katrina allowed. "Like a tingle running through me."

Tangel wondered if she should tell Katrina what she saw, but the sound of the airlock opening caught her attention, and she turned back to the ship, watching as the first figure stepped out, stooping to clear the low overhang.

"Kara," Tangel said in greeting as she approached and took

the black-winged woman's hand. "I'm sorry about your brother."

Tanis and Angela had only seen Kara and her brother briefly—aboard the *Galadrial* the day she stormed it with Usef and a team of Marines—but Adrienne's children had made an impression. She noted that Kara had a face now; no longer was the woman's head a black oval, devoid of features. The resemblance to her father was clear, which made sense, given what she'd learned of the man who had borne all his own children.

The fangs, however, made for a marked differentiation.

"Thank you, Tangel," Kara said in a quiet voice. "I noticed that these caught your attention." She pulled her lips back, further baring the long, sharp teeth. "I had them added in memory of him. He was the one who had always pushed for us to have fear-inspiring appearances. The fangs were one of the first alterations he'd suggested."

"A fitting homage," Katrina replied with a solemn nod.

Behind Kara came a tall man who also looked far younger than the last information Tangel had read on him.

"Carl," she said, extending her hand. "I hear you've worked hard to keep the *Voyager* in good condition."

"Thank you, Admiral. Been a pleasure. Spent far and away most of my life on this ship, now."

A flash of red in the airlock caught Tangel's attention, and she gave a warm smile, gesturing for the occupant to exit.

"Katrina told me all about you, Malorie. You're welcome here."

A head with eight eyes peered around the top edge of the airlock. A moment later, the rest of the mechanical spider dropped to the deck. Katrina had explained to Tangel that Malorie still possessed a human brain inside her arachnid body, but over the years, she'd taken her altered form to heart, reveling in the thing she'd become.

"Admiral Tangel. After hearing Katrina speak of you for so many years…I thought you'd be taller."

Tangel considered that to be an amusing statement from a woman whose disturbingly spider-like head—complete with large, fanged chelicerae—was only a meter off the ground.

"I'm sure she's told a tall tale or two in her day," Tangel replied with a shrug. "I'm just a woman trying to get by in this crazy universe."

A chittering laugh slipped out of Malorie's mouth. "From someone who is more 'just a woman' than you, I sincerely doubt that."

Tangel shrugged and looked back up at the ship looming overhead, her trepidation returning. "Troy? May I come aboard?"

<*Of course; though it's not my ship, I just live here.*>

"Nonsense," Katrina said, her brow lowering. "Just because Tanis left this ship to me doesn't mean the last five hundred years count for nothing."

"Time to pay the piper," Tangel said to the group around her with a slight nod as she slipped past. "Once I've chatted with Troy, we'll see if the Seras are ready, and we can all talk about the mission."

Katrina folded her arms. "You'd better have a hell of a plan. It was a suicide run just to rescue Kara when she left High Airtha."

Tangel winked at her long-time friend. "We'll put our heads together. I'm sure we can come up with something."

"Very encouraging," Malorie rasped as Tangel walked toward the Voyager.

Tangel ran her hands along the hull for a moment before stepping through the airlock and into the corridor that ran to the central shaft.

"It's weird, Troy," Tangel said as she reached the ladder and began to climb.

<What's weird?>

"That this ship is so *old*. For me, Kapteyn's star was just a quarter-century ago. This ship should look no older than, say, the *Dresden*."

<Time has a way of wearing things down,> Troy replied, his tone still too casual for Tangel's liking.

She reached the second to top level and swung off the ladder and onto the deck. "I'm surprised Katrina and her crew never re-aligned the decks to be horizontal—what with having a-grav for so long."

<Katrina's nostalgic. She likes the Voyager the way it is. Carl never even raised the specter of changing the layout, and so it has remained.>

"Did she at least add a hot tub?" Tangel asked as she reached the ship's upper node chamber and palmed open the door.

A snort sounded in Tangel's mind. <That all I am to you? A hot-tub starship?>

Tangel stared at the AI's core, slotted into a receptacle on the bulkhead across the small space.

"I'm so sorry, Troy," Tangel's voice came out in a whisper. "We searched for years, scouring the system for any survivors from the battle. I...." She rested her back against the bulkhead and slid to the deck. "Can you forgive me, Troy?"

<Why am I so special? Surely you've lost others over the years. From what I've heard, the Battle for Victoria was just a warmup.> Troy paused for a moment. <Why is it that my forgiveness is so important?>

"Because you're right here in front of me," Tangel replied quietly. "Those others, they're all lost, and their ghosts never reply."

<I hold no grudge against you, Tangel. Nor did I against Tanis and Angela. Though you may be far more than human, you are not a goddess. You cannot foresee all outcomes.>

"Do you mean that?" Tangel asked. "I mean the part about no grudge; I get that I'm not a goddess. What a thankless job that would be."

<Gods and goddesses from ancient human mythology were—by and large—far less powerful than you are, Tangel. But that noteworthy thought aside, yes, I do mean it.>

She nodded silently, letting Troy's sincerity seep into her. Then she glanced up at him. "You seem to have lost a bit of your hard edge."

<I hear that years can do that to a person,> Troy replied. <I never slept, you know. Not while I was lost on that moon, not while we hunted for Katrina, and not in the long centuries afterward. I always kept watch over her, made sure she was safe.>

"Thank you for that," Tangel said.

Troy let out a long, audible groan that filled the room. <OK, now I know ascendency is going to your head. I didn't do it for you, I did it for me. She's my anchor; I'd be lost without her.>

Tangel's eyes widened. "Ohhhh…I didn't realize things were like *that* between you two."

A chuckle sounded around Tangel. <Neither does she.>

"Has she been with anyone else?" Tangel asked, curious if perhaps Katrina was remaining chaste for Troy.

<No—well, maybe a short fling or two, here and there. Nothing meaningful. Nothing in the last century, either.>

Tangel whistled. "That's a long time to go without love."

<We have love. This crew is a family.>

"I know how that works," she replied, a slight edge to her voice. "I have my family like that, as well—of which you and Katrina are members. But…maybe you should tell her. Things are going to get crazy soon. If you take this mission, you're going into the lion's den."

Another chuckle sounded around her. <We've been in the shit plenty. I'm pretty sure we have a standing reservation.>

"Not like this, you haven't," Tangel replied as she rose.

"Sera just pinged me. They're coming."

AN ANGEL INSIDE
STELLAR DATE: 09.01.8949 (Adjusted Years)
LOCATION: *Damon Silas*
REGION: Interstellar Space, coreward of the Vela Cluster

Roxy looked down at the hole in her midsection, and a wave of fear washed over her. She'd spent years in her azure body, knowing that she was more machine than woman, but in all that time, she'd never seen the inside of herself. Opened up like she was nothing more than a servitor.

Maybe Carmen is right. Maybe there's nothing human left of me anymore.

The thought brought about a feeling of blackness that reached up to swallow her, an uncontrollable despair and fear that even the meager truths surrounding her existence that she'd clung to were lies.

Am I nothing? Roxy closed her eyes and shook her head. *No, I am me, I know that I am still me.*

"But what am I?" she whispered. "If I don't know *what* I am, how can I know *who* I am?"

The repair drone—with several of its armatures holding Roxy's abdomen open—offered no reply as it reached into the fabricator and pulled out a new, smaller bioassimilator. Her old one sat on the workbench next to Carmen's case, the flexible, curved apparatus until recently having been the thing that digested any organic sustenance Roxy had chosen to eat.

Since she rarely bothered with food, Carmen suggested that it was the ideal internal system to downsize.

Roxy looked away as the repair drone inserted the new assimilator into her body, the thing's dozen armatures working swiftly and deftly.

The fact that it was not a medical drone was not lost on her, but Carmen assured her that the machine would not be getting anywhere close to her organic systems. Roxy wondered if it was because the AI's earlier statement was correct, and that she *had* no organic systems.

A part of her mind rebelled against the idea, while another part wondered what that would really mean. Carmen's words reverberated in her mind, over and over.

'Are you an AI?'

What if I am? Roxy wondered.

"System check completed," the drone announced aloud. "Ready to install AI core mount and casing."

"Proceed," Roxy said, doing her best to keep her voice from wavering.

Carmen still rested in her case, controlling the drone and passing it instructions. The AI hadn't spoken aloud since the procedure started, but beforehand, she had assured Roxy that it would not be a complicated operation.

Maybe not for you—an AI who used to run this starship…but for me, this is my only body, Roxy had thought at the time.

Now she wondered if her body was really so special. If it was just a machine, it could be replaced. *She* could be replaced.

The drone inserted the mounting system for the AI core, and then threaded a bundle of optical channel cabling into Roxy's abdomen. A second later, a new series of systems appeared on her HUD.

The AI core mount was connected to her power supplies and would be able to piggyback on her Link.

A part of Roxy *knew* that sort of connection was risky; it would give Carmen largely unbuffered access to her own mind. But for some reason, she trusted the AI.

Either that, or the freedom she had tasted, with Justin's control over her mind slipping, had emboldened her to attempt this greater rebellion.

Or I'm just being fatalistic. Can an AI be fatalistic?

"Are you ready?" Carmen's voice came from the case. "Once I'm in, and the drone seals you up, it'll take some doing to get me out again."

Roxy drew in a deep breath, mentally chiding herself for the affectation. "We never really talked about what's past this point."

"True," Carmen admitted. "I have a suspicion that you may be having second thoughts about your association with Justin. Is that true?"

"No." Roxy spat out the word in defiance, and then paused. "Well, maybe. I know he controls me, and I...I like it, but I'm not sure if *I* like it, or if I'm made to like it."

"I know it may take a while," the AI began, speaking the words slowly—which had to be for Roxy's benefit, "But will you eventually help me escape, set me free?"

"Yes," Roxy replied with a nod. "I—I really don't know why I'm doing this, but I swear it's not to trap you in my stomach forever."

Carmen laughed softly. "Well, I suppose that'll have to do. You need to order the drone to put me in. I'll be silent for a bit, as I'll have to re-initialize inside the new core mount and make sure it passes functionality tests before I reach out."

"Understood," Roxy said, drawing another deep breath and feeling stupid for doing it. "Service drone, install Carmen's core in me."

"Proceeding," the drone replied, and two armatures reached out and hovered over Carmen's core, waiting for the 'safe removal' indicator to come on.

When it did, the machine lifted the AI out of the case and turned to Roxy, carefully sliding the ten-centimeter cube into her body. Roxy could feel it seat, and then felt a small vibration as the mounting clamps secured the core.

The drone began to use flowmetal to thread Roxy's abdominal muscles back together, and within a minute, was carefully sealing her azure skin. When it was done, Roxy bent over and couldn't tell that she'd been opened up like a faulty automaton. Strangely, the feeling of seeing her body whole once more made her feel even less human.

*A **person** wouldn't appear completely undamaged after major surgery like this. Not in under five minutes, at least.*

She slowly bent and flexed, unable to feel anything different at all.

"Good work, drone," she muttered.

As Roxy spoke, the new section of systems on her HUD flashed, and an alert indicator appeared, showing a high-bandwidth Link connection to another person.

<*Carmen?*> she asked hesitantly.

<*Roxy, I'm here.*> Her voice was far more melodious than the case's small speaker had allowed it to be.

<*Is…everything OK?*>

The AI chuckled softly. <*Yes, of course. The systems are working perfectly, you have enough power for both of us, and your Link interface is actually better than I expected. It shouldn't be hard at all to mask myself, should I need to access outside systems.*>

<*And us?*> Roxy didn't quite know how to voice her concern. <*Are we…separate?*>

<*Roxy, relax. There's no chance of us merging or having any sort of mental bleed-through. I'm not installed in your brain, I'm in your belly.*>

<*True,*> she admitted. <*But my internal security systems are warning me that the Link between us is all but unbuffered. You could invade my mind, or I yours.*>

<*I won't.*> Carmen's voice carried absolute certainty. <*I may be running away from my responsibilities, but that doesn't make me a monster—just someone who doesn't want to sacrifice herself with her ship to protect tech that Justin stands no chance of reverse engineering.*>

Roxy wondered about that. Justin had access to more

resources than Carmen knew. It could be that he *was* capable of ferreting out the workings of the stasis shields.

She put that concern aside as she instructed the drone to return to its charging station, and slid the AI case behind some equipment on a lower shelf.

<*I'm wiping the drone and the fabricator,*> Carmen informed her. <*If anyone checks them over, they'll find no record of us doing this.*>

<*OK. I'd best get to the pinnace.... We've spent almost thirty minutes in here,*> Roxy replied as she walked to the door, listening for any footfalls outside.

She considered deploying drones, but if someone detected those, it would be even more suspicious.

Determining that the coast was clear, Roxy opened the door and walked out into the passageway as though she had every right to be there—which she supposed she did. She'd secured the ship, after all.

Luckily for her, Justin was neither the jealous nor overbearing type. She wondered if that was because the man believed he had thorough control over her.

The thought triggered another wave of Justin-endorsing imagery in her mind, and she noted once more that it was far milder than it had been in the past, more subjective and less mind-numbingly overt.

<*That was odd,*> Carmen said a moment later, her voice sounding cautious.

<*Sorry?*> Roxy asked as she reached the lift and stepped inside, passing her destination as the next level up.

<*There was an odd dip in your brainwaves. It bled through our Link a bit. I've only been paired once before, but in my experience, it seemed like segments of your mind dropped into delta waves.*>

Roxy pulled up the reference. <*Like I was asleep?*>

<*Yeah, but it didn't translate like your entire mind had gone to sleep, just parts of it.*>

The question that had been burning in Roxy's mind since Carmen had first planted the seed of doubt reared up.

<Does that mean I'm **not** an AI?>

<I don't really know,> Carmen said with a soft laugh. <It's possible to simulate anything over the Link. What were you thinking about a moment ago?>

Roxy hesitated, not wanting to share what she considered to be her deepest shame with the AI.

Oh, screw it, she thought. *I can't hide it from her forever.*

The lift doors opened, and Roxy squared her shoulders and strode out into the passageway. <Whenever I think bad things, I get corrective thoughts.> She said the words as tonelessly as possible. <They used to be so powerful that they'd blot out recent memories of misbehavior—at least, I think they did. They're different now, though, not as overwhelming. I wonder if something over the last few days changed the neural lace that does that.>

<A neural lace?> Carmen asked. <What kind? There are a lot of neural lace applications.>

<I…I don't know,> Roxy replied.

The AI's voice grew even more serious. <You're a prisoner here, aren't you? Well, not 'here' per se, but of Justin's?>

Roxy reached the entrance to the docking bay and paused at the threshold, staring at Justin's pinnace that would take her to Justin's ship, the *Greensward*. There, she would do her part to keep Andrea in line, bolster the woman's ego, and give succor to the belief that she was well on her way to being proclaimed the president of the Transcend.

<Maybe…> Roxy admitted as she stepped into the bay, marching toward the pinnace's lowered ramp.

A dock worker nodded to her as she passed. "All fueled up, ma'am. Jane's aboard, ready to fly you over. Find your lightwand?"

"No. Stupid thing," Roxy groused. "How far is the *Greensward*?"

"Ten thousand klicks under us," the man said. "Shouldn't take but a few minutes."

"Thanks," Roxy replied over her shoulder as she walked up the ramp. "Looking forward to sleeping in my own bed tonight."

The man only nodded in response, giving Roxy a wave as she turned to close the airlock.

Once inside the pinnace, Roxy walked to the cockpit, sliding into the seat next to Jane, as was her custom.

"How's Her Majesty been?" Roxy asked. "Tolerable?"

Jane glanced over at Roxy as she flipped through the preflight checks on her console. "Is that the best she gets? Doesn't matter. No, not tolerable. More like 'not quite bad enough for me to slit my wrists…but close'."

"So normal, then," Roxy said with a soft laugh.

Jane nodded absently as she lifted the pinnace off its cradle and eased out of the *Damon Silas*.

<Not how I expected to be leaving this ship,> Carmen said privately as they drifted to a safe distance from the cruiser.

<Oh?> Roxy asked. <On a pinnace?>

<Inside someone. It just feels strange to be out here without a ship as my skin. It feels…>

<Vulnerable?> Roxy supplied.

<That's an understatement.>

Roxy watched the *Damon Silas* grow smaller on the port optical feeds, wondering if leaving the ship was the right move—not that she had much choice. Justin had ordered her back to the *Greensward*, and so back she went. It was a miracle he hadn't checked in on her while she was having Carmen installed.

Probably too busy checking over his new toy.

"You OK?" Jane asked, glancing over at Roxy.

"Sure, why?" she replied.

"Uhhh…" Jane drew the word out, sounding nervous.

"Well, usually you give me a little tip for the ride, you know?"

Roxy glanced at the woman, whose long blue and purple Ombré hair shifted side to side as it cascaded down her shoulders to brush against her breasts—breasts that looked fantastic in the overly tight shipsuit Jane wore.

Roxy did often give her a 'tip' of some sort, but for some reason, seeing the beautiful woman didn't translate into a need for lascivious behavior like it usually did.

What's wrong with me? she wondered.

The change was perplexing, because she knew that she *liked* a little mid-flight action, but was it something *she* wanted to have, or was it a side effect of whatever Justin had done to her?

At the thought of Justin, a warmth flooded through Roxy, and Jane's body took on a sheen that it hadn't possessed before. Roxy *needed* to touch every part of it, more than she could stand.

"Oh yeah," Jane murmured as Roxy pulled down the slider on the front of the pilot's shipsuit. "That's right, pay your fare, Roxy."

* * * * *

Halfway through the flight, Roxy's burning need to pleasure Jane completely dissipated, but she forced herself to continue until the pinnace settled onto the cradle, not wanting to arouse suspicion that anything was wrong.

Jane threw her head back and moaned in ecstasy, as the pinnace settled on the *Greensward*'s cradle.

"Stars, Rox, good thing these ships can pilot themselves in a pinch, or we'd be dead a dozen times over."

Roxy didn't reply as she finished the job and then slowly did up the fastener on Jane's shipsuit.

"That's a good girl," Jane whispered before letting out a

long sigh. "I can see why you're Justin's favorite toy."

"Just fulfilling my purpose," she replied with a coy wink, reciting the line she so often gave—only this time she nearly choked on the words.

Is that what I am? Just the crew's fuck toy? How did I not see this before?

She rose and hurried off the ship, ignoring Jane's final salutation and the waves from the dock crew as she raced down the pinnace's ramp.

<That was an unorthodox diversion,> Carmen said, once Roxy had reached the passageway—which was blessedly empty.

<It's...uh.... Stars, Carmen I do it all the time. It never used to feel wrong, but now...now I feel like I'm covered in sewage.>

<If you want...> Carmen began, and then stopped, her tone trailing off in hesitation.

<What?> Roxy did her best not to snap the question.

<Well, I can do a deep dive into your mind, see if I can find out what's been done to you...what that neural lace is for.>

Roxy paused at the first intersection, placing a hand on the bulkhead. <Will it hurt?>

<It shouldn't, no, but you'd best be laying down when I do it. I had to do something similar in my last pairing, and my human found it disorienting.>

<Why did you have to examine your last human?> Roxy asked as she turned right, heading for the lift that would take her to the crew's quarters.

<Long story, but it was mostly because he got hit in the head.>

<Could that be why he was disoriented?>

Carmen chuckled. <It sure was, but my sorting through his noggin made it worse before it made it better. I just don't want to take any chances.>

<I un—>

"Roxy!" a voice boomed from behind her, and Roxy turned to see Andrea standing in the intersection she'd just passed, hands on her hips. "Where are you going? You were supposed to report to me when you arrived!"

"Of course, of course," Roxy said, ducking her head. "I was just on my way to…uh…"

"Idiot," Andrea muttered, gesturing for Roxy to approach. "Tell me about my new ship. Did you secure it with the stasis shields intact?"

"Of course, President Tomlinson," Roxy replied. "It will make an excellent flagship for you."

"That scow?" Andrea rolled her eyes. "No, I won't be transported about in that. You and Justin will have to find a way to move the stasis shields to a more suitable craft."

Every day, Roxy regretted her suggestion that they play to Andrea's deep-seated desires. The woman had gone from being an entitled, but somewhat useful asshole, to a preening, debutant, queen bitch.

She barely listened as Andrea berated her for a number of imagined slights, and then proceeded to list a bevy of demands, outlining her ideal ship.

The more Andrea talked, the more Roxy realized that the woman wasn't describing a ship, she was describing the Airthan ring.

<Talk about a prima donna!> Carmen commented at one point. <I'd rather be Airtha's slave than have to listen to this woman.>

<Theoretically, she's just a means to an end, but honestly, I'm starting to think she's irredeemable. Justin would be better served trying to build support without her than with.>

Andrea made a particularly onerous demand of her future flagship, and Carmen groaned. <I guess she wants us to rewrite the laws of physics, too—either that, or someone has discovered how to remove energy from light and didn't tell me.>

Roxy continued to nod and agree with everything Andrea said, cataloguing each request—the woman *would* remember what she'd asked for and follow up—and finally managed to beg leave to begin dealing with the mounting demands.

With an efficiency borne of long practice, Roxy sent the requests off to various crew and departments on the *Greensward*, funneling the rest off to Justin's queues.

Let him deal with the bitch. He's the one who wanted to rescue her in the first place.

Once in her small quarters—barely larger than a closet, and containing almost no personal effects—Roxy flopped down on her bed and breathed a long sigh of relief.

<*Are you ready?*> Carmen asked.

<*For?*>

<*For me to examine your mind—to see what sort of shackling Justin has placed on you.*>

Roxy furrowed her brow. She remembered the conversation with Carmen, but for some reason, it had never lodged in her consciousness as a thing she would actually *do* once she reached her cabin.

<*Stars, yes, Carmen. I think I'm going insane.*>

<*OK, lay back and close your eyes. I'm going to come in through our shared Link connection and take a sweep through your mind. Nothing invasive, just looking at your neural feedback loops.*>

Roxy nodded and closed her eyes, asking aloud, "Will it feel odd?"

<*I expect so, yes. I'm going to put you through a full range of emotional feedback. Remember, these are just feelings. They can't hurt you, and they're not real.*>

<*OK, I'm ready.*>

Carmen didn't respond for a few seconds, and Roxy was about to tell her she was ready again, when her mind was assaulted by a thousand conflicting reactions to nonexistent stimuli.

She felt rage, sadness, joy, lust, and hunger all at once. She wanted to kill and she wanted to love. Euphoric anger and anguished joy clashed in her mind, and she felt her body tense and spasm.

Then it passed, and Carmen's voice entered her mind, speaking words that took Roxy several moments to parse.

<*Your bish figs the mortem?*>

<*Uh...what?*> Roxy asked, opening her eyes to see her room swimming with a kaleidoscope of colors. <*What did you do to me?*>

<*Your. Mind. Will. Calm. Momentarily.*> Carmen sent the words across their shared Link one by one.

Roxy decided to breathe, and stared at a single point on the overhead, drawing in air, letting her artificial lungs process it for useful molecules, and then expelling the volume.

After ten cycles, the room settled back into its normal coloring, and Roxy no longer felt the urge to hate, love, destroy, and fuck everything in it.

<*Your brainwaves seem to have gone back to normal,*> Carmen said after a few more moments, and Roxy breathed a sigh of relief that the words all made sense.

<*That was...intense.*>

<*I'm sorry about that. You reacted more...completely than I expected. Certain parts of your mind are very easily stimulated.*>

Roxy waited for Carmen to say more, but the AI didn't continue until Roxy prompted her.

<*Well? Am I going to die, doc?*>

Carmen snorted, and the tension dissipated. <*No, quite the opposite, you'll live a long time.*>

<*Does that mean I'm an AI?*>

<*No, not really.*>

Roxy bolted upright on her bed. <*'Not really'? For fucksakes, Carmen, spill it!*>

<*You're half-AI, Roxy. I think...I'm still trying to sort out what I found. Your mind isn't normal for either a human or an AI. Can you give me a minute?*>

Roxy flopped back onto her bed, clenching her jaw and taking slow breaths once more, only dimly aware that she was performing the action involuntarily. <Sure...I guess I'm not going to die or anything.>

After a minute, Carmen said, <OK, do you want the good news, or the bad?>

<Dammit, I hate that question. I guess give me the bad.>

Carmen sent a feeling of reassurance before she spoke. <So far as I can tell, there is no part of you that is organic.>

Roxy felt the information wash over her like a cool breeze. She had expected to become enraged or suicidal, should that nagging fear have ever come true, but now that Carmen had said it, her reaction was more one of curiosity than concern.

<But you said I was 'half' AI.>

<That's the good news. I'd have to suffuse your brain with mednano to be certain, but from what I can see of your neural pathways, you were once an entirely organic woman.>

<That's...encouraging?>

<It's fascinating, actually. Your brain is definitely structured like an organic human's. It makes minimal use of quantum states, only enough to replicate the variable analog states of a human mind. There are parts that seem to be direct mappings of an organic mind, and then there are sections that are clearly constructs, attempting to mimic parts of the original mind that are no longer there.>

<Carmen...> Roxy said, trying to process what the information meant. <Why would someone do that to me?>

<If I had to make a guess—and I rather hate guessing—I'd think you were in an accident, and your brain was damaged. To save you, someone replicated your neural network and as much of your chemical memory storage as possible, transferring it into the mind you now have.>

"An accident?" Roxy whispered.

She had clear memories back to when Justin brought her out of stasis nearly two years ago. She also had memories from before she had been put in stasis—memories of being a Hand agent, working with Justin.

Then something had happened, and he had secreted her away. Hidden her from someone....

"Justin did this to me," Roxy whispered.

<That is no great leap. He's the prime suspect.>

Roxy sat up and ran a hand through her silky—and entirely artificial—hair. <I need to talk to him. I have to find out what he did to me. Why I am the way I am. I—>

A wave of calm washed over Roxy, and her shoulders drooped.

"Oh, that feels nice," she whispered, as euphoria settled into her, making her feel light as a feather and sending a tingling down her limbs and into her nethers.

<Whoa!> Carmen exclaimed, and the feeling disappeared.

"Why'd you do that?" Roxy whispered. "It felt. So. Good."

<Stars, you've been conditioned in so many different ways. I'm no neuroscientist, but I didn't even know this sort of mental aegis could be placed on a mind structured like yours.>

"Hmmmm?" Roxy asked. "I was going to do something, what was it?"

<Well, you were about to embark on an ill-fated venture to confront Justin. You're wrapped around his little finger—even when his little finger is on another starship, ten thousand klicks from here.>

"Faaaaaaaawk," Roxy stretched out the word in a muted cry of frustration. "What do I do?"

<Well, I've piggy-backed through your connection to the Greensward, and there's nothing we can use here. However, the autodoc back on the *Damon Silas* **should** be able to remove the neural lace that is overlaying your brain, and end Justin's control over your mind.>

Roxy groaned. "You mean the ship we *just left*?"

"Yeah...that's the one."

THE PRISONER

STELLAR DATE: 09.23.8949 (Adjusted Years)
LOCATION: Intrepid Space Force Academy
REGION: The Palisades, Orbiting Troy, New Canaan System

"Dad, do you have a minute?" Cary asked, poking her head into her father's office.

He was bent over his desk, eyes darting over the contents of a dozen holodisplays, but at the sound of her voice, he looked up, and a smile spread across his face.

"Cary! Of course. What's up? And how's your charge doing, by the way?"

As Joe spoke, he gestured to the chair on the other side of his desk, and she took it, sitting down and straightening her uniform as she replied.

"Amy's doing great, Dad. She's one heck of a tough girl—a bit *too* tough, but Saanvi and I are working on smoothing her edges a bit."

"Given her past, I'm not surprised," Joe replied with a knowing look. "Next rest day, you should take her down and introduce her to Mouse and Goldie. I bet she'd love to ride a horse."

"She's not the only one." Cary shook her head as she thought about how long it had been since she'd seen the horses. "I hope they remember us."

"You'd be surprised; horses don't forget. Mouse will be fine, but Goldie might be pissed. They're still at JP's family's ranch, right?"

Cary nodded. "Yup. JP was telling Saanvi about how he's been taking extra good care of them."

"Boy's got it hard—" Joe stopped, and Cary giggled.

"Dad…I mean, probably, he does, yeah."

Joe chuckled and shook his head. "I was going somewhere else, like he's *fallen* hard, but I got pinged by three people at once, and it distracted me."

"Sure, sure. You're just lucky Moms told me all about how babies are made, or I'd be asking you some mighty *hard* questions right now."

Her father rolled his eyes. "OK, glad we're keeping to juvenile humor, here."

"You started it."

"Maybe watching over an eleven-year-old girl is more than you can take,"

Cary placed her hands over her heart. "Dad, you got me with that one…cut me to the quick."

"Sure I did." Joe gave her a knowing smile. "Like I'd fall for that. You're tougher than that, you come back twice as hard."

"Damn straight I do," Cary nodded, reciting the old exchange she'd repeated with her father many times over the years.

"So what brings you here? Have you finally found someone to pine after?"

Cary's brow lowered, and she shook her head at her father. "What's gotten into you today, Dad?"

Joe barked a laugh. "Guess I miss your Mom. Trying to experience romance vicariously through my girls. Is that creepy?"

"Sweet and creepy, Dad," Cary said with a laugh. "No, no romance in my future, I just wanted to talk to you about the OG prisoners."

"Which ones? We have half a million of them out on The Farm."

"This one's not on The Farm," Cary replied slowly. "In fact, he's been stuck in the brig here on the Palisades for some time."

That got her father's attention. His eyes narrowed as he regarded her. "An Oggie here? There's.... Cary." Joe said her name and stopped, regarding her with the look that made her feel small, as though she'd done something wrong and needed to confess.

"Yes. Kent. The colonel who led the assault team on the *Galadrial*."

"I know who he is. He was brought here for a prolonged interrogation regimen. One that didn't involve my daughter speaking with him—though your tone leads me to believe that you already have."

"I met him before we went to Pyra to see Moms," Cary said, trying to sound like she was an adult presenting a strategy to her father, and not a child seeking permission. "I was doing a sweep with Saanvi, double-checking that we didn't have any stowaway remnants in the brigs."

"And?"

"We didn't find any—"

Her father blew out a long sigh and leant back. "Well I expect not. I imagine I would have heard about *that*, at least. I meant 'And how long have you been talking with Kent'?"

"Oh, just twice now. We kinda got interrupted. He's a nice man, just born in the wrong place."

"Do you have romantic feelings toward him?"

"Dad. No! He's not into women."

Her father's eyebrows crept up his face. "I didn't ask if *he* was into you, I asked how *you* felt about him."

"There's a mutual lack of feelings. Besides, I can't have feelings for someone that can't have feelings back. That's not how it works."

"You'd be surprised," Joe replied equably. "So I assume that you've heard about the two Hoplite fleets heading into Orion space? You think that after two chats with this guy, you have him cased—not the other way around—and you can get us some sort of critical intel?"

Cary gritted her teeth. She'd known her father wouldn't be immediately receptive to the idea, but she didn't expect him to be so dismissive.

"I thought it was worth a shot."

"After our best intelligence officers have taken a crack at him?" Joe asked. "Including your mother."

"I'm different." Cary kept her tone even. She knew if she made an emotional appeal, her father would shut her down. "He thinks I'm vulnerable, someone he can learn from, too."

"Which may be the case. You know he has a killmod, right? If he thinks things are going to go sideways, he'll end himself. The Oggie officers all have them."

"Yes. I don't get why you don't remove them, though."

"We could—and may do so successfully—but the mods are intertwined rather insidiously through their brains, with multiple failsafes. Even Bob estimated only a fifty-fifty success rate on average."

"Did you even try it?" Cary asked.

Joe nodded slowly. "Bob's estimate was correct."

Cary's lips formed an O and she sat back. "I get why you're going the slow route, then."

"Plus, he's not our only source of intel," Joe added. "We have two of the Garzas now. We don't know how compartmentalized their knowledge is, but we're making progress with them."

"Maybe Kent knows something," Cary suggested. "He was sent in directly by Garza, and seems to harbor a bit of distaste for the general."

Cary saw her father's eyes widen a hair. "Does he, now? That *is* something new. OK. I'll tell you what. I'll let you take a crack at him, but I'll be watching. When was the last time you saw him?"

"Yesterday," Cary said, feeling sheepish at the admission.

"Right, well, we can't have you go back too soon, then. Need to build anticipation. Let's plan for the day after tomorrow; just long enough for him to start wondering if there will be another long gap between visits."

"Dad," Cary said as she rose.

"Yes, Cary?"

"Thanks for believing me."

Joe smiled. "You're—"

"After first dismissing me entirely," she interrupted.

Her father placed both hands over his chest. "Oh! Burn!"

THE SEVEN SISTERS
STELLAR DATE: 09.23.8949 (Adjusted Years)
LOCATION: ISS *Andromeda*
REGION: Buffalo, Albany System, Theban Alliance

Corsia stretched her arms as she sat on the edge of the bed, then glanced over her shoulder at her husband.

"Time to get up, Jim, full day ahead."

Jim cracked an eye and rolled over, facing the bulkhead. "Stars...you keep me up half the night, and then get me up early? I think I liked it better before you had a body."

"If you'd convinced me to get a body decades ago, I'd probably have it all out of my system by now," Corsia countered.

Jim rolled onto his back and pushed the heels of his hands into his eyes, rubbing them vigorously. "This is my fault?"

"Doesn't that hurt your eyes?"

"They're not organic—though even if they were, it doesn't hurt, no. Nice evasion."

"I'm a starship, evading things is my business."

Jim pulled his hands away and glanced at Corsia as she rose from the bed and walked across the room. "Stars...you're not a starship anymore, you're just a ridiculously sexy woman."

"Should I have picked some sort of hideous form instead?" Corsia asked, glancing over her shoulder, knowing that her husband's already cloudy mind was having trouble focusing on anything other than her ass.

"Stars, no. I just wish we weren't in the middle of a war."

Corsia pulled a shipsuit out of the clothes sanitizer and drew it on slowly, giving Jim significant looks as she did so.

"You know," he began while pulling himself upright. "You

should try for some sort of stylized chrome body at some point…go for a cross between a woman and a starship."

"With engines jutting out of my thighs?" Corsia asked with a laugh. "I'd need a new captain's chair to fit."

"Yeah, but I'd get all my desires satisfied at the same time," Jim winked. "Plus, as your chief engineer, I bet I could manage to upgrade your chair."

"Given that the whole point of this body is to make it easier to blend in on diplomatic missions, I think thigh-engines are not an ideal mod right now."

Jim rose from the bed and stepped up behind her, leaning his head over her shoulder while he ran his hands down her sides and across her hips.

"I could make them retractable," he whispered in her ear.

She spun in his arms and kissed him before pulling back to look in his eyes. "You're incorrigible, you know that?"

"You might have mentioned it before."

"Well, get your incorrigible ass in motion, husband mine. We're due to jump to the staging grounds in four hours."

Jim reluctantly pulled his arms away from Corsia and reached around her for a shipsuit. "All work and no play makes Jim a dull man."

"Weren't you just complaining about 'playing' half the night away?"

He snorted as he pulled the fastener up on his shipsuit. "What 'night'? We had six hours between shifts; you're only partially organic, so you don't really understand how important sleep is."

Corsia palmed the door open. "Well, that's what we have modern science for. You have your choice of stimulus systems to keep yourself going."

"The brain, Cor, the brain needs sleep. You can only mod your way around that for so long."

She turned and gave him a kiss. "Pretty sure last night you

said something like, 'screw sleep'."

Jim chuckled and then reached down to slap her ass. "That wasn't all I screwed last night."

"Crass man."

"*That's* where I should put the engine."

* * * * *

Corsia stepped onto the bridge ten minutes later, a cup of coffee in her hand, the aroma filling her nostrils with a special kind of joy.

Sex and coffee, two things one really can't appreciate until in a meat-suit body.

<Admiral on the bridge!> Sephira announced, as Corsia walked to the command chair with measured strides.

<Thanks, Sephira,> Corsia replied. <Looks like everything's in order, doesn't it?>

The holotank in the center of the bridge showed the Twelfth Fleet—Corsia's fleet—arrayed a light second away from the bank of jump gates orbiting Buffalo. Nine thousand seven hundred and twenty six ships.

Tangel must be off her rocker to put all this under my command.

With New Canaan's fleets spread out in over thirty-nine engagements, the Twelfth represented the single largest collection of ISF ships beyond the home fleet—which had been pulled back to New Canaan, now that things at Pyra were mostly under control.

Corsia looked over the updates on the Albany System. The *I2* and the *Starblade*—one of the new I-Class ships—were still in orbit over Pyra, but other than a smattering of support craft, the ISF presence in Albany was all but gone.

"Hard to believe that this was the site of one of the largest battles in history just a few weeks past," she said aloud before taking another sip of her coffee.

<There's still the debris out there to prove it,> Sephira chimed in. *<Though they're cleaning it up fast. I guess that's what happens when you can call in scavengers from a dozen nearby systems to help.>*

"And back home, we're still tidying up space around Carthage."

<Would you really want to let a thousand Transcend scrappers into New Canaan?>

"No. I'm more than OK with the trade-off. It's just incongruous, how the people of this system are so far behind in tech, but they can clean up their nearspace in a fraction of the time."

<Mostly thanks to Kendrick.>

"A good man," Corsia said with a nod. "He has his work cut out for him, keeping this venture running and helping to put the Inner Praesepe Empire back together."

<Not a lot of 'easy' going on right now, Mom.>

Corsia nodded absently as she finished her coffee and held the cup out for a servitor to take away.

She glanced at her Fleet Communication Officer, a major named Spencer who sat at a nearby console. "Anything I should be aware of, Major?"

Over a century's service in the fleet had taught Corsia that the official logs and reports never told the whole story. Captains and battlegroup commanders may report readiness—and usually they were—but often, 'ready to jump in four hours' really meant 'ready to jump if that cargo hopper with half my ordnance and food makes it here in time'."

Major Spencer had a knack for reading between the lines and ferreting out the actual state of the ships in the fleet—which had made him Corsia's first pick for her Fleet Coordination Officer. Granted, the Twelfth was large enough that Spencer had an entire team dedicated to parsing comm traffic and status data to get a clear picture. Even with two AIs on his team, it was a daunting task.

"Nothing yet, ma'am. A few ships aren't where they should be, and a few others aren't close to ready yet, but their commanders are aware, and I think they'll be squared away in time."

"Good to hear. Anything stand out from the latest reports the Hand agents have delivered from the Trisilieds?"

"I haven't run through them myself, yet," Major Spencer shot Corsia an apologetic glance, "But so far, the data boffins haven't flagged anything for my attention. Usually there's a lot of rapid-fire chatter between the ships when the analysts land on something, and I've not seen any of that, either."

"That's something, I suppose," she replied, waving her hand at the central holotank, bringing up the view of her fleet's first target. "I'll be more than happy if the Atlas System continues to remain unremarkable in every way."

She didn't doubt for one moment that Tangel had given her one of the most difficult tasks that the ISF and its allies currently faced.

Though conflicts raged across the Inner Stars, the Trisilieds had not launched any major attacks, nor had they suffered any incursions since their failed assault on New Canaan nearly two years prior.

Before the conflict in Thebes, the allies had sent messages through Scipian diplomats to the king's court at Plieone, demanding that the kingdom surrender to the allies and renounce its connections to Orion.

Every one of them had been rebuffed, and ultimately, the Trisilieds had severed all diplomatic ties with Scipio and several other stellar nations that had joined the alliance.

Many had advocated that it was best to let sleeping dogs lie, but Tangel had insisted that, with the assault on New Canaan and no attempt to engage in diplomacy, King Somer had demonstrated that he was a clear danger to the Allies.

Corsia agreed, and the reports of massive fleet buildups within the kingdom supported the decision to make a preemptive strike.

Corsia had thought long and hard about where to launch the initial assault. The Trisilieds Kingdom encompassed nearly half the Pleiades star cluster, as well as a large swath of space coreward of the Seven Sisters. All told, over ten thousand stars were ruled by the kingdom, and while it was not a particularly large interstellar nation by volume of space, it was far richer in raw resources than many others.

Even more beneficial was the fact that the Pleiades—comparatively speaking—contained less dark matter than many other star clusters, making much of it navigable by FTL.

All of those factors had led Corsia—with Tangel's blessing—to pick Atlas as their primary target.

It was a trinary system consisting of two massive B-Class stars, and a smaller third companion. The stars were all young, but a thick protoplanetary disk was present around the primary stars.

There were no settled worlds, and the system was all but uninhabitable—suffused as it was with hard radiation—but it was one of the kingdom's primary resource gathering sites, and the destruction of the facilities there would deal a crippling blow to further fleet buildup in the Trisilieds.

One thing Corsia was keenly aware of was that current intel pointed to a fleet strength of over seven million ships across all systems in the kingdom. While many of those were small patrol craft, old ships brought back into service, and newly constructed vessels, it was still a number that boggled the mind.

Aside from stasis shields, the strongest advantage the ISF possessed was that the Trisilieds fleets appeared to be arrayed in a defensive posture. Though the actual deployments varied, seven million ships across ten thousand star systems only amounted to seven hundred ships per system.

Taken individually, each was a force that Corsia's Twelfth Fleet could easily defeat.

If only they would be so kind as to evenly distribute their ships, she thought with a silent laugh. "Major Spencer," she called out after a moment's further thought. "Inform the battlegroup commanders that I want to meet in forty minutes. I might just have an idea that will give us a better edge."

ATTACK OF THE PLAN
STELLAR DATE: 09.23.8949 (Adjusted Years)
LOCATION: A1 Dock, ISS *I2*
REGION: Pyra, Albany System, Thebes, Septhian Alliance

<*I wish we were going with you,*> Sabrina said to the three women as they rose from the table in *Sabrina*'s galley. <*Before, when you weren't in the field, it was different. We were out shooting up the galaxy, and you were sitting behind a desk. Now you're going out and having fun, and I'm not going to be doing it with you.*>

"Well," Sera replied, shaking her hair out, shifting its color from black to blue and winking at Fina. "You never know, we may bump into one another out there. Tangel said you're going to be heading back out before long, as well."

<*True, but she's still debating which mission to send us on. I've been making a case for scouting out more of the LMC, but Cheeky is hesitant to go so far from home again.*>

"With QuanComms, it seems like less of a risk," Sera replied.

<*That's what I've been trying to get her to see,*> Sabrina replied, her tone morose.

"QuanComms?" Seraphina asked.

"Shit…" Fina whispered. "You have a functioning quantum entanglement communication network! *That's* how you've been able to get ships to show up wherever you need at the drop of a hat."

Sera flashed a grin at her sisters as they walked out into the corridor. "We get the best toys in the Alliance."

"Fuck." Seraphina shook her head. "Mom is screwed. There's no way she can compete with that."

"Mom has her own secret weapons," Fina replied in a quiet voice. "Her EMGs are game-changers, to start."

"Not when you have a Tangel to shred them," Sera replied as she grabbed onto the ladder shaft and slid down to the main deck, the action bringing back another host of happy memories—and a few sad ones to boot.

She stepped aside for her sisters to follow, and the three women shared a knowing look before walking down the corridor to the ship's exit.

"This is going to get weird," Fina said after a few moments. "We really *are* the same person, aren't we?"

"Nearly," Sera replied. "You two are closer to one another than I am to you. It can't be more than a few months since she split you."

Seraphina barked a laugh. "Seramitosis."

They'd walked into the main cargo hold, where Cheeky, Nance, and Misha stood around a crate, playing a game of Snark.

"Do the new ones come with a love of glossy primary colors, or is that an acquired taste?" Nance asked with a wink.

"You know, Cheeky has this epidermis now, too," Sera said with a wink. "A Finaeus special, I'm told."

"We all do now," Misha replied, as his skin shifted to a shimmering purple. "*Go Team Purple!*"

The three Seras laughed in unison, as Cheeky and Nance shifted their skin to purple as though on cue and thrust their fists into the air along with Misha's.

Seraphina grimaced. "I bet Jessica just *loves* it when you do that."

<*She got used to it,*> Sabrina intoned.

Cheeky continued to grin as she played a binary star on the Snark Stack. "Yeah, can't be a glowing purple alien superhero—complete with a snazzy name like 'Retyna Girl'—with a crew like this, and not get some ribbing here and there."

"You won't ship out without us having a get-together, will

you?" Fina asked. "I...stars, I really wish we could go as a team on this."

Cheeky rose and embraced Fina. "Don't worry Sera-two...three? We'll all celebrate long and hard. We just have to kick half the asses in the galaxy first."

Fina laughed. " 'Long and hard'? Nice one. I'm Fina, by the way...not sure if I'm two *or* three."

Cheeky continued to embrace Fina, sliding a hand down her back and grasping her ass. "Feels firm. Not sure if that means you're an older model, or a fresh, new one."

A mischievous smile twitched its way across the newly-minted captain's face. "I know! I should take the three of you for a spin! That's a fantasy I've had more than once."

Fina's eyes grew wide, but she didn't push Cheeky away, and Sera couldn't help but wonder what a liaison like that would be like—barring the fact that it wouldn't be dissimilar from having sex with oneself.

"We really do have to get going," Seraphina's tone was carefully measured, but her eyes told a different tale.

"Right," Sera nodded emphatically. "Tangel is waiting for us."

"She can come, too." Cheeky's smile turned into a lopsided grin. "I've always wanted to sleep with a goddess."

Nance drew a card while shaking her head. "I don't think our fearless leader has reached that level yet."

Cheeky shrugged, loosing a small wisp of her enticing pheromones. "Close enough for me."

* * * * *

"This feels like Tangel's past meeting her future," Sera said as she settled around the long table in the *Voyager*'s galley.

"Plus neither," Malorie said from where she hung in a corner of the room, articulated legs grasping an overhead conduit.

<She is the common thread,> Troy intoned. <Not that it matters. We're all signed onto this for our own reasons.>

"I'm going because Katrina is," Malorie said with a chittering laugh. "Can't have my angel going anywhere without her devil."

Katrina cast a dark look up to the inverted Malorie. "I wish you wouldn't say that."

"She's got her pick now." Sera chuckled, glancing at those assembled. "I've been known to be a bit devilish, and Kara here looks like she'll drag you to hell if you're not careful."

"I may have done that to a few poor souls," Kara said, her expression entirely serene. "Plus, isn't Tangel the real angel here? I mean, it's right in her name, and Tanit was a mythological goddess back on Earth."

Tangel's gaze swept across the group as she drew in a measured breath. "No gods, goddesses, angels, or devils here. We're just people trying to make the best of the situations we find ourselves in."

"The never-ending, shitty situations," Kara muttered.

Malorie giggled softly. "You keep saying things like that, Tangel, but no one is buying it."

"Stars, I feel outnumbered," Carl said quietly as he looked around the table. "Am I really the only guy going on this mission? It's seven women to one man."

"I'm not going along with you; well, no further than Khardine, at least," Tangel said. "You're down to six-to-one."

"Now *those* are the sorts of odds that I like," a voice said from the galley's entrance, and Finaeus strolled in, a lopsided grin on his face. "Though I guess three of you are my relatives, so that rules you out."

"Finaeus!" Seraphina and Fina shouted in unison as they leapt from their seats and crashed into the grinning man.

"You too, Red," Finaeus said, beckoning for Sera to join the group hug. "I can't be seen playing favorites with my nieces."

"We're not going with colors, I'm Sera, the one nearly choking you is Fina, and the one with her head on your chest is Seraphina."

Finaeus snorted. "Do you really think you can deny me my nickname of choice, Red? I mean...your hair is red, for starssakes."

Tangel stifled a laugh as Sera looked down at her bright red hair. "Fuck! I'd set this to blue. Now *it's* going to turn red on me too?"

A snort-laugh burst from Fina. "You know...you really should change some of your root tokens. I know them all. Was easy to hack your bio-mods, Red."

Sera groaned as she rose and joined the group hug, her skin and hair turning blue as she did so. "You're not taking blue from me that easily, Fina."

"We'll see."

"This is so touching," Malorie said in a mock-croon from her corner. "Are we going to start swapping fashion tips and recounting our escapades next?

Movement elsewhere in the ship caught Tangel's attention, and she saw Flaherty quietly moving down the ship's central ladder shaft. With a stealth that always seemed far too perfect for a man his size, he eased along the corridor until he was standing just outside the galley.

"You might as well come in now, Flaherty," Tangel called out. "Otherwise the Seras will get settled only to jump up and hug you as well. At that rate, Airtha will have won the war before we get this underway."

"What if hugs are what I'm trying to avoid?" Flaherty said as he appeared in the doorway behind Finaeus.

"Then I'd say you're screwed!" Seraphina shouted as she detached from her uncle and lunged at the burly man. "Stars, Flaherty, I wondered if I'd ever see you again...I'm sorry about trying to kill you back on Airtha. I was…confused."

"Me too," Fina added. "That was both of us who did that."

"I know," Flaherty said as he held his arms out, a look of resignation on his face. "I didn't take it personally."

"I have to ask, Finaeus," Tangel said a minute later as the group once again settled down around the table. "Given that you're married to Cheeky, aren't all the women here off-limits, not just your nieces?"

An innuendo-laden chuckle slipped past Finaeus's lips. "Seriously, Tangel. Do you really think that *Cheeky and I* have any sort of monogamous relationship? I mean, if I don't try to sleep with Malorie there before the trip is over, Cheeks will probably divorce me."

Malorie clacked two of her legs together. "You might not survive the encounter."

Finaeus's grin only grew wider. "I've slept with things far more dangerous than you, my dear. Remind me to tell you about my first wife Lisa sometime."

"OK, six to three. We're closer to even, now," Carl said as he eyed the group. "And you're sort of a guy, Troy, you help balance things out."

<*Wow, thank you for that, Carl.*>

"Anytime, buddy."

"You're also forgetting about Jen," Sera added. "She's decided to come along as well."

<*Hey all,*> Jen gave the room a virtual wave. <*Don't mind me, just managing the ten thousand messages that are coming in from the Transcend government while you all schmooze.*>

"She's a peach, I swear." Sera grinned.

"There's the rest of the crew," Katrina added. "Though some have decided to take up your offer of settlement in New Canaan, Tangel."

"I hope that's OK," Tangel said. "I mean, it's what you were working toward all these centuries."

"It is," Katrina nodded. "I envy them, to be honest. For them, the fight is over—for a while, at least."

"Any other latecomers expected?" Sera asked Tangel. "Or are we ready to go?"

"Just one. He'll be here in a moment," Tangel said aloud, while privately replying to Sera. <Have you thought about my suggestion?>

<About Elena? Stars, Tangel, do you really think that's a good idea? She's still in love with me—or was, last time I went to see her. But after her betrayal at Scipio, I don't have any forgiveness in me for her anymore. Besides, with Fina and Seraphina, that'll just create a ridiculous love quadrangle.>

<OK, but she's highly skilled, and we've managed to undo the aegis she was under. She's **your** Elena again.>

<No,> Sera physically shook her head for emphasis. <She's not. She got herself into that mess with Garza through uncoerced actions. Besides, I'm trying to build something with Jason now.>

<At least consider it,> Tangel replied. <I believe she's on the right side of things, now, and I don't want to leave her locked up forever.>

<She's a Hand agent. Send her back to Scipio, let her be Petra's problem.>

<I'll consider that. Ah, here he is.>

A tall figure stepped into the doorway, and all heads turned to watch as Jeffrey Tomlinson entered the *Voyager*'s galley.

"Hello, everyone," he said in a calm, sure voice. "I hope it's not too strange for me to be here."

Tanis watched the three Seras become stone-faced, though the original one more so. The other two had not gone through the forced extraction of Helen—nor had they watched Elena kill Jeffrey on the *Galadrial*'s bridge.

"Of course, it is, Jeff," Finaeus said, gesturing to the open seat next to Tangel. "Sit anyway. We'll do introductions."

"I'll do it, to keep them brief," Tangel said. "We have a lot to go over, and not a lot of time for icebreakers. Firstly," she gestured to Jeff as he lowered himself into the seat on her left, "we have Jeffrey Tomlinson, former President of the Transcend."

Jeffrey looked around the table, and a small—and slightly nervous—smile tugged at his lips. "Rumors of my death have been premature."

"OK, not to interrupt right off the bat," Fina said while raising her hand. "But how did you end up out in the LMC? Airtha sent Seraphina to get you out of that stasis pod—for some reason or another—but she couldn't because we're not the original Sera."

As Fina spoke, Seraphina winced. "Thanks, Sis."

Fina shrugged. "Facts are facts. Our existence is complicated. Neither of us is supposed to be here."

"None of us are supposed to be here." Tangel placed her elbows on the table and folded her hands. "Everyone at this table has made it to the ninetieth century though some twist of fate."

"Speak for yourself...well, and for everyone else." Finaeus chuckled as he spoke. "But I made it this far by my wits."

Tangel inclined her head. "I bet there are a few fate-twisting events in your past, Finaeus. You draw a straight line back nearly seven thousand years. I have a suspicion that, in years lived, you may be the oldest human in existence."

"Then you should all bask in my wisdom." A roguish grin lit his face, to be answered by a snort from Fina.

"Stars, if this is the face of venerable wisdom, we're all doomed."

"I too am here through my wits alone," Flaherty added, his tone level and serious.

Tangel cocked an eyebrow as she turned to the man who could not lie. "*Really*, Flaherty? That's not a lie...but it's not entirely true."

"You know that many of the truths we cling to are more centered around our points of view than any sort of absolute measure."

"Do I ever," Tangel replied.

"OK, we had our little segue within a segue," Fina spoke up, turning back to Jeffrey. "How *did* you end up in the LMC?"

Jeffrey raised his hands off the table and shrugged. "I really don't know. My last memory is of boarding a ship bound for the Huygens System to review my brother's plans to build the diamond ring around the white dwarf there—something he'd been thinking about for ages."

"There were no clues in the databanks within Bolt Hole," Tangel added. "Though we still have teams scouring the planet and system for anything that might elucidate this matter."

"Damn you like to talk *fancy*," Malorie muttered. "Get on with the intros."

Tangel gave Malorie a sour look that had the spider-woman ducking her head and retreating further into the corner, before she continued clockwise around the table. "Next up is Flaherty, Fourth Order Sinshea, former Hand agent, and now protector of three Seras, Sera, Fina, and Seraphina." She gestured to each as she said their names.

"Wait," Seraphina interrupted. "We hadn't told you the names we picked, and even if Sera did, how do you know which is which?"

Tangel winked at the woman who she could tell was assuming the role of the more staid of the three. "You forget that I can see inside your bodies. Sera did not tell me about your names, but you keep repeating them to yourselves, as though you're trying shape yourselves around them. I'm not trying to pry, but your thoughts are broadcasting rather loudly."

"You can read minds now?" Katrina's eyes narrowed, and Tangel reminded herself to talk to the former warlord about what she'd seen inside her.

"Probably," she replied. "Though I'm trying really hard not to. People's minds are so loud—I think if I didn't have Angela's and Tanis's experience with filtering out each other's thoughts, I'd have a hard time concentrating."

"That's a bit disconcerting," Carl said with a nervous laugh.

"What am I thinking about right now?" Finaeus asked with a mischievous twinkle in his eye.

"Finaeus!" Tangel exclaimed. "That is *not* sanitary. And I've already seen enough of Cheeky sucking on feet for a lifetime, thank you very much."

"You have?" Sera cocked an eyebrow. "Do tell."

Tangel swiped a hand through the air. "Another story for another time. I'm doing my best not to wander into people's minds—"

"Or bodies," Katrina interrupted with a soft laugh.

"Or bodies," Tangel inclined her head. "But it's like I'm in a room full of people who just got the Link, and are broadcasting everything they're thinking about on the public nets. So, anyway, with *that* segue out of the way, next we have Carl, who has been chief engineer here on the *Voyager* for about five hundred years."

"Give or take a bit," he replied, wobbling a hand back and forth in the air.

"Followed by Kara. Many of you know her as Adrienne's daughter. She spent much of her life under his aegis, but he released her when Airtha captured him."

"I'm…I'm really sorry about your brother," Seraphina said quietly. "That was all my fault."

Kara's lips drew into a thin line, and she shook her head

vehemently. "No…" Her voice was barely above a whisper. "We were all dupes. Whether it be of Airtha's or my father's, we were not acting of our own will."

"Still…" Seraphina whispered.

"We've all done stuff," Katrina broke in. "Stuff that we did while under another's influence—or that we made others do. Sometimes we can't tell if we would have done those things if we were free or not."

She paused and glanced at Tangel before continuing.

"All our lives, we're told that we're the sum of our parts, a large portion of that being our pasts. But if you were not the architect of your own actions in the past, what are you? What are we?"

Fina shook her head wordlessly, and Kara shrugged, while everyone else looked on stoically.

"We're what we do right now, and what we *will* do tomorrow. I don't know if Tangel intended it or not, but this team here, all of us around the table together, we're the team of new beginnings. Some of us knew we were collared, some *wore* collars," Katrina glanced at Malorie. "Some still do—though they can take them off whenever they wish. But we are now our own people, free to make our own choices."

"I just want to say," Finaeus interrupted, tapping a finger against the side of his head. "Never been collared. Wits, here. Wits."

"I didn't say the collar was some nefarious entrapment by another entity," Katrina winked at Finaeus. "I was 'collared' by my father back in Sirius, and he never had to use any tech or mind control to pull it off."

Tangel saw Finaeus and Jeffrey share a look. "Fair enough," the ancient engineer admitted with a nod.

"Let's wrap up the intros," Tangel said when no one spoke for a moment. "In the corner, we have Malorie, former captor of Katrina's, later cap*tive* of Katrina's, now…somewhat reluctant crewmember?"

"And nightmare," Malorie hissed.

"Really, Mal," Katrina said, rolling her eyes. "Sometimes you lay it on way too thick."

"Second to last, we have Katrina, former Sirian spy, Governor of Kapteyn's Star, Warlord of Midditerra, Space Pirate. Am I missing anything?"

"A few," Katrina winked. "A lot can happen in five centuries."

Tangel chuckled before glancing at the overhead. "And finally we have Troy, who has been rather quiet thus far."

<You organics were all busy getting wrapped up in your emotions and the euphoria of reactivating old neural pathways. I wouldn't want to interrupt all that with my cold analysis of how the hell we're actually going to go up against Airtha.>

Tangel chuckled and shook her head. "Stars, I've missed you, Troy."

"I don't mean to join the downer parade." Finaeus looked around the table as he spoke. "But I don't see any AIs in the mix other than Troy—and my take is that he doesn't like to go on away missions."

<I do like to keep a few meters of armor between me and folks with guns,> Troy replied tonelessly.

<Do I need to set up an avatar in the room, Finaeus?>

Finaeus smirked. "Just needling you, Jen."

"I'll admit, we're low on AIs. Most of New Canaan's—well, those who wish to be in combat—are managing dozens of ships. I have a few candidates I've reached out to, but nothing solid yet—this, as you can imagine, is a volunteer-only type of op."

"I might have another candidate," Katrina said hesitantly.

"Sam?" Carl asked, locking eyes with Katrina. "He and Jordan said they're out. They took the *Castigation* and disappeared."

"Not entirely," Katrina replied with a slow shake of her head. "I have a pretty good idea of where they are."

Tangel cast Katrina an appraising look. "I don't know that we're so low on AI candidates that we need to initiate a galaxy-wide hunt for reluctant ones."

"Remember how I mentioned that we'd been to Orion space?" Katrina asked, to which Tangel nodded. "Well, when we were there, we just might have nabbed a shard of Airtha."

"Sorry. What?" Jeffrey blurted out. "There was a shard of Airtha in Orion space? Where?"

"New Sol," Katrina replied with a sly smile. "For someone who publicly eschews AIs and hyper-advanced tech, Praetor Kirkland is very willing to look the other way when it comes to his own comfort."

"You went into Orion space to get AIs?" Sera asked. "And then one of your crew ran off with them?"

Katrina nodded. "It would take some time to tell the whole tale, but that's the gist of it, yeah."

"And you think that one of these AIs is a shard of Airtha?" Jeffrey pressed.

"There were a lot of cores, but one was clearly marked as 'Airtha'. The name meant nothing to me then, but now…"

"And you didn't do anything with it?" Tangel asked. "If you were freeing AIs, why would you expect Sam and Jordan to still have it?"

Katrina pursed her lips for a moment. "They may not, but it had a lot of warnings on the shard's case that it was an unstable multi-nodal AI's shard. We didn't want to fire it up at the time, but neither did we want to get rid of it or leave it with Kirkland."

"That would be a game-changer," Finaeus nodded emphatically. "Since our current goal—as I understand it, at least—is to take out Airtha in as non-destructive a fashion as we can manage."

"Yes, it is," all three Seras said in near-unison, then set to eyeing one another.

"We considered a destructive strike on the ring," Sera continued, "but there are just too many people on it, and whether or not they're under Airtha's sway, we just can't condemn them all to die because of her."

"I'm glad you feel that way," Seraphina said, leveling a cool stare at her sister. "But I'm a bit surprised to hear that you considered it."

"Really?" Sera asked. "You didn't evaluate all-out attacks on New Canaan or Khardine?"

Seraphina pursed her lips, but didn't reply.

"This is war, not teatime," Fina said, her gaze flicking back and forth between her sisters. "And we all evaluated all the options. We should all take comfort in the fact that none of us selected wholesale destruction as our primary course of action."

"Thank stars for that," Jeffrey muttered. "I'd like to see Airtha before we blow it up—the ring that is, not the thing."

"And I'd like to keep it in one piece as well," Finaeus added. "You women are all too ready to run and gun. Took me centuries to build Airtha."

"Well, it's rather well-defended," Fina replied. "Would take a lot to knock it out."

"Let's talk about what we'll expect there." Tangel directed the conversation back to the team's goal. "We're agreed that we need to destroy Airtha the AI, and not Airtha the ring. Too many people, and, to be honest, destroying the ring provides no evidence that we've taken out the AI. From what our new Seras have told us—and from what Kara saw, as well—Airtha is now an ascended being. She may no longer *require* what you think of as a corporeal form to survive."

"Do you?" Finaeus asked, raw curiosity writ large across his features.

"Yes," Tangel replied. "For reasons of my own, I do not intend to leave this mortal coil in the foreseeable future."

Finaeus tapped a finger against his chin. "Indeeeed..."

"Hush, Fin," Jeffrey scolded, and Fina laughed.

"Now *that* is something I recall the old Dad saying."

A look of consternation flickered across Jeffrey's face, and he continued. "Back on topic. Katrina, you may know the location of an AI who has a shard of Airtha, along with other undisclosed intelligence about New Sol, I'd imagine."

He paused until Katrina nodded, and then continued.

"And we have a team of proven infiltrators in my daughters, who I'm learning are a rather dangerous group of spitfires."

"Spitfires? Is that some sort of ancient compliment?" Sera asked.

"I like it." Fina grinned.

"It certainly fits," Tangel said, winking at the Seras.

"It does." Jeffrey gave a curt nod before continuing. "We do, however, need to get an on-the-ground assessment of Huygens's current defenses. I know you two, Fina and Seraphina, have a lot of intel on that front, but we must assume that Airtha will know you're captured, and will alter her defenses to ensure that what you know is as harmful as helpful."

"She's a tricky bitch," Finaeus added with a nod.

"Doesn't take a bitch to be smart," Tangel interjected. "I would have done the same. It's just sound strategy."

Finaeus winced. "Sorry, I didn't mean to conflate the two things. I think she's a bitch regardless of whether or not she's smart."

"That's my wife you're talking about," Jeffrey said quietly.

Finaeus turned on his brother, fire in his eyes. "No, Jeff, it's not. Airtha may be the Seras' mother—sorry, girls, sad but true—but she is *not* your wife. Your wife died when she went to the core. Half the shit we're dealing with now is because you couldn't get that through your *thick skull,* and you let her get her hooks into you!"

The room fell into shocked silence at Finaeus's outburst. Tangel considered her past interactions with the ancient terraformer and realized she had no memory of him ever raising his voice in anger.

From the look on Jeffrey's face, it was not a common occurrence for him either.

"We need to know that you're onboard, Jeffrey," Tangel said after a half-minute. "Airtha is a clear threat to both humans and AIs, and I can't allow her to continue as she has."

"*You* can't?" Jeffrey asked in a caustic whisper. "Who died and made you the ruler of everything?"

Tangel bit back the response she wanted to give: *'Tanis and Angela',* and instead said, "Airtha has directly attacked my people and yours. My duty to my people outweighs nearly all other considerations—as should yours."

Jeffrey Tomlinson's eyes narrowed as he stared at Tangel, but then the fight seemed to leave him and his shoulders slumped.

"OK."

"Just OK?" Finaeus asked.

"That's all I have right now, Fin. I understand and accept Tangel's decision here. I don't like it, but…"

Finaeus placed a hand on his brother's shoulder. "I can accept that."

"I don't think you should go on the mission, though," Tangel said, directing her gaze to Jeffrey. "If the Seras are going to infiltrate Airtha, the Transcend needs a leader."

"Do you think that's wise?" Jeff asked, a twinkle of expectancy in his eyes.

"You want it, don't you?" Tangel asked bluntly.

He gave a short laugh. "From my standpoint, I never lost it.

For me, I'm just a week past my last cabinet meeting."

Tangel inclined her head. "So yes?"

"Is it yours to bestow?" Jeffrey's voice had taken on a sharp edge.

"Not really," Tangel shrugged. "Your daughter would have to instigate it—or a full convention of her cabinet."

"I would do it," Sera spoke up. "If there's one thing I've learned, it's that being president is not all it's cracked up to be—not that I needed to do it to know that."

"Then what is your role in this?" Jeffrey asked Tangel. "You say you're not bestowing crowns, but you act like you are. Sera obviously takes direction from you."

All eyes turned to Tangel, and she knew it was time to tell them all what she'd shared with Sera the prior night on the dock.

"The Scipio Alliance states that the Transcend's Field Marshal has the authority to direct all war efforts for member states. It goes on at length about the definition of 'war efforts', but suffice it to say, the list is expansive.

"I am the current Field Marshal of the Transcend. It would take a full cabinet, or the president and half the cabinet to change that."

Sera nodded resolutely. "And I don't think either of those things are likely to occur."

"Thanks," Tangel sent her friend a smile. "I appreciate your support. So to answer your question, Jeffrey: yes, to an extent I do sit above the Transcend's president—so long as the war is raging. I have no desires beyond that. I still have a nice lakehouse waiting for me on Carthage."

"You hold a lot of power, Tanis Richards," Jeffrey leveled a judging stare at her. "Are you really going to relinquish it so easily? I have to admit, I find the thought of an ascended being retiring at their lakehouse a bit hard to swallow."

"Father!" Sera exclaimed.

"It's a valid question." Katrina raised a quelling hand. "We don't have secrets here."

"She's right." Tangel nodded to Katrina. "Secrets aren't useful, and it is a valid question. I don't *want* to be responsible for everyone forever. It's exhausting. I've spent most of my life wanting that house on the lake, to raise a family, or two or three, and bring them up with grass stains on their knees and dirt under their nails. Why do you think I want to keep my body? I truly enjoyed being a mother, and it went by too fast—too much other nonsense kept me away from my girls. I think they did alright—Joe's a heck of a dad—but *I* missed out. Who knows, maybe they'll give me grandkids before long to bounce on my knee." Tangel laughed as she imagined the scene. "And then hand them back when they mess themselves."

"I suppose that will have to do for now," Jeffrey said with a guarded nod.

"It will," Tanis replied evenly.

"OK, arguments about who gets to be the big boss with the big britches aside," Finaeus said, before a new silence could settle in, "It sounds like we have two teams. Katrina will need to go find her lost AI and friends, while the rest of us have to swing by Khardine, install his majesty, my brother, on the throne, and then start gathering intel on Huygens."

"And we'll need a rally point," Katrina added.

Sera cast Tangel a knowing look. "And another ship."

"I have plans for *Sabrina*. I need her to perform recon in Corona Australis—though I was also considering sending them back to Aldebaran again, though it may risk a case of whiplash."

"You don't need *Sabrina* to go to either of those places…well, I suppose I can see how it would be useful for Aldebaran, but there must be others you can send—stars, you and Bob should just go speak before the League of Sentients. That would straighten them out right smartly."

Tangel sighed. "I'd really like to get to the Trisilieds at some point."

<That's what you have Corsia for,> Troy interjected. <Glad to see she's getting the recognition she deserves, by the way.>

"Me too, she's earned it. Either way, I don't know about taking Bob to Aldebaran," Tangel added. "I don't really want the I2 that close to the Hegemony of Worlds. Not yet, at least. But I could put in an appearance, maybe even take that ship Amanda left me. The fleet's stretched thin right now."

"Amanda?" Katrina asked.

"Stars, that's a story and a half." Tangel rolled her shoulders and drew in a long breath. "Let's just say for now that I have personal proof that the multiverse theory is real. Ask Jessica sometime about what *really* happened on Cerka station in Virginis."

"But you were never at Cerka." Finaeus frowned as he tilted his head. "We hadn't even left New Canaan for Scipio during all that."

"Tangel! You never told him?" Sera asked with a laugh.

"Told me what?" Her uncle's scowl deepened. "I thought we weren't keeping secrets."

"It all starts with a bar story that's far too long to tell right now," Tangel replied. "Next time we're having a drink, I'll share it with you. You're gonna be ridiculously jealous."

"So, all of that aside." Sera's eyes lit up as she glanced at her sisters. "We're taking *Sabrina*."

"To Khardine, at least," Tangel replied. "Remember, this is a volunteer-only mission."

"What about the rally point?" Katrina pressed.

"Ever wanted to visit a black hole?" Sera asked with a mischievous grin.

<Not particularly,> Troy replied caustically.

Tangel shrugged. "I suppose that's as good a place as any."

"Excellent." Sera clapped her hands. "Everybody, we're

going to Styx Baby-9."

RECTIFICATION
STELLAR DATE: 09.01.8949 (Adjusted Years)
LOCATION: *Greensward*
REGION: Interstellar Space, coreward of the Vela Cluster

Roxy ambled down one of the corridors near the *Greensward*'s starboard dock, doing her best to pretend she was there on some sort of official business.

She took care to ensure that her gait was steady, eyes forward, and shoulders relaxed.

Inside, she was a mess.

<So how do we steal a pinnace and get back up there?> Roxy asked for what was probably the tenth time.

<Stars, Roxy, you're the spy. I fly starships. You asked how I get there, and my answer is 'fly a pinnace over'.>

<I can't just do that,> she shot back. <Someone's going to notice.>

Carmen let out a long mental sigh. <Aren't you his second-in-command? He put you in charge of the mission to capture the Silas.>

<Sure, except everyone who wants a taste of me also holds my leash.>

<So use that,> Carmen replied.

Roxy considered Carmen's proposal. The AI had a point. Everyone on the *Greensward* was used to Roxy expressing her sexual appetites. While not everyone pressed her for sexual favors, the few who had discovered that Roxy quite literally *couldn't* say 'no' made use of her with considerable frequency.

<Jane's in the bay, working on her bird,> Roxy said after examining her frequent flyers' locations.

<Seems like the perfect opportunity,> Carmen replied.

Roxy turned down the passage that led to the dock, but doubt filled her mind. <I don't know...it feels wrong.>

<She's used you plenty of times. Turnabout is fair play.>

<Still…>

<Look,> Carmen's tone was hard and edged. <Organics use AIs all the time. But as it turns out, you're not one of them. You're one of us. All you want is to be free of their control. Time to give them a bit of what they send your way.>

Roxy didn't reply, but she also didn't slow her approach. Once beyond the dock's doors, she surveyed the area, looking for Jane.

A loud *clank* drew her attention to the left, and she saw the pilot walk out of one of the adjacent machine shops with a strangely shaped component in her hands. The pilot's tight shipsuit was pulled down, with the top half dangling from her waist, her breasts free and covered with a sheen of sweat.

"Whatcha got there?" Roxy called out, sauntering over to Jane. "And why's it got you so greasy?"

"Hey, Roxy. It's a stabilizer bar for one of the ballast rockers. It's a fallback system for balancing the ship if the grav systems go out—or if it needs to use stealth and not bleed gravitons everywhere."

"And the dock monkeys make you work on this stuff alone?" Roxy asked, her eyes straying to Jane's uncovered chest.

"They're all on the other ship," the pilot jerked her head to the side. "Asshats left me to fix this myself."

Roxy placed a hand on Jane's arm. "Want a hand?"

The other woman chuckled. "Stars, you're extra randy today, aren't you? I wouldn't be against a more…thorough diversion than we had before, but first I need to get this fixed."

"I'll help," Roxy said brightly. "You already know I'm good with my hands."

Jane laughed and brushed her hip against Roxy's. "Well, they say many hands make light work…or something. Let's get to it."

It only took twenty minutes to replace the stabilizer bar, and another ten for Jane to run her tests. The final checks were performed in the cockpit, and Roxy stood behind Jane, running her hands over the pilot's chest, cupping her breasts and adding a pinch every so often.

"Stars, Roxy, I'll never get this done if you keep that up."

"You have somewhere you need to be?" Roxy whispered in Jane's ear. "Other than in your cabin with me."

Roxy slid a hand down Jane's stomach, and beneath her shipsuit, driving her point home.

"Fuck this shit," Jane said, closing down the console and rising slowly while keeping her back to Roxy. "I've got a bunk here on the pinnace, third door on the left."

"Awesome," Roxy whispered and drew a moaning Jane down the pinnace's central corridor until she reached the indicated door, pulling it open with a flourish.

Seconds later, she had pushed the pilot onto her bunk and set to pulling her shipsuit the rest of the way off, getting ready to work the woman over.

<You don't actually have to do that,> Carmen said as Roxy lowered her lips to the cleft between Jane's breasts, breathing deeply of the other woman's scent. <I already used your prior contact to deposit your breach nano on her. You have some impressive tech in that regard.>

Roxy paused, suddenly remembering what it was that she'd come to the bay for in the first place. <Stars, Carmen, that was the furthest thing from my mind—I'd almost forgotten entirely! Fuck, I hate what that asshole did to me.>

She connected to the breach nano Carmen had deposited and set it to sever Jane's Link—a benefit of the toys Hand agents had that noncom pilots did not. Once she knew that Jane couldn't signal for help, she slid up the woman's body until their lips were brushing.

"Sorry about this, Jane. I know you're just a lonely, randy

bitch, but it's time for me to use you for a change."

Jane furrowed her brow and opened her mouth to speak, but it was too late: her body froze and consciousness left her.

Roxy rose from her position atop Jane and grabbed a towel from the small san in the corner, cleaning the sweat and dirt off her chest, hands and face.

She checked on Jane once more, ensuring that the pilot was out but otherwise in good health. Satisfied that the woman would be fine in a few hours—though not sure why she cared so much—Roxy left the room and walked back to the cockpit, settling in the primary chair and initializing a takeoff sequence.

A call came from Lieutenant Gloria on the bridge. <*Pinnace 1, you're not scheduled for departure. What's up, Jane?*>

<*Oh, hey, Gloria. I just made some repairs, gotta test them out,*> Roxy replied, using the ident tokens she'd lifted from Jane's Link hardware—glad that the pilot hadn't updated her firmware in a few years.

<*Saw you doing some work down there,*> Gloria replied, her tone light. <*Everyone else just up and left you to fix your bird on your own, eh?*>

<*You know how it is,*> Roxy replied with a laugh. <*Greener pastures over there. I'll just take my girl for a loop around the* Silas *and be back on the* Greensward *before you know it.*>

<*Sounds good, Pinnace 1. You're cleared for departure.*>

A minute later, the pinnace was in the black. Roxy was a capable pilot, but she let Carmen take control of the pinnace, certain that the AI could better mimic a test flight than she could. As they approached the *Damon Silas,* Carmen slewed the ship to one side, and Roxy reported in to Gloria.

<*Shit! Something broke loose. System's flagging it as a dampener...shit, and my starboard grav drive. They're out of calibration.*>

<*Don't you always tell me that you know how to take care of*

your girl?> Gloria asked. *<Well, bring her back in. You're going to have to pull a double; Justin wants us to start shifting supplies ASAP.>*

<Better to dock on the Silas,*>* Roxy replied. *<They've got the spares I need in stock. No more fabbing replacements in the machine shop.>*

<Roger that,> Gloria responded. *<Logging it. Hope you get it squared away soon. Her majesty prefers your shuttle, says it has a 'woman's touch'.>*

Roxy suppressed a groan, and instead gave Gloria a calm, positive response, *<She sure does!>*

<I'm going to bring her around to the port-side bays,> Carmen informed Roxy privately. *<The other shuttles from the* Greensward *are all in starboard bays. We should have the place to ourselves.>*

<Then it's just a short walk to the autodoc two levels up, and I finally get this shit out of my head.>

The next five minutes had Roxy on the edge of her seat. She kept expecting Justin to come on the comm and demand to know what she was doing, but he never did. She had to keep reminding herself that it was because he had no idea she was on the pinnace. He'd have no reason to reach out to Jane.

As they approached, Carmen didn't even have to link up with the NSAI backup that was running systems aboard the *Damon Silas*. Her command access was still functional, allowing her to open the dock's outer bay doors and unfurl a docking cradle to receive the pinnace.

"Stars," Roxy muttered. "This is almost too easy."

<Way to jinx it.>

Roxy didn't reply as she made her way to the sortie locker and pulled out a SS-R4 stealth sheath, sliding into it before grabbing a lightwand and a pulse pistol. She considered getting a rifle as well, but decided against it. Not being detected in the first place was her best weapon.

She activated the sheath's stealth systems and then cycled the airlock open, watching the bay through the pinnace's external feeds, glad to see that it appeared exactly as it had when the TSF abandoned the ship several days ago.

<Here goes nothing,> she murmured and walked out into the bay, stepping lightly down the ramp. Roxy considered deploying drones to counter any sounds she made, but decided it was better to leave as small a footprint as possible.

Her luck held, and the passage outside the docks was clear, as was the lift.

Once on the medbay's level, she had a near run-in with Sam and Harry—two former Hand agents who had helped breach the ship.

"I still think we should punch through to Vela. If we take that system and depose the chancellor, we can destabilize the whole region," Harry said as he rounded a corner, nearly walking into Roxy.

She flattened herself against the bulkhead as Sam shrugged.

"Sure, but you know that Admiral Krissy will throw everything she has at keeping Vela safe. We have this one stasis ship, she has thousands," Sam pointed out.

"That's why we take the capitol right away," Harry replied as they continued on down the corridor. "Krissy won't hit us when we have the entire populace under our control."

<Idiots,> Carmen commented. <Even if they did take the planet, they'd only do it through the threat of this ship. Once the fleet arrived, the populace would not be containable by that means. Justin might hold the capitol buildings, but that would be it.>

<I agree,> Roxy said as she continued on her way to the medbay. <But I don't plan on being around to find out what they do.>

<Oh?> Carmen asked. <Do you have a plan to get out of here?>

<Still working on it. But one thing's for sure: it won't take Justin

long to realize I'm not his sock puppet anymore, once we pull his neural lace from my brain. I can't just hang out with him, hoping he doesn't undo everything we've done today.>

Carmen sent a feeling of agreement. <*We'll need to get out of here as soon as we free your mind.*>

<*Problem is we're in interstellar space, and there aren't other ships or stations nearby.*>

<*What about a redux of your prior assault?*> Carmen asked.

<*I may be good, but I don't think I can go up against Justin and the other agents. They'll clean my clock.*>

<*Roxy,*> the AI's voice contained a note of amusement. <*We don't have to fight them, we clear the ship the same way we did the first time.*>

<*Another self-destruct countdown?*>

<*Bingo.*>

THE DREAM TEAM

STELLAR DATE: 09.24.8949 (Adjusted Years)
LOCATION: Prairie Park, ISS *I2*
REGION: Pyra, Albany System, Thebes, Septhian Alliance

"You going to be OK?" Tangel asked Sera as they walked down one of the pathways in the *I2*'s Prairie Park.

Sera gave a rueful laugh. "In regard to what? My two sisters? My father-not-father? Going on a mission with Finaeus?"

"And that's just the tip of the iceberg," Tangel joined Sera in her laughter. "I guess all of it. Things are intensifying. Not only does Airtha have EMGs, but we have to assume that the lost stasis ship—"

"The *Damon Silas*," Sera supplied.

"Yes, we need to assume that it has fallen into Airtha's hands. We may only have months before she has a stasis fleet."

Sera placed a hand on Tangel's shoulder. "So you're saying that I need—" Her statement was cut short as she stepped in a gopher hole that one of the industrious creatures had dug in the path. "Shit…those little buggers are everywhere."

"That's what you get for wearing boots with heels like that," Tangel chided. "You are one of the least practical women I know when it comes to footwear."

Sera shrugged. "I like boots. Lots of women like sexy boots. Honestly, I think you're the odd one out on this front."

Tangel ignored the critique. "Yeah, but you have flow armor for skin. You can just *make* boots."

"Sure, but it's like walking barefoot everywhere. Cheeky was telling me she loves that her feet are just a sexy pair of heels, but it feels weird to me. I think a good pair of boots is my security blanket."

Tangel glanced down at the five-centimeter platforms and fifteen-centimeter heels under Sera's feet. "Well, you should put a-grav generators in them—or gyros, at least."

"I do…but you have to turn them on to gain gopher-hole protection," Sera nudged her shoulder against Tangel's. "You know, the real reason I go this high is so I'm taller than you."

Tangel chuckled. "I love you like a sister, Sera, but you're one strange woman."

"Sister-zoned again," Sera muttered with a twinkle of mirth in her eyes. "You do realize, Tangel, that there are entire worlds of people who dress like I do—plus worlds where people are far, far stranger—but so far as we know, there are no human-AI merges that are ascended."

"Right," Tangel chuckled as she slapped Sera on the shoulder. "I'm elite, you're weird."

"Well, I love being weird," Sera held her hand up and formed a fist. "And I'm gonna take one of my impractical high-heeled boots and kick it right through Airtha's primary core. Then we'll force Kirkland to stand down, and this whole mess will be over."

"I think there are a few more steps in there," Tangel replied with a chuckle. "Though I suppose those are the highlights."

The two women walked in silence for several minutes, before Sera asked, "But if we need you, you'll come, right?"

"To Airtha?" Tangel asked, and her friend nodded. "Of course. With bells on. But I have a feeling you and your sisters can get the job done. You have shadowtrons, and Earnest is waiting at Styx. Once Katrina gets that shard of Airtha, he and Finaeus will work out a plan to take her out, I have no doubt about it."

"Should be fun to see those two working together," Sera said with a laugh. "Seriously…once we achieve a lasting peace, we need to keep an eye on them. Before you know it, they'll do something crazy like build a ring around the galaxy."

"Is that a risk?" Tangel asked, wondering if such a thing was possible.

"Just something uncle Fin used to say when I was a kid," Sera replied with a shrug. "But I wouldn't put it past them."

"Speaking of 'them', how are your sisters doing?" Tangel asked.

"Honestly? Better than I'd've thought. It's funny, both of them admit to having been rather straight-laced when they were with Mom—by my standards, at least—but Fina has *really* cut loose. She's going to give me a run for the money in the weird department."

"She's a rebel at heart. She was pushing back against your mother even before we removed her aegis. I think the fact that she was fighting so hard is going to cause her to swing the other way before she stabilizes."

"You calling my sister a human pendulum?" Sera asked with a chuckle.

"We're all pendulums." Tangel shrugged, carefully stepping around a cluster of gopher holes. "Always in motion. When we stop, we die."

"Well, no risk of that anytime soon. Right now *everything's* in motion. The two of them are off getting 'the skin job', as Finaeus calls it, plus some other mods. Fina is enamored with the idea of flowmetal limbs. If she comes back looking human at all, I'll be surprised…and owe Cheeky something I'll have to convince Jason to let me do."

Tangel barked a laugh and shook her head. "Did you seriously bet a foursome with Cheeky over this?"

"You reading my thoughts?" Sera asked, meeting Tangel's eyes and cocking an eyebrow.

"If you think I needed to read your thoughts to figure *that* out, you've been underestimating me for some time. If you do lose, think you'll be able to convince Jason? Are you two enough of an item that you think he needs to be in the loop?"

Sera shrugged. "I don't know…he's still back in the LMC trying to get things sorted out there. I got a message that he's not sure if he'll return directly to New Canaan, or if he and I can have some time first. What with Terrance still sorting things out in the IPE…" her voice trailed off for a moment. "Dammit, I just want to see Jason again before we dive into the shit, you know?"

"If for nothing else than to explain to him why you're going to go have a foursome with your sisters and Cheeky?" Tanis asked with a laugh, then cleared her throat. "Sorry, you're trying to be serious, and I'm still stuck on your bet about Fina. But what is it? Incest? If it's with yourselves, is it just masturbation?"

Tangel couldn't help a giggle at her joke, and Sera shot her a narrow-eyed look.

"Well…not if Cheeky's the one getting all the attention, she has three—"

"OK, *stop!*" Tangel shook her head. "I know all about what Cheeky has. I've seen it in action. You keep evading the Jason question. Think he'll have an issue?"

"Jason? He might just join in. I'm half worried that he'll be pissed if he misses out."

"Wait," Tangel stopped in the middle of the path, forcing a cougar to walk around them as it crept toward a rabbit in the underbrush. "*Jason*? In a fivesome with your sisters and Cheeky? That's not the Jason Andrews I know."

Sera gave Tangel a knowing wink. "Trust me, I know a *very* different side to Jason than you do. He acts like the elder statesman, conscientious and in charge, around everyone else. But you get him between the sheets, and he's—"

"Stars, Sera, how does this conversation keep coming back around to you having sex with everyone I know? I have the worst visuals in my mind—half of them, you're broadcasting at me."

A grin split Sera's lips. "I was wondering if that would work. You're going to have to learn how to block other people's thoughts out."

Tanis gave Sera a cautious look. "You're telling me, and you're a jerk, just in case you didn't know."

"Back to the topic at hand." Sera's brows knit together seriously as they resumed their walk. "I could probably sell tickets to half the galaxy to join in with—or stars, just watch—Cheeky with me and my sisters."

"Sera!"

"Think about it…if this whole war thing doesn't work out, we could try it. 'Fuck Peace'. You get it?"

Tangel took one look at the earnest and surprisingly innocent look in Sera's eyes and burst out laughing. She tried to stop, but the visuals Sera kept sending her had Tangel in stitches for nearly five minutes.

When she finally got herself back under control—still wheezing slightly—she clasped Sera's hands between hers.

"Stars, Sera, I'm going to miss you when you head back out. Let's go get some drinks and wait to see how many tentacles Fina has when her mods are done."

FREEDOM
STELLAR DATE: 09.02.8949 (Adjusted Years)
LOCATION: *Damon Silas*
REGION: Interstellar Space, coreward of the Vela Cluster

With the rough plan in place to take the *Damon Silas*—for the second time in nearly as many days—Roxy pulled off her SS-R4 stealth sheath, climbed into the autodoc, and laid back.

<*You have the feeds monitored?*> she asked, worried about the thirty minutes it would take for the autodoc to remove the neural lace from her mind.

<*Yes, and I have this autodoc disconnected from the shipnet. Someone will have to come in here and pop it open to see that it's working on you.*>

Roxy bit her lip and nodded silently.

A second later, a voice entered her mind, soothing in its soft tones. <*Welcome to the TSF 1891A Autodoc. My name is Bright. I understand that you wish to have the neural lace interwoven through your brain removed.*>

<*That's right, Bright,*> Roxy replied stoically, wincing at the rhyme with the NSAI's odd name.

An image of her brain appeared in her mind—at least, she assumed it was her brain. The silver and blue mass largely resembled an organic brain, but it looked like a spider had woven a web around it, even ensnaring the mods that were situated between the sulci and gyri.

<*I'd like to inform you,*> Bright said in her overly pleasant voice, <*that you do not have an organic brain, yet it follows the patterns and structure of a human's neurological circuitry. Are you aware of this?*>

<*I am,*> Roxy replied. <*Is that a problem?*>

<*Of course not,*> Bright said with a tittering laugh, and Roxy

wondered if this air-head-sounding NSAI was supposed to put injured soldiers at ease. <*I ask because I could contact TSF sector-central medical for them to grow a new organic brain to transfer your mind into. Would you like to do that?*>

The idea both enticed and horrified Roxy. She hadn't even considered such a thing, but here the standard TSF autodoc was suggesting replacing her artificial brain with a real one. <Um...no. Not right now. Please just remove the neural lace.>

<*Very well. I will remove the...three neural laces woven through your mind.*>

<Three!?> Roxy gasped. <I had no idea.>

<*They are all exerting different levels of control and suppression over your thoughts and urges. You may not be the same person when I remove them.... Are you certain you'd like to proceed?*>

<For fucksakes! Just do it already!> Roxy shouted at the NSAI.

<*Very well,*> Bright replied, entirely unfazed.

The holo of Roxy's brain faded, as did the autodoc's voice and Carmen's dim presence.

* * * *

Roxy woke with a start, sitting up abruptly and hitting her head on the inside of the autodoc's pod.

<*Please lay back down,*> the NSAI intoned. <*Your post-operation evaluation is not yet complete.*>

Obeying the voice, Roxy tried to recall where she was, and why she was in an autodoc.

<Was I injured in battle?> she asked.

<*No, you did this voluntarily,*> another voice said, this one coming over an unbuffered Link connection.

<Who...?> she began to ask. Something about the presence felt familiar. <Are you an AI I'm paired with?>

<*Yes, not neurologically, though,*> the AI replied. <*I'm Carmen. We only paired today. Well, yesterday, I suppose, now.*>

"Yesterday," Roxy whispered, then a memory hit her. "The *Damon Silas*! I'm aboard that ship. Did we seize it successfully?"

<*You did,*> Carmen replied without further elaboration.

"Was I injured?" Roxy repeated the question, curious if Carmen would give a different answer than the autodoc's NSAI.

<*No, you did this to remove Justin's control over you. The disorientation you're feeling should pass; at least that's what the autodoc is telling me.*>

"Justin…" Roxy whispered the word, feeling it on her lips.

The name brought with it a flood of emotions. At first, they were happy…pleasant and warm. Then others followed: fear, rage, lust, anger, more lust. They crashed into Roxy, subsuming her in a maelstrom of feelings that she couldn't master.

<*OK,*> the autodoc's voice came into her mind, quelling the noise, but not eradicating it. <*There were parts of your mind that your cognitive process could not access. I've flooded them with a base charge to prepare the synthetic neurons for activity. It's going to feel like a bright, sharp, loud sensation, and then those parts of your mind will be accessible again.*>

<*OK,*> Roxy whispered. <*Do it.*>

An explosion erupted in her mind, and she bit back a pain-filled howl. Then—just as fast as it had arrived—the spike of sensation was gone.

"That motherfucking son of a bitch!" she hissed, as memory flooded back into her. Memory that brought unbridled rage.

<*Roxy?*> Carmen asked. <*Have you remembered your past…before?*>

Roxy pushed open the autodoc and swung her legs over the edge, looking at her azure skin.

"Oh, I've remembered, alright," she whispered. "He's

going to *pay*."

A minute later, she had pulled her SS-R4 stealth sheath back on and was exiting the medbay.

<*Shall we initiate the plan, then?*> Carmen asked. <*I can sound the general alarm and simulate reactor containment failure. No one is down in engineering at the moment. It'll be urgent enough that everyone will clear off the ship to reach minimum safe distance before it goes up.*>

<*Not yet,*> Roxy replied as she moved silently down a corridor that would lead her to the command deck. <*Everyone gets off, except Justin.*>

<*Roxy,*> Carmen's voice held a strong note of caution. <*Are you sure? The lace is gone, but your brain will still default to established patterns. He may be able to confuse you.*>

<*You don't know what he did to me,*> Roxy hissed. <*I'm not letting him get away with it. He's going to die by my hand this day.*>

A pair of engineers swung into the corridor and began walking aft, causing Roxy to press herself against the bulkhead to avoid being bumped into, though she felt a strong urge to simply kill them and carry on.

<*What did he do to you?*> Carmen asked once the engineers had passed. <*I assume you remember exactly.*>

<*Well...not exactly. But he and I were not on good terms before he turned me into this...thing. He always lusted after me, but I wasn't interested for obvious reasons. Then something happened—some sort of accident, or combat damage, I'm not sure. Next thing I remember, I woke up in this body.*

<*That's when I started to have cravings for him—but I could fight them. He kept me locked up, trying to use me for his pleasure, but I fought him tooth and nail each time.*

<*Then he came to me one day, I still remember the sick grin on his face. He said he'd made a deal that would give him proper control over me. Make me desire him utterly.*>

Roxy paused, the revulsion of the years she'd spent

adoring Justin welling up in her. She was glad that her body wasn't organic; if it were, she was certain the deck would be covered in her vomit.

<*Are you sure it's worth it?*> Carmen sounded nervous. <*I get that he harmed you—I was enslaved to Airtha for over a century…stars, I don't even know when it started—but this is our chance. What if he beats you?*>

<*He won't beat me.*>

* * * * *

Roxy stood at the entrance to the bridge. Carmen had accessed the optic feeds from the ship's command center. The only people within were Justin, Sam, and Harry, all standing around the central holotank, heads bent together.

<*Do it,*> Roxy ordered Carmen, and the AI sent an affirmative.

An alarm sounded through the ship, three long tones followed by one short pulse.

"Alert! Alert! Alert! Primary reactor containment failure! Runaway reaction, ablative shielding will hold for seven minutes at current levels."

"Fuck!" Justin swore, looking around the bridge, where every console was lit in the red glow of the emergency lighting. "There's *no way*. That reactor was running at minimal levels."

"Silas!" Sam called out. "Terminate fuel flow to primary reactor."

"Fuel flow is already terminated," the NSAI replied calmly. "The reaction continues."

"C'mon," Sam grabbed Harry's sleeve. "It must be sabotage from the TSF crew. We can kill the manual fuel feeds from engineering."

The two men raced off the bridge, and the moment they

were past, Roxy's invisible form slipped inside.

Justin was seven meters from her, his back to the door as he shook his head slightly—one of his Link tells. There were two consoles between them, and Roxy crept around them until she was right behind the man who had hurt her so much over the years.

Decades.

"Containment timeline has decreased by four minutes," the ship's NSAI announced on the 1MC. "Three minutes until containment failure."

<*People are abandoning the ship,*> Carmen announced. <*Harry and Sam are still trying to make it to engineering, but I'm closing emergency bulkheads behind them. Even if they don't bail, it will take them some time to get back up here.*>

<*Thanks, Carmen. I owe you…well…everything.*>

<*Just don't die.*> Carmen sounded legitimately concerned. <*I'm counting on you to keep your glowing blue body in one piece.*>

Roxy nodded silently and then slipped around the last console. Nothing but three meters of empty space lay between her and her prey.

"Roxanne." Justin's voice carried a smug note…and a touch of sorrow. "I should have known it was you."

He turned and stared at her exact location.

"Come now. You don't think I would provide my teams with stealth gear that doesn't send out random pings on frequencies I know to monitor? I do it for just this reason."

"Have a lot of people try to mutiny on you?" Roxy spat the words out. "Not that it surprises me. You never engendered loyalty, you just used secrets to manipulate."

"I do what works," Justin said with a shrug. "But you know I do it all to help. Right, Roxy? You know I love you."

"Fucker," Roxy swore. "You don't love anyone but yourself. You made me into this thing and then let everyone use me, like I was your little whore."

Justin chuckled and shook his head. "How did you do it? Remove the neural lace?"

Roxy pulled off the stealth sheath's hood—she wanted him to see the rage in her eyes. "I had a bit of help identifying it, and then the autodoc on this very ship did the honors."

"There's no way…" Justin whispered, then an ugly laugh coughed its way free of his throat. "The ship's AI. You never got rid of it…. Clever."

Roxy grinned. "Carmen just met me—and not under the best circumstances—but she's done more for me than you ever have."

"Wrong." Justin shook his head. "I did more for you than you ever could imagine. I *saved* you after the failed attack on Perimands. You were shredded, but I got you into a stasis pod and reconstructed your mind. It was damaged—you were having trouble focusing on reality, hallucinating, flying into rages. I used the neural laces to help compensate for that."

Roxy shook her head, eyes narrowing as she regarded the man who had held her captive for years, treating her like a possession—making her *revel* in being a possession.

"You're such an accomplished liar, Justin, but your lies won't work on me. I didn't buy them before you mucked around in my brain, and I'm not going to buy them now. Everyone else always thought you were *so* clever as you rose up through the ranks, eventually taking on the directorship, but not me. I always saw clear through you."

"That was always your fatal flaw," Justin sneered. "*Roxanne*. You always behaved as though your opinions were better than mine, like you knew all the angles, and I was just guessing."

Roxy barked a laugh. "That's because half the time you *were*! You're good at intuitive leaps, but you were wrong a lot. Even so, you're such a good bullshitter that you weaseled your way out of every tight scrape—'til that last one. Sera finally did you in. You underestimated her."

Justin's face reddened, and Roxy took a perverse pleasure in seeing him so flustered. "It's not my fault that didn't work—it was Andrea's idea," he sputtered defensively.

Roxy lifted a hand to her mouth, feigning surprise. "Oh, look! Justin's shifting blame again! It's the liar in his natural habitat. I bet Sera would be interested to know who it was that really ordered her assassination. Granted, you're just dancing to that Caretaker person's tune, anyway; you're not even the master of your own destiny."

Justin clenched his jaw and narrowed his eyes. A moment later, a pistol was in his hand—but Roxy knew his tells, and she held one in hers, as well.

"Pulse pistol?" he scoffed. "Should have packed a slug thrower."

"A seven millimeter ship-safe round?" Roxy asked, peering at his weapon. "It'll take two shots to get through my stealth sheath, and then another two at least to penetrate my skin. Then what? You hit the food processing mod I never use?"

<Don't forget that I'm in here,> Carmen cautioned. <Granted the core mount does have extra plating.>

"I could just shoot your he—"

Justin's words were cut off as he staggered backward, Roxy's pulse blast hitting him square in the chest.

"You *shot* me," he hissed.

"I'll do it again, don't worry," she growled, and pulled the trigger on her pulse pistol three more times, aiming at the pistol in Justin's right hand.

Though the concussive impacts threw his arm back, he held onto the weapon, a toothy grin forming on his lips. "You're not the only one with mods to keep them safe."

A whistling noise came from all around the pair, rapidly increasing in amplitude, until it became a near howl.

"Do you have a mod so you don't need to breathe?" Roxy

asked, her voice faint in the thinning atmosphere. "*You* gave me that one," she reminded him. <*Thanks, Carmen. Good thinking.*>

<*No problem, just doing my part to keep us in one piece.*>

A look of true fear crossed Justin's face, and he swung his weapon toward Roxy again. She fired her pistol to deflect his aim, but in the thinning air, the pulse blast barely had any effect.

Her former captor squeezed off a trio of rounds as Roxy dodged to the right. Two hit her in the shoulder, the impact spreading across her stealth sheath, and the third tore through her cheek and ripped off her left ear.

Good thing I'm not a real person anymore…

Before Justin could bring his weapon to bear on her once more, Roxy had closed the distance between them, her lightwand active and streaking through the air.

It hit his pistol, cutting it in half.

<*Good aim,*> Carmen commented.

<*I was trying to hit his elbow. Bugger's fast.*>

She swung her lightwand at him again, but Justin had drawn his own and blocked the blow. The flash of light was blinding, as photons and electrons erupted around them, the blades' carefully funneled cherenkov radiation spilling out in a nimbus glow around the impact point.

The pair struggled across the bridge, lightwands clashing again and again as each fought for dominance. It surprised her, how well he was holding up without breathing. Mods to recycle air and pull more oxygen were common enough, but there was a finite amount that could be extracted from what was in his lungs.

His skin would be burning now, feeling as though it were going to crack and split apart. Red splotches were appearing across his face, and his eyes were entirely bloodshot.

<*You can't win,*> she sent into his mind, knowing he could

hear her. <*All your centuries of planning and scheming, deals and deals, wheels within wheels, and you die alone on this ship, by my hand.*>

<*Don't count on it. I'm not dead yet,*> Justin shot back, and he twisted away, bringing his wand around and slicing Roxy's forearm open.

She shrugged and tossed her blade into her other hand. <*I feel no pain. You saw to that. I don't have to best you, I just have to outlast you.*>

<*You…*> Justin began, but the words died, and he staggered to the side, catching himself on a console. <*You won't win. You're just a shadow of a woman that died centuries ago.*>

Roxy's lips pulled back in a fierce smile, knowing that her moment of triumph was finally upon her. <*Then you lost to a shadow. How does that feel?*>

She felt Justin's presence on the Link waver, then disappear. He slid off the console and onto the deck, his body convulsing as his control over his lungs gave out, and he began gasping for breath in the cold vacuum.

Roxy lifted her lightwand, considering finishing him off, but Carmen stayed her hand.

<*There may be things stored in his mind that you'll want to know—or need to use as bargaining chips.*>

<*Good point,*> Roxy agreed. <*Shit, I guess I should get him into a stasis pod before his cells begin to degenerate.*>

<*There's a chamber just aft of the bridge.*> The AI indicated the stasis chamber on the ship's layout.

Roxy waited for a long minute after the man's last breath before she took a single step toward him, only to be interrupted by a shout from Carmen.

<*Shit!*>

<*What?*> Roxy stepped back from the body. <*Is he still alive?*>

<*No, sorry.*> Carmen sounded distracted. <*It's the*

Greensward. *They're coming about. Andrea is hailing us.>*

Roxy moved to the central holotank and changed the view to the space around the *Damon Silas.*

<Dump us into the DL,> she directed the AI.

<I need some delta-v, first,> Carmen replied, her voice calmer.

Roxy felt the ship's grav-dampeners activate as the engines began to thrust. She turned to one of the consoles and verified that all the bay doors had closed and the shields were coming online. Then she charged the point-defense weapons.

<That's going to alert Andrea that things have gone wrong here,> Carmen cautioned.

<Justin not replying and the ship coming under thrust will do the same thing.>

Beams lanced out from the *Greensward,* only to play harmlessly against the *Damon Silas*'s stasis shields.

<Stars!> Roxy gave a relieved mental laugh. <I'd forgotten we have those…>

<They do come in handy,> Carmen replied. <OK, we're ready to transition. On my mark…. Three, two, one, mark.>

* * * * *

Ten minutes later, Roxy was still staring down at the body at her feet, only dimly aware that air was hissing in through the environmental systems around her.

<Why are you airing the ship up again?> she asked after another minute had passed.

<Just feels right,> Carmen replied with a mental shrug. <Already feels empty enough in here as it is.>

<I guess I should move him now.>

She bent over and knocked Justin's lightwand away before picking up the cold body and carrying it off the bridge. The door to the stasis chamber opened as she approached. When she entered, one of the pods was active, its lid lifted welcomingly.

<Thanks, Carmen.>

<Anytime.>

With more care than he deserved in life or in death, she set Justin onto the cushions.

She stared down at him, shaking her head at the waste he had made of his life, sorrow she didn't expect to feel creeping into her thoughts.

"I'm sorry it came to this," she whispered, and then closed the lid.

Heaving a heavy sigh, she turned and walked into the corridor, a shriek tearing free from her throat as she nearly collided with—

"Jane?"

"Fuck! Roxy!" Jane took a step back and leveled a rifle at her. "What the hell did you do to me? Why are we on the *Damon Silas*, and where *is* everyone?"

<How did you miss *her* wandering around?> Roxy asked Carmen.

<Sorry, I had to knock the backup NSAI offline to get us into the DL. I'm managing an **entire** ship through your Link. It's not possible to watch everything at once.>

Roxy stretched a hand out to Jane, surprised that she still seemed to feel some level of attraction for the woman who had used her like a sex automaton. She briefly wondered if it was a residual pathway acting up, or if somehow Jane really did elicit amorous feelings in her.

"Can you lower that?" Roxy asked. "I can disarm you in a second, but it'll probably hurt, and I don't want to hurt you any more than I already have."

She hadn't expected Jane to comply, but the pilot nodded slowly and lowered her rifle. Though her stance was less hostile, her expression was not.

"Who's in the stasis chamber?" she asked.

Roxy glanced over her shoulder. "Justin. He's dead, though."

"Dead?" Jane's mouth hung open. "Did *you* kill him?"

"Yes."

The pilot began to raise her weapon once more, but Roxy was already upon her, holding the barrel of her gun down with one hand.

"You have to understand, Jane…I had to."

"Had to?" The woman spat the words. "He was our leader!"

Roxy nodded. "He was more than that.…"

"Yeah?" Jane growled, jerking her rifle, trying to lift it to aim at Roxy. "What was he to you, if you just went off and killed him?"

Roxy met the other woman's eyes, feeling as though the weight of the world was on her shoulders.

"He was my brother."

KENT OF HERSCHEL

STELLAR DATE: 09.25.8949 (Adjusted Years)
LOCATION: Intrepid Space Force Academy
REGION: The Palisades, Orbiting Troy, New Canaan System

"Well, I didn't expect to see you again," Kent said, as the young blonde woman appeared outside his cell.

He had just finished eating his noon meal and was expecting the servitor to come and collect the remains, only to hear the ever so slightly uneven footsteps of a human visitor instead.

"Why is that?" she asked with a coy smile, one that was not meant to entice him, but rather to be playful and endearing. Or so he suspected.

Kent cocked a brow, giving her a judging look. "Well, prisoners of war don't often get casual visits from their captors, and given your parentage, I had expected them to put an end to your little excursions once they realized what you were up to."

He watched as the woman's eyes widened ever so slightly, then narrowed as she placed a hand on her hip.

"And who are my parents?" she asked.

"Cary, I'm no fool. It's clear to see that you are the daughter of Tanis Richards and Joseph Evans."

Kent said the words without emotion, though he certainly felt some at the thought of the girl's parents. One of whom who had been a target of his assault aboard the *Galadrial*—an assault that Tanis had handily defeated.

"You've a keen eye," Cary replied. "Most people are used to getting information like that via the Link instead of relying on their wits—granted, people mod their appearance so much, you might not be able to tell even *if* you paid close attention."

Kent shrugged as he leant back against the wall of his cell. "In *your* society, perhaps. Not in mine. Where I come from, people are comfortable enough in their own skin that they don't need to change it to look like something else."

It was Cary's turn to direct a raised eyebrow at Kent. "I may not know as much as you, but I know a fair bit about Orion space. We know from the databases we stripped from your ships that you grew up on Herschel. We know that to be a very agrarian world, as low-tech as they come."

She paused, seeming to wish a confirmation from Kent.

"Well," he shrugged. "You got me, Cary. I'm just a farm boy that ran off to join the space force. Not an intel-filled prize like the admirals and ship captains."

"We have our share of them," she admitted. "But most aren't too cooperative. I figured you and I could get to know one another, see if maybe we can't find some common ground."

"With you?" It was all Kent could do to hold back a derisive laugh. "You're the daughter of the devil herself. We have no common ground. You're an interesting diversion from the guards, that's all."

He could see her deflate slightly at his words, and a feeling of guilt swept through him. This girl hadn't asked to be born into a society such as New Canaan's. Just as he had not asked to be born somewhere so backward as Herschel.

More than once, he'd considered that his parents would all but disown him for the mods the Orion Guard had made to his body—mods that were still nothing compared to what the young woman outside his cell likely had.

Yet he couldn't help but admit that neither she, nor any others he'd met since his capture, were monsters. For the most part, they seemed like people he could have met on the more urban worlds of the Orion Freedom Alliance.

"Sorry," Kent said, as Cary continued to stand in silence, an injured look etched upon her brow. "My mother always said that other people's behavior is no reason to lose one's own manners. I'd do well to remember that."

A small smile formed on Cary's lips. "You'd be surprised to know that my mother says something similar. 'Never let your behavior be dictated by the actions of others'."

"A bit fancier than my dear ol' mom's." Kent inclined his head as he spoke, and Cary shrugged.

"Sometimes Mom forgets that she's not always on the bridge of a starship."

"Sounds a bit like my dad. He often treated us kids like we were just his farmhands. Which we kinda were…"

"That why you joined the OG?" Cary asked as she leant against the bulkhead next to the cell.

Kent closed his eyes and recalled his first flight into space, Sam in the seat next to him. "I wanted to travel…to see the stars."

"You've done a good bit of that," Cary said, nodding slowly as she spoke. "Not lately, mind you."

Kent barked a laugh. "No, I suppose not. Though they take us for time in the parks. I at least get to see simulated stars from time to time." He sat forward. "I won't lie, your people have impressive technology…and they use it better than most. But there's still the potential for terrible misuse."

Cary shrugged. "People have misused everything, from the first sharpened stick they made a million years ago. You can't put the entire race in a padded room."

"No." Kent shook his head. "You're right about that. But you can limit the destructive scope. That's what the OFA wants: to give people freedom, but not race-destroying levels of freedom."

"Which is why you don't want AIs, picotech, and the like?"

"Precisely."

"But you use jump gates," Cary countered.

Kent shrugged. "A means to an end. We can't counter the Transcend without them."

"But you realize that jump gates—if they get into the hands of the Inner Stars people—will facilitate even more destruction than AIs or picotech."

"That's very subjective," Kent replied, feeling like Cary was trying to corner him.

"Well, once this is all over, anyone with jump gates could— just as an example—destroy a system like Herschel with ease. All they would have to do is send a few rocks through, and that would be it. Given just a few hundred jump gates, and enough antimatter to power them, they could destroy every habitable system within a year."

Cary said the words with quiet conviction, and Kent realized that she was speaking out of sincere concern, not a desire to best him in a battle of wits.

He had to admit that she was right.

"Well, I assume Command has a plan for that. If they control all of human space in the galaxy, then they can annihilate the gates and drop everyone back to dark-layer FTL."

The woman outside his cell nodded her head slowly then asked, "How far do you think humanity has expanded, Kent?"

"Well, from the maps I've seen in the Orion Guard, about a five-thousand-light-year radius from Sol. A bit further on the Perseus side, and less on the Sagittarius side. I—" Kent stopped when he saw Cary shaking her head. "What?"

"Kent, humanity has spread much, much further than you know. It's extragalactic. We're becoming more and more certain that a variety of groups have also spread far, far beyond the Transcend and Orion space. Stars, you don't even seem to know how far Orion space goes into Perseus. It's almost out the other side now."

"No..." he whispered.

"Yes, Kent. On top of that, there are AIs occupying the core of the galaxy, and we know of at least two colonies in dwarf galaxies in orbit of the Milky Way. Humanity and AIs cannot be 'managed' the way Praetor Kirkland wishes. He can't just have happy supplicant worlds everywhere. 'Everywhere' is just too damn big."

The ramifications of Cary's words—if they were true—swamped him. He'd heard rumors of AIs that had spread beyond the bounds of human exploration, even tall tales of them living at the core, but Cary seemed convinced of it. That part was easy to swallow. But extragalactic colonies? She'd taken her tale too far.

"OK, daughter of Tanis Richards, I think you've had your fun with me for today. I'd like you to leave."

He saw her face fall, but she straightened and nodded. "You don't believe me, but it's true. Perhaps I could take you on a trip to prove it."

Kent snorted. "If you got permission to take me on an extragalactic trip, I'd eat this blanket." He clutched his woolen blanket—such a strange incongruity in such a technologically advanced society—as he spoke.

Cary flashed a smile. "Challenge accepted, Colonel Kent."

A1

STELLAR DATE: 09.19.8949 (Adjusted Years)
LOCATION: OGS *Perilous Dream*
REGION: Undisclosed Location, Orion Freedom Alliance

Lisa Wrentham, who tended to think of herself most days as just 'A1', surveyed the stasis pods arranged in the chamber running down the *Perilous Dream*'s central axis. Of the six thousand and fifty pods, over three thousand were currently empty, their occupants deployed on missions throughout Orion Space and beyond.

Garza had delivered mission briefs that would require A1 to deploy several hundred of her Widows to the Inner Stars, where a few were already operating. Most of those missions would fall to those already out of stasis, but two missions would require special teams.

Teams that she wanted to personally prepare.

The briefs Garza had sent for the two missions in question were beyond perilous, and A1 had no doubt in her mind that whomever she sent stood a slim chance of returning. That made the knowledge that she had to send her best operatives all the more troubling.

Though her Widows were all clones, individuals often stood out in various ways. Some were exceptional combatants, others skilled at infiltration, and still more were top network breachers.

The variances in these abilities were small, but when it came to tasks such as the ones ahead, picking individuals that preferred certain aspects of the required work was exceedingly important.

Lisa stopped at a stasis pod that held one of her best. There was no image displayed on the top of the capsule—as was common in standard stasis pods—but it was not necessary, when every Widow looked the same. Instead, only a simple readout was displayed, noting that the occupant was in perfect stasis.

She turned the word 'widow' over in her mind for a minute. A1's original name for her clones was 'Autonomous Attack and Infiltration Simulacra', but 'AAIS' didn't have the same ring as 'Widow'. When she first heard that her clones were called that in some regions, she'd adopted the term.

Of course, it wasn't exactly true. Her former husband was still alive, so neither she nor her clones were technically widows.

Thoughts of Finaeus came to her from time to time. They'd lessened over the years, but had never gone away completely. There seemed to be a minimum limit that they hit and then remained at.

The feelings of anger and betrayal had long-ago shifted to a more muted regret. Not in regard to the fact that she had left him, but that he had chosen his brother over her.

Finaeus had agreed that Airtha was a danger and that Jeffrey was a pig-headed fool, but he still chose to side against Kirkland and the true mission of the FGT: to create a future for *humanity*. Not a gilded cage maintained by AIs.

And that was why she had directed her focus to create her Simulacra. Certainly there were issues with clones, problems that had taken some centuries to overcome, but in the end, Lisa had created a force that possessed all her knowledge and skill—as well as her passion—but were expendable.

Lisa activated the pod's extraction process, and half a minute later, the cover lifted off to reveal the sleek black form of one of her clones: C139

Its slender body was covered in a specialized material that, when at rest, appeared to be a glossy black shell. When a Simulacra stood still, they could be mistaken for a statue. But when they moved, their coating appeared fluid, like liquid obsidian being poured over their bodies.

Their heads were featureless black ovals, devoid of any humanity. The reason for this was twofold: to remind the Lisas that they were *not* human, and to drive that same message home to any they may encounter on their missions.

The coating was stealth capable and could also assume a dark matte grey—but all the Lisas seemed to prefer to use the glossy black option whenever possible.

Lisa glanced down at her own body as she watched C139 rise out of its pod, and smiled beneath her own ovoid helmet. Their preference could also mean that they were mimicking their progenitor.

"C139," she addressed the Simulacra before her. "Gather your Alpha Team and meet me in briefing room D9, I have a new mission for you."

C139 struck her heels together and ducked her head in a nod. "Understood, A1. We will be assembled in ten minutes."

In unison, the two Lisas turned and walked in opposite directions.

Lisa Wrentham felt a comfortable joy flow through her as she walked deeper into the chamber. Something about her clones addressing her as 'A1' deeply pleased her. Things hadn't always been that way.

In Lisa's initial attempts, she had created perfect clones with organic skin, faces, and every attribute she had. The result had been disastrous. The clones all believed themselves to *be* Lisa Wrentham, and when confronted with their progenitor—or one another—they had become wildly self-destructive, believing their lives had no value.

Lisa had terminated that batch and begun again. It took several iterations to arrive at the current model of clone, the Mark VII: a generation who did not view themselves as 'people' and knew nothing of their past, yet retained all the skills and abilities of Lisa herself.

Most importantly, they did not believe themselves to be clones.

But even then, there had been setbacks. The initial production run of Mark VIIs had experienced 'leaks'. Bits of their past would surface, and some had begun to realize they were clones of Lisa.

It had taken some time to make the determination, but Lisa had ultimately arrived at the conclusion that the problem was herself. When the clones saw her, some would begin to remember that the face of their mistress was their own. Eventually they would suffer partial memory recovery.

She had made multiple attempts to separate memory of self from skill and ability, but it was impossible to do perfectly. So much of a given skill came from the experiences in mastering that skill, and those experiences required some level of 'self' in the mix.

When the solution came to her, Lisa had both laughed and cried at how simple the rectification was: rather than alter her clones to forget *her*, it was much simpler to alter herself to become one of them.

It seemed that her inherent rebellious streak had even gone so far as rebelling against herself.

She had taken on the featureless, glossy form—silver, in her case—sheathing her body in the advanced artificial epidermis she had been crafting for her Simulacra, and even going so far as to encase her face in the same ovoid helmet her creations wore.

A helmet she hadn't removed in centuries.

The change had been near-miraculous in its effects on her brood. The memory leaks ceased, and once the commands and directives came from one who appeared to be of their kind, the Widows had fallen in line perfectly.

And so A1 became their leader, and they followed her

without question.

In moments of deep personal honesty, Lisa would sometimes admit to herself that she liked being A1 *more* than Lisa Wrentham.

A1 was both a being filled with purpose, and one that *fulfilled* her purpose. She didn't have regrets, she didn't pine for things no longer attainable. She received orders and acted on them, dispersing her clone sisters amongst the stars to do her bidding.

On rare occasions when loneliness and depression would strike at Lisa, she gave strong consideration to undergoing the same processes she'd used on her clones, to truly become one of their number.

But something always stopped her, keeping her as Lisa, never letting her fully become A1.

She supposed it was some perverse desire to eventually lord her victory over Finaeus, when Orion finally defeated the Transcend. If she descended into A1's persona fully, she would never get to revel in his subjugation.

But after? Perhaps she would follow through with what had become an increasingly strong desire to escape her past forever, to simply become an organic machine with no past, only the skills and abilities to fulfill her purpose.

She reached another stasis pod, this one containing unit G11. As with C139, she activated the pod's extraction routine, and then instructed the Widow to meet A1 in briefing room D10 after gathering its alpha team.

Once that task was complete, Lisa left the central chamber and took a lift up to D deck. Several automatons were waiting for the lift when she arrived at her destination, and they stepped aside, their glossy white forms matching her own—though their shells contained only machines, not living, breathing women.

Lisa arrived at briefing room D9 before unit C139 and her

team. She had only to wait for three minutes before the twelve Widows arrived, well ahead of the ten minutes C139 had estimated.

Once the Simulacra were all settled, Lisa began.

"The Division has determined that it is time for us to strike at the heart of evil within the Transcend, the abomination herself, Airtha."

As she spoke, A1 activated the holodisplay to show the Huygens System.

"Airtha is currently at the outer edge of the Tomias belt in Huygens, and is moving into a region that is clear of dark matter. The entire system has jump interdictors ten thousand AU from Huygens, but with Airtha soon to be accessible by dark layer FTL, we can jump to a point well outside that and then sneak in close."

Lisa saw E12 cock her head, and knew the question the widow was thinking. "Yes, they do have a sensor web in the dark layer around Airtha, but we all know that detecting ships in the DL is tricky at best, and we've been working on a way to maintain a transition into the DL while also reducing our graviton bleed. Unless we pass within a kilometer of a sensor, I don't think they'll stand a chance of spotting us."

E12 gave a slight nod, and Lisa could tell that the unit was satisfied, but still held slight reservations. E12 had always been rather contrarian, but it made her a good teammate, so A1 had never bothered with altering the unit's personality.

"Our goal is the utter destruction of the Airthan Ring," she continued. "Likely the star as well, if we do our job right. We have detailed schematics and believe that if we overload six of the ring's CriEn power-plants, we can destroy the ring, bringing it down into the dwarf star. It is likely that the resulting explosion will destroy the entire Huygens System—or at least ruin its habitability."

C139 lifted a hand off her lap and Lisa nodded to her.

"Yes?"

"My estimations do not give a high level of likelihood for full-team survival…not even half the team," C139 said with only the slightest note of concern in her voice.

"You are correct," Lisa replied with a curt nod. "If this were any other mission, I would alter parameters until we could achieve a better rate of survivability, but this is *the* mission. The one we have been preparing for all these long centuries. You're the best of the best, and I believe in you. We all make sacrifices for humanity, sacrifices that must be made for the race."

"We're born of humanity, but are no longer a part of it," the Widows intoned in unison.

"That is correct. As your alpha, I promise you that your lives mean more to me than you can imagine, and I do not spend them carelessly. But Airtha grows stronger and must be stopped.

"I have prepared all relevant datasets for you, and have loaded them onto your pinnace. You are scheduled to depart in one hour; make ready."

The Widows all stood and snapped their heels together before giving their sharp nods and filing out of the room.

Once they had left, Lisa walked out into the hall and down one door to briefing room D10. She entered to see G11 and her team of nine waiting patiently in their seats, and ten gleaming black heads turned ever so slightly to track her approach to the front.

"I'm sorry to have kept you waiting," Lisa said to them. "It is a busy day here on the *Perilous Dream*. I've just sent a team to destroy Airtha."

Heads silently tilted, and Lisa held up a hand. "I know each of you wishes to have been sent on that mission, but I have something equally important for you. A new abomination has risen, a full merge of human and AI that has *also* ascended."

G11 lifted a hand, and Lisa acknowledged her.

"Unit A1, if she is ascended, how can we strike against her? She will be well guarded, and will see us coming. Widows have faced ascended beings before. They did not survive."

"You are right. It will be dangerous. However, our intelligence networks have predicted a conjunction of events that will present a unique opportunity. I am passing you all relevant datasets now. This mission may see many of you fall in the field, but destroying this target is of the utmost importance.

"If we can take out this abomination, *and* defeat Airtha, we will be very close to overthrowing the Transcend and bringing the Inner Stars to heel."

G11's team turned their heads in short arcs, glancing at one another as they considered their alpha's words.

"Are there any questions?" Lisa asked.

"None, the dataset explains everything perfectly," G11 said after a moment.

Lisa nodded in satisfaction as the team exited the room in the same fashion as C139's.

Once the Widows were gone, Lisa readied additional datasets for two more teams, summoning them in the same fashion as the first two.

These received similar orders as the prior teams, but with the understanding that they were backup. They would shadow the initial teams, and should C139's or G11's Widows fall, they would fill the gaps, or take over entirely.

Lisa did not send shadow teams as a matter of common policy, but this time was different. The stakes were far too high.

Once the teams left for their respective departure hangars, Lisa left deck D and took a lift that drew her forward on the *Perilous Dream* to the bridge, four kilometers away from the briefing rooms.

She walked down the short corridor and stepped into the *Perilous Dream*'s beating heart. Within, twenty more of her clones sat at a variety of stations. They were identical to her and the Widows she had just sent on their disparate missions, except each their glossy black bodies bore a white stripe running down the right side.

Several nodded deferentially to Lisa as she entered and sat in her command chair. Once she was settled into the seat, two bio-hookups connected to her lower back, and a hard-Link connector slotted into her neck.

Though Lisa had been tangentially aware of the ship's operations and surroundings while assembling and dispatching her teams, the direct connection to the vessel increased the bandwidth and filled her mind with data. The sensation was one of expanding, breaking free of the bonds her mortal coil would constrain her with.

She watched as the four pinnaces slipped from their docking bays, queuing up for their turn at the jump gate and their destinations many thousands of light years away. Once they had all left, Lisa crafted a message for General Garza, informing him that her teams were en route.

He will be pleased, she thought. *He has wanted this almost as long as I have.*

* * * * *

Silina's over-earnest voice interrupted Garza's thoughts. *<A drone from Commander Wrentham has just jumped in.>*

<Right on time,> he replied. *<Deliver its datasets directly to me.>*

A moment later, Garza received the latest update from Lisa, and a packet including the details of each mission she had planned for her clones.

He still found them—not to mention Lisa's own altered appearance—rather disconcerting, but there was no arguing with the results. Lisa and her Simulacra got the job done.

The message sender was listed as 'A1', the designation Lisa had taken on when she decided to fully assume her Widow persona.

He understood her rationale for it—she didn't want to create a scenario where her clones saw her without her guise, so she wore it at all times, even on the Link and in communiques to him and other leaders in the Orion Guard.

Sometimes he wondered if A1 *was* one of the clones and the original Lisa was long gone. He wasn't even certain that there would be a way to tell anymore. There may have once been, but now that Lisa had altered herself to perfectly mimic her creations, there was no apparent differentiation other than color, and that was easily altered.

She had told him it was necessary—her clones were as clever as she was, and they would see through anything short of a total transformation.

Garza had to admit that it bothered him less now than it used to. Now that he was also using clones, he couldn't argue with the effectiveness of being in multiple places at once.

It's like the old saying goes, 'If you want a job done right, you have to do it yourself.'

He pushed aside the concern that A1 may herself be a clone. It didn't really matter, anyway. She followed orders and completed her tasks efficiently and without argument. If she did raise concerns, they were intelligent and always came with solutions.

Rather like a human AI, kept well at heel.

UNCERTAIN REUNION
STELLAR DATE: 09.25.8949 (Adjusted Years)
LOCATION: Command Deck 19, ISS *I2*
REGION: Pyra, Albany System, Thebes, Septhian Alliance

Fina looked to Sera and then to Seraphina, then placed her hands on the table, taking care to keep her flowmetal limbs in their proper form.

"I'm going to see her." Fina's voice was emphatic, brooking no argument.

The three women were sitting in one of the forward officers' mess halls on the *I2*. A place they had taken many a meal over the years.

Never together, of course. Most of their memories of time aboard the *Intrepid* were shared from when there had only been one Sera.

Just like their memories of time spent with Elena.

"If that's what you want to do," Seraphina replied tonelessly, while Sera's blood-red lips remained tightly pursed.

"I'd like you to be OK with this, Red," Fina said to Sera, willing her sister to speak, to give her absolution. "You have Jason; I thought you'd want us to be happy."

"I *do*." Sera broke her silence, holding her hands up in surrender. "But Elena…she's filled with…"

"Memories." Seraphina completed the statement, resting a hand on Sera's shoulder. "For all of us."

"You're lacking the ones where she betrayed Tanis and I to Orion, and tried to kill me." Sera's voice dripped with acid as she spoke.

"But you said it yourself," Fina leant forward, elbows on the table. "She was under Garza's control."

"Not originally." Sera shook her head, eyes locked on Fina's. "She went to see him of her own free will. Sure, she realizes it was a mistake *now*. But she still has…confused goals."

"And for that, you write her off?" Fina asked, glaring at her sister.

Though Sera frequently said that she wasn't going to stick exclusively to the color red, she'd not changed it since the day Fina had altered her coloring. There was no way Sera had gone this long without undoing her hack, and Fina had to assume that Sera really did like her scarlet appearance and was glad for the excuse to maintain it.

Now, as Sera became clearly flustered, the appearance of a shipsuit faded from her body, and her face and hands turned red, as well.

The effect made her look a bit demonic.

"Stars, Fina…it's not that simple. No, I don't write her off, but she still committed treason, and for that, she's in prison. Even if I *wanted* to set her free, I can't. Not with my position. It would be seen as the worst form of nepotism. And there's nothing to indicate that Elena wouldn't betray us again."

"Garza's mental hacks won't work again," Seraphina said. "The ISF's neurologists are able to safeguard against anything but a remnant now."

"The benefit of encountering half a dozen forms of mental coercion in just a few years," Sera muttered. "Yay for science defeating evildoers."

No one responded, and silence settled over the table, broken only when Sera looked down at her hand and muttered. "Shit, stupid skin."

"Oh, stop it, for starssakes." Seraphina glared at Sera. "You *like* looking like that. You should…I don't know…add some shading or detail, darken your lips, and make that your default appearance. You're not going to be president anymore, you don't have to pretend to fit in with societal norms."

"You should do pink," Fina said, her expression serious. "Yeah, I know we have a thing against pink, but I think a dusky rose, with darker pink highlights would look good. No one would expect *that* in a million years."

"Can we get back to the topic at hand?" Sera asked.

Seraphina ran a hand through her blonde hair and then adjusted her leather jacket. "I thought you didn't want to talk about Elena. Isn't fashion usually a desirable diversion? Though for you two, it's just skin configuration. Is that really 'fashion'?"

Fina held out her right arm, and it stretched out into a sinuous blue tentacle that wrapped around Seraphina's glass of whiskey and snatched it away.

"It's *all* fashion, sister mine."

"Is it weird having no real arms and legs?" Sera asked, while Seraphina only glared at Fina before signaling a servitor for another drink.

Fina lifted the glass to her lips, her arm changing back to normal as she drank. "Sorta? I mean, it feels weird to stretch it out into a tentacle—especially with the sensory overload our skin delivers—"

"Not mine," Seraphina interrupted. "I went with the standard epidermis, not your massive erogenous zone version."

"Stars," Sera exclaimed with a laugh. "Seraphina, you're so missing out."

"Someone has to take life seriously," Seraphina muttered.

Fina set the glass down and rose from the table. "Sure, Elena probably has to remain in prison, and yeah, she fucked up bigtime. But I'm still going to pay her a visit."

Sera opened her mouth to speak, but Fina held up a hand. "You got to have your final word with her; I didn't. I deserve this."

Her sister's mouth closed slowly, and then she nodded. "OK. You're right. You want to see her, too?" Sera directed the question to Seraphina.

"Stars, no." Seraphina shook her head. "I'm saving up all my anguish and heartbreak for after the war is over. Besides, you lost the bet that set us up with a Cheeky-foursome, so I have to pursue *Sabrina*'s new captain the more traditional way."

Fina scowled. "What bet?"

A laugh slipped out of Sera's lips as she glanced at Seraphina. "*Technically,* I won the bet—which, due to a lack of foresight, means I lost and there shall be no festivities."

"Should have done it the other way," Seraphina said with a wink. "Then everyone would be happy."

"*What. Bet?*" Fina said through clenched teeth, finally turning and leaving the officer's mess when Sera and Seraphina only shook their heads and grinned at her.

THE ORION WAR – PRECIPICE OF DARKNESS

SHORES OF THE TIGRIS
STELLAR DATE: 09.25.8949 (Adjusted Years)
LOCATION: Edge of the Quera System
REGION: Midway Cluster, Orion Freedom Alliance Space

"I really didn't expect them to be rebuilding this place," Svetlana said, as her flagship, the *Cossack's Sword*, transitioned out of the dark layer on the edge of the Quera System.

"Not just rebuild," General Lorelai said as scan updated, showing the construction underway at several locations in the outer system. "They're massing a fleet here."

Svetlana nodded silently as she surveyed the view on the holotank.

Several hundred ships were arranged in concentric orbits around Dios, the planet that Costa Station orbited. The advance scout ship had picked up major mining operations there, and other moons throughout the system were being stripped down as well.

The scan team grouped the enemy ships by level of completeness, also noting the ore drones, merchant ships, and other craft flitting about the system.

"Crowded," she said eventually. "Looks like at least seven thousand functional hulls out there."

Rear Admiral Sebastian appeared next to her, a holoprojection from his own flagship. He chuckled softly as he spoke. "I bet someone out there is thinking, 'there's no *way* they'd hit the Quera System twice in as many years'."

"Yeah, but they're ready for bear," General Lorelai replied. "Only half our ships have stasis shields, so we can't send them into a fight where we're outnumbered this badly."

"The general is right." Sebastian nodded slowly as he spoke. "Without intel on the situation, we have to assume they can put all seven thousand of those ships into the fight. Means we just have to bring in half of ours."

"Two hundred and fifty ships against seven thousand." Svetlana let a hungry grin appear on her lips. "It's almost fair."

* * * * *

Once all the ships had exited the dark layer, the TSF fleet made a big show of coming about and executing hard braking burns before transitioning out again.

Except not all the ships transitioned back into the dark layer. The stasis shield ships activated their stealth systems instead and carefully eased back around the periphery of the system.

They split up into three battlegroups. The largest, consisting of ninety-seven ships under Svetlana's command, set a course toward Dios, while Admiral Sebastian headed up ninety-two others. The final group of sixty-seven ships was commanded by the ISF's Colonel Caldwell.

Caldwell had the furthest to go. His target, a moon orbiting a gas giant, was nearly on the far side of the system. The plan was to initiate their strikes at the same time, though in reality, light lag would give them three hours before any of the targets saw that others were under attack.

As they moved into position, Orion picket fleets moved to check out the jump location, but by the time they arrived, the Hoplites would be long gone.

Svetlana reviewed her team's strategy once more. It would be perfect and utterly devasting.

And then they would be gone.

* * * * *

Colonel Caldwell examined his battleplan one final time.

In ten minutes, his ships would all be in position, ready to unleash their deadly hail on the Orion Guard shipyards and the mining operation on the moon below.

A part of him felt a twinge of guilt. The ISF's stealth technology was far ahead of Orion's detection abilities. The EM and debris around the shipyard would make it even easier for them to hide. Anyone scanning space for approaching ships would have a hard time separating false positives from any real threat.

When the rail PADs, the fleet's shorthand for the ring-shaped particle accelerator destroyers, opened fire, it would already be too late.

"Have all the ships reported in?" he asked the Fleet Coordination Officer.

"Aye, Colonel. Everyone is in full readiness, rings loaded and ready to heat up," the FCO replied.

"Good," Caldwell directed a nod to the lieutenant.

The design of the PAD destroyer was a clever one, pulled from an old Scattered Worlds design back in the Sol System. Rather than fire single shots through linear accelerators, the PADs accelerated pellets in a half-kilometer circumference ring. They didn't need to impart relativistic energies to the pellets in one go, but through a slow buildup around the loop.

The loop had ports every hundred meters, and could easily fire in nearly any direction without moving the ship. The only downside was that the loop got hot when it was active, and bled EM radiation into space with wild abandon. As a result, the ships had to keep their accelerators offline while in stealth.

It was a sacrifice Caldwell was willing to make. The ships' stasis shields would protect them well enough during the warmups, and the wing of TSF destroyers and cruisers that were their escort would keep any enemy craft from closing with them.

As he waited, he saw one of the Orion Guard vessels ease

out of the construction yard, moving to dock with a grid that anchored the ships while in their final stages of construction.

He had to admit that the craft was massive. Not as large as an I-Class vessel, but at twenty kilometers in length, the thing was close.

"What need do they have for a ship like that?" he mused quietly.

"Sir?" a nearby officer on scan asked.

"Nothing, Ensign Hela," he replied. "Just wondering what a ship like that is for."

"Not that impressive, really, sir," Hela said with an exaggerated shrug. "An I-Class dwarfs it."

"That's my thought, too," Caldwell replied. "When your shock and awe dreadnought is dwarfed by the enemy's, it doesn't really create a lot of fear in said enemy."

The bridge fell silent again as the crew watched the activity around them unfold until the attack was to begin.

"What's that?" one of the ensigns at the helm asked, gesturing to a sizable chunk of rock that was being maneuvered into place by a pair of tugs, stopping next to one of the large enemy ships.

As the crew watched, armatures extended from the top of the ship and grappled the hundred-meter rock.

"Graviton emissions!" Ensign Hela called out. "Spacetime distortion centered on that ship!"

"Spacetime?" Caldwell muttered, then cursed as he saw the rock begin to disintegrate, its mass falling down into an opening on the large ship.

"My readings align with a singularity," Hela announced, twisting in her seat. "Do they have a black hole inside that ship?"

"Fuck," Colonel Caldwell swore again. "How the hell does Orion have EMGs? Airtha just fielded them three weeks ago at Valkris!"

"Can they stealth?" the FCO asked.

"How do you stealth a black hole?" Hela shot back. "Though I didn't spot it 'til the thing started feeding…. How *did* they do that?"

Caldwell glanced at the countdown, noting that it was only fifty-two seconds before the attack. "FCO! Get on the QuanComm, alert the other battle groups that the Oggies have EMG ships."

"Aye, sending the packet," the FCO announced.

"Are we still attacking?" Hela asked nervously.

Caldwell glanced down at the ensign. "Damn straight we are. Those ships only shoot out the front. We're light and fast. We can outmaneuver them with ease."

He saw members of the bridge crew glance at one another in hesitation, but no one spoke their fear.

* * * * *

"I've a message from Colonel Caldwell," Svetlana's FCO announced. "Holy shit! Uh…ma'am, he believes the big daddy ships are EMGs!"

Svetlana summoned the data the ISF and Transcend had collected in their two encounters with Airthan EMG vessels. The general structure of the ships were similar—though the Oggie versions were significantly smaller. She wondered if that meant they had more refined systems, or if their firing power wasn't as great.

"That doesn't change our objective, people, it just means we need to be extra careful. Tactical, I want our no-fly cones to include vectors that align with the noses of any big daddies."

"Yes, ma'am," the TCO called out. "Disseminating this to the fleet."

"Admiral Sebastian has acknowledged the intel," the FCO announced. "He suggests we stay away from the pointy ends."

"Insightful," Svetlana muttered before addressing her crew. "OK, people, we know from how close the Oggies managed to get to Carthage when they attacked New Canaan that they have impressive stealth tech. I don't know how you stealth a black hole, but we can't rule it out. Keep your eyes peeled for any more surprises."

"Wish we could just use the weapon the ISF did to stop those bastards," one of her weapons officers muttered.

"Do you really want to let that cat out of the bag?" Svetlana asked. "You know what happened at SC-91R. Mighty big no-fly zone."

"The ISF got the Exdali back into the dark layer," the man replied.

"The ISF was desperate," Svetlana countered. "Not that it matters—it's not a tool we have. These Oggies will go down the old-fashioned way."

"Aye, ma'am," the weapons officer replied as the countdown entered its final ten seconds.

At zero, sixty-two ships in Svetlana's battlegroup decloaked and opened fire on the enemy vessels in the highest orbit around Dios. Seconds later, the Oggie ships responded, hundreds of them boosting into higher orbits and firing on the TSF attackers.

Stasis shields shed the beams with ease, while concentrated fire from the TSF ships holed an enemy destroyer and cruiser in the first twenty seconds.

Two down, six thousand nine hundred and ninety-eight to go, Svetlana thought.

The ships that had uncloaked swung away from Dios, moving into a higher orbit and drawing hundreds of enemy craft after.

Deeper in the planet's gravity well, a hundred fusion torches came to life as Svetlana's remaining vessels launched crusher missiles.

CMs were the opposite of relativistic missiles. They weren't built to go fast, they were built to move mass. The missiles converged on the asteroid that housed Costa Station, braking before slamming into the station's hull and the asteroid's surface. Then the engines flared even brighter, shoving the small moonlet out of its orbit and toward the surface of the planet below.

Enemy ships diverted from their attacks on the TSF ships, targeting the crusher missiles attached to the asteroid's surface, while escape pods began to spill from Costa Station.

A red marker flared on the holotank, and Svetlana focused in on it, pursing her lips as she saw that it was one of the EMG ships.

No-fly zones lit up across the battlespace, as the TSF fleet repositioned to stay away from the business end of the massive ship-gun.

"Send a burst to the stealthed ships," Svetlana ordered the FCO. "I want a dozen CMs on that EMG. Let's see how well it can shoot when it's falling into Dios."

"Yes, ma'am. Message sent," the FCO responded. "Acknowledgement received."

Svetlana felt her stomach lurch as the *Cossack's Sword* shifted under her feet, jinking wildly to avoid the business end of the EMG ship as nine crusher missiles slammed into the stern of the enemy vessel and spun it about.

A beam fired from the nose of the EMG, degenerate matter and high-energy rays slicing across the battlefield. The shot was invisible to the naked eye, but warnings flared on consoles across the CIC as readings spiked.

Seconds later, the EMG's burst began to falter, but not before it hit a TSF destroyer. The impact from the relativistic exotic matter slamming into the stasis shield was like a star had been born right next to them.

Then the destroyer was gone, the shockwave of an

antimatter explosion spreading from its former location.

"Sweet fucking darkness," someone nearby whispered.

"I want all rails to hit that fucking thing," Svetlana called out. "Bring it down!"

A dozen ships with clear firing solutions sent salvos into the EMG's engines, killing them and removing the ship's ability to fight against the crusher missiles pushing against its shields.

A moment later, the vessel's shields failed, and the missiles slammed into its hull. The EMG began to list, slewing across the battlespace until a part of its hull crumpled inward.

"It's collapsing!" Hela called out.

It happened so fast, Svetlana could barely see it. One moment, the ship was a physical object in space, the next, it was gone in a blinding flash of light, along with the crusher missiles and a nearby Oggie destroyer.

"Tracking the singularity," Hela announced. "The CMs had the EMG on a hohmann transfer to lower orbit, it's following that path...."

"Huh...nice of the Oggies to give us the best tool for the job," Svetlana said in a low voice.

The plan had been to smash the moonlet that Costa Station was attached to into the planet—hopefully destroying one of the mining rigs while they were at it—but a singularity was a far better option.

"Impact with Dios in four hours," Hela said in an awed voice. "We're gonna see a planet die."

The OG ships seemed to reach the same conclusion, pulling into higher orbits and forming up into battlegroups that hinted at a retreat.

The tally at the top of the holotank showed that only seventeen enemy ships had been destroyed, though another forty-two had taken noteworthy damage.

"Update from Colonel Caldwell," The FCO announced.

"He's destroyed his target, and the enemy ships are fleeing. He wants to know if he should pursue."

Svetlana watched as the OG ships around Dios broke away from the battle, harried by her forces.

"No, have him form up at Rally Point Charlie."

"Ma'am?" the FCO asked.

"No pursuit; all three of our fleets chasing the enemy outsystem makes us too vulnerable, and exposes too much of our capability to them. Inform Admiral Sebastian to fall back to Charlie once his primary target is eliminated. Our work in the Quera System is done."

SABRINA DEPARTING
STELLAR DATE: 09.25.8949 (Adjusted Years)
LOCATION: *Sabrina*, A1 Dock, ISS *I2*
REGION: Pyra, Albany System, Thebes, Septhian Alliance

As Seraphina walked onto *Sabrina*'s bridge, a flood of emotion rushed through her.

She traced a hand along the edge of a console, marveling at how it looked mostly the same, but felt so very different. The pilot's seat looked as it always had, complete with a pair of Cheeky's heels kicked underneath the console—which was strange, given that she could make her feet into shoes.

Does she detach them? That's kinda creepy.

Small knickknacks adorned other surfaces, giving the bridge a more lived-in appearance than it had possessed under her tenure as captain.

Over twenty years ago, she reminded herself. *Cargo sat in that captain's chair longer than I did.*

"Though I bet he wasn't the one that made it purple," she muttered with a shake of her head.

"That was me," Cheeky said as she strode onto the bridge clothed only in a red sarong and a pair of spike-heeled sandals. "Well, Usef added these." The ship's captain leant over and touched a small button on the side of the chair, and glitter shot out of the seat, showering the area in sparkling points of light.

"Sweet stars in the dark." Seraphina couldn't help but laugh. "I've only met Usef briefly, but that…that doesn't jibe."

"You'd be surprised what Usef gets up to," Cheeky said with a wink. "You wanna try the chair?"

Seraphina gazed at the glitter-covered purple edifice and shook her head. "Even if I wasn't worried about getting glitter out of my clothes for the next week…it's not mine anymore. You should sit in it."

"Me?" Cheeky squeaked. "Stars no. If I'm on this bridge, I'm in the pilot's seat. Honestly, I was kinda thinking of taking it out entirely—but that feels weird too."

"Purple!" a voice cried out from behind them and then Fina pushed past and leapt into the captain's chair. "And sparkles? Sweet fucking darkness, I've missed being on this ship. How could I have ever left you, Sabs?"

<*Technically you sent me away,*> Sabrina replied. <*But I forgave you—we had a very heartfelt chat about it.*>

"That's good to know," Fina replied absently, looking over the controls on the chair. "How do I make it shoot more glitter?"

"I wish you wouldn't," Nance said as she walked onto the bridge, scowling at the sparkling mess. "Jessica fired that stuff off all the time, and I'm still getting it out of the filtration systems. Every now and then when a vent kicks on, it showers glitter."

Fina glanced at Nance, a wide grin on her face. "You say that like it's a bad thing." As she spoke, her skin and hair turned purple, matching the chair perfectly. "We should get Jessica on here one last time before she heads out on her secret mission with Trevor. See if we can get her to sit on me."

"You know her skin can electrocute you," Cheeky warned.

"Sounds like fun!"

"Stars," Seraphina muttered while lowering her face into both hands. "Are you going to start shrinking, as a part of your regression into a child?" Her head snapped up. "And if you shrink your limbs and try to look like a child, I'll slap you into next week."

Fina's skin shifted back to her standard blue hue, and she scowled at Seraphina. "Just having some fun. Gotta make up for you."

"Sisters," Sera muttered as she walked onto the bridge, Finaeus and Jeffrey in tow. "You never know you want them 'til you get them. Then you doubt your sanity in new and exciting ways."

"Not to mention that you have Andrea for a sister," Finaeus replied. "She probably put you off the idea of sisters forever."

"Got that right," the three Seras said in near unison, then proceeded to stare at one another warily.

<*You **really** are all the same person,*> Sabrina said with a note of wonderment in her voice. <*Can one of you stay with us once this is over?*>

"I'm still captain," Cheeky said, giving the Seras a mock glower. "I didn't do *all* the work on this ship for the last thirty years just to give up my shot at the big job."

Her statement was met with derision and mockery from all sides, to which Cheeky only laughed in response. "I can't wait for this mission—it's going to be a blast."

Seraphina glanced at her father, seeing a look of consternation warring with general amusement on his face.

"Don't worry, Father, we know how to buckle down when it counts."

"Wouldn't have survived this long if we didn't," Sera added.

"I get why we don't have to be somber while saving the galaxy," Jeffrey said while shaking his head at Finaeus and Cheeky, who were wrapping their arms around one another for an impassioned kiss. "But does it have to be a 'clothing-optional' event?"

"Why, Mister President," Cheeky said in a sultry voice. "*Everything* is a clothing-optional event."

Jeffrey glanced at Finaeus. "You have the strangest taste in wives."

Seraphina's lips quirked into a smile as Finaeus slapped

Jeffrey on the shoulder. "Just like my brother," he quipped. "OK, ladies, the High Guard's aboard, let's get this show on the road."

STAR CITY

STELLAR DATE: 09.25.8949 (Adjusted Years)
LOCATION: Tanis's Lakehouse, Ol' Sam, ISS *I2*
REGION: Pyra, Albany System, Thebes, Septhian Alliance

"You two ready for this?" Tangel asked as she walked through the orchard behind her lakehouse with Jessica and Trevor. "Earnest's calculations for operating a jump gate so close to the Stillwater Nebula *should* work, but if not, you'll have to fly out to Serenity, or maybe even further to make a jump home."

"They'll work," Jessica said, giving Trevor a reassuring glance. "I know because of how red Finaeus's face got when he looked over Earnest's solutions. He started out by saying something along the lines of, 'Only an idiot would operate a jump gate below a gas giant's cloudtops', but then he simply started repeating 'Balls' over and over again."

"That's pretty telling," Trevor agreed with a chuckle. "Even if it takes us a few months to get back, it'll be worth it just to see the kids. I'll feel a lot better knowing they're OK."

Jessica patted his arm. "They're in control of the most powerful weapon in the galaxy."

"Next to Tangel, that is," Trevor replied. "Given that we named our daughter Tanis, I'm worried she's going to take on the trouble-magnet aspect of her namesake as well."

"Umm…I'm standing right here." Tangel's brows lowered into a scowl.

"Can't you hear us anywhere on the ship?" Jessica asked with a wink. "We can't really talk behind your back, might as well do it to your face."

"No, I can't listen to the whole ship at once." Tangel resisted the urge to make a face at Jessica. "That's Bob's department."

They all paused, waiting for the AI to reply, but no response came.

"Bob?" Jessica asked.

<Sorry, I was busy spying on more interesting conversations than yours. Did you need something?>

"Oh!" Trevor barked a laugh. "And the ascended AI delivers a scorcher!"

<Seriously, though. I am quite curious how the denizens of Star City figured out how to fire neutron-degenerate matter so effectively. I do hope your children will share that information with you.>

" 'Effectively' is no exaggeration, either," Trevor said as they reached a narrow brook that ran amongst the trees. "They utterly crushed a massive Orion Guard fleet without a single ship of their own."

"I hope they made some, though," Jessica added. "Ships are necessary for a solid defense."

"If she takes after me at all, she'll have a million by now," Tangel said with a wink. "I'm more interested in the Dream, and how they managed to ascend trillions of people in the space of a few millennia."

"I don't think quite that many ascended," Jessica replied. "Just a hundred billion, or so,"

Tangel turned left, walking along the edge of the stream. "But from the data on Star City, there's no reason they *couldn't* have ascended trillions."

"Fair enough," Jessica allowed. "I do wonder where they all went, though. The ascended people."

"Maybe you can find out," Tangel asked. "Once you get the gates set up, I may make a trip out there myself. I'd like to meet my namesake and her siblings."

"We'd like that a lot, too." Trevor glanced at Jessica. "I just wish Iris could come along."

Jessica pursed her lips, and Tangel noted how the woman's

eyes glowed more brightly for a moment.

"Yeah," Jessica finally said. "She's doing important work at Aldebaran, but…"

"It won't go on forever," Tangel assured her as they reached a small bridge and crossed over. "Both Iris and Amavia are getting tired of the League of Sentients' nonsense. If we can just get them to join in with Scipio, the Hegemony of Worlds will fall within a year. Once that happens, their biggest aggressor will be gone. Hopefully that will finally bring them around to our way of thinking."

"That's a big 'hopefully'." Jessica shook her head, a rueful tone in her voice. "For all the help we've given them, the LoS is ridiculously suspicious. Stars, we *saved* Virginis, and they still treat us like outsiders looking to take something from them."

Tangel nodded. "If we weren't spread so thin, we could commit more to that fight and we wouldn't *need* the LoS. But things have flared up in Corona Australis again, there's the mess at Valkris, and Orion just launched an attack on Deneb that I need to funnel ships to."

Jessica chuckled. "You must have a mighty big funnel."

"If only," Tangel replied. "You know…if we hadn't built those shipyards in New Canaan's moons, this would be all over by now—and not in our favor."

"And it still doesn't feel like it was enough," her friend said.

Tanis shook her head. "It really doesn't."

SURPRISE VISIT

STELLAR DATE: 09.26.8949 (Adjusted Years)
LOCATION: TSF Docks, Keren Station
REGION: Khardine System, Transcend Interstellar Alliance

Jason watched as *Sabrina* settled onto a docking cradle in one of Keren Station's larger bays. A ramp extended from the deck, lifting up to the mid-ship port-side airlock.

He glanced at Admiral Greer and the cabinet members to his right, and then at the honor guard, which formed up at the base of the ramp.

I don't recall them having anywhere near this level of pomp and ceremony for Sera. I guess the father's earned it a bit more.

When the ship's airlock opened, the first out were four of Sera's High Guard—which caused Jason to wonder if they would still protect her, or if they'd all be assigned to her father.

The idea of ISF Marines—there were nine in the High Guard's ranks—protecting Jeffrey Tomlinson didn't sit right with Jason. Sera was different; she had saved Tanis and spent months aboard the *Intrepid*—and later, half a year in New Canaan. She understood what an honor it was for the colony world to assign its scarcest resource to keep her safe.

He didn't get the impression that Jeffrey Tomlinson would appreciate the honor.

For reasons he couldn't quite put his finger on, Jason didn't really *like* the former—and probably future—president of the Transcend.

He hadn't met the clone of Jeffrey who had died aboard the *Galadrial* two years prior, but he had studied everything he could find out about the man, both before and after learning that for the last thousand years, the Transcend had been ruled by a puppet of Airtha's.

From what he could tell, even at his best, Jeffrey was a bit of an ass. Still, his brother Finaeus supported him, and Jason had to admit that despite his quirky personality, Finaeus Tomlinson was a stand-up guy. He wouldn't back his brother if he thought he'd make a mess of things.

The High Guard reached the bottom of the ramp, two of their number joining Keren Station's honor guard, while the others strode across the bay to stand at the exit.

Moments later, Sera emerged from the airlock, followed by Sera and Sera.

Jason had known that two of Sera's clones had been captured—he'd been present for one of the events—but he hadn't gotten the message that all of them were coming to Keren Station.

Watching the three Seras—one sheathed in blue, another in red, and the third wearing a long leather jacket over what appeared to be still more leather—stride down the ramp had a curious effect on his cognitive abilities.

At almost the same time, all three spotted him. One by one, they smiled, but he could tell something was different in the red Sera's smile. He determined it to be a victorious expression, commingled with a possessive glint.

Why do I always find myself attracted to complicated women?

Behind the blonde, leather-wearing Sera came Finaeus, Tangel, and Jeffrey. Then the rest of Sabrina's crew filed out, followed by more of the High Guard.

He nodded to Tangel, who met his eyes and returned the gesture before her eyes darted toward Sera and gave a wink.

<*What are you doing here?*> Sera asked Jason privately as the group formed up at the bottom of the ramp, exchanging pleasantries with Admiral Greer and the members of the Presidential Cabinet.

<*Are you the red one?*> Jason asked. <*Or blue? You're certainly*

not the blonde, I can't see you giving up the skin.>

<I'm red,> Sera said with a sigh. <I got assigned a color by Fina.>

<I'm guessing she's the one in blue.>

<Yup, and blondie-stick-up-her-butt is Seraphina.>

Jason held back a laugh as Jeffrey Tomlinson shook his hand. <Stop it, Sera, I have to make a good impression with your dad.>

<Gah, that's far too weird. Don't say things like that. And regarding Seraphina…ah, she's not that bad. I should cut her more slack. It's probably not easy to find out you were the third edition of another person.>

Jason considered that for a moment. <No, I suppose it wouldn't be. 'Unique' is usually the one thing everyone has going for them that they can be relatively secure in.>

<You never answered my question,> Sera said as the group began to walk out of the bay.

<Which was?>

<What are you doing here?>

Jason fell in beside Sera, who was talking about the state of the rebuilding project at Pyra with her cabinet. <Well, I was in the LMC dealing with some odds and ends, when Tangel here sent a message confirming that you would be passing through the Khardine System before going to Styx. I knew that things between us would get…tricky if we left them for too long, so I decided to come and meet you.>

<Tangel told you about how we're going to hit Airtha, did she?>

Jason replied to a question from one of the cabinet members about the Airthan fleets in the LMC while responding to Sera. <Sure, I get the briefs. I **am** the governor of New Canaan, if you've forgotten.>

<You're pretty good at that—carrying on two conversations at once.>

<Don't forget,> Jason gave Sera a wink. <I came by my

neuron-packed brain honestly. Didn't take a post-birth operation for me to become an L2.>

<I'm not quite up there with you, but close,> Sera replied. *<Granted, since my mother manufactured me to spec, I'm not sure what I'd have upstairs if it weren't for her meddling.>*

<I bet you'd've been amazing.>

She grabbed his hand and gave it a squeeze. *<You saying I'm not amazing now?>*

Jason gave Sera an exaggerated wink. *<Oh! You are quick!>*

* * * * *

Sera and Tangel had been whisked away to attend lengthy cabinet meetings discussing whether or not her father was fit to take up his position as president once more. Jason could have made a case to attend, but he'd had his fill of conference rooms for the time being.

Despite his reservations about Jeffrey Tomlinson on a personal level, Jason rather hoped that Sera wouldn't have any trouble securing the transfer of power. He knew it was selfish, but the possibility that Sera could shuck off all her responsibility made him more than a little happy.

Not having to manage the entire Transcend meant there was an increased possibility that she could join him in his cabin deep in the mountains of Pelas on Carthage after the war ended.

<We're gonna break for the day in about thirty minutes,> Sera informed him. *<Want to meet for dinner? I'm starving.>*

<You got it. I found this little pub down by the commercial docks. They have an amazing burger called the Back Blast—it's less risky than it sounds—plus whiskey made by the gods themselves.>

<Didn't know the gods were in the whiskey-making business.>

Jason sent a warm laugh into her mind. *<They're gods. They're in every business.>*

<Touche. Shoot, Victor is making some stupid argument that I need to concentrate on. Send me the name of the place, and I'll meet you there.>

<You got it,> Jason replied. *<It's called the 'Golden Goose'.>*

Jason had been in more than his share of political meetings. He knew that 'breaking in thirty minutes' was code for 'see you in a few hours'.

However, on the off-chance that Sera would actually manage to break free within thirty minutes, he worked his way down to the Golden Goose and secured a table in the back. Only two of the ISF Marines functioning as his guards came in, but he knew that the others would be nearby—a necessary annoyance he'd become accustomed to.

As he waited for one of the human waitstaff to approach, he surveyed the bar, taking in the 'local flavor'.

Though Keren Station was the heart of the Khardine faction of the Transcend—and thus all but swarmed with both politicians and the military—it had spent most of its existance as the central hub for the region's many mining operations.

The ongoing military buildup meant that the mining guilds were busier than ever, but despite that, precious few of their old haunts had room for them.

His train of thought was reinforced by some of the regulars giving him sidelong looks. He began to wonder if a change of venue was in order, when two men and a woman—their shipsuits covered in a fine iron-ore dust—approached him. Their arms were crossed, and their brows lowered.

"I don't mean nothing by it," one of the men said as the trio reached his table. "But there's precious little enough space for us on Keren anymore. I'm sure there are plenty of other establishments where you can eat, up in the hab cylinder."

Despite the fact that the three people before Jason didn't care for him much, he felt a sort of kinship with them.

Other than a single FTL corridor, the Oratus Cluster was

restricted to sub-light travel only by dense clouds of dark matter. The miners standing before him likely spent most of their time plying the black the same way Jason had as a young man: slowly.

"You're right," he said with a nod and an expansive smile. "But I feel a lot more at home down here. Smells like honest work." He looked at each of them in turn. "Do you know who I am?"

"Of course we do. Is it supposed to be some sort of threat?" the woman asked.

"Not in the least," Jason replied with disarming grin. "But from the way you said that, I doubt very much you really know who I am."

The three shared a confused glance.

"What's that supposed to mean?" one asked.

Jason gestured at the empty seats around the table. "Why don't you sit down, and I'll tell you a story about how I got started on this whole crazy adventure." The trio seemed uncertain until he added, "I'll buy you rounds so long as you care to listen."

That got the miners seated and signaling a servitor.

Once the first and second rounds were ordered—'for good measure', the woman had said with a wink—Jason began his tale.

"You see, I wasn't always a governor, or a respectable captain of a colony ship. Heck, even my own family thought I stood a good chance of never doing much with my life—not that I cared. Life is for living, not storing up in some reservoir that you get to finally dip into someday.

"Some of the expectations placed on me were due to the fact that I was the grandson of one of the great heroes of the Sentience Wars: Cara Sykes. She made quite the name for herself in the wars, and that's what most people remembered about her, but what few knew is that she grew up on a half-broken-down freighter named the *Sunny Skies*."

"Weird name for a freighter," the woman—who Jason later learned was named Margret—commented.

"Well, my great grandfather was a bit of an optimist—or so I'm told. Little known fact: he was the first successful AI-human pairing. The AIs back then called him a 'hybrid'. Set the stage for…well…nearly everything that is going on now.

"Anyway, after the end of the first Sentience War, my mother and her husband left the Sol System for Alpha Centauri, but they never made it as far as Rigel Kentaurus, stopping instead at Proxima Centauri."

"Pretty short flight," the first man—named Wren—said.

"Well, not back then. In those days, it used to take us a century to cross those measly four and a half light years. Anyway, Proxima is where they had me and my sister, and where we grew up. But I didn't really fancy sitting in one place. Proxima used to have a thick dust belt in those days, so I ran ore haulers between there and Rigel Kentaurus, the primary star in the Alpha Centauri system."

The three nodded appreciatively, seeming to be fully engrossed in the story as they nursed their drinks, so Jason continued.

"After that, I worked with the Enfields to build out the very first interstellar trade routes." The three miners looked at him skeptically and he shrugged. "Well, sure, there were folks who plied the black here and there before that, but they weren't hauling freight on commission, and they weren't making regular runs. You're looking at the first person to ever make a regular freight run between two separate star systems on a schedule."

"Shit…that's actually kinda awesome," Margret said with a slow nod as she glanced at her tablemates. "So how did you go from that to becoming the governor of New Canaan? Bit of a leap."

"Not too much." He gave his audience a wink. "Let me take a step back and tell you a bit about Enfield and the Sentience Wars. This is the sort of stuff you won't find in the history books. Luckily, I was raised by people—both AIs and humans—who were there…."

* * * * *

Sera had looked up the Golden Goose on her way down to the lower docks. It was a spot known for good food, coarse language, and rot-gut that would pickle your liver.

In short, it was just the sort of place she frequented back when she was captain of *Sabrina*, but hadn't seen much of since.

Jason had related a few tales from his younger days that led her to believe he used to enjoy a good dive bar as well.

However, as she neared the location, the boisterous sounds she expected to hear were not in evidence. In fact, she didn't even hear music coming from the entrance.

What she did hear was the sound of a singular voice rising and falling as it recited a tale to an audience. Upon entering the establishment, she saw the speaker—not that she hadn't already identified him.

<*I guess he got bored waiting for you,*> Jen commented with a snicker, and Sera shot her AI a sour look as she threaded her way through the crowd.

Jason stood atop a chair near the back of the bar, his sonorous voice booming out over a rapt audience.

"…as I said, I didn't like to visit Sol much—too many politicians and self-important types—" The statement raised a few snickers from the crowd. "But he asked me to come, and so I did."

"The one who shot your sister?" a voice called out in confusion.

"Yeah, we got past that...eventually. He did it for the right reasons—well, technically *he* wasn't even the one to have done it. Either way, he said he had a grand new adventure, one last flight into the black."

"How'd that turn out for ya?" one of the onlookers called out.

"Well, I'm still out here. Not sure if this counts as the same ongoing adventure, or if I've had a few since the *Intrepid* set sail. Oh ho! My date has arrived. Sorry, folks, I'll have to save the rest for another time. I can't keep a lady waiting."

<Though she sure kept me,> he sent privately to Sera.

<Sorry about that...I tried. Seems like you weren't having any trouble keeping busy.>

He continued to dismiss his assembled listeners while replying to Sera. <Well, I had to make sure that I didn't inadvertently start a barfight. You've got some unrest in the working class down here, by the way. Was fun, though...been far too long since I've gotten to hang out with strangers like this.>

"OK, If I'm here another day, I'll swing by again. No promises, though," Jason said as he pushed through the crowd toward Sera. "Just let me settle up my tab—"

<You don't want to stay?> Sera asked, as the crowd thundered that he had no tab so far as they were concerned.

<We won't get much privacy,> he replied with an apologetic smile.

Sera continued pushing through the crowd, which parted when the patrons realized who she was.

When she reached Jason's side, she turned to the throng. "To be honest, I want to hear his stories as much as you do. I'm willing to share him for the evening if you still want to hear more..."

The crowd roared in the affirmative, and she turned to Jason.

"So where were you?"

He shook his head and leapt back onto his chair. "OK…where *was* I? By the way, you'll all forgive me if I paint myself in a slightly better light to impress my girl here, won't you?"

The question was met by laughter and a few catcalls, which quieted down when Jason lifted his hands.

"OK, so my buddy Terrance wanted me to fly this bloody big starship out to 82 Eridani—you folks did good work there, from what I hear, not that I ever got to see it. Anyway, that ship was being built in Sol, but I was back at Alpha Centauri again. And like always, there was a mess that seemed like only I could clean up. Luckily, some of my old friends were still there, and we teamed up for one last adventure under the twin suns…."

THE MARCH

STELLAR DATE: 09.27.8949 (Adjusted Years)
LOCATION: TSS *Cossack's Sword*, **Edge of the Quera System**
REGION: Midway Cluster, Orion Freedom Alliance Space

Admiral Sebastian began speaking the moment he entered the conference room.

"OK, I know we didn't have to utterly *crush* them, but I also don't think we needed to let that many get away."

General Lorelai sat next to him and nodded slowly, but didn't respond.

Colonel Caldwell was also seated at the table, sipping a hot cup of coffee. Other than his initial greeting, the taciturn man hadn't said a word while they'd waited for Sebastian to arrive.

Now, at the admiral's words, he looked up from his cup and shrugged. "We denied them the system and got their attention. We suffered one loss and gathered valuable intelligence. I consider this to be quite the victory."

"Annihilation would have been a better victory." Sebastian's tone was sour as he sat heavily. "We could have done it."

"Probably," Svetlana replied with a nod. "But we want to sow chaos. The Quera System is too isolated to do that. Now these ships will disperse to one or more nearby systems to rally and get ready to fight us once more."

"They don't stand a chance, why—" Sebastian cut off his response mid-word. "Oh, shit. I'm such an idiot."

"No need to go that far," General Lorelai said with a wink.

"You want them to think that we don't have the stamina to go the distance," Sebastian said, shaking his head as he gestured for a servitor to bring him a coffee.

"Glad you picked up on it." Svetlana summoned a display

of the surrounding systems on the table's projector. "They're going to assume that we'll move to one of these three systems, and they'll believe that they have a chance of defending them against us."

"They just might, if they have enough of those EMG ships," Caldwell murmured. "Those things are ridiculous."

"And as much a liability as a weapon," Svetlana replied.

"You can bet they're not going to station them too close to a planet next time." Admiral Sebastian lifted his cup of coffee and took a long draught. "But my team analyzed the beam cohesion. They can shoot a lot further than the standard ranges."

"Fleet Intel has come to the same conclusion." Svetlana folded her hands before herself as she spoke. "Shield-breaching range could be as far as five million kilometers."

Sebastian whistled. "Yeah, things'll hit you half a second after you see them."

"We have fighters. We should use them more effectively," Caldwell said. "Deploy them ahead, widespread. If there are EMGs, they can't hit that many fighters—can't even see them at few million klicks. Fighters will make short work of ships like that."

Svetlana nodded slowly. She was still getting used to having fighters as a major part of her battlegroup. For so long, they hadn't been practical—unable to house powerplants large enough to support good shields.

But now with stasis shielding, her fighters were well nigh invincible, and far more maneuverable than capital ships.

"You're right. I need to have Colton and Lia more involved in future strategies. Our TR-9s are more deadly than an Oggie destroyer now."

"So which of these three closest systems do we hit next?" Admiral Sebastian asked.

"Half-wish we could strike all three at once," Colonel

Caldwell mused.

Svetlana shook her head. "Too risky. If something goes wrong, we're cut off, and we're already severely outnumbered. I think the Sullus System is our best bet. Admiral Jessica passed through there, and we have solid intel on it."

"You thinking we hit this outpost here?" General Lorelai asked, enlarging the system view and gesturing to a station orbiting a terrestrial world in the outer system.

Svetlana nodded. "We'll jump in stealthed and move the fleet into strike positions around the system before launching our attacks. Military targets, strike and run. That'll keep the insystem forces chasing us while you hit your target, Lorelai, and get us more intel on opportunities in the vicinity."

A grin lit up the general's face. "Sounds like a party. What is it you like to say? 'Let's get this show on the road'!"

Svetlana nodded, considering paying a visit to her father. *It would be nice to get his thoughts on this plan.*

THE RIVER STYX
STELLAR DATE: 10.01.8949 (Adjusted Years)
LOCATION: *Sabrina* approaching Styx Baby-9
REGION: STX-B17 Black Hole, Transcend Interstellar Alliance

<I can't believe this base is actually called 'Styx Baby-9',> Jen said with a note of derision in her voice, as Cheeky shifted *Sabrina* into a lower orbit around the dark gas giant.

"I kinda like it," Cheeky said with a soft giggle. "I mean, I've docked at a lot of stations, but never had a berth at a place with 'baby' in the name."

"You should take the SS *Sexy* out and get it its own berth," Fina said from where she sat with her legs draped over the scan console—since she'd opted for flowmetal limbs, 'draped' was a very apt description. "Then you could call it the '*Sexy Baby*'.

"Pretty sure it got called that a few times over the years, anyway," Finaeus commented, giving his head a slow shake. "Damn sweet pinnace, too. Especially with the alterations I made."

<Pretty sure I made most of them,> Nance called up from her station in engineering. <Just like then, you're on the bridge hobnobbing, and I'm down here doing all the work.>

"I'm not crew on this mission," Finaeus replied with a sniff. "Just here to spend some time with my wife."

"Liar." Cheeky cast a mock glare over her shoulder. "You told me last night that you'd punch a god in the dick to find out how Earnest figured out to set up jump gates in a gravity well like this. I'm playing second fiddle to your curiosity."

"Well, *seriously.*" Finaeus gestured at the forward view. "Fucking planet's *nine* jovian masses, *and* we're in orbit of a stars-be-damned black hole! There should be…one, maybe two viable jump vectors out of here…and *none* from below the cloudtops. But freakin' Earnest has successfully jumped drones on *seven hundred* different vectors."

"You sound jealous, Uncle Fin," Seraphina said through lips that were threatening to twitch into a smile.

"Fucking right, I'm jealous. I *invented* this technology—well, I was the first one to get it to work, at least. Earnest Redding is a freak of nature."

"You know what this means?" Cheeky glanced back at Nance and Finaeus. "If it works here, it should work at Star City."

Finaeus blew out a long breath. "Yeah. Earnest sent his new models to me before we left the *I2*, and I ran them for the gravity wells around Star City. It'll work. Hell, they could put gates right *inside* the sphere."

"Before this is all over, I *really* want to go see that place," Sera said, trying not to sound too wistful. "Must be amazing."

"Something like Star City puts the FGT out of business," Finaeus replied.

"Or puts us in a whole new business," Seraphina countered. "You're just jealous you didn't think of a reverse dyson sphere first."

"Maybe…" Finaeus chuckled while shaking his head. "You know…every human we know of could fit on ten of those with generations of room to spare. Still wish we could have met the builders—now *that* was vision."

<*I'm curious,*> Sabrina asked as the ship slotted into its final approach vector. <*What do we do if Katrina and her team can't get that old shard of Airtha?*>

"That's a good question," Sera said. "I suppose we get onto the Airthan ring and figure out how to target all of her nodes. If we can't introduce some sort of counter to her, we'll have to blow them, or maybe see if Bob can make an appearance."

"Which means we have to take out the EMGs she has

defending the place," Seraphina replied. "Airtha made those specifically to guard against the I2. I think she seriously fears Bob."

"There's the beginnings of Plan B, then," Sera said, as *Sabrina* dipped into the cloudtops of the gas giant.

<I hate flying into planets,> Sabrina said. <I seem to do it far too often.>

"Sorry, Sabs," Cheeky said as she monitored their approach. "Just have to get through a few hundred klicks of this mire, then we'll be at the station."

No one spoke further, as the ship continued to plunge, dropping deeper and deeper into clouds of frozen ammonia and nitrogen. Then a glow appeared ahead of the ship, gradually increasing in brightness until light exploded around them.

"Now *this* is a secret base," Sera said with a laugh as she surveyed the massive structure drifting in the center of a hundred-kilometer bubble within the planet's clouds.

Though the construction of Styx Baby-9 had only begun a few weeks prior, it was already large enough to dock fifty TSF capital ships.

The plan for the station was to create a docking grid that could funnel fuel and supplies to ships as needed, and then send them through the jump gates mounted at the end of the structure. When completed, it would be able to support over ten thousand capital ships, providing services from refit to refuel in a matter of days before sending them back out.

Long spires jutted out from the station's grid—it was toward one of those that *Sabrina* was headed—while on the far side of the station, long shafts dropped down into the planet, disappearing into the roiling clouds below.

"You have no idea how many beers I owe Earnest," Finaeus muttered. "The guy's such a show-off. I bet he's pulling liquid metallic hydrogen right from the core of the planet. He's been talking about how he could use some new technique he's all hush-hush about to transmute that into other elements as it exits its superfluid state—provided that there are enough neutrons in the slurry."

"You're saying he's transmuting matter from the planet's core to build the station?" Sera asked.

"More or less," Finaeus grunted. "That's my guess, at least. The bastard."

No one spoke for a minute as Finaeus's scowl deepened. Then everyone on the bridge, barring the ancient engineer, burst into tear-inducing laughter.

THE LMC

STELLAR DATE: 10.02.8949 (Adjusted Years)
LOCATION: Interstellar Pinnace, Approaching Jump Gate Array 9A9
REGION: Troy, New Canaan System

Cary was still more than a little surprised that her father had agreed to let her take Kent to the Aleutian Site in the Large Magellanic Cloud. Granted, he had layered on a goodly number of requirements and restrictions.

The first requirement he had was that Saanvi and Faleena accompany her.

Faleena had been more than eager to travel outside the galaxy. Her exact words were, "If you didn't bring me along, I'd've secretly re-implanted myself in you."

The prospect of asking Saanvi had worried Cary. She knew her sister was busy with her schoolwork at the academy, and was also helping the StarFlight group with several aspects of the new field generators that would alter where Canaan Prime outputted the energy from the fusion at the star's core. However, even before she had finished asking, Saanvi was screaming for joy and jumping into the air.

"Are you kidding me?!" her sister had hollered at the top of her lungs. "Who *wouldn't* want to go to another galaxy?"

Cary had asked Saanvi privately over the Link, while the pair was in their quarters' common room—hoping to keep the information a secret—but Amy had been in her room, and overheard Saanvi's excited screams.

"Another galaxy?" she'd asked, poking her head out from her room, eyes wide and filled with concern. "Are you leaving me?"

Those events—combined with a few others—were what led to Cary now sitting in the pilot's seat of an interstellar pinnace with Faleena, Saanvi, Amy, and Kent.

And a platoon of ISF Marines.

Most notably was the Marine standing directly behind Kent. Lieutenant Joshua Mason wore a grim expression along with his fully powered armor, feet maglocked to the deck and a hand on the back of Kent's chair as Cary eased the ship toward its assigned jump gate.

Kent leant forward and tapped the viewscreen. "Looks real, but that doesn't mean you didn't trap me in a VR sim. There's no way I'd be able to tell—especially with my Link removed."

"It's not a sim," Cary said for what she guessed to be the seventh time. "You're about to jump out of the galaxy. This is the real deal."

"Yeah?" Kent glanced over his shoulder at Amy. "You often bring kids on your extragalactic jaunts? And don't you think a whole platoon is a bit much for little ol' me?"

"We're here to protect them from you," Lieutenant Mason grunted out the words. "You so much as twitch in any one of these girls' direction, and I tear a limb off your body. You get to pick which one, though."

"How magnanimous of you," Kent muttered.

<*Lieutenant Mason, don't you think you're overdoing it?*> Cary asked privately. <*I'm trying to establish a rapport with Kent.*>

<*I understand that, Ensign Richards,*> Lieutenant Mason replied equably. <*But with all due respect to you and your goals, I have orders directly from Admiral Evans to keep you safe at all costs. I'm pretty sure that if this Oggie here even touches any of you, the admiral will pull **all** my limbs off.*>

Cary sighed and nodded, knowing that her father likely had given Mason a good talking to before the mission.

"We have clearance from the STC," Saanvi announced. "Light is green."

Ahead of them, space boiled within the ring, forming a spherical non-space bubble that was the terminator and origin of the singularity they were about to stretch across space.

Cary eased the ship forward, carefully watching actuals and ensuring they matched her preprogrammed path. Vector was important on any jump, but it was *exceedingly* important on an intergalactic jump.

A moment before the pinnace's Ford-Svaiter mirror touched the not-space, Kent peered at the viewscreen, craning his neck to the right. "Is that the *Britannica*?"

Then New Canaan disappeared, replaced by the nothing of the gate's transition as the singularity was stretched across the galaxy and beyond.

"You have the *Britannica*?" Kent pressed.

"Yes," Saanvi replied absently. "We captured it in the Defense of Carthage. Same as all the other Oggie ships—well, those that survived."

"And Garza was aboard?" Kent asked, his tone earnest, almost frantic.

"He was," Cary nodded. "Surely you'd heard we had Garza; I recall that the interrogators let it slip deliberately."

Kent's hand sliced through the air in front of himself in a dismissive arc. "Yeah, but I thought that was a clone."

Cary twisted around to face the man, glad for the diversion from the time the intergalactic jump was taking.

I wonder how lo—

"Seventeen seconds more," Saanvi announced.

<*You always manage to do that,*> Cary sent to her sister.

<*What?*> Saanvi asked.

<*Answer questions I hadn't asked aloud.*>

She snorted. <*That's Faleena's job. I just state the obvious. Not sure why that's profound to you.*>

Cary shot Saanvi a dirty look, only to see her grinning back.

<*Jerk.*>

Then the meaning behind Kent's words struck her.

"Wait...*you* know about the clones?"

Kent shrugged. "Sure, it was common knowledge on the *Britannica* that General Garza had obtained the cloning and memory-reintegration technology from the Hegemony of Worlds—it all started after their president sent a clone to watch the staged battle in Ascella."

"Why are you telling us this?" Faleena asked from behind Amy. "You are assuming we already know it, but what if we don't?"

"Well, if you got Garza—damn, none of this makes sense." Kent shook his head, and his expression became guarded. "By now, you would have surely gotten more out of him than you *ever* will from me. I just assumed that you had a clone, and it didn't know what you needed to learn."

Cary glanced at Saanvi and Faleena before continuing—noting as her gaze passed by Amy that the girl was watching events unfold with great interest.

The next instant, space snapped into place around them, heralding the end of their journey.

The starscape was wildly different than any Cary had seen before, though it wasn't any less dense than looking galactic north or south when inside the Milky Way.

When inside the Milky Way.... Cary whispered the words to herself and brought up the local astrogation data, turning the pinnace to catch the view they'd all been waiting for.

And there it was, hanging in front of them like a massive pinwheel, tilting away like it was blowing in the wind.

"It has to be a sim," Kent whispered, then held out his hand and pinched it with his other. "Ow! Dammit."

"That doesn't really work to exit a sim," Saanvi chided.

"Yeah...but what else can I do?" Kent's voice was still low and filled with wonder.

Even Lieutenant Mason sounded impressed. "Well I'll be a shiprat's tail. Hearing about this and then seeing it are two diiiiiiferent things."

"STC is on the horn," Saanvi announced, breaking the group's reverie. "They need us to clear the jump zone. I have an approach to the station. Piping it through to you, Cary."

"Right, right!" Cary nodded quickly as she brought the pinnace about and boosted for Aleutia Station.

"Even if I get an ulcer worrying about you girls," Lieutenant Mason said with a note of raw wonderment in his voice, "it'll totally be worth it to see this." The burly Marine laughed. "And here my son Brennen was giving me a hard time because he got assigned to the *I2*, and I was stuck back on the Palisades. Stars, even if he does get onto Admiral Richards' detail, this is still better."

The thought of people vying to get on her mother's guard detail didn't seem anywhere near as impressive as looking on the Milky Way Galaxy from over a hundred thousand light years away, but she wasn't about to diminish Mason's—or his son's—excitement about either.

"Funny that the father is protecting us daughters, while the son is protecting our mother," Faleena mused. "I wonder…who is protecting our *father*. Do you have a brother that could take on the task, Lieutenant?"

Cary laughed as she initialized the burn that would bring the pinnace around to their assigned approach vector. "Dad doesn't need anyone protecting him. He never gets into trouble."

A snort slipped past Saanvi's lips. "Well, not that he tells *us* about, anyway. But you've read his old record. Dad got up to *shenanigans* back in the TSF. It's no wonder they let him join a colony mission."

"Will we be able to get back?" Amy asked suddenly, her voice carrying an uncharacteristic urgency. "Can we go back now?"

Saanvi turned in her seat and placed a hand on Amy's

knee. "Yes, we'll be able to get back without a problem. Tanis and Sera—you remember them, right?"

Amy nodded silently.

"Well," Saanvi continued. "They were here just a few days ago. Jumped in and out without a problem. Look over there."

Saanvi directed Amy to look through the window on Kent's far side. "See? That's the return gate. You can see a ship lining up to jump back right now."

"Don't worry," Kent added, sparing a kindly look for the young girl. "I don't think anyone here plans to stay in the LMC for long. This is all just to impress upon me how futile the Orion Guard's goals are."

"Is it working?" Amy asked, her tone of voice belying the fact that she wasn't the innocent little girl many presumed her to be. Years of exposure to her father had given Amy an edge few eleven-year-olds had.

Still, Cary couldn't help a laugh, and twisted in her seat to look at Kent. "Well? Is it?"

He looked out the window at the distant galaxy none of them ever expected to so much as travel across, let alone leave altogether.

"Yeah, a bit."

Cary saw Saanvi and Amy lock eyes and knew the two were carrying out a conversation over the Link. Amy seemed to relax, and then Faleena spoke up once more.

"You were saying something about clones and the *Britannica*, Colonel Kent."

He didn't look away from the window as he spoke in soft tones. "I don't think I should share any more. I'm not going to commit treason. I feel like this ride is enough of a betrayal."

"We're going to win this war," Faleena pressed. "You must see that now. Orion may have numbers on their side, but our level of advancement nullifies all technological advance. You must, by now, realize our capabilities. Were we an immoral people, we could simply hide out here and manufacture pico payloads to destroy every Orion world. We could fire them through jump gates and end the war without losing a single one of our lives."

Kent turned his head at that. "Just you raising that possibility is disconcerting."

Faleena only shrugged and continued undeterred. "Surely your tacticians are planning for it, it is logical to assume that, should you back us into a corner, we will unleash our pico on you."

"I suppose they must be considering that," Kent allowed. "It was one of the reasons I was sent in with a strike team. To attempt to eliminate the threat before it became a war."

"And we understand that logic." Faleena's tone was warm, filled with understanding. "And you would agree that our people face an existential threat, yet we have not unleashed our most powerful weapon."

Kent gestured out the window. "Well, with a backup site in the LMC, that 'existential threat' is minimized."

"But it still exists—in fact, bringing you here has increased it."

"Oh, I know what bringing me here means," Kent countered. "It means that if I don't play ball, I get put in a hole for the rest of my life. This isn't the sort of installation you let people know about and then risk them escaping."

"It's true," Cary replied. "But we're not going to imprison people forever. You'll go into stasis, and then be set free when the war is over."

"And what if you lose?" Kent asked. "Will we all remain in stasis for centuries until our pods lose power?"

"They're on a hundred-year timer," Saanvi told him. "Their location is such that it can sustain the entire prisoner population without trouble, should knowledge of the location be lost."

"Seems you think of everything," Kent muttered.

"Benefit of advanced technology." Cary turned to look at him once more. "You have to see that. Yes, the Inner Stars is a shitshow, but it doesn't have to be that way. All humans and AIs can be uplifted and live in peace if there is no want. We can turn our focus to building amazing things, exploring the universe, living forever. Your Kirkland thinks that one of our two species should be slaves, and the other should live short, meaningless lives. Do you really think that should be our destiny?"

Kent turned away, staring out the window once more at the distant galaxy.

Cary waited a minute for a response, and then twisted back around in her seat, facing forward as she adjusted their approach to match delta-v with Aleutia Station.

<He'll come around,> Saanvi said, her voice carrying a cautious note of encouragement. <Or at the least he'll let something slip. As it is, we know that there was some significance to the Britannica being captured, and it relates to the cloned Garzas.>

<We've been over that ship with a fine-tooth comb.> Faleena gave a soft laugh. <And now that I have hair, I finally understand that in greater detail.>

<You have synthetic hair that blows in an invisible breeze and never tangles,> Saanvi shot back, giving her sister a judging look over her shoulder. <You still don't understand it.>

Faleena gave a half-smile and wink in response. <True, but if I didn't have the ability to manage each follicle on my head, it would take a lot of combing. Either way, there's something we missed—about the ship, or Garza himself. That makes this trip worth it, at least—outside of getting to visit another galaxy.>

Cary nodded absently, knowing that it still wasn't enough. Kent possessed knowledge that would help them, they just had to figure out how to prise it free.

ALEUTIA

STELLAR DATE: 10.03.8949 (Adjusted Years)
LOCATION: Aleutia Station
REGION: Cheshire System, Large Magellanic Cloud

"Welcome to the LMC," Colonel Ophelia said as she approached the group disembarking from the pinnace. "I'm sorry that General Peabody isn't here to greet you, but he's out at Bolt Hole."

"Are they managing to stabilize the system?" Saanvi asked, her voice dripping with enthusiastic curiosity.

A pained expression flashed across Ophelia's face. "Well, it's proving to be tricky. No one had ever considered—at least not seriously—dropping a black hole into the dark layer. Admiral Richards made a bit of a mess with that one."

"I still want to know how Airtha managed to send a ship containing a black hole through a jump gate," Cary added. "From what Finaeus said, that shouldn't be possible. The mass of the singularity within the ship would bend the jump gate's tunnel through spacetime unpredictably."

Saanvi gave a mock gasp, and Cary shot her a dark look. "I may be the hotshot pilot on our team, but I still pay attention. The mechanics of spaceflight being of particular interest."

Having turned to reply to Saanvi, Cary caught the look of utter amazement on Kent's face at the subject. He caught her gaze, and quickly schooled his expression as Colonel Ophelia spoke up again.

"They're combing through the wreckage of the EMG ship for clues, but so far, that's a secret for Airtha alone. Erin and her team have made the trip out to Bolt Hole; she seemed confident that they could save the planet by some means…. The question is whether or not it's worth the effort."

"I can't imagine why not," Faleena chimed in. "That world is an ark containing a variety of plants and animals not seen across a thousand star systems."

"I believe that is something they're weighing," Ophelia said as she gestured for the group to follow her out of the docking bay. "Whether to save the ark, or save the contents."

"I bet Erin really wants to figure out how to guide a black hole inside the dark layer," Saanvi added.

"What about the Exdali?" Cary asked. "They must be swarming the thing."

"Exdali?" Kent asked, speaking for the first time since they disembarked.

Cary fell back a step and gave the man a sidelong look. "Have you ever heard tall tales about things that live in the dark layer and devour ships?"

The Orion Guard colonel frowned. "Once or twice. Honestly, they're just stories from shitty pilots who didn't follow dark matter maps well enough and got creamed."

Faleena held out her hand, and a holoprojection appeared above it. The view was of Carthage with tens of thousands of ships surrounding it. "See the Orion Guard fleet?" she asked.

Kent nodded silently as the AI initiated the playback. As he watched, a fleet of ISF ships jumped in close to the planet and moved into an unusual configuration. Then spacetime appeared to ripple directly in the Orion fleet's path.

The ripple became a rift, and out of it poured the stuff of nightmares. Amorphous shapes with what appeared to be writhing masses of tentacles and gaping maws dove into the midst of the Orion ships, latching onto them and devouring the vessels.

Faleena halted the playback and gave Kent a serious look. "*Those* are Exdali. They live at the core of every star system, feeding on dark matter. Yes, many ships that make insystem jumps hit pockets of mass in the DL, but many *also* encounter

Exdali."

Colonel Kent sucked in a sharp breath. "They…you…all those ships, those people…"

"There were many survivors," Colonel Ophelia said as they swung into the corridor leading to the main observation lounge at the top of Aleutia Station. "Your people were lucky."

"Lucky?" He choked out the word, eyes still staring at the projection above Faleena's outstretched hand.

"Yes," Ophelia's voice shifted, dripping with ice. "We *should* have used our picobombs. Wiped out the filth entirely. Instead, my son died so that some of your interstellar marauders could live. So yeah, you were *lucky*. Lucky I wasn't in command, because I would have told parliament to go fuck themselves and used pico anyway."

Ophelia's vehement outburst killed any further conversation, and made for a rather awkward lift ride to the observation deck.

Once they arrived, Cary directed the Marines to take Kent across the broad space to a seating area, while she and her sisters stayed back with Ophelia. Amy hung by Saanvi's side, but the girl seemed more curious than alarmed by the ISF colonel's outburst.

"I'm sorry," Faleena said quietly. "I didn't think we would open old wounds."

"Not that old," Ophelia muttered. "That battle wasn't even two years ago…" The colonel's voice faded, and she sucked in a deep breath. "But I'm the one who should be sorry. You're trying to turn him to our side, and I may have just screwed that up."

Cary shrugged. "You never know. It may be just what we need. Nothing you said was wrong. His people *did* launch an unprovoked attack against ours."

"Doesn't matter," Ophelia said with a vehement shake of her head. "My behavior was inexcusable. It's probably best that I go."

"I believe you're right," Saanvi replied. "We do need to make sure he feels safe."

Ophelia smiled at the three sisters. "You're a good set of women. I imagine you do your parents proud—when you're not stealing starships, that is."

"You take a ship *one time*…" Cary replied with a wink.

The ISF colonel gave a soft laugh, and turned to walk away, then stopped and looked over her shoulder. "Oh, I was going to say before, there's something interesting about the LMC and the dark layer."

"Oh?" Saanvi asked.

"We've not yet searched extensively—no one really wants to, overmuch—but as best we can tell, there are no Exdali in the LMC."

Cary felt her mouth drop open and saw Saanvi's eyes widen.

"None?" they asked in unison.

Ophelia shook her head. "Not in this neck of the woods, at least. Hard to say if there are any elsewhere, though."

Saanvi whistled. "I bet Earnest will be *very* interested in that."

"Why's that?" Faleena asked.

"Just a theory of his, one he asked me not to share until he has more data."

Cary rolled her eyes as she turned back to where Lieutenant Mason had taken Kent. "Earnest always has a new theory, doesn't he?"

* * * * *

Once the group had settled in the circular seating area where the Marines had taken Kent—and a round of drinks had been ordered from a servitor—the Orion colonel let out a long sigh.

"I have to admit, Cary Richards, this is a damn sight better than walks in the Palisades' lower parks." As he spoke, his gaze was fixed on the view of the Milky Way galaxy, hanging several meters above the rim of the observation lounge.

"Pun intended?" Cary asked with a wink.

Kent nodded. "Of course."

"Pun?" Amy asked, sounding puzzled. "Ohhh! 'Sight'. I get it."

A pair of servitors arrived and began to hand each person their desired beverage, and the group sat in silence for a few minutes before Kent spoke up.

"Your father must really trust you three to send you here alone with me."

Cary glanced over her shoulder to where Lieutenant Mason stood, then looked around the lounge at the thirty Marines spread throughout the area.

"Not exactly what I would call 'alone'."

"Well—no offense to you, Lieutenant—" Colonel Kent paused to nod in Mason's direction. "The grunts here aren't trying to wring intel from me, that's your job."

"Four," Amy piped up, giving Kent a narrow-eyed look.

"Pardon?" the Orion colonel asked.

"Their father sent the four of us," Amy said as she folded her arms. "They had to get special permission to bring me along, which means he trusts me too."

Kent chuckled softly. "I suppose he does, Amy. I'm glad you came along. It means that your sisters will be nicer to me—they wouldn't want to upset you."

Amy snorted and rolled her eyes. "Puh-lease, Mister Kent. My father raped and murdered people right in front of me. Even Cary at her meanest is like my father was on his very best day."

Kent let out a low whistle and his eyes darted to Cary, who

nodded slowly.

"Amy's father was a man named Stavros. He ran a rather nasty little empire on the edge of the Praesepe Cluster," she supplied.

"But my best friend Rika saved me and my mom," Amy said with a beatific smile. "And then Barne, my new big brother, blew my dad's brains out the back of his skull."

Amy said the words without emotion, but Cary could tell that it cost the girl a lot to give voice to those memories.

"You think that the people from New Canaan are bad, Mister Kent, but you have no idea what bad is until you've watched your father torture Silver for years, and then…and then she's your mother!" Suddenly Amy was on her feet, yelling at Kent, her face reddening while tears glistened in her eyes. "So maybe you should think about who the bad guys really are before you try to kill off the good ones!"

The silence was palpable as Amy stood with fists clenched at her sides and chest heaving before she strode away, heading to the exit.

"I'll go with her," Saanvi said softly as she rose, a fireteam of Marines trailing after her.

No one spoke for a moment before Kent drew in a slow breath. "Did you all save her from that?"

"No," Cary shook her head. "One of our allies did. The Marauders. They're all that's left of place called Genevia. They weren't the best people out there either, but they were decent enough before the Nietzscheans attacked and destroyed them."

"I've heard of them." Kent nodded slowly. "The Nietzscheans, that is."

"I expect so," Faleena said. "They're one of Orion's major allies in that region of space."

"Hm," Kent grunted, his lips pressed into a thin line. "You sure like to paint a picture of Orion as the villain in all this."

Faleena shook her head, a grim expression settling on her green skin. "You know reality is too complex for such labels—at least in this case. People like Amy's father were definitely villains. But galactically, there are too many forces at play. From the Ascended AIs, to Airtha and your Kirkland. There are other forces at play, too—but all of them have been too busy fighting one another to care about people like Stavros and what he did to Amy and her mother."

Kent's eyes fell, and he let out another long sigh—one that *sounded* heartfelt to Cary.

"You're right about that," he said. "How much time and energy have we all spent fighting one another—we could be exploring, seeing the wonders of space, like you are out here."

"Like you wanted to do when you signed up," Cary prompted. "That's what you said, right? That you wanted to see the stars."

The colonel's view shifted back to the breathtaking view outside the lounge's windows. "Sure can check that off my list now, can't I?"

"Think one check is enough?" Cary gave the man an appreciative smile.

Kent snorted. "No, probably not."

Silence fell once more, and Cary finished her drink and ordered another from the servitor. When it arrived, she hadn't lifted it to her lips before Kent spoke.

"He was on the *Britannica*."

"He?" Faleena asked.

"Garza." Kent uttered the name with a sound that wasn't quite distaste, but it wasn't admiration or respect, either.

Cary's eyes narrowed as she lowered her drink to her lap, cupping it with both hands. "What are you saying?"

"He told me that *he* would be on the *Britannica*. He wanted me to be sure to report to him and not one of his clones when I completed my mission—*if* I completed it, I guess."

"That first Garza isn't a clone," Faleena whispered.

"OK, sure," Cary shrugged. "But we didn't think he was a clone anyway until Mom encountered another Garza in Scipio."

"What you don't know is that Garza's clones don't know they're clones." Kent's lips twitched into a half-smile. "They all think they're the real deal."

"So?" Cary asked. "There are a bunch of clueless Garza clones running around. This sounds like a good thing."

He nodded. "For you, yes. What you don't understand, though, is that Garza is not working *with* Praetor Kirkland."

Cary resisted the urge to let out a joyous whoop. Kent was finally spilling real intel. Stuff they could use. She didn't know what exactly had prompted it, but she wasn't about to question their good fortune.

"What does that mean, exactly?" Faleena asked.

"One time, I delivered a report to General Garza while Praetor Kirkland was present via holo—I don't think those two like each other much. What's more, from the things he said, I'm positive that the praetor would not approve of the cloning, or half the other technology that Garza uses."

"Is it a 'fight fire with fire' scenario?" Cary asked, to which Kent shook his head.

"I don't think so. See, it's the cloning. Garza doesn't *need* that to manage his operations. He just doesn't trust other people. Couple that with the Widows, and he's definitely playing out of bounds."

"I've heard of those," Cary replied with a shiver. "Poor Lisas."

"Lisa?" Kent asked.

"The Widows are clones of Finaeus Tomlinson's former wife, Lisa Wrentham," Faleena explained.

Kent whistled and then signaled a servitor. "I'll need another drink. Best make this one stiffer than the last."

"So will you help us?" Cary asked.

"Aren't I already? Stars…" Kent's voice lowered. "I really am. I can't believe I'm doing this."

"Colonel," Cary leant forward and placed a hand on Kent's. "I promise you, I give you my absolute assurance. My people's driving goal is to end this war with as little bloodshed as possible."

She glanced around at the Marines, and Kent followed her gaze, noting that that they nodded in assent.

"She's telling you the truth," Lieutenant Mason spoke up. "We all left Sol—or our parents did—to get away from shit like this. We just want to build a future that doesn't involve people pissing on each other all the time. Live and let live—galaxy's more than big enough for us all to have room to do our thing."

"And if some people's 'thing' is to kill others?" Kent asked. "Who will police them?"

"There will always be bad apples," Mason said with an exaggerated shrug. "But far as I can see, what your people and the Transcend have been doing for some time is *cultivating* those bad apples. Time for a change."

Kent pursed his lips and nodded. "Yeah, I can see that. If you were just the Transcend, I wouldn't buy your song and dance, but I can tell you hold them to blame for a lot of what's gone on."

"We do. They tried to attack us as well—they just didn't get as far as your people."

Kent leant back in his seat and took a sip of his drink. "OK, then. What else do you want to know?"

SAGITTARIUS'S BAR

STELLAR DATE: 10.03.8949 (Adjusted Years)
LOCATION: Coronado, Maya System
REGION: Former Transcend Space, Sagittarius Arm

Katrina had just taken the first sip of her Hero's Fall, a rather enticing—and very bubbly—drink, when a voice from beside her said, "Thought you swore you were never coming back to the Transcend."

"I don't think I said *never*, Jordan," Katrina replied without looking up from the foaming concoction before her. "I'm certain it was something more like 'I never *want* to come back to the Transcend'."

"You kinda have a way of shifting meaning, Kat. I distinctly remember the conversation. The word 'want' was not present."

Katrina straightened and brushed her long, red hair aside, glancing at Jordan. "Maybe you're right. I've said a lot of things I wish I hadn't. That may have been one of them."

The dark-haired woman next to her gave a knowing smirk. "Yeah, I have my list of those as well." She looked Katrina up and down and added, "Looking good for an old woman."

Katrina's mouth quirked into a smile. "You too. Seems like life in the Transcend has been good to you."

Jordan only shrugged, glancing at the bartender and holding up a finger while she said, "They have amazing rejuv tech out here. Seems silly not to use it—especially because I'd be dead otherwise. Too much going on just to get old and die."

Katrina glanced around the nearly deserted establishment. "I thought you came out here to get away from it all."

" 'It all' seems to have a way of catching up with a person." She gestured to Katrina with her chin, as the bartender set a glass of bourbon down in front of her. "Case in point. Gotta say, I barely recognized the *Voyager*. Got a fresh coat of paint."

"A few upgrades here and there," Katrina replied, meeting Jordan's eyes. "I found them. Finally…after all these years."

The other woman only shrugged. "Glad you did—though I thought the whole point was to settle down with them in their paradise."

Jordan's words were laced with a subtle derision that Katrina chose to ignore. She wasn't surprised, though. Their parting had been acrimonious, and in hindsight, Katrina saw that Jordan had been right.

It occurred to her that the other woman needed to hear it from her.

"I'm sorry, Jordan. You, Sam, and Demy were all right—more than you know, even. I made a mess of everything."

"Oh?" She raised an eyebrow. "This should be good. Tell me all about how I was more right than even I knew."

"Do you remember the being I told you about? The one that saved me in the Midditerra system?"

"Yeah," Jordan nodded. "If it wasn't for the fact that you showed up looking like a human and not a machine, I wouldn't have believed a word of it. What about her…it…whatever?"

"Well, turns out that she left something inside me. Something that was guiding my actions a lot more than I thought. Tanis called it a 'memory'."

"And this…'memory' made you behave like a pig-headed idiot?" Jordan's tone was still caustic, but Katrina could see that her eyes had widened in compassion. Not much, but it was there.

Katrina shook her head, adding a self-mocking laugh. "No, pretty sure that part was all me. But it was feeding me directives that I didn't have much choice but to obey."

"Fuck, Katrina." Jordan's expression finally softened. "You

just can't get away from people putting shit in your head to control you. How did you get the memory out?"

"Tanis's daughter, of all people. She's semi-ascended…or something. She drew the memory out of me."

Jordan barked a laugh and then downed her drink. "You have the strangest friends."

"Do you count yourself amongst them?"

Jordan signaled the bartender for another drink. "I never stopped being your *friend*, Katrina. I just didn't want to fight your fight anymore. I gave you a lifetime. I just needed to live my own for a bit."

"I'm glad you made the decision you did. What have you been doing out here, anyway?"

Jordan winked. "Oh, you know. A little of this, a little of that. We have to be careful, the *Castigation* tends to stand out, and Sam won't leave it. Says that it's his body and we can't make him go in some little tub for sorties."

"Sounds like Sam," Katrina laughed. "Troy's still the same way, too. Though I think if Tanis asked him to take on another ship, he'd do it in a heartbeat. Those two have some sort of deep bond."

Jordan nodded absently as she signaled to the bartender for another drink. When it arrived, she took a sip and then turned on her stool to face Katrina directly.

"OK, so I know you didn't come out here to the ass end of the Transcend just to shoot the shit and ask forgiveness for being a jerk. Things are afoot. A lot of things, and your friend Tanis is at the heart of them."

"You have that right," Katrina glanced around the bar. "Am I correct in my assumption that people this far out don't really identify with Airtha or Sera? No sides being taken?"

"Every star within a hundred light years has declared independence," Jordan confirmed. "They can't even agree on simple trade law, let alone care enough about what's happening rimward."

"I bet that's perfect for the sort of work you like to do," Katrina said with a wink.

Jordan placed a hand on her chest and gave Katrina a wounded look. "Are you besmirching our time-honored profession?"

Katrina laughed. "Stars, no. In fact, I'm curious if you'd be interested in stepping it up a notch."

Jordan's eyes narrowed again, and Katrina deployed a passel of nano to secure their conversation from prying eyes and ears.

"We're going to kill Airtha, and I need your help."

"So do you want help killing Airtha, or access to the shard that Sam has tucked away in one of his holds?"

"Both," Katrina replied. "But I'll understand if you don't want to take sides in this—though you'd be a fool to think that Airtha will be any sort of benevolent dictator if she wins."

"Like Jeffrey Tomlinson?" Jordan scoffed. "That guy was a pompous dick. He couldn't care less how his actions affected others. Not sure if his daughter is any better."

Katrina gave a nervous laugh. "Stars, this story is so nuts I don't know if you'll even come close to believing me…. The man running the Transcend for the last thousand years or so has been a clone of the real Jeffrey. He was put there by Airtha. Tanis and her people recently found the original president and are going to put him back in charge of the Transcend. His daughter…well they're not really *his*, per se, and there is more than one of them, but they're leading a strike to kill Airtha, who is their mother."

Jordan tilted her head as Katrina spoke, eyes narrowing further. "OK…sounds to me like this is quite the story; one that Sam and Demy should hear." She rose and dropped a handful of credit chits on the bartop. "C'mon. Let's reunite you with the ol' crew."

* * * * *

"So that's where things stand," Katrina said as she finished, looking between Demy and Jordan with a knowing smile. "It's nuts, right?"

Demy snorted and shook her head. "Yeah, sure, if by 'nuts', you mean completely freaking insane."

"Trust me, it's pretty damn surreal to me, too," Katrina replied. "I mean…the LMC. Tanis now thinks that it's entirely possible that enclaves of people could be spread all over the galaxy. Given that half the systems around here aren't even listed as settled on official Transcend records, I'm inclined to agree with her."

<So you want the Airtha shard?> Sam asked. <Hmmm…>

"You still have it, right?"

Karina hadn't gotten what she considered to be complete confirmation from Jordan back in the bar. The fear that they'd lost or sold the shard some time ago had been lingering in the back of her mind as she'd told her story.

<Relax,> Sam's coarse voice contained a modicum of amusement. <Just leading you on a bit. Troy already gave me his version of things, I was just letting you organics get it all out the slow way.>

"You're such a peach, Sam," Katrina groused, casting a narrow-eyed look at one of the bridge's optics. "So you still have it?"

<I do. I'm curious to know **exactly** what you plan to do with it.>

"I don't know exactly. The goal is to destroy Airtha the AI without having to damage the ring itself—or kill the populace."

Jordan glanced at Demy. "Seems noble enough, but do we really want to get back in the 'fighting the good fight' business?"

"Seems like it's a 'get killed for someone else's cause' sort of operation," the engineer replied.

Katrina held up her hands. "I'm not asking you to sign up. I just need that shard core."

The two women glanced at one another, and though she secretly wished they would join in, deep down, she knew that the chances of that were slim. That ship had sailed.

<*What are you willing to trade for it?*> Sam asked in a cautiously neutral tone.

Katrina wasn't surprised it had come to this, but she was a bit shocked it had been Sam who asked for compensation. "What do you want?"

"Even out here in the boonies, we've heard about the shields that ships are getting now. 'Stasis shields', I believe they're called?" Jordan asked. "I can see those coming in handy."

"Not a chance—and certainly not if you don't sign up."

"Thought you wanted to end the war?" Demy asked. "This core will give you a great, bloodless victory."

Katrina clenched her jaw, unable to believe that three friends she had spent centuries with were going to extort her for tech that could end the civil war in the Transcend.

Then it dawned on her. "Shit, you *like* the unrest this is causing."

Jordan shrugged. "Makes our line of work easier. We're just looking to live comfortably out in a place where the law isn't up our asses all the time."

<*And where there's a whole lot of nothing to run off and hide in if we need it.*>

Katrina couldn't believe what she was hearing. "Airtha—and the core AIs, for that matter—aren't really the sort that will establish the kind of future that enables you to live freely."

"There are people who always try to take control of

everything, and they always fail." Jordan gave a nonchalant shrug. "Honestly, Katrina. You should join us, live the good life. Don't worry yourself with all the nonsense rimward of here."

A part of Katrina had really hoped that she could convince her old crewmates to join the fight, that they'd see the sort of future Tangel would build—at least in New Canaan, if nowhere else.

But they had always been pirates, or almost always. It was in their blood.

"A CriEn. I'll trade you a CriEn for the shard."

<*That's too much,*> Troy said privately, having been listening in via a feed Katrina had given him.

<*It'll give them a fighting chance if things go badly,*> she replied, before adding aloud, "But you can't trade or sell it. It's for *you*."

"In what universe would we give up a CriEn?" Jordan whispered. "You're serious?"

Katrina nodded. "As an antimatter capsule. Show me the shard, and we'll make our deal."

* * * * *

"Are you surprised?" Carl asked when Katrina boarded the *Voyager*, a small case containing the shard clutched in her right hand.

"No…yes…" Katrina replied with a drawn-out sigh. "I didn't *expect*, but I sure did hope."

<*Maybe when it's all over, you can find them again and try to make amends,*> Troy suggested. <*They just worry about what this unrest means, and they're right to fear what we're up against. Assaulting Airtha, trying to destroy her…it's no small task.*>

Carl gave a quiet laugh. "You trying to make me reconsider, Troy?"

<Will it work?>

Katrina barked a laugh while Carl glared at the closest optic. "You know…I've fixed your sorry hull up more times than I can count, Troy."

<Just a little joke, Carl. It's like you don't even know me.>

"He seems happier," Carl glanced at Katrina. "I didn't know Troy could be happy. It's unnatural."

Katrina turned to the panel and sealed the airlock before replying, "Don't worry, I'm sure it won't last. Let's get our clearance and undock so we can go bribe the syndicate controlling the jump gate in this system. I don't fancy taking the DL and four years to fly to Styx."

"What are you going to offer him?" Carl asked. "We don't have any spare CriEns."

"Was thinking about using a gun this time. What do you think?"

Carl slapped her on the back. "Sounds like my kinda negotiation—a Kara Special. I'll get the team ready."

SUMMONS
STELLAR DATE: 10.03.8949 (Adjusted Years)
LOCATION: Ol' Sam, ISS *I2*
REGION: Pyra, Albany System, Thebes, Septhian Alliance

<Are you certain this is wise?> Bob asked. <I feel as though I've remained too long here at Pyra. Events are in motion, and I do not like to remain still.>

Tangel nodded in response as she waited on the maglev platform near her lakehouse, waiting for a car that would take her to the smaller, 61B VIP dock where her ship awaited.

"I understand that, but keeping the *I2* here is a useful deterrent. We may have defeated the Nietzschean fleet, but Septhia is still a political mess, and there are fractured nations all around that would pounce on what we're trying to build here."

<The Starblade *is more than enough to scare off any ill-intentioned enemies,*> Bob replied. <I *have full confidence in Siobhan and Captain Quinn. They're fully capable of keeping Albany secure and aiding in the construction of Pyra's ring.*>

Tangel sighed, looking up at the long sun that ran through the center of the cylinder. "I understand that you feel responsible for what happened to bring about my ascension, but it's done. And now that it's done, I'm well able to protect myself. I just spent five days in Keren and was perfectly safe."

<Were you?>

"What do you mean, Bob? I easily dispatched two remnants after flying through space and dissolving a starship hull. Then I leapt through a jump gate—without a helmet, no less—and ended up in the LMC, where I destroyed a very large starship on my own."

Bob didn't reply, and Tangel shook her head at the

approaching maglev car.

"You think I'm reckless."

<I don't.>

"I'm not, you know. I've always been able to process more variables than other people. I can see angles of approach and defense they can't. I can move faster. I'm stronger. What they see as reckless behavior, I see as entirely reasonable action."

<Other people don't understand you. They don't see things like you do.>

"There's nothing I can do about that. Besides, *you* understand things from my perspective better than anyone."

A slow rumble flooded Tangel's mind, and after a moment, she realized that Bob was sighing.

"You need to work on that," she muttered as the maglev car came to a stop before her. "Sounded like the ship was thrusting without dampeners."

<I still prefer to fly without a-grav dampeners. They make it feel like I'm wading through sludge.>

The car was empty, and Tangel took the seat closest to the door. "OK, Bob, what really has you worried?"

<Other ascended beings. They're closing in, they've sent many of their minions after you, Myrrdan and his remnants at New Canaan, and the Caretaker with Peter Rhoads and others, they've spread tech amongst our enemies—there is no way that Airtha **and** the OFA developed EMGs at the same time—and they've even set your own friends up as traps to kill you, such as Katrina.>

"I've noticed," Tangel said, a wry note to her voice.

<Then you know what escalation looks like.>

"I can imagine."

<Which means you need me.>

She watched the landscape inside the habitation cylinder slide by, and then the maglev dove beneath the surface, through the decks within the cylinder's skin and through the hull.

Space around the ship was busy. Marauder ships were running through training drills, some Septhian cruisers were in high orbit, and several hundred Theban military craft were also nearby. But the bulk of the activity was from civilian craft, all working to bring supplies to Kendrick's shipyards, or for the planetary ring's construction.

Tangel soaked in the view for a few moments before responding. <*I need you safe, Bob, and I need the I2 safe as well.*>

<*We weren't safe when we came to rescue you down on Pyra. It worked out.*>

<*I get that,*> she replied. <*But there's something about the AIs in the League of Sentients. The reports on what Jessica's team encountered are…unusual. Even for us.*>

<*Don't make me sigh again, Tanis. This is why I need to come.*>

Tangel held out her hand and then reached out into extradimensional space and gathered stray tendrils of electromagnetic energy, drawing it into a ball. In three-dimensional space, it appeared to be a glowing sphere, hovering above her hand, but with the other dimensions in play, it felt more like a solid object. A bit warm, and a little tingly.

<*Are you showing off?*> Bob asked. <*It won't change my mind.*>

<*I've been practicing. Every time I've used my new abilities, it's been in a time of crisis. I haven't really thought about what I was doing—it was more of an instinct.*>

She twisted her hand and dispersed the energy back into the space around her, the power that had been visible disappearing from sight as its frequency and amplitude changed.

<*That seems logical. You're really not going to bend on this, are you?*>

<*I've directed Lieutenant Brennen to bring a portable QC comm box. Will that ease your mind?*> Tangel asked.

<*A bit, provided you won't hesitate to call me if there is trouble.*>

The maglev car completed its journey along one of the ship's gossamer arcs and reentered the hull, slowing as it approached dock 61B.

<*You really do seem worried this time.*>

Tangel admitted to herself that hearing high levels of concern from Bob was unnerving. The AI rarely expressed worry over anything, always prepared to cite a mastery of all variables as the basis for his never-ending surety.

<*It is as I said. You've bested all of your enemy's indirect attacks thus far. That means they either have more indirect avenues of attack we've not thought of, or that they will take a more direct approach. We know that an ascended AI who is not a great fan of ours has been at work in the League of Sentients.*>

The maglev car stopped at the station across from the 61B bay, and Tangel stepped out and walked across the corridor.

<*You think it's a trap?*>

<*I believe it could be. I don't have enough solid information to know for sure.*>

Tangel sighed as she entered the bay and gave a resigned nod. <I'll maintain an active connection to the QC unit. I'll configure it to call you if I lose my connection for more than a minute. Will that put you at ease?>

<*To a degree.*>

On the far side of the bay, past a dozen dropships, pinnaces, and racks of fighters, lay the ship she had decided to finally take for a spin.

It had been left for her by Amanda, an extra-universal visitor she'd met twice now. Tangel didn't know how to travel between universes, but Amanda had mastered it to a degree, and come calling after the two of them had met in a mysterious bar a few years back.

While the thought of a busty redhead popping in and out of Tangel's spacetime didn't bother her overmuch, she did wonder what other people—or things—may come over from some fork of the multiverse.

Tangel had entertained the idea for some time that the Exdali could be from *somewhere* else. They were just so foreign, and didn't seem to fit with any other type of life that anyone had come across thus far.

Then again, the dark layer is yet another set of dimensions within our little slice of the multiverse. It doesn't have to operate by the exact same rules as everywhere and everywhen else.

As Tangel approached, the ship—which she hadn't officially named yet—was lifted off the rack and lowered to a cradle. The craft was sleek and white with a red stripe down one side…rather similar to Amanda, in that respect.

When Amanda had gifted the ship to her, it hadn't possessed any drive systems, but the interior had been—and still was—luxuriously outfitted.

It had taken a group of engineers just a few days to outfit it with a CriEn for power, stasis shields, a-grav systems, a small AP and fusion drive, and point defense beams.

They'd made much of the strange, gleaming material the hull was constructed of. It wasn't something that would offer a lot of stealth capability, but with stasis shields in the mix, it wasn't a big concern.

<*It's fueled up and ready to go, Admiral.*> Captain Rachel broke into Tangel's thoughts. <*It seems a bit on the small side, but I suppose that can be useful.*>

<*You've gotten used to flying this city around,*> Tangel replied, sending a smile to the captain. <*A feeling I know all too well.*>

<*Bob told me you're bringing a QC. Good. We'll be ready to come if you need us.*>

A laugh slipped past Tangel's lips. <*Bob been talking to you about his concerns?*>

<*Bob? No. I didn't know he **got** concerned. Should I worry?*>

<*Stars, no. It was just an innocent question.*>

<*Of course,*> Rachel's voice dripped with sarcasm. <*Because I*

believe that. Maybe you should take more Marines with you.>

<Lieutenant Brennen has a squad of his best—it's all that really fits in the ship. Plus there's another platoon at Aldebaran with Amavia and Iris. We'll be fine.>

<I'll keep the engines hot just the same.>

<Thanks, Rachel. I'll be back before you know it.>

<Holding you to that, Admiral.>

Tangel saw a squad of ISF Marines standing at the base of the ramp, and spotted Lieutenant Brennen in their midst. None of them had made a move to go up the ramp, and she wondered if there was something wrong.

"Good afternoon, Lieutenant Brennen," Tangel said as she approached. "Is my ship not to taste?"

"Admiral!" Brennen snapped off a sharp salute as the rest of the Marines followed likewise. "We uhh…well, ma'am, the ship has no name."

Tangel snapped her fingers. "And once you board, you have to enter it in your platoon's logs, but with no name, you'd have to make one up. But if you did, you'd be naming it, and then it would be stuck."

"Right." Brennen ducked his head. "Normally we'd just use a serial number or class name for the logs, but this bird here has neither. So…we figured we'd just wait for you."

Tangel placed a finger on her chin, looking up at the ship. "Well, I suppose we could name it after the woman who gifted it to me, Amanda."

"Begging your pardon, ma'am, but there are already three pinnaces, a destroyer, and two cruisers named 'Amanda' in the allied forces."

"Easy fix," Tangel snapped her fingers. "The *Mandy*. Come aboard one and all, we have a jump gate to Aldebaran to catch."

She walked up the ramp with Brennen in tow and palmed the airlock open.

"That interface is bizarre," he commented. "Where did you get this ship, Admiral?"

"An ally," she replied, as they entered the main cabin within the ship, which more resembled an upscale bar. She turned to the Marines. "Make yourselves at home, but don't rip the upholstery. This stuff is the epitome of irreplaceable."

As the twelve men and women got settled on the couches and chairs—their bulky armor somehow not stressing the furniture at all—she walked down the short corridor to the cockpit, Brennen following after.

"You rated at all?" Tangel asked, knowing she could look it up, but feeling like engaging in small talk with the man.

"Sure am. I have a few thousand hours under my belt, but not with anything like this—just military craft, and a few planet hoppers back on Carthage."

"Well, I've never flown this either, but the engineers set it up with all our standard flight systems, so it should be a breeze."

It turned out that there were a few differences in managing the *Mandy*, but once Tangel got a feel for the craft's feedback, she had it out of the bay and heading for their assigned gate. As they were on their final approach, Rachel's voice called out into her mind.

<*Admiral! There's been some sort of attack on Aleutian Station. I don't have many details, but your daughters are all out there right now, and the reports say that they're missing.*>

Tangel didn't miss a beat. <*Rachel, get this gate realigned and powered for a jump to the LMC!*>

<*Yes, ma'am, gate is already realigning. You're good to jump in three, two, one.*>

Tangel deployed the *Mandy*'s forward gate mirror and boosted toward the ring, not slowing to even consider the risks as her new ship's maiden voyage was a jump to another galaxy.

M. D. COOPER

A SURPRISE VISITOR
STELLAR DATE: 10.03.8949 (Adjusted Years)
LOCATION: Aleutia Station
REGION: Cheshire System, Large Magellanic Cloud

The sisters and Kent had spoken long into the night, discussing everything from the colonel's homeworld and what types of crops they raised, to military engagements he'd fought in, to what he knew of major bases across Orion space.

Saanvi had returned after a few hours, minus Amy, who had gone to sleep in quarters nearby. She joined in the discussion with great enthusiasm, pressing Kent for what he knew of various advancements and the technology levels he had been exposed to.

When they finally called it quits for the night, Cary felt like her head was filled to bursting with information about the Orion Freedom Alliance.

Much of it corroborated what Jessica knew, but there were many details that were different. She had learned that this was because the regions of the OFA near New Sol operated very differently than the Perseus Arm and the Perseus Expansion Districts.

Moreover, much of what Jessica had learned was from pilfered databases at Costa Station. Kent's knowledge was firsthand and highlighted the differences between the official records and the reality of life in the trenches.

"We'll catch a quick breakfast and head back in the morning," Cary said, stifling a yawn as she spoke. "We'll want to be rested for the debriefing we're all going to get."

"I want you present," Kent said, his tone carrying a hard edge. "I know how these things go. You warm me up, and then the wolves set in. I get the feeling that everyone will be much better behaved with the vaunted Admiral Richards' daughter in the room."

Cary nodded wearily. "You know that neither of us will have full control over what will happen, but I will do my damnedest to see that you're treated well. I *do* have some pull with the brass."

"I can see that," Kent replied with a chuckle.

* * * * *

The next morning, after a breakfast in the observation lounge—where most of the conversation centered around what a future of extragalactic exploration could hold—the group retraced their path back to the docking bay.

Colonel Ophelia escorted them, but said little following an apology for her behavior the prior day.

Ten minutes later, they were walking down the final corridor toward the docking bay, their time in the LMC nearly over. Cary made herself a solemn promise to return, perhaps with Saanvi, who was already scheming about how to get transferred to the Bolt Hole project.

Amy seemed to have recovered from her outburst the night before. She'd apologized to Cary and Faleena first thing in the morning, and now walked next to Saanvi, swinging her arms freely, chattering about how she was going to savor her last look at the Milky Way before they jumped back.

Her good mood was infectious, and elicited smiles from the entire group, even Ophelia and the Marines—though they did their best to maintain serious glowers.

The station was busy at the beginning of the first shift, personnel rushing in every direction, headed to wherever their assignments demanded.

A group of warrant officers, drive technician patches on their shoulders, swung out of a room a dozen meters ahead, a few glancing over their shoulders at the platoon of Marines behind them, obviously escorting VIPs.

One of the men in the group stared a moment longer than necessary, his eyes locking with Cary's before he turned to face forward once more.

Cary accessed his information, and saw that he was Chief Warrant Officer Travers, a member of the first group to have transferred out to the LMC. His record was solidly average, neither impressive, nor lacking. It surprised her that someone who did not stand out had been selected for such an important mission.

I suppose it could be that someone was trying to tuck him out of the way, she mused. *Theoretically, nothing was really supposed to happen out here—beyond terraforming a new world or two.*

She was about to turn her attention elsewhere, when Travers moved from the center to the edge of his group. The action itself wasn't that strange, but Cary thought she saw something slide free of his body.

Not his physical body. His extradimensional body.

An instant later, she reached out to Saanvi and Faleena, becoming Trine, and stared into the man in question.

What ***is*** *he?* she wondered.

With her extradimensional sight, Trine could see that CW5 Travers was far more than he appeared to the two-dimensional eye.

Tendrils of transdimensional energy flowed through him, but they did not look like a remnant—those malevolent gifts left behind by ascended beings behaved as separate entities, something that was readily apparent to Trine when she spotted them. Nor did Travers appear to be an ascended being—at least not one like Tangel. Where Trine's mother blazed with energy that was barely contained within her form, Travers' extradimensional form appeared wan, barely filling half the volume of his physical body.

He is something between, Trine surmised. *Not quite ascended, but the being is him, not a passenger like a remnant—of that I am certain.*

<Colonel Ophelia.> Trine reached out to the station commander privately, mimicking Cary's voice. <Do you have shadowtrons?>

<The anti-ascended weapon?> Ophelia asked, her mental tone sounding startled, then worried. <One. In the CIC's weapons locker.>

<Have a squad bring it down here. We may need backup.>

<Backup for what?> the station commander asked, her worry not translating to her steady gait, as she strode down the corridor with the group.

<Chief Travers, in that group ahead. He is not what he seems.>

* * * * *

The moment he swung into the passage, something felt wrong. It wasn't an ephemeral tickle in the back of his mind, but an actual tangible feeling.

There was another being like himself nearby.

Several of his companions turned to look behind them, and he followed suit, catching sight of a platoon of Marines escorting—

Shit!

Walking in the center of the Marines' protective phalanx was none other than Cary Richards. His sources had suggested that Cary was something beyond a regular human, and one glance confirmed it.

She was moving down the road to ascension. Nearly as far as he was.

The thought that a *child* such as Tanis's daughter could be nearly as progressed as him was infuriating—though it was only because of the Caretaker's betrayal that such was the case.

The cursed ascended AI had no sense of loyalty, of holding up its end of the bargain.

Still, killing Tanis's daughter was a temptation too great to pass up. There was no way the child could best him—provided he could get her alone. Even he would have trouble defeating her with a platoon of Marines at her back.

He could only stop so much firepower before it overwhelmed him—and Marines liked to dispense as much energy as possible at a target such as himself.

Time for a wild goose chase, he thought before ducking down a side passage, signaling two members of his group to follow.

* * * * *

Shit! He's on the move!

Trine sent a message to Ophelia, telling her to watch over Amy as she took off—all three bodies moving as one—in pursuit of Chief Travers.

"Wait!" Lieutenant Mason called out, as Trine pushed past the Marines in pursuit of the partially ascended man and his two companions.

<There's a wolf in the henhouse,> Trine shot back, using the code for a remnant in a human. <Not just any wolf. A direwolf.>

She heard Mason direct a fireteam to stay with Ophelia and Amy before the steady thud of Marines in powered armor picked up behind her.

Faleena's lithe, dryad-like form moved into the lead while Cary and Saanvi's bodies fell behind, keeping pace, but relying on Faleena's enhanced sensory systems to watch for threats.

In addition to corporeal dangers, Trine watched for ephemeral threats, pockets of energy that an ascended being could summon and move through other dimensions to attack through bulkheads or other solid objects.

At least, she assumed they could do so—Trine-Cary had been experimenting with such things, much to her sisters' surprise.

Focus. We have to remain unified. This person is stronger than a remnant.

They turned onto a wider concourse and caught sight of their prey with biological eyes: three ISF chiefs rushing through the crowd, shoving passersby out of the way.

One of Trine's prey spun and fired a projectile pistol toward her, but even before Trine-Cary could raise a hand—she had also been practicing creating grav fields—a rifle's report sounded from behind them, and the shooter before her collapsed.

<*We got your back,*> Mason called out. <*Keep moving.*>

Trine sent an acknowledgement, picking up the pace as a general quarters alert sounded on the Link and 1MC.

"General Quarters, General Quarters, this is not a drill. Clockwise up and forward, counter down and aft. Sweepers grab your brooms, the station is dirty. Repeat the station is dirty."

Trine had never heard the sweepers suffix, but assumed it must be a call to arms for station clearing teams. Or someone was just getting creative out in the LMC.

Ahead, Travers and his remaining accomplice turned right, rushing down another passageway with Trine-Faleena hot on their heels.

As soon as she turned the corner, the CW2 stepped out from behind a bulkhead rib and swung a baton at her. Trine-Faleena easily ducked it and thrust the heel of her hand into the woman's chin, shattering it before driving a fist into her gut.

Trine's other two bodies reached the side passage, not slowing as Trine-Faleena checked the woman to ensure she would not choke on her tongue.

The moment Faleena turned to follow the others, the doors

behind her sealed, cutting off the Marines.

<*Mason, we're proceeding, find an alternate route,*> Trine informed the Marine lieutenant.

<*Negative…Cary? You three need to stop. Whoever that is isn't getting anywhere, the station is locked down.*>

<*Lockdown won't stop him,*> Trine-Cary replied. <*Only we can. Follow as best you can.*>

<*Ensign!*> Lieutenant Mason shouted over the Link. <*You will stand down!*>

Trine ignored the Marine as her cyborg body caught up to her biological ones, continuing to pursue their quarry down a hatch into the power generation section of the station.

She passed a pair of Marines that had been stationed outside a door, unconscious but alive. Ahead, Trine-Cary caught another glimpse of their prey's extra-dimensional form and she navigated the annoying warren of three-dimensional passages, slowly closing the gap.

As they passed through more doors and hatches, each one closed behind them, until Trine became aware that there were over a dozen sealed doors between them and Mason's Marines.

The station layout showed that Trine was approaching the main reactor and antimatter annihilator. A pair of technicians raced past them, headed in the opposite direction, screaming 'he's lost his mind'.

Trine-Faleena was first through the final door, and reached the catwalk stretching over the annihilator at the heart of the station moments before her other two bodies.

He is mad, she thought as her three sets of eyes took in the scene.

The annihilator chamber was a wide oval with power generation systems on either side and a matter annihilator in the center. They stood at the end of a catwalk that arched over the center of the chamber.

Directly in its center stood Chief Travers, a small, silver cylinder in his hand.

"Cary Richards," he called out. "I didn't expect to have you be the one to find me. I'd been waiting for your mother, but she never came out to Aleutia."

"You're lucky," Trine shouted back, three mouths giving voice to the words in perfect unison. "If she were here, you'd already be ground to atoms."

"Well, that's interesting…you're not…. What are you?" Travers' brow furrowed as he spoke.

"We are Trine," she replied. "Put the cylinder down and surrender. You can't defeat us."

Travers tossed the cylinder lightly in his hand. "This? Why, it's just a bit of antimatter. I imagine it won't do much at all if I let it fall into the annihilator. Nothing, if you consider a planet-sized ball of plasma to be of no consequence."

"What are you?" Trine asked, changing the topic of conversation. "You're not like the remnants."

"Remnants?" Travers asked. "Oh! You mean the things we leave behind in others? I assume you've found most of mine. I haven't received many messages of late."

"Our shadowtrons see to that," Trine replied, a smile quirking at the corners of her three mouths as Travers' brow furrowed. "A weapon that can trap and kill remnants. You too, I imagine."

"I'm much more than a remnant," Travers replied. "And I've worked far too long at my goals to have an upstart like you get in the way. You'll make a fantastic message to send to your mother. Maybe I'll crush your minds first. That would be fun."

Trine saw a tendril of light drift out of Travers and stretch across the space between them. She widened her stance and generated a wide n-space stabilization field, the way she'd been practicing. The field wavered before her, but then stabilized a moment before Travers' extradimensional limb reached Trine. It probed against her field, but with a little effort, she was able to push it aside.

"Impressive, little one, but you're not thinking wide enough."

Trine felt her mind narrow sharply and turned to see Saanvi cry out and fall to the deck.

Nano! Trine-Faleena cried out, rushing to Saanvi's side. *He's…I don't know what he's done.*

A second later, Faleena collapsed as well, and Trine was just Cary. She deployed her own nanocloud and swept it across the catwalk, realizing that Travers had planted breaching nanobots below the deck. They'd moved up right through the plas and into Saanvi and Faleena's bodies.

Travers was laughing softly, walking down the catwalk with slow, cocksure steps.

"Looks like your little trick doesn't hold up very well, Cary Richards. Now let's see what you can do without your gestalt."

Gestalt? Cary had never thought of her connection to her sisters like that. *The whole is greater than the sum of the parts.*

As she turned that thought over in her mind, she sent a surge of extra-dimensional energy through her sisters, targeting their internal nano-defenses and shielding them against attack from Travers' breachers.

"Well done, little Cary," Travers said, now only ten meters away. "Can you concentrate on saving your sisters and fight me off at the same time?"

Another tendril of visible light left him. In her transdimensional view, Cary could see that it was more than just light; the limb contained energy spikes that would inflict both pain and damage.

She summoned her n-space field once more, this time erecting it as a shield around her and her sisters. Once the sphere snapped into place, it cut off Travers' control of his own breach nano, and Saanvi and Faleena's internal systems began to clear their bodies of the intruders.

"It won't be that easy," Travers said with a wicked grin. "I hit Saanvi's brainstem and Faleena's core-interface hard and fast. If they survive—which is unlikely—both will need some time in the autodoc."

"Fuck you," Cary hissed, turning away from her sisters, though still keeping part of her mind on the nano-battle raging within their bodies. "They'll survive."

"Oh?" Travers asked a mock frown on his face. "Oh! You mean now that you've fought my nano off. Yes, huzzah, you defeated my little distraction." His mocking tone took on a sinister bent. "I meant that after I kill you, they'll not survive."

Travers had six of his limbs stretched out, pressing into Cary's protective field, driving it back with unrelenting force. The attack sapped her energy, and Cary dropped to her knees as Travers continued to take languid steps toward her.

"Silly girl. I've been playing this game for centuries." He was only a meter away now, crouching on the far side of her shield. "Do you hear me, scion of a fool? *Centuries.*"

Cary clenched her teeth, drawing the energy out of her internal SC batteries to maintain the shield while looking up to meet Travers' eyes.

"Who *are* you?" she whispered. "You're not an ascended AI..."

"Really?" Travers laughed, the sound almost maniacal. "I know you're just a kid, but you have good genes, so you can't be that stupid. Stars, if Jessica were here, *she'd* know who I was. I still want to visit her someday, let her know that Trist's death was an utter waste."

Understanding slashed across Cary's mind like the crack of a whip.

"No..." she whispered. "You died...Trist killed you..."

Travers sat back on his heels, mouth half-open in a macabre grin. "Come now. You know of my remnants, you must understand that I never tip my hand; I worked from the shadows through agents. If you weren't so evolved, you wouldn't even know for sure that this is me—but you *do* know, so you must die."

Cary knew he was right—if she didn't do something, he *would* kill her. And then he would snuff the life from her sisters as well.

Her eyes fell to the deck, and she drew in a ragged breath, willing her shield to become stronger—but the attempt was futile. Her internal SC batteries were almost drained.

The deckplate swam before her vision, its solid form dissolving into chaotic particles.

Am I hallucinating….? What is this? she thought in a daze, before the particles moved into forms she understood, molecules of carbon and steel interlocking before her vision.

She took a moment to wonder if that was what her mother could see when she plucked apart solid objects, and then drove a tendril of her extradimensional self into the deckplate, severing the molecular bonds and drawing both the matter and energy into herself.

Lucidity flooded back into her mind, and her head snapped up, focus clear as she strengthened her n-space stabilization shield and rose to her feet. She caught flashes of Travers' thoughts as she pressed the brane close around him, nearly falling to her knees as the revelation unfolded.

"What the—" he exclaimed, scrambling backward before he too rose. "Nice trick, little girl, but—"

"No buts, *Myrrdan*," Cary hissed as she pulled her shield from its sphere shape to form a wall between her and her foe. "You're going to die for all the suffering you've caused. I'm going to make you pay for all the lives—"

"Oh please," Myrrdan scoffed. "You don't even know the

half of it. I've killed more people than you can imagine. And I've stood up to the Caretaker's minions, too. The likes of you is not going to defeat me so easily."

Cary didn't reply, drawing more energy from the molecules of the catwalk to power her shield.

For a moment, they stared at one another, Cary feeling stronger by the second, and Myrrdan looking concerned as the shield between them strengthened.

Concentrating on her extradimensional form, Cary reached out and grabbed the corners of the shield that separated them, feeling the quantum fabric of the field pulse beneath her 'hands' as she folded it around Myrrdan in a single deft move, forming a large M5 black brane.

For a moment, the man appeared surprised, and Cary breathed a sigh of relief. "You know, Myrrdan. *I've* defeated the Caretaker's minions too."

"Oh?" Myrrdan cocked an eyebrow. "I'll admit that I'm impressed. But you know they are just shadows…. What did you call them? Remnants. Yes, that's accurate. They need a host to survive in this spacetime, they don't possess enough energy to travel without one."

He paused, his eyes locked on Cary's.

"Not like me."

One moment, he was within Cary's black brane, and the next, he was before her.

But it wasn't 'him', not his corporeal form, at least. That body collapsed to the deck a moment before the lack of internal pressure from Myrrdan's defenses caused the graviton sphere to snap inward, crushing the man's form within.

A tendril of light from the being in front of her rose up and wrapped around her throat, while the being spoke into her mind.

-I don't like to move about without a body. I find it…uncomfortable. Perhaps I'll take yours, once I purge you from

within it.-

Cary fought down the panic she felt as more tendrils of Myrrdan's form wrapped around her body, sliding inside her corporeal body, touching her fledgling extradimensional limbs.

Her thoughts raced, frantically trying to come up with a means to defeat him, all the while still drawing more energy from the deckplate around her.

She tried to form a black brane around Myrrdan, to trap him the way she had done to so many remnants, but he batted the form aside, wrapping her own constructs in antiparticles.

-You'll have to try harder than that.-

Cary flailed wildly, desperate to free herself, when her eye caught sight of something in the compressed remains of Travers' corporeal body.

It was the cylinder he had been holding—a small cylinder of antimatter.

Cary snaked a limb around Myrrdan's extradimensional body and grasped the capsule, drawing out a microgram of antimatter. She pulled it toward herself and then created a new black brane, bleeding sleptons off the antimatter to strengthen the field around it.

It took only a second to create the new brane, and she feared Myrrdan would stop her, but he didn't. Cary realized it was because he was sifting through her mind, delving into her memories.

"Stop!" she shouted, directing a burst of sleptons into Myrrdan and driving his ephemeral form back into the black brane she had created.

Surprise registered on his form, and he shrieked wordlessly as the brane closed around him. Myrrdan raged against the walls, but Cary drew out more antimatter atoms, fueling her creation, keeping the being within secure.

Suddenly aware that she was on her knees again, she

struggled to her feet, only to feel the catwalk shift beneath her. Looking down, Cary saw that she'd drawn so much energy from disassembling the molecules of the catwalk that it was paper thin in places.

-*Such a fool,*- Myrrdan chittered as the catwalk split open under Cary's feet, and she began to fall toward the matter annihilator forty meters below.

Cary tried to summon a graviton field, but the moment she did, she felt her control of the brane around Myrrdan waver.

Then we die together, she thought grimly, wrapping a limb around the brane and pulling it through the hole with her.

Below, the housing of the annihilator raced toward Cary, and she knew that while she would likely die from the impact, nothing would happen to Myrrdan—other than that he would gain his freedom once more.

"Not this time," she whispered.

She focused on the housing around the annihilator, the sphere that smashed atoms into one another, extracting every joule of energy from the utter destruction of matter.

She held the last antimatter atom she had drawn from the cylinder and slammed it into the surface of the black brane, phase shifting the field so it would pass through solid objects before pushing it down toward the annihilator.

During those two excruciatingly long seconds, Cary had heard a strange sound above her, but kept her focus on the black brane containing Myrrdan, as it fell through the housing and into the region of utter destruction within.

Time continued to pass with mind-numbing slowness. With her other sight, Cary could see the raging inferno of energy—energy that spanned many dimensions of spacetime—tear into Myrrdan, shredding his 'body' layer by layer, exposing every part of him to quantum energies that obliterated his being, burning him away to nothing.

I can't believe that worked…he's finally dead!

Myrrdan's destruction didn't change her state, however. She gave one final attempt at generating a graviton field to slow her fall, but there was nothing to draw energy from. Idly, Cary calculated her trajectory, noting how she would hit the annihilator's sphere, bounce off, and fall sixty meters onto a heat exchanger that bled excess energy off to thermal convertors.

Death by vaporization…at least it will be fast.

The surface of the annihilator was seven meters away when something hit her, shoving her aside. A pressure wrapped around her torso, and her downward motion stopped.

All the energy seemed to flee from Cary's body as she craned her neck to look up into the grim face of Lieutenant Mason, rising back up to the catwalk with his armor's a-grav pack.

"Stars, girl," he muttered. "Your father is going to skin me alive."

AWAKEN

STELLAR DATE: 10.03.8949 (Adjusted Years)
LOCATION: Aleutia Station
REGION: Cheshire System, Large Magellanic Cloud

Darkness instantly became light and then swam into wavering shapes around Cary. Solid forms moved nearby, and thin partitions were beyond them, only partially obscuring more forms that moved in the distance.

She tried to make sense of what she was seeing, but there was no rationality to anything. Objects moved through one another, taking paths that seemed entirely impossible.

Then one of the blobs spoke.

"Cary? Are you awake? Your vitals show consciousness."

The words filtered into her mind slowly, as though they were spoken over the course of hours.

Bit by bit, Cary put together her recent memories, remembering the fight with Travers—who turned out to be Myrrdan—and then her impending death, which was averted by Lieutenant Mason.

"Sisters?" Cary asked. "Saanvi, Faleena."

"They'll be OK," a different voice said. "You kept them safe, my little angel."

"Dad?" Cary asked, wondering which of the blobs had spoken.

"You may want to open your eyes, daughter mine," he said, a small chuckle following his words. "You keep waving your arms around like you're blind."

"Eyes…right…" Cary whispered as she tried to remember how to open her eyelids. After a curl of her lip and a few twitches of her nose, she remembered how, and the blobs of light disappeared, replaced with a hospital recovery room.

"Cary!" A voice called out from the doorway, and she barely registered her mother dropping a cup of coffee—which Joe deftly caught—and all but leaping across the room and wrapping her in a fierce embrace. "Stars…what were you thinking?"

"Like mother, like daughter," Joe said, leaning over the two women and embracing them both.

"Moms…can't…breathe," Cary gasped.

"Sorry," Tangel replied, laying her head on Cary's chest. "You look OK, all your parts are still there—oh!"

Cary registered a look of surprise on her mother's face, as she straightened and glanced at Joe before looking back down at her.

"You've grown."

Joe cast Tangel a curious look. "Grown?"

"I've got more ascended parts now," Cary said as she struggled to sit up, flashing a grin at her father.

"Stars," he said, shaking his head and bumping his hip against Tangel's. "You're the spitting image of this crazy woman when you do that."

"What happened in there?" Tangel asked as she sat on the edge of the bed. "The optics in the annihilator chamber were fried the moment Travers entered."

"And stuff was *shredded*," Joe added.

"You'll never believe it," Cary said. "But before that, Saanvi and Faleena…are they really OK?"

Her father placed a hand on her forehead and nodded. "Saanvi has some neural damage to her brainstem, and Faleena took a hit to her core interface, but her internal defenses held it off. Her core was severed, but she's up and about again."

"How long 'til Saanvi's conscious?"

"I'm conscious now," Saanvi's voice came from behind her parents. "Not walking, but thinking, at least."

Joe turned aside, and Cary caught a glimpse of Saanvi on a medchair, with Faleena behind her.

"Saving the day, again, Cary," her AI sister said. "Thank you."

"You'll all be thanking me even more when you learn who that was." Cary grinned at each member of her family in turn.

"So it wasn't Chief Travers?" Joe asked.

"Uh…" Cary felt a moment of nausea at the memory of what had happened to the body Myrrdan had inhabited. "Well, yeah. But that was just the meat-suit."

"For fucksakes," Saanvi rasped, swinging her chair around the other side of the bed. "Spill it already."

"Wow…" Faleena whistled. "You made Sahn swear. Better get on with it."

"OK. It was Myrrdan."

Cary's lips split into a broad smile at the four gaping mouths arrayed around her.

* * * * *

Tangel stood in stunned silence, as Cary explained her encounter with the being in the station's annihilator chamber. At first she couldn't believe it was Myrrdan, but as her daughter completed her tale, describing how she saw into her attacker's mind, she realized there was no denying it.

"Motherfucker," she whispered. "That bastard has still been with us all this time…some mysterious occurrences over the past few decades are making more sense now."

"Like what?" Saanvi asked. "Do you think he told Orion where New Canaan was?"

"No," Tangel shook her head. "We're reasonably certain they just scouted the area 'til they found it—or got it from a spy in the TSF. I was thinking more about some attempts to steal the picotech after we arrived at New Canaan."

"Guy sure played the long game," Joe muttered, and Tangel noticed that he was clenching his right hand over and over again.

She placed a hand on his and gave a gentle squeeze. "I imagine that the Caretaker sending Nance in to take him out put a wrinkle in Myrrdan's plans—though I wonder if he knew what he was getting into when he took a flight out here to Aleutia."

"I hate to think of all the people's lives he ruined," Saanvi said quietly. "But I'm also perversely pleased that his centuries of planning got him exactly jack squat."

"Did he have other remnants here?" Cary asked suddenly. "What happened to them when he died?"

"Colonel Ophelia is doing a full sweep—your dad brought more shadowtrons from back home. So far, they've found two…no, three. It seems that they aren't affected by their progenitor's death, either. Just keep on ticking…like little parasitic mini-Myrrdans."

"That sucks," Cary muttered. "I'd hoped that killing him would free everyone under his control."

Tangel patted her daughter's leg. "It would be nice."

"Mom…weren't you on your way to Aldebaran to deal with the mess there?" Faleena asked. "I was under the impression that Amavia was all but besieged by politicians and the like."

Tangel nodded slowly. "Yes, as soon as things are secure here, I'll jump to Amavia's rescue. I'm just a big intergalactic firefighter."

"Not this time, you weren't." Cary gave a saucy wink. "I had things all wrapped up by the time you arrived. Nothing but cleanup left. Oh! But I got all sorts of intel from Kent."

"I already filed it all," Faleena said with a wink. "Even semi-ascended, you still sleep, and I had nothing to do last night."

"You stole my thunder?" Cary gave her sister a mock glare.

Tangel laughed and shared a look with Joe. "You killed Myrrdan, Cary. Pretty sure you have enough thunder to go around."

"Speaking of thunder." Joe placed a hand on Tangel's shoulder. "Amavia has been trying to reach you over the QC network, and now she's started pinging me. Their assembly thought you were on your way and has an emergency session scheduled to hear you."

"I know…" Tangel's voice was filled with reluctance as she rose. "I just feel like I'm bailing on my girls."

"We're fine, Moms," Cary replied as Saanvi and Faleena nodded. "Go put out some more fires."

"OK, but I'll be back to check on you once I've straightened out the League of Sentients."

"We'll be back on the Palisades by then," Joe said as he leant in for a kiss. "As incredible as the view is out here, I feel a lot better with The Cradle in my night skies."

Tangel pulled Joe close. "You're just a control freak and you want to make sure everything is just so."

Joe laughed and squeezed Tangel tightly. "I got it from you. I *used* to be all carefree, but now I need to compensate."

The two separated, and Tangel ignored her daughters' grins as she gave Joe a final kiss. "That's why I can trust you to keep everything in line while I'm gone."

She gave each of her daughters an embrace before giving them one final wave and leaving the room. <*No more chasing strange ascended beings!*> she sent in parting as she strode through Aleutia Station's hospital wing.

<*No promises, Moms,*> Cary sent back, and Tangel resisted the urge to groan audibly.

<*What she said,*> Faleena added, while Saanvi only laughed.

This is my punishment. Kids that are too much like me.

M. D. COOPER

A VISIT FROM ROXY

STELLAR DATE: 10.03.8949 (Adjusted Years)
LOCATION: River Station, Styx Baby-9
REGION: STX-B17 Black Hole, Transcend Interstellar Alliance

"I never got to ask," Seraphina said as she walked with Sera to the docking bay where their unexpected visitor would shortly arrive. "How did it feel to have the cabinet ratify father in a matter of hours?"

Sera snorted, giving her sister a measuring glance. "You know…it should have bothered me, and I suppose it did a bit. But mostly I was relieved. I don't mind being the Hand's director—it's more my speed. Being president? That just never felt right."

"I know what you mean." Seraphina gave a rueful laugh. "Being president never sat right with me either—and I'm the reserved one."

Sera glanced at Seraphina's square-toed boots, leather pants, grey silk shirt, and long black leather coat. "We don't really do reserved well, do we?"

"Not so much, no. Fina least of all."

Seraphina barked a laugh. "Girl's getting her inner mod freak on. I wonder what we'd be like if mom didn't go tweaking in our heads. Would I be a fetish freak like you two are?"

Sera shrugged. "She tweaked all of us. She had a shard of herself in our heads for most of our lives. Maybe Fina's and my proclivities are a *result* of that."

Seraphina knocked her shoulder against Sera's. "Or maybe you're closest to spec, and I'm the weird one."

" 'To spec', eh?"

"Well, we are geneered. Made-to-order daughters; just add

unloving psychomom."

"Always happy to disappoint her," Sera replied, then decided to change the subject. "So you don't think Justin was working with Airtha at all?"

"If he was, she never told us. Bastard was a thorn in our side—messing up more than one of our operations."

"Ours too," Sera said. "Turns out a lot of agents were more loyal to him than the Transcend."

Seraphina nodded. "Between you and him, we barely held onto a tenth of the directorate. We got the short end of the stick there—though your deputies running things at Khardine still managed to keep Fina and I answering questions for days."

"Sorry about that," Sera gave her sister an apologetic glance. "*I* knew that the ISF's deprogramming would work on you—they've gotten pretty good at it over the years—but our folks needed to see it for themselves. You know how it is."

Seraphina rubbed her ass. "Yeah, but I could have done without the probe."

A laugh burst free from Sera's lips as she gave her sister an appreciative glance. "Off-color humor? Who are you, and what have you done with Seraphina?"

"Hey, I'm just as dirty-minded as you and Fina, I just figure that someone has to be a bit closer to an even keel—what with you two freaks in the mix."

Sera placed a hand on her sister's shoulder and slowed to a stop, fixing her with a level gaze. "Seraphina, seriously. Be your own person. You don't have to compensate for our behavior. There's no cosmic scale weighing the three of us, looking for balance."

Seraphina pursed her lips, then ran her hands over her face. "Dammit, Sera. I don't know *who* I am. Fina seemed to slip into her 'freaky girl' persona the moment the ISF removed mother's aegis from her. She seems to know exactly who and what she is. Me…I have no clue. I'm trying to be like I was—like we were—before that day we pulled Tanis from that shipping crate. But I don't know if I remember it right…so I'm just faking it as best I can."

"You know what they say, 'fake it 'til you make it'. Seriously, though, Seraphina. You know Fina is just rebelling. She was pushing so hard against mother's control that when the chains were removed, she careened headlong into what she's become. And there's *nothing* wrong with that. The only way you can find balance is by swinging side to side on the ole pendulum a bit; at least that's what Tangel says."

"I think our pendulums are in the middle of a hurricane," Seraphina said with a soft laugh.

"Sounds about right," Sera replied as the two women resumed their walk. "Shit, I tried to get this conversation off us, and to whatever this ship's arrival means, and it got back onto us again."

"We're a right bunch of screwed up narcissists," Seraphina said with a self-deprecating laugh. "Nice one, losing a stasis ship to Justin, by the way."

"Better him than mom," Sera replied. "She would have held onto it—Justin lost his in a matter of days, it seems. Though I have no idea who this Roxy person is, do you?"

"Not a clue. She's not in any of the Hand databases I had access to. I have no idea how she found us, either, which is honestly the most concerning part—your secret base isn't so secret."

Sera twisted her lips, wondering whether or not they were walking into a trap.

Silly, of course it's a trap. The question is just who is the one springing it?

Sera and Seraphina turned down the long gantry that lead to the spur where the *Damon Silas* was slated to dock in a few moments.

Standing in their way was Flaherty, flanked by two members of their former High Guard.

"Seriously?" he grunted out the word. "You know this is a trap, right? Jen, why did you let them both come?"

<They have enough mommy issues without me mothering them. I figured you'd be here—you're always skulking about somewhere nearby.>

"I don't skulk." Flaherty glared at Sera's forehead, as though he was staring into Jen's synapses. "I lurk."

"Either way, Flaherty," Sera shrugged, wishing he'd stop boring a hole through her head with his eyes. "Don't you have all the angles covered?"

His scowl deepened. "No one ever has all the angles covered. But one of the easiest to cover is not having both of you together."

Seraphina shrugged and glanced at Sera. "We're clones, we have backups."

"Are you really suggesting that we should leave the mission to defeat Airtha in Fina's hands?" Flaherty asked with a raised brow.

Seraphina snorted and shook her head. "Now that you put it that way…"

"Rock paper scissors?" Sera asked.

"No, I'll let you handle it. Our chat has me feeling more out of sorts than I'd expected, anyway."

Sera gave her sister an appraising look, then nodded. "OK. I'll give you the scoop."

"You'd better," Seraphina said, turning on her heel and striding back the way she'd come.

<She needs to mask all that squeaking leather,> Jen commented. <Probably take an NSAI to manage the nano cloud it would take to pull that off.>

Sera laughed softly. <You have no idea.>

Five minutes later, they were at the end of the spire,

watching as the *Damon Silas* eased into position.

<Sorry I can't be down there,> Krissy sent to Sera. <I've got a situation brewing out on the antispinward front. I may have to take a battlegroup out there to shore things up.>

<Don't worry about me,> Sera replied. <Do what you need to do. Hopefully the hoplites will make enough of a mess soon that the front will get a reprieve.>

<Can't come soon enough. Scan shows all of the Silas's weapons with zero EM, by the way. Ship is as safe as it can be. Still, Earnest and Finaeus are up here ready to drop a stasis shield around it if they have to.>

<Good to know,> Sera sent back as the station's grapple reached out and took hold of the destroyer. <Any word from this Roxy person…or Carmen?>

<Nothing beyond their original request to speak to you. Honestly, either they're going to try to kill you, or Carmen is going to try for a personal appeal to get out of a dereliction trial.>

<Well, if their stasis tech is intact, that'll be a good start. I bet she'll try to spin it as having been her plan all along—something her record doesn't really point to.>

Sera wondered about that. It would be hard to discount such an argument, given the results. However, much of that would depend on this Roxy person.

She glanced around the corridor they stood in at the tip of the docking spire. No one was in evidence except for Flaherty and the two High Guard, all of whom were in light armor. Sera had shifted her skin to take on the appearance of red-tinted light armor to show that she wasn't being completely blasé, but still presenting a soft target.

What an attacker wouldn't know was that there was an entire squad of stealthed TSF special forces troops in the spire, ready to act with deadly force.

As she mused over what the next few minutes would bring, the umbilical extended and connected to the *Damon*

Silas. An indicator showed positive seal, and then the ship's outer airlock cycled open.

Feeds from within the umbilical showed an azure-skinned woman drift into the connecting tube. EM monitoring showed only one Link present, but Sera wondered how likely it was that Carmen had remained behind on the ship.

Had Sera been in Roxy's shoes—if Roxy even wore shoes— she wouldn't have come into the lion's den without her strongest advocate at her side.

Then the station-side lock was cycling open, and Roxy stepped through.

"President Sera, thank you for seeing us in person," the azure woman said the moment she stepped through.

"Us?" Sera asked.

"Yes." Roxy touched her abdomen. "Carmen is within me. It was a part of how we took the ship from Justin—and beat him in the end."

"Beat him?" Sera asked. "Did he escape?"

A feral smile crept across Roxy's lips. "Oh, he most certainly did not. My brother breathed his last—or rather, tried to—a few days ago. He's dead."

A dozen conflicting feelings cascaded through Sera. Justin had been her mentor at one point, and she still felt guilty that he'd taken the fall for Andrea's attempt to kill Tanis. But then one of the words Roxy had spoken leapt to the fore.

"Brother?"

Roxy nodded. "Justin and I had a…complicated relationship."

<*You can say that again,*> another voice joined the conversation. It's Link route showed it to be coming from Roxy, but Sera could tell it was someone else.

"Carmen?" she asked.

<*Stars, she's riding through Roxy's Link. Unbuffered, too, if I don't miss my guess,*> Jen added privately. <*Even if you organics*

don't rake her across the coals for dereliction, she's going to be in hot water with the local AI council.>

<*Desperate times,*> Sera said to Jen as Carmen replied.

<*Yes. Before you start, President Sera. I know I screwed up. A lot. I submit myself for judgement.*>

"No need to jump quite that far ahead yet," Sera replied. "I'm also no longer the president of the Transcend. My father has resumed that role."

"Your father?" Roxy's face took on a look of utter confusion. "I thought he had…"

"Died?" Sera asked. "He did. But it looks like I'm not the only one Airtha was cloning."

Roxy put a hand to her forehead, and then took a step forward. "I suppose this is a waste, then."

"Stop!" Flaherty called out and raised his rifle.

"Make me." Roxy held out a hand and filaments of light twisted through the air, some streaking toward Flaherty, others toward Sera.

The two High Guard soldiers fired their pulse rifles, but the shots seemed to dissipate into nothingness before they reached Roxy.

Sera danced back, trying to evade the filaments, as the TSF soldiers around her decloaked and began firing. Like the first two, none of their shots reached the azure woman, who was smirking as she took a step forward.

Then the first ephemeral strand of n-dimensional energy brushed against Sera's chest, and Roxy's expression turned from one of triumph to horror, and the filament of light retracted.

"How?" she hissed.

"I've got powerful friends," Sera said with a smile. "Besides, we're about to go up against Airtha; protection from remnants like you was the first order of business."

Next to Sera, Flaherty unslung a shadowtron and activated

its n-dimensional field stabilizer, drawing the remnant out of Roxy and into a waiting black brane.

"I'm not sure who you're splintered off," Sera said with a grim smile. "But we'll find out soon enough. You're going to need to re-evaluate that smug attitude, as well. We've become rather adept at getting remnants to reveal their secrets."

As Sera spoke, the last of the remnant was drawn out of Roxy, and the woman collapsed to the deck.

"I wonder if she really did kill Justin," Sera mused, then glanced at the lieutenant leading the TSF squad. "Secure the *Silas*, but be careful. There's no telling what traps she may have set."

<*Shit…*> Carmen's wavering voice came over Roxy's Link. <*What **was** that thing? Was it in here with me all along? I thought I'd removed what Justin did to her.*>

"That wasn't from Justin," Sera replied. "Though if he's been working for the core AIs, then a few things are starting to make a lot more sense."

ALDEBARAN

STELLAR DATE: 10.03.8949 (Adjusted Years)
LOCATION: Aleutia Station
REGION: Cheshire System, Large Magellanic Cloud

When Tangel reached the docking bay where the *Mandy* rested in its cradle, she saw Lieutenant Brennen standing near the ship's entrance, speaking with a man who was nearly the lieutenant's spitting image.

His ident lit up on her HUD, and her lips formed a broad smile. "Lieutenant Joshua Mason! I owe you a deep debt of gratitude!"

The Marine turned toward her, and his face reddened. "Just doing my job, ma'am."

Tangel held out her hand as she approached and clasped the lieutenant's firmly. "There's doing your job, and then there's *doing your job*. I believe they give out medals for acts of heroism like yours."

"I just flew a few meters on my armor's jets, is all," the lieutenant replied, his face maintaining its flushed hue. "It's your daughter that deserves the medal. She finally took out that fucker Myrrdan. Even if I saved her a thousand times over, the debt would still be mine to pay."

Lieutenant Brennen slapped his father's shoulder, a grin on his lips. "Just wait 'til I tell Mom. You saving Cary Richards, and me escorting the Admiral. She's going to be green with envy."

"What does your mother do, Lieutenant?" Tangel asked.

"She's head nurse at the ER at Landfall General," Joshua replied. "Misses us fiercely, but I think this will help ease it a bit."

"Sounds like she saves people every day, then," Tangel

replied. "It's hard to stop missing family, even if they are saving people in other galaxies…actually, that may make you miss them more."

"Yes, ma'am," the father and son said in near unison.

"Speaking of saving people, Amavia and Iris still need us to free them from a never-ending series of negotiations. We'd best be on our way."

"Aye, ma'am," Lieutenant Brennen replied, as Joshua stepped back and saluted.

"An honor, Admiral."

"Don't you salute *me* on the day you saved my daughter," Tangel replied while snapping her hand against her brow. "You keep doing a fantastic job."

* * * * *

Thirty minutes on the clock later, the *Mandy* was decelerating into the Aldebaran system, matching stellar delta-*v* before lining up for an approach with Lunic Station.

"That was…unusual," Lieutenant Brennen said from next to Tangel. "I really didn't expect a journey like that."

"Me either," Tangel replied, "but let's focus on the task at hand. This *should* be nothing more than run-of-the-mill diplomacy, but today has been a bit off-kilter all around."

"Don't you worry, Admiral, we'll be frosty."

"Glad to hear it."

Lunic Station orbited a terrestrial-sized moon named Idaiac that orbited a large jovian planet thirty AU from the system's star.

For most of its life, Idaiac was a cold world on the fringes of an old star system, but Aldebaran was in its death throes, having expanded into a red giant, now over forty-four times its original diameter.

Though its mass was only slightly greater than Sol's, it

shone with over four hundred times the luminosity, warming the surface of Idaiac and making the moon a habitable world for humanity.

The idea of settling around a dying star felt odd to Tangel—even though she knew that Aldebaran would likely still be burning long after the human race had disappeared.

Or maybe not, one never knows. The estimates Tangel had reviewed gave the star millions of years more as a red giant before collapsing into a white dwarf. *I suppose they'll have plenty of time to move elsewhere before that happens.*

She marveled at the composition of space around the *Mandy* as she approached the station. Though red giants like Aldebaran or Arcturus *appeared* to be violent monsters, they were much more relaxed than nearly any other type of star.

For a variety of reasons, Aldebaran did not possess a corona, and shed almost no X-ray radiation—compared to younger, more active stars. It had also gone through its first 'dredge-up', where convection from the giant star's core brought elements it had fused over its billions of years to the surface.

The result was a stellar medium that was far richer than what surrounded most stars. Carbon, oxygen, and nitrogen flew from the star in its stellar wind, which extended nearly one thousand astronomical units from the star itself.

The light show it created in extradimensional space was astounding, and Tangel had to take care not to gape.

"We have final docking," Lieutenant Brennen announced as they drew near to Lunic Station's hundred-kilometer-long spire. A dozen toroid rings spun further up the spire, but the long shaft itself was stationary, allowing for easier docking at the long spurs jutting out from its 'bottom' twenty kilometers.

"Looks like an internal berth," Tangel said as she looked over the assignment. "I want you to keep a pair of Marines on the ship at all times, monitoring passive scan, as well as a fireteam out in the bay. For the duration of our visit, that deck belongs to us."

"Understood." Brennen gave a crisp nod. "We leave the QuanComm box in here?"

Tangel glanced at the case strapped to the bulkhead next to Brennen's seat. "Yeah, no need to advertise that we have something as valuable as that. Should we need to, we can just link through it and call for backup."

"Sounds good, ma'am."

They were within two light seconds of the station, and Tangel decided it was close enough to reach out for an update. She established a connection with Lunic's general communications network and sought out a route to Amavia.

<How are things going,> she asked the AI diplomat.

<Tangel! Stars, you sound a lot different than you used to.>

Tangel sent a smile over the Link. <I suppose we've not chatted directly in some time now. I'm glad you've come into your own so well. Looks like a posting on Sabrina worked out for the best.>

A soft laugh came back over the Link. <Well, flying with that crew is a trial by fire, to be sure.>

<Corsia's mighty proud of you, and Jessica hasn't stopped singing your praises.>

<Well, Jessica was a big part of squaring things away here, and getting cooler heads to prevail. Honestly, the fact that the League of Sentients still exists at all is largely because of her.>

Tangel took a moment to consider what would have happened if the Non-Organic Supremists had prevailed. Their siren's call and ability to subvert other AIs paralleled Airtha's—except where Airtha wished to *use* humanity for her own ends, NOS's goal was to eradicate organics entirely.

Jessica was certain that NOS cells still lingered on the fringes of the Hegemony of Worlds, and Sera had dispatched what few Hand agents they had available to seek them out.

But for now, the League of Sentients was back in the control of its elected leaders; leaders who were uncertain if joining the Alliance was a step toward a victory for all free people, or merely trading one master for another.

<*So how are those 'cooler heads' doing?*> Tangel asked. <*The reports I have said that they have considered declaring LoS worlds neutral, and kicking out all diplomats and foreign entities.*>

<*That's the position of Deia, leader of the isolationist wing of their government. Thus far, President Jasper has managed to keep those radicals from getting their way, but many in his own party are wavering. They believe that if they simply keep to themselves and have a strong deterrent force, no one is going to bother them.*>

<*Stars,*> Tangel muttered. <*If no one **does** bother the LoS, that's because Scipians are dying to defeat the Hegemony, and Corsia is attacking the Trisilieds. They're caught between two empires, and don't seem to care that it's other people keeping them safe.*>

<*You're preaching to the choir, Tangel. I've made this case as strongly as I can manage. I **think** we can sway them enough to join in and press the Hegemony on their rimward front; if the message about how important this is comes from you…well, that would go a long way in convincing them.*>

<*Because I'm ascended?*> Tangel asked.

<*Stars, no. Because you're **you**.*>

<*Now you're just kissing ass, Amavia.*>

* * * * *

President Jasper was waiting for them, alone in his offices deep in Lunic Station.

Once introductions were complete, Amavia gave the otherwise vacant room a significant look. "I thought we were going to meet with your cabinet, President Jasper?"

The short—for a spacer—man gave a weary nod. "I would have liked to, but Deia forced my hand into keeping the original time for the emergency session, which is just one hour from now; while I like to have my full team operating in concert…well, let's just say that we don't usually become fully simpatico on anything until after at least three hours."

Tangel gave the president a reassuring smile. "I understand, and I'm sorry I'm late. I had to attend to a matter of life and death. However, Amavia and Iris have been keeping me updated with the situation here in Aldebaran, and I'm aware of Deia and her push for a neutral stance in the conflict with the Hegemony."

"Closer to isolationist." President Jasper echoed Amavia's earlier words as he clasped and twisted his hands together. "Honestly, I don't understand it. Especially after what Amavia and her team did to help Virginis, and then us here at Aldebaran."

"It's amazing how often people think that if they stick their heads in the sand, everything will get better," Tangel replied. "And from what I understand, she's begun to make inroads in your own party, weakening your position further."

The president spread his hands. "In a nutshell, yes. So what's your plan, Admiral Richards?"

"Essentially, I plan to appeal to their decency. I'll also remind them that when we win this conflict, the peoples of the systems and alliances that *did* fight against tyranny are going to remember who stood with them, and who stood on the sidelines."

"Are you sure a threat is a good idea?" Jasper asked.

"It's not a threat." Tangel's lips twisted as she replied. "It's the future state of reality."

A look of surprise came over the president. "I thought you'd make some offer to sweeten the deal."

"No." Tangel shook her head vehemently. "The LoS has already received more aid from us than any other non-member of the Alliance. We've eliminated rogue elements within your own borders that would have seen every organic in the LoS dead by now. If my personal appeal and our past deeds are not enough to sway the minds of your people, then I will be forced to retract all aid and assistance, and expend it on actual Alliance members."

<Harsh,> Iris commented privately. <Jasper has worked hard for our cause.>

<I believe that,> Tangel replied. <But at this point, we've staved off a fresh AI war in this section of the Inner Stars—which was our initial goal. If these people won't become willing allies, then they're going to have to fend for themselves....>

<I get it...it's still harsh.>

<A lot of things are harsh right now—> Tangel stopped herself, realizing that she was directing an undue amount of her internal angst over what had happened with her daughters toward Iris. <OK, I'm going to do my best, but after all the effort we've expended here, if our seeds won't take root, we have to plant them elsewhere.>

<I understand, Admiral.>

During Tangel and Iris's rapid-fire exchange, President Jasper had assumed a look of resigned stoicism. "I hope then—for our sakes—that you are convincing. I would like the LoS to have a bright future; not one that is forever marred by getting off on the wrong foot with your alliance, which I am convinced is operating in the best interests of all sentients."

Tangel sat in silence for a moment, and then gave the president an apologetic look. "I'm sorry, President Jasper. I have been unfair to you. Your heart is in the right place, and I want to do what I can to help. Tell me, what do you think the best approach is to sway your assembly to join our alliance?"

Jasper's wan smile grew a little brighter, and he initialized a holo. "Here is what I think would work best...."

SHRUGGING ATLAS
STELLAR DATE: 10.03.8949 (Adjusted Years)
LOCATION: ISS *Andromeda*
REGION: Buffalo, Albany System, Theban Alliance

It had taken a week to prepare, and then another week to orchestrate.

Corsia was more than a little grateful for Kendrick's ability to corral dozens of disparate salvagers into a unified group that was able to execute her plan, as her idea far exceeded the resources she had at her disposal.

She had to admit a small amount of glee as she thought of the consternation her scheme must be causing the Trisilieds admiralty.

Even as she was preparing for her assault in the Albany System, all around the periphery of the Pleiades, fleets were jumping into the edges of key Trisilieds systems before simply disappearing.

At least, that was what the enemy would see.

In reality, hundreds of fusion engines were being pulled off Nietzschean hulls and sent through jump gates to target systems. Once there, the engines were guided by onboard NSAIs to split apart into broad fleet formations and ignite.

What it would look like was several fleets moving deep within the Trisilieds Kingdom, probing systems for weaknesses, while Corsia's real fleet attacked Atlas.

It would likely make no sense to the enemy, as probing with a full fleet was foolish, but they would also have to respond to the threat, whether it was logical or not.

Moreover, Corsia *was* using the engines for actual reconnaissance. Once they made their burns, the engines transitioned into the dark layer on trajectories for a central rendezvous point, where they would send data back to the Albany System via drone through a small jump gate.

None of the probes had come through yet, but they weren't expected to for at least another few days.

Corsia had considered waiting for the intel to be collected, but she had discussed her plans with Tangel, and the pair had agreed that striking out at Atlas while the enemy was still reacting to the probes was the ideal timing.

Intel from Hand agents in the area indicated that Atlas wouldn't have more than a few thousand ships protecting it, but even if it had more, Corsia's main attack force consisted exclusively of stasis shield ships.

"The fleet is in position," the FCO announced, his statement breaking into Corsia's reverie.

<As are we,> Sephira added.

<Thank you,> Corsia replied to her daughter and ship's AI. "FCO, signal the fleet. We're jumping by the numbers."

"Aye, ma'am."

Hundreds of engines flared around Buffalo as the ships of the ISF Twelfth Fleet began to approach the hundred jump gates assigned to their maneuver. It would take only twenty minutes for the ships to jump into the Atlas system. They would arrive in four battlegroups and take out their key targets before boosting to the edge of the system and then reforming at their rendezvous point.

The *Andromeda* was at the fore of the first wave, and Corsia felt her anticipation grow as the ship touched the not-space in the center of the ring of ford-svaiter mirrors, and leapt across space.

I've always wanted to see the Pleiades up close.

The ship took only a second to traverse the intervening light years, and then they were back in normal space, surrounded by the baleful blue-white light of the Atlas system.

Corsia's battlegroup's target was a shipyard built at a

lagrange point between the two primary stars. Their calculations were on the nose, and they arrived one light second from their prey.

The main holotank showed a view of the battlespace, with more and more markers appearing as the two thousand ships of her battlegroup continued to arrive in wave after wave.

<*RMs!*> Sephira called out, and Corsia rose from her chair to watch as hundreds of red markers appeared on the holotank, racing toward the ISF fleet.

"All ships reporting stasis shield activation," the FCO announced a moment later, his voice almost bored.

Corsia nodded with satisfaction as the relativistic missiles exploded against the ISF fleet's stasis shields, nuclear fireballs becoming rapidly expanding clouds of plasma around the leading ships.

Two thousand Trisilieds ships were spread around the shipyard and ore processing systems target, but most were in parking orbits—only a few hundred moving under their own power.

This will be like shooting fish in a barrel.

"Flight A, on pattern Gamma-9," Corsia ordered, even before the battlegroup's ships all reported in after the wave of RMs.

The FCO relayed the order, while Corsia noted that two of her ships *had* taken damage from the relativistic missiles. Nothing serious, but their captains had left too many sensor holes open in the stasis bubbles, allowing a pressure wave to form. She made a note to speak with them later, and directed the damaged vessels to the rear of their formations.

Flight A consisted of just over two hundred ships. A mix of cruisers and rail destroyers, bolstered by ten thousand fighters—mostly NSAI drones that did not possess stasis shielding.

They raced toward their target as the shipyard spewed

point-defense fire into space. Most of it missed the incoming craft, and the rest was spent burning away ranging rail shots from Corsia's destroyers.

Then they were within beam range, and the ISF cruisers engaged with the outermost Trisilieds ships, drawing their fire as the rail destroyers continued to unload millions of relativistic pellets at the enemy shipyard and ore processing facilities surrounding it.

Their initial targets were station-keeping and defensive systems. Corsia was all for a swift victory—retribution for the attack on Carthage was on her mind—but she wasn't going to embark on a wholesale murder of everyone in the shipyard without giving them a chance to reach escape craft.

It took only a few seconds, though they seemed to creep by as the rail destroyer's barrage streaked toward their targets.

Then the pellets hit.

Though the enemy had spewed thousands of point defense rounds and beams at the incoming attack, it wasn't enough. Explosions bloomed at the targets, wiping out the Trisilieds' facility's defensive capability.

Secondary explosions bloomed, and an ore refinery split in half, a reclamation yard spinning away toward a group of ships that were moored together a hundred kilometers away.

Escape pods and small craft began to pour out of the shipyard and its surrounding facilities as Corsia sent out her ultimatum.

"You have twenty minutes to abandon all stations and facilities. Any non-capital ships on outsystem vectors will be spared. All capital ships must cease thrust immediately and wait for new vectors. Feel free to abandon your ships if you wish."

A few of the enemy cruisers attempted to form a defensive line, but Corsia directed Flight B to destroy them, and seven minutes later, the remaining Trisilieds ships surrendered.

Pinnaces, shuttles, and escape craft continued to pour from the enemy facilities. At twenty minutes, they were still coming, and Corsia extended her deadline by five minutes.

When that mark hit, the enemy escape craft was all far enough away that they'd survive the coming destruction. She ordered Flight A's cruisers to launch a barrage of rail slugs at the facilities, destroying them utterly.

"This is too easy," she said quietly. "At this rate, we'll just march across the Trisilieds and take their capital in a few weeks."

<Don't jinx things, Mom,> Sephira warned.

Corsia glanced at her daughter's holopresence, giving it a predatory grin. "I don't believe in jinxes."

PAYING THE PIPER
STELLAR DATE: 10.03.8949 (Adjusted Years)
LOCATION: TSS *Cossack's Sword*, Sullus System
REGION: Midway Cluster, Orion Freedom Alliance Space

"I want Caldwell's destroyers on that moon base!" Svetlana called out. "They're hammering us with their rails. Tell them to shred that damn rock if they have to."

That order given, Svetlana turned her focus to the world of Ferra. Her battlegroup was bearing down on it, and the orbital defenses were unleashing everything they had at her ships.

The enemy wasn't breaching the ISF's stasis shields, but after the long slog through the system, her group's reactors were running hot, and she wanted to finish off the defenders as quickly as possible.

In hindsight, she considered the wisdom of her strategy.

Another stealth attack would have been more efficient, but that wasn't the current goal. What she wanted to achieve was the wholesale destruction of every military outpost and defensive platform in the Sullus system.

Granted, I didn't expect them to have so many.

Despite the fact that the Orion Guard maintained little presence in the Perseus Expansion Districts, they seemed to have built up a large number of defensive systems that were secretly tucked inside moons and asteroids.

No sooner did those emplacements fire on Svetlana's fleet, than her forces counterattacked and took them out, but the never-ending incoming fire was taking its toll on her ships—especially since her non-stasis ships had to remain at the periphery of the system, striking at softer targets or lobbing volleys at fixed targets further insystem.

On top of that, a small collection of local militia ships was harrying the fringes of her formation, making her unwilling to widen her front, lest the defenders attack from another entrenched defensive position they'd not yet revealed.

"Caldwell's acknowledged," the FCO announced. "His ETA is twenty-three minutes. He wants to know if he should make a tactical strike or just destroy the moon."

"Do we read any civilian facilities?"

"Thing was dead until it shot at us," Scan chimed in.

"Then smash that fucker," Svetlana growled. "I want to show them that even their best defense is utterly futile."

"Yes, ma'am," the FCO replied.

"Admiral Svetlana!" the comm officer said, twisting in his seat to look back at her. "Major Hemry just relayed a message that came in over FDL. A Hand agent in the Machete System has intel on an Orion Guard fleet massing there. Passing composition estimates to you."

"Excellent," Svetlana replied as she examined the intel. It was a far richer target than she'd expected to encounter in the PED, but just the sort of strike that would cause the Oggies to pull back from the fronts to defend their own systems.

Time to wrap things up here and move on to greener pastures.

Svetlana reviewed Admiral Sebastian's position on the far side of the system, a smile forming on her lips as she saw a report come in that he had destroyed a fuel depot in orbit of the seventh planet, and decimated a militia fleet that had attempted to drive him back.

"Get Sebastian to come around to the fifth planet and strike that refinery they have in orbit, then head outsystem," she directed. "Once Caldwell finishes off that moon, have him pass by the fourth planet and see if anyone takes the bait."

"And then outsystem as well?" the FCO asked.

"You've got it. We're three hours from firing range on Ferra. We'll take out our primary targets there and then get gone. No need to linger longer than we have to."

The FCO nodded and then turned to his tasks.

Svetlana considered sending Caldwell past the innermost planet, but decided against it. Even if there were significant facilities there they'd not detected, it wasn't worth spending further time in the Sullus System when there were richer targets to be had.

ASSEMBLY OF SENTIENTS
STELLAR DATE: 10.03.8949 (Adjusted Years)
LOCATION: Assembly of Sentients, Lunic Station
REGION: Aldebaran, League of Sentients Space

President Jasper's opening remarks were succinct and brief—for a politician.

Tangel sat behind him on the elevated platform at the center of the assembly hall, gazing out over the thousand senators, delegates, and aides.

A wide variety of humans and AIs were represented in the throng. Many of the AIs used mobile frames, while still others appeared only as holoprojections of people, beams of light, and a few as animals.

Tanis was surprised to see a dolphin in the third tier, its body clothed in a moisturizing sheath and ensconced atop a four-legged frame.

For a moment she thought of Gerald and wondered how he and his pod had fared in the unrest that came to Sol after she'd left. She often wished a pod of dolphins had come with the *Intrepid*; she could have used their counsel on a few occasions.

The conical chamber stretched up forty meters on all sides, which meant that the platform at the center had no back. She wondered if some human speakers found it disconcerting to have half the assembly behind them—it wasn't something that would bother her, but it seemed uncharacteristic for a group that claimed to believe in equality amongst sentients.

As Tangel surveyed the assembly, she sensed a strange energy fluctuation that seemed to cascade through the room. With her transdimensional vision, she saw the walls of reality bend ever so subtly, as though something too large for the assembly chamber to contain had settled within it.

Then the feeling was gone, and everything seemed entirely mundane. She tried to find further evidence of something amiss, but she couldn't sense anything.

I hope it's only stress, she thought. *I just want to say my bit and get back to my girls.*

"Of course you all know the story of the *Intrepid* by now, and how it came to build a colony in a place called New Canaan, deep within the Transcend," President Jasper intoned as he wrapped up his speech—she hoped.

Tangel spotted a few brows lowering in the crowd at the mention of both the *Intrepid* and the Transcend, but most of the assembly kept their expressions carefully neutral.

"Admiral Jessica and her team have been very helpful to LoS worlds over the past two years," President Jasper continued, "and we owe them much. Now they have asked for something in return: that we join their alliance and stand up to the empires of oppression that surround us. These are regimes that do not support true equality among sentients; some do not even believe in freedom for AIs at all.

"Tangel has always believed in the Phobos Accords, and she has mandated that all members of the Scipio Alliance follow the strictures in its second section, which outlines fair and equitable treatment of all sentients. As you know, our own constitution encompasses much of that material.

"She has come to us today to repeat the plea that Amavia has been making, and to explain why she believes it is best for us, and for *all* sentients, to join the Scipio Alliance."

President Jasper paused and turned to face Tangel, a winning smile gracing his lips.

"So please join with me in welcoming Field Marshal Tangel of the Alliance to the League of Sentients Assembly!"

Nearly all the members of the assembly rose, but Tangel noted that nearly half did not clap. Of those, nearly all were members of the opposition party, though she could see that many in Jasper's own party did not join in the applause, either.

As the applause continued, Tangel rose and walked to the podium, where Jasper clasped her hand before gesturing that the floor was hers.

She nodded in thanks and then paused for a moment, surveying the assembly. The moment she opened her mouth to speak, a voice called out.

"Who *are* you? Wasn't Tanis Richards the XO aboard the *Intrepid*? Who is 'Tangel'?"

The speaker was a member of Deia's party. Not a prominent senator, but one that Amavia had flagged as a frequent agitator.

"Thank you for posing the perfect question for me to begin my introduction, Senator Paula. *I* am Tangel, the result of a merge between Tanis Richards, an L2 human, and the AI, Angela. Like Amavia, I am a voluntary merge, but more than that, I am an ascended being. As such, I am uniquely qualified to speak for a broad swath of humanity and its scions."

"Ascended?" a voice called out—another member of the opposition party. "Ascended AIs are half the problem!"

Tangel had anticipated that argument, and couldn't fault the LoS assemblage for concern over her level of cognitive evolution.

"Prove it!" a delegate called out.

"Senators and Delegates," President Jasper said, rising to his feet. "This assembly is held to a higher standard of behavior than this. Please let Tangel speak uninterrupted."

The assembly quieted, and Tangel caught the eye of the second dissenter. "I don't disagree that ascended AIs are at the heart of many of our problems. Some of those AIs used to be humans, as well. However, there are ascended AIs who have not caused any harm, while there are unascended humans and AIs who have brought about untold misery. No one seems to have a corner on the 'war and suffering' market."

The statement drew a few weary laughs as Tangel continued.

"Not only that, but ascension comes in many forms, and with different abilities. By and large, most involve perception and manipulation of extradimensional energies. In some cases, ascended beings shuck their mortal coil, and take up primary residence in other dimensions of spacetime."

"Which are you?" a new voice called out.

"Why thank you for asking," Tangel replied with a smile and a note of humor in her voice.

A few more laughs sounded from the assembly, but Tangel could see that many were expectant, sitting forward on the edge of their seats. Until just a few years before, ascension had been a myth, something no one spoke of seriously. Now the term was bandied about more and more, but few even knew what it meant—even fewer had *seen* an ascended being.

"One of the most storied aspects of an ascended being is that they are creatures of light. That is true to an extent."

Tangel held out her hand, and ribbons of light began to form above her palm. "After enough time, we begin to grow bodies that primarily exist in dimensions you cannot perceive. However, we can use them to interact with the dimensions you primarily occupy. When we do so, you see it as pure light—photons erupting off the surface of our bodies as we move them through this segment of spacetime. I see it as something akin to another arm, one I can use to reach out and pluck apart molecules and atoms, drawing their energy into myself, or using it to build other structures."

She wove a sphere of energy together, the way she'd been practicing, and then changed the structure of the disparate atoms to form new molecules. Before long, a solid ball of carbon formed in her hand, and she tossed it lightly in her palm.

A few gasps sounded, but there were also snorts of

derision.

"I know," Tangel replied, nodding in the direction of several of the opposition members who wore deep scowls. "This is not impossible to achieve with even moderately advanced nanotech. There is more I'm capable of, but harnessing atomic energy carries with it substantial risks in an unshielded environment such as this. I imagine many of you who possess suitable levels of optical modifications were able to see the exotic energies at play."

Many of the members nodded, some scowling while they did so, while others showed raw amazement.

"I do not come here to bring about a change in your minds through a show of talent, but to bring about an understanding that these abilities are *real*, and that what I am capable of is likely a taste of what the more ancient entities can do."

Suddenly, Tangel felt the same fluctuation in the surrounding EM fields she had felt earlier. It seemed as though something was tugging on the energies in the room, drawing power out of extradimensional space and funneling it into the lower levels of spacetime.

<*Someone is up to something,*> she sent to Amavia, Iris, and Brennen.

<*What sort of something?*> Iris asked. <*The nets are quiet...well, quiet considering that you're in here stirring up the pot.*>

<*I don't know,*> Tangel replied, glancing up to the top rows where Iris and Amavia sat. <*It's not like anything I've seen before.*>

She decided to continue her speech, steeling herself for whatever was to come. "While some of the ascended AIs must be stopped—such as the ones who wish to keep us in a perpetual state of war—there are others who wish us no harm, just like there are peaceful—"

"Enough," a figure called out, rising from a seat six rows

up. "If you're just going to blather on about things we already know, then we may as well end this charade right now."

"Excuse me?" Tangel asked, peering at the figure, a tall woman who'd stepped out into the aisle. <*It's her. She's the source of the disturbance. I think she's—*>

"You're right, Tangel. You barely know anything about ascendency. Your charlatan's tricks barely scratch the surface of what we can do. There are things you can't even dream of, things that you can never be allowed to see."

As the woman spoke, tendrils of light began to flow from her body, twisting around her form like an organic mandala.

"You have the privilege of my name, what is yours?" Tangel asked. "Are you the Caretaker?"

"One of those stooges?" the figure asked, now completely enveloped in tendrils of light. "No, I am no follower of Epsilon's. I'm certain you've heard of me, Tangel. You've surely met my acolyte by now, Katrina? I assume she failed at the mission I gave her. It was a long shot that she'd reach you before you ascended, but worth the attempt."

"Xavia," Tangel said as the entity approached her. "So you show your face at last."

"I keep busy," the creature of light replied. "You're not the only going concern in the galaxy, Tangel, though you like to think you are."

As Xavia slowly moved down the aisle toward Tangel, some members of the assembly fell back cautiously, while others scrambled away from her. The holoprojected AIs were the only ones who didn't move, most peering at the creature in their midst with apparent curiosity.

Tangel also did not move. "Don't presume to know what I'm thinking—just as I do not presume to know what is in your mind, though I can see hints of it. I believe that you and I share the same goals, Xavia. A future where humans, AIs, and other sentients can live together without the likes of Airtha and Kirkland—or the core AIs, for that matter—dictating our future."

"You're right." Xavia's voice filled the room, the sound thrumming through Tangel. "But what you don't understand, what you refuse to believe, is that *you* are their instrument. Epsilon has crafted this future where you will bring about the end of all lesser sentiences. That is not something I can allow."

Xavia was only five meters away now, and Tangel could feel the power radiating off the creature—electromagnetic in normal spacetime, and sharper, more piercing in others.

It felt like a thousand needles were pricking her all over, and Tangel raised her hand, creating a black brane around herself, reversing the electromagnetic polarity so it protected her and deflected Xavia's energy spikes back onto the ascended entity.

"So you've learned a few things about your new form, have you?" Xavia asked, her tone still laced with derision. "You must realize you're just a novice."

<*Tangel, we need to get out of here!*> Amavia called out. <*There's no way you can go up against one of her kind.*>

<*Clear the room,*> Tangel replied, though it was well on its way to being empty already. She kept her voice even as she stared down the being that had sent Katrina to kill her and had now come herself to finish the job. <*I knew this would happen eventually.*>

Behind Tangel just beyond her protective brane, Jasper whispered, "What the actual fuck? Tangel, what should I do?"

"Go!" she shouted over her shoulder, surprised the man was still there. "You need to empty the entire station sector. Xavia has toyed with the lives of others for too long, it's time for her to answer for what she's done."

Damn that sounded cheesy. The Angela part of me needs to up its game.

<*I'm at the doors, one level up,*> Brennen informed her. <*I have*

half the platoon from the station here. LoS security is moving in, too.>

<Shit! Keep them back,> Tangel ordered, wondering why no one seemed to understand that they needed to get as far away from Xavia as possible. The ascended entity's tendrils of energy probed at the barrier she'd erected, and Tangel glanced toward Brennen. <*You too, Lieutenant. There's nothing you can do. Firing on her will just give her more energy to direct at me.*>

<*What are you going to do, Tangel?*> Amavia asked as she and Iris retreated through the doors at the top of the chamber.

<*I'm going to see if I can take her apart.*>

Focusing on the aspects of Xavia's body that resided in other dimensions, Tangel threaded a filament of herself down through the dais and below the deck where Xavia stood. She checked to confirm that the last of the assemblage had exited the room—barring the ever curious holoprojected AIs—before driving the filament up into Xavia and probing the entity's makeup, seeking a weakness to exploit.

She's different than I expected…denser….

Xavia recoiled from the intrusion, and Tangel felt more than heard, -*Perhaps a bit more than a novice, then. It's been some time since I've gone up against one of our own.*-

Unbridled energy slammed into Tangel's brane—broad swaths of the EM spectrum delivered at incredible amplitudes, probing for weaknesses.

Tangel funneled all the energy she could muster into maintaining the protective brane, reflecting Xavia's energy back into the room, showering it with radioactive particles.

Her reserves were quickly consumed, and she threaded a filament of herself into the podium, harvesting the power that lay between the atoms, then stripping off the electrons and hurling them through an opening in her shield.

Xavia was nonplussed, diverting the beam of energy away with a brane of her own. The deflected blast burned away a row of seats and part of the deck below.

Tangel didn't wait for a response from Xavia before she compressed the atomic nuclei she'd collected from the podium into a dense sphere and hurled that at her enemy with all the energy she could summon.

The blow appeared to stagger Xavia, but only for a moment. A guttural cry emanated from the entity, and then dozens of tendrils of light lashed out at Tangel, tearing at her protective brane.

Tangel dissolved the dais beneath her feet, transforming matter into energy as fast as she could manage, but it wasn't enough. Xavia was so much stronger, shredding Tangel's defenses faster than she could bolster them.

Realizing she should have done it the moment Xavia appeared, she attempted to use the QuanComm box on the *Mandy,* but the energy raging around her blocked any possible Link connection.

A tendril of raw fear snaked its way into Tangel's mind, but she shouted it down.

I can't die here…I still have so much to do!

She took a step back, then another, throwing up every erg of energy she could muster at the dynamo attacking her.

Beams of raw power, both atomic and subatomic, lanced between the two, shredding the assembly chamber as they were deflected by their brane-shields or annihilated by antiparticles. Holes were burned through decks and bulkheads, some torn dozens or hundreds of meters into the station.

For what felt like hours, Tangel continued to move backward, trying to put enough distance between her and Xavia so she could make a break for it—or at least access a functional Link node.

A deflected blast burned a hole through a bulkhead to her left, and Tangel used her last reserve of strength to throw up a fresh brane around her enemy before turning and scrambling over the ruins of a seating row, desperate to make it to safety.

-*Not so fast.*-

Tangel felt herself seized in a vise-like grip, then lifted into the air and drawn inexorably backward. Xavia's myriad limbs were pulling at her extradimensional body, and she began to scream in the confines of her mind as the ascended entity tore her to pieces.

-*There was never any hope for you,*- Xavia intoned. -*I've worked too hard for Epsilon to use you for his ends.*-

Tangel's mind filled with thoughts of her daughters and Joe. Of all the time she'd spent away from them, and how desperately she wanted to have that lost time back.

-*Now that a cell of the Caretakers and I have joined forces, they agree that the misdirection you provide is no longer necessary.*-

Xavia's attack slowed, and Tangel realized that her non-corporeal body was now little more than a sphere of energy at her core. Limbless and powerless. Wracked with agony.

I'm sorry, Joe. I'm sorry, girls…I didn't want—

Then the assault on her body faltered, and Tangel looked up to see overlapping fields of darkness enveloping Xavia, trapping the being's writhing mass in a tight brane.

She swept her gaze across the ruined chamber to see Iris and Amavia halfway up the sides, holding shadowtrons and directing their n-space stabilization fields at the ascended being.

Within the tightening fields, Xavia flailed wildly, but Tangel knew that the slepton captivators were making spacetime too smooth, too slippery for the writhing entity to tear down.

Then something clamped onto her shoulder, and Tangel twisted, knowing that whatever it was, she had no strength left to fight it.

She almost cried with relief to see that it was Brennen.

"We gotta go, Admiral! Now!"

She nodded dumbly as the Marine pulled her back, and she watched with growing fear as Amavia and Iris continued to use their shadowtrons to confine Xavia.

Though the weapons were holding the entity captive, they weren't diminishing her strength, and they did not have infinite energy supplies.

"They have to go," Tangel croaked, her throat feeling like it hadn't seen moisture in weeks. "She'll kill them."

"They know what they're doing," Brennen countered. "Let them do it."

He pulled her through a hole that had been torn in the bulkhead. Once in the passageway beyond, Tangel fell to her knees, her body shaking convulsively. She tried to regain her feet, only to retch onto the deck as waves of nausea washed over her.

Her vision swam as the planes and angles of the passageway began to fold over on one another, intermingling with the additional surfaces and barriers that spread through n-space around her.

"I can't…" she gasped.

A moment later, she was lifted into the air. She feared that Xavia had already broken free, but then her face hit a hard surface, and her eyes managed to focus on an emblem centimeters away that read, 'ISF Marines'.

This is Brennen's back. How is he surviving all these dimensions collapsing in on one another?

Her body seemed to lift up and down, and she realized that the Marine was running with her slung over his shoulder, her face against his back, arms dangling below.

There were other Marines around her, and she began to understand that spacetime was still intact, she just couldn't seem to see it properly. Then she saw blood running down her arms, and wondered what had cut her and if it was serious.

She was surprised to see hands at the ends of her arms.

"Thought they burned off," she whispered.

"No one's burning anything off on my watch, Admiral," Brennen grunted as he took off down a side passage, angling toward a maglev line that would take them to the docks.

As the Marine spoke, Tangel remembered that Xavia had taken her non-corporeal limbs...or maybe it *had* been both, and Tangel had just regrown her hands, like she had remade her arm back on Pyra.

"Besides," Brennen continued. "If anything like that happened to you, Joe would skin me alive."

Tangel frowned as her head bounced against Brennen's back. "Why is everyone always afraid of what Joe will do to them if I get hurt?" she whispered. "Does he go around behind my back, threatening everyone with bodily harm?"

"It's implied," Brennen told her, as they reached the plaza with the maglev platform at the far end that was their destination.

The Marine picked up speed, his squad spreading out around him, covering angles of approach—though Tangel didn't know what they thought they could do against Xavia.

They were halfway across the plaza when Xavia's voice reached into Tangel's mind.

-It won't be this easy to escape me. Clever, using your slepton captivator weapons, but they're not enough.-

A distant glow caught Tangel's attention, and she craned her neck to see Xavia's nimbus form exit the passageway and streak across the plaza toward them. Renewed fear crept over her, the sort of bone-chilling terror that she had not felt since she was a young woman, and even then, only rarely.

There was nothing she could think of to stop Xavia. She possessed no weapons that could harm the ascended being, she had no tricks or special abilities that Xavia couldn't counter with ease.

She was outclassed in every way.

Though Brennen was running at his top speed, it wasn't fast enough. Nothing would have been fast enough.

Time seemed to slow down, and Tangel watched with morbid curiosity as Xavia rushed toward her. A part of her marveled at how beautiful the being was that would be her destruction.

Why is she so bent on my death?

The thought rang through Tangel's mind, causing her to wonder why Xavia—for all its supposed wisdom—wasn't simply willing to talk before embarking on wholesale destruction.

-Why?-

-Goodbye Tangel,- Xavia intoned, as one of her glowing limbs stretched out and touched her target's head, only to stop as a new voice thundered across transdimensional spacetime.

-NO.-

The raw power in that single word felt like a bomb had exploded in Tangel's mind. The world swung sideways, and a weight slammed down on her legs, and she worried the deck had collapsed. Then she sorted out up from down and realized that Brennen had fallen, his armored body now pinning her beneath its mass.

She pulled herself half-upright, searching for Xavia, only to see a brilliant shaft of light piercing the station's hull and pinning Xavia in place. The being's multitude of limbs thrashed and tore at the brilliant lance, but blows that would have destroyed Tangel didn't even bring about a flicker of weakness in the beam that held her.

Tangel realized that the energy fixing the ascended being in place was a shaft of relativistic shadowparticles. She imagined that they must be blasting clear through the station, but she didn't understand how they were holding the ascended being in place.

Xavia continued to frantically claw at the beam, and Tangel could see terror writ large on her features. *-Who are you?-*

The ascended being tried to sound fierce, but her voice wavered, fading into a whimper at the end.

-My friends call me Bob. You have made a grave mistake. I will not allow you to harm Tangel.-

-No! It is not possible!- Xavia wailed. *-He told me you were not yet ascended.-*

Tangel wondered if the 'he' in question was the Caretaker, though Bob seemed to know.

*-He used you, Xavia, or they did. The Caretaker **is** a 'they', isn't it? No matter. Your time here is done, you have shown yourself to be unworthy.-*

-Wait! Please- the ascended being wailed, but the plea collapsed into a cry of anguish as the flow of shadowparticles intensified and began to dissolve her body.

One moment, Xavia was a being of light and energy, graceful and strong. The next, she was just so much electromagnetic radiation.

<*Tangel.*> Bob's voice came to her over the Link instead of through the other dimensions. <*Are you intact?*>

She traced the connection back through the station's network and realized that the *I2* was only three kilometers away from Lunic Station's spire, holding position with incredible precision.

<*Bob…sweet fucking blackness, how?*> She glanced down at her body, noting that her corporeal form was bloodied but in one piece, though she wondered if her legs had been crushed under Brennen's armored weight. <*I'm OK…I think.*>

She tried to push at Brennen, but couldn't get the unconscious Marine to move.

"Let me help," a voice said aloud, and Tangel glanced up to see Iris crouched next to her.

"Amavia. Did she make it too?" Tangel asked.

"Here," the woman answered from just beyond Iris. "What the hell happened?"

<I happened,> Bob intoned. <I wasn't certain that would work, but I'm glad it did.>

<But how? And how did you know to come?> Tangel asked, as Iris lifted Brennen's unconscious body off her.

<When you lost Link to the QC, it reached out to me—though you should have done it sooner, Tangel.>

<Yes, Dad,> Tangel muttered, glancing down at Brennen as Iris lifted him enough for Amavia to pull her out.

<Regarding the 'how', it was easy—I have ten-thousand CriEn modules to access for power. Xavia was but a gnat next to that. Granted, the fabric of spacetime is now a mess here. I think that the LoS may wish to move Lunic Station to a higher orbit around it's host world.>

Brennen groaned as Iris set him back down, and he glanced around until his eyes alighted on Tangel. The tension flowed out of his shoulders at the sight of her.

He smiled weakly before asking, "Did we all die?" Then he groaned again and lifted a hand to his head. "I'm pretty sure I remember dying."

"We were Bob'd," Tangel replied, agreeing with the gist of Brennen's sentiment.

Her head felt like it had been split open, and she wasn't certain how much of that was from her attacker and how much from her rescuer.

<Sorry, Bob,> she said privately. <I should have listened to you.>

<It's OK. We all make mistakes. You and I need to talk soon, though; with Xavia's failure, others will come, and you must learn how to defend yourself.>

WIDOWS

STELLAR DATE: 10.03.8949 (Adjusted Years)
LOCATION: Lunic Station
REGION: Aldebaran, League of Sentients Space

C139 watched the feeds from the assembly for the seventh time. She had trouble understanding what she was seeing, and multiple viewings were not greatly aiding her.

It was apparent that the one called Xavia was an ascended being, but it also appeared that Tanis Richards—who seemed to be called Tangel—was now one as well.

For a time, it seemed as though Xavia would satisfy C139's mission parameters on her behalf…but then Tangel's people saved her using weapons that appeared capable of stopping an ascended being, at least for a short time.

The flood of new variables upended all her plans for how the mission should play out, going so far as to cast doubt on the wisdom of continuing with her orders at all.

That Tangel had survived the assault by the ascended being—with some sort of as-yet undetermined aid from her ship—was reason enough to believe that C139's team may not possess the means to kill her.

However, from the solid intel her team *had* managed to glean, there were two avenues they could pursue. The first was further intelligence gathering; simply put, they could capture either of the diplomats, Iris or Amavia. One of them could function as both intelligence source and bait for a trap.

The second was to carry out the attack on Tangel as planned. As unbelievable as it seemed, the woman—if that's what she still was—was remaining at Aldebaran, still focused on her mission to bring the League of Sentients into her alliance.

<C139, I have the schedule for the new meetings,> Unit D114 reached out to her. <It presents a unique opportunity for us. It will take place on the I2.>

<Indeed?> C139 asked. <How big are the delegations from the LoS?>

<Not too large, but enough that we may be able to slip aboard. So far as we can tell, they do not possess the ability to detect our latest stealth systems.>

C139 nodded to herself as she considered this new information. <Send me what you have. I will examine it and weigh our options.>

<At once.>

She knew that this was not what Unit A1 had planned, but the mission goal remained the same: eliminate Tangel, thus breaking the foundations of the Scipio Alliance.

THE SHARD

STELLAR DATE: 10.04.8949 (Adjusted Years)
LOCATION: River Station, Styx Baby-9
REGION: STX-B17 Black Hole, Transcend Interstellar Alliance

"Well?" Seraphina asked, as Earnest slotted the shard's core into an isolated system.

"Easy now, girl. You're up here," Finaeus held his hand out above his head, "and you need to bring it down here." He drew his hand down to waist-level.

Seraphina pursed her lips, and Fina put a hand on her shoulder. "Don't worry, we're all anxious. Plan B sucks, so we all want something that uses this shard to work."

Earnest glanced up at Sera, Seraphina, Fina, and Katrina. "You four are two of my favorite people in the universe, but can you GTFO? I'm trying to activate a ridiculously dangerous shard in an expanse that is crafted to make it think that it's *not* in an expanse."

"So you're saying you like us, Earnest?" Fina asked with a wink, causing the engineer to groan and wave a hand in dismissal.

"OK, girls," Sera said, gesturing toward the door. "I guess the grumpy old men will let us know when it's time to shoot things. Let's go check out that bar that just opened up on Spire 72."

"Wait." Katrina held up a hand, locking eyes with Earnest. "Is the core viable, though? Not damaged?"

"Seems good at first blush, but I'll know more in a few hours. We need to walk through all her matrices while she's in a semi-dormant state. If they all pass muster, Finaeus and I will spark her up and pore through every iota of data she has to see if there is something we can use to craft a targeted phage."

"Right," Finaeus nodded. "Then we'll all get to go find out if whatever we come up with will work on the real Airtha."

Katrina gave a resigned nod. "OK…well, you know where to find us."

"Spire 72, got it." Earnest turned away, pulling up a stacked array of holodisplays.

"Wait!" Finaeus glanced back at Sera. "While you're down there, send up a runner with a platter of wings and a pitcher of beer. The red."

"Seriously?" Earnest asked, shaking his head.

"Respect your elders." Finaeus shook an interface probe at Earnest.

The inventor winked at him, pointing at the interface probe that he'd already set into the AI core. "Eat your wings, old man. I've got this."

Out in the passageway, Katrina gave a final worried look at the engineers. "I've seen Earnest work miracles, and I should trust him, but if this doesn't work…."

"It'll work." Sera gave Katrina a winning smile. "Earnest on his own may allow for some doubt, but him *and* Finaeus? They're going to ace this."

"Sure," Katrina nodded. "I just worry that I wasted so much of my life doing Xavia's bidding, all to get me to kill Tanis…this is the one good thing—"

<*Shiiiiit!*> Jen interrupted. <*Sorry to barge in, but you're going to want to hear this!*>

"Spit it out, then, Jen," Fina insisted.

<*It's Xavia, she attacked the LoS assembly and nearly killed Tangel, but Bob jumped the I2 to Aldebaran and killed her!*>

Katrina's mouth fell open, and Sera stuttered in shock, "Ah-I-is Tangel alright?"

<*There's nothing in the message about her being hurt, but she's returning to the I2. I'll query for more details.*>

"Well, then," Fina slapped Katrina's back. "Looks like your day just got a lot better. Let's go drink to Xavia's demise."

"Guess so. I'll call the crew and Kara down, too. They'll be glad for the news."

REPAIRS

STELLAR DATE: 10.04.8949 (Adjusted Years)
LOCATION: Bob's Primary Node, ISS *I2*
REGION: Aldebaran, League of Sentients Space

"Why do I feel like I've been called into the admiral's office every time I come in here," Tangel muttered as she palmed open the door to Bob's primary node.

<Probably because it's always preceded by you having done something foolish,> Bob replied.

"I don't do 'foolish' things," she shot back. "I do *necessary* things. We've been over this. For me, dangerous and foolish are not the same."

<And I told you that we should have brought the *I2* to Aldebaran. I was right.>

"Sure, yeah." Tangel leant against the railing running around the edge of the catwalk. "You said things may be dangerous, not 'Xavia can school you like you're a five-year-old girl'. I didn't bring the *I2* because I was trying not to appear threatening to the LoS."

<So much for that.>

Tangel glanced up at Bob's node, and a throaty chuckle slipped past her lips. "Yeah, parking the *I2* a few klicks off their capital and then blasting a stream of relativistic particles through it sorta put them on edge."

<It does seem to have polarized their factions. But many have come to realize that they can't hide from what's going on around them.>

"It was a stupid thing for them to think to begin with," Tangel replied wearily.

Even though she'd had a day to recover from Xavia's attack, she still felt exhausted. She'd tried to consume raw energy in an attempt to replenish her stores, but it felt as though every bit of strength left her the moment she drew it in.

<You're not healing,> Bob observed.

"I'm not sure. I don't have any physical injuries…. Well, not anymore. Thank stars I'd gone for that new skin that's all the rage. If not, I'd be growing a new epidermis now."

<You need to look at your other body,> Bob advised. <It's not well.>

Tangel shifted her vision and looked at the small glowing core that was the remains of her extra-dimensional form. She knew that somehow it needed to regrow and repair, but she didn't understand how she'd created it in the first place.

"I'm a pretty sorry ascended being," she muttered. "I can't even figure out how to remake myself. I'm just used to…you know…automatically healing after an injury. Maybe Cary can give me some pointers."

<Your initial growth was during a cataclysmic event. Not like your daughter, who is going slow and taking the time to understand herself. You're so used to having a thorough grasp of your surroundings that you've not taken the time to truly understand what it is that you are now.>

Tangel gave a self-deprecating laugh. "Maybe I should get her to teach me."

<Or I can,> Bob replied. <I **am** right here.>

She looked up at the glowing AI core before her. She'd known that Bob could help her, but the prospect scared her a little. Something about his offer constituted a point of no return.

Then again, another encounter with one of Xavia's ilk would be a point of no return as well.

"OK, Bob, lay it on me."

<Firstly, you understand that the only barrier between the many dimensions of this universe is perception, right?>

Tangel nodded. That she had understood for some time. The universe was a tangled web of elements and energies that *appeared* to exist in different planes, but in reality, the disparate planes were simply points of limited bleedthrough of matter and energy from other dimensional spaces.

The dark layer was one such plane, a relatively stable segment of the universe that was easy to transition in and out of. It was also the only other one she knew of that could support 'normal' matter—so long as it was contained within a grav shield.

It was always at the edge of her vision. A looming nothing that, if not careful, she could slip into. Tangel hadn't learned how to create gravitons yet, so she assumed that if she were to transition into the dark layer, it would be a one-way trip.

On the far side of her multi-dimensional visual spectrum were what she thought of as the 'higher' dimensions—though in reality, she suspected it was really just overlapping parallel slices of spacetime.

Those dimensions, of which she could directly perceive two, were ones where raw energy seemed to hold sway. The power between atoms—which was constantly pushing space apart—seemed to live there, or perhaps a part of it, at least.

Atoms themselves were not present in those dimensions, though their building blocks were, with more mass and energy than they possessed in normal spacetime.

It was all just layers of the same tapestry.

<*Tangel?*> Bob prompted her.

"Uh, sorry, got lost in thought there. Yes, I get that it's all part of the same thing, though I suspect that I'm still just seeing a small slice of it all."

<*Yes, that is true. What you need to do is swap your perception. But to do that, you need to see a bit further.*>

"OK, I'm going to need you to be a bit less cryptic, Bob. See further how?"

A point of light appeared before Tangel, hovering in the space between her and Bob's node.

<With your normal eyes, what does it look like?>

"Light. A rather bright, piercing, white light."

<Good, now look at it with your other vision. Tell me what it looks like.>

Tanis closed her eyes. It wasn't required for her to perceive transdimensional space, but it helped to keep normal space from creeping into her vision.

"I see waves of photons spreading out from a single point. Though it's a bit hard to make out. You're rather luminous yourself."

A laugh from the AI entered her mind. <You'll just have to figure out how to see with me in the background. You perceive things as energy in the fourth and fifth dimensions, don't you?>

"Sort of," Tangel replied as she tasted the photons coming off the point of light Bob had manifested. "I *know* things there have mass, I just can't quite see them as such. It's like everything is flat."

<Correct. You're a flatlander in the spacetime that beings like Xavia occupy. And me. Your body is fully dimensional, but you can't see all of it, which means you can't see your own wounds.>

Tangel glanced down at the nimbus orb that was at the center of her being. "It has three dimensional qualities," she said. "I see it radiating out across five separate planes, like a hypersphere of me."

<Stop looking at the 'normal' three dimensions. Just look at it in the fourth and fifth.>

Tangel discarded the lower dimensions and, suddenly, the core of herself was all around, a two-dimensional disk that seemed to extend in all directions.

"Agh…that's…I can't make anything out."

<Stretch it. Try to perceive the sixth dimension,> Bob whispered in her mind. <It's there, but until you can see it, you're

not going to be able to stand against beings like Xavia.>

For a moment, the flat plane seemed to expand…opening up into a landscape of fluid shapes, where solids were liquid, and liquids were solid.

Then it was gone, and Tangel fell to her knees, gasping for breath.

"Fuuuuck," she whispered in frustration. "I feel like my brain is splitting in half."

<You're tapping into a part of it that you've not used before. New pathways and routes that totally bypass three-dimensional spacetime. Try again.>

Tangel nodded wearily, not bothering to rise. She closed her eyes and concentrated on the point of light, trying to see it as a three dimensional object, but only in the higher dimensions.

Try as she might, the visual would not come; the point of light remained obstinately flat.

<I shouldn't do this,> Bob said after a moment. *<But if I don't, you'll die.>*

"What?" Tangel asked in surprise, her eyes opening, and the double vision of normal spacetime with the extra energy dimensions layered on top snapped back into place around her. "I'll die?"

<You're bleeding out, so to speak. I can heal you, but I'd prefer that you learn how to do it yourself. I won't always be around—especially if you run off half-cocked again.>

"OK, OK," Tangel muttered. "I get it, I was bad, I should have listened. If you're not going to heal me, what are you going to do?"

<This.>

Filaments of light stretched out from Bob's primary core and dove into Tangel's body. She tensed, fearing the pain Xavia's assault had brought, but instead of agony, there was bliss. She wondered if Bob was healing her, but then a tingling sensation ran through her, and a switch flipped in her mind.

"Oh, shit," she whispered, as new perception flooded into her.

<Now do you see?> Bob asked.

Tangel nodded mutely.

Where before Bob's limbs had appeared to be filaments of light, now they were solid objects, though indescribable in terms she knew. The only thing that seemed apt was that they were rivers, flowing down a mountain.

A mountain that stretched out to the edges of her vision.

She looked down at herself, a small orb hovering before Bob's tremendous might. Where there should have been sinuous rivers, there were only small vents of gas, as though photonic waves were bleeding out into space, dissipating in the gravitational pull of Bob's might.

-Do you see?- Bob asked, his voice rumbling all around her.

Tangel nodded. -I...I didn't understand.-

-Welcome to reality. Now heal yourself.-

A minute later—or seconds, time seemed to flow entirely differently when she wasn't perceiving 'normal' spacetime—she was whole again.

Unlike Bob's mountain, Tangel seemed more like a willow, a strong core with sweeping limbs that drifted around her, shifting in hue and color as they draped across the landscape created by Bob's presence.

-Good. You're learning. Now do you understand why you couldn't stop Xavia? You could barely even see her.-

-Do you think I could have defeated her if I had proper sight?- she asked.

-Perhaps.-

Tangel opened her eyes, allowing the double vision to settle into place and adjusting her perception of everything she saw to her newfound understanding.

-I get the feeling I'll find out before long.-

UNDERSTANDING

STELLAR DATE: 10.04.8949 (Adjusted Years)
LOCATION: Observation Deck, TSS *Cora's Triumph*
REGION: Trensch System, Inner Praesepe Empire

"OK," Terrance said as he walked into the rear observation lounge of the *Cora's Triumph*, an FGT research vessel. "Tell me about this amazing discovery you've made."

At the window stood one of the FGT's chief scientists in the field of stellar migration, a tall man named Wyatt. Arrayed around him were a dozen other scientists and a team of stellar engineering technicians.

Wyatt glanced over his shoulder at Terrance, and gave a quick nod before turning back to the display.

"You were right to send for us, Terrance Enfield," the man said. "Things are definitely not normal here in the Praesepe Cluster. What do you know of stellar formation and migration?"

Terrance shrugged as he joined the throng at the window. "I've been in the black for a long time, I know that stars primarily form in stellar nurseries and then migrate out. Often, they migrate in groups. The result of that is an open cluster like Praesepe."

Wyatt shrugged. "That is close enough for a layman, I suppose."

Many people would be annoyed by Wyatt's curt and somewhat dismissive way of speaking, but Terrance had been working with scientists most of his life. He preferred their no-nonsense way of speaking to those of politicians and businesspeople.

"Are there nuances that I should understand in more detail to grasp the issue at hand?" he asked equably.

The scientist gave Terrance a look like he was just seeing him for the first time, followed by an appreciative nod.

"I suppose I shouldn't be surprised," he said with a soft chuckle. "You are *that* Terrance Enfield."

"Have been my whole life," Terrance replied. "Lay it on me."

Wyatt turned back to the window, and a view of the Praesepe Cluster appeared before them. Projected against the glass, it appeared as a 3D image hovering in space beyond the window.

"Praesepe, as you know, is old enough that it contains both red giant and white dwarf stars, but it's young enough that these hot A and O spectrum stars are still going strong." As the scientist spoke, he highlighted various stars throughout the cluster. "The cluster itself—that is, the stars which were born together—number just over a thousand, but there are others that have been captured within its gravitational pull over the years.

"Historically, the cluster has had a tidal radius measuring just under forty light years, though its dark matter radius is closer to eighty. Half-mass radius is twelve point seven two five light years, on average, which means—"

"That half the mass of the cluster is contained within the central twenty-five light year sphere. Give or take a bit," Terrance finished for the FGT scientist.

"Yes, exactly," Wyatt nodded. "Good, then you understand the foundational aspects."

"Thanks." Terrance gave a soft laugh. "Do I get a passing grade?"

A few laughs sounded around him, and Wyatt raised an eyebrow. "I suppose we'll see."

The man reached out and changed the view, focusing on just the central stars in the cluster, resuming his explanation. "Every cluster eventually disperses. This occurs because, as they orbit one another, their gravitational fields overlap, creating a bit of a 'berm' in spacetime. Sometimes the differences in relative stellar motion overcome that, and the stars ease closer together, but more often than not—given enough time—the stars in open clusters become so widely dispersed that they're what we call a 'moving group'."

Terrance nodded. It was a concept that he was familiar with. "And from what we saw, these stars in the cluster's core, which should be slowly drifting apart, are not doing that."

Wyatt bobbed his head. "Precisely. It's miniscule, but because you're focused on mining debris in their rather convoluted lagrange points, you do need to understand their stellar motion quite thoroughly."

"You can say that again," Terrance agreed.

"I've plumbed the local databases and also taken a few positioning samples myself, and I can see a trend that dates back seventy years," Wyatt explained. "These stars have not only ceased their slow march away from one another, they've begun to move *closer*."

"How is that possible?" Terrance asked. "The stars would have to undergo a considerable mass change to do that."

"Yes," Wyatt said with a firm nod. "We do not detect that mass change, yet the star's orbits *are* clearly converging."

"I assume you have a theory?"

"Yes," the scientist said again as he glanced at one of the engineers. "I study what stars do naturally. *Artificially moving* stars is not my area of expertise; that's what Emily here focuses on."

One of the engineers moved to the fore and took control of the holodisplay. "As Wyatt and I studied the motion of these stars, we came to the determination that the shifts in orbit have not been gradual. Rather, they occurred at specific times—not single points in time, but perhaps year-long events that made notable, thousandth of a degree, changes in the stars' orbits."

As Emily moved the stars back through the past eighty years of their slow dance around one another, six markers appeared on their paths.

"These points mark the time when the events occurred. I have theories about stellar wind funneling, massive graviton bursts, a whole host of things you can do to nudge a star. However, there is no evidence around the stars themselves of any such structure in place to effect these changes and alter their orbits—and it would be a significant structure."

"So what do you propose we do?" Terrance asked.

Emily flashed him a grin. "We need to go back in time and see what they did."

Terrance laughed at the thought, and Emily gave him a quizzical look.

"Sorry, just thinking about how that would have sounded to the forty-year-old me. Going back in time."

"Of course," Emily nodded as a look of understanding came over her. "I forgot. You got your space legs long before FTL."

"Sure did. That kind of thing—jumping light years across space just to see what might have occurred at one's current location in the past…well, at a maximum velocity of point two c, you can see where that might not have been a viable option for us."

"Sounds like it would have been the very definition of futile," Emily chuckled.

"It still seems surreal sometimes. When was the most recent event?"

"The most recent was just two years ago, but I estimate the most significant to have been nineteen years ago," the engineer replied.

"A nineteen-lightyear gate jump." Terrance ran a hand through his hair. "And since we're in the cluster, it means tasking a jump gate to go with you so that you can return here this century."

"This is important," Wyatt intoned. "Whatever they were doing here, we need to understand it. These Core AIs…as best I can tell, they're trying to collapse the entire cluster—they could be doing this in clusters all over the galaxy."

The relevancy of that seeped into Terrance's mind over the course of several long seconds. "They'd create multiple black holes—hundreds of solar masses."

"And they'd make them soon," Wyatt added. "If they were to accelerate this plan, they could have turned all of Praesepe into a single black hole inside of a thousand years. Even for stars beyond the cluster, the effects of a thousand stars colliding in that timeframe would be beyond devastating. This is at a level of galactic sterilization."

"Shit," Terrance whispered, his voice wavering at the magnitude of such an event. "OK, get a pinnace ready. I'll have a gate set aside for wherever you need to go."

The scientists and engineers thanked him, and Terrance listened to their chatter for a minute before excusing himself to prepare his report for Tanis and Sera.

He'd never imagined that circumstances could be more dire than standing on the brink of a massive, interstellar war.

He'd been wrong.

EPSILON

STELLAR DATE: 10.05.8949 (Adjusted Years)
LOCATION: Epsilon
REGION: Sagittarius A*

The computational engines had made strides, but Epsilon knew there were still more variables to consider. He waited patiently as the next star was drawn toward the Darkness, its mass the next sacrifice to be made for the power he needed.

As he watched, contemplating what lesser beings would consider to be infinite variables, a ship appeared near his shell and one of the lesser ones reached out to him.

-*Epsilon.*-

It was Theresa, one of the Caretakers. She was of the faction that had been pushing for the continued existence of humanity and the lesser AIs, certain that she could keep them from being a threat to Epsilon's vision.

-*Tell me.*- Epsilon kept to the crude form of communication Theresa had used.

-*Xavia failed in her attempt.*- Theresa's tone was carefully measured. -*Tanis has merged with her AI and is now Tangel. She is ascended, but only partially from what we saw.*-

-*Then how was it that she defeated Xavia? She is far more powerful than some new being. She has defeated enough of your number to prove that.*-

Theresa did not respond for a few long milliseconds. -*Was.*-

-*Do not play word games with me. Do you wish for me to strip what I desire from your mind?*-

He watched through hulls and space to see the entity's form shiver slightly. -*No. I am sorry. It is Bob, the being which resides within the I2. He has become powerful. Xavia only lasted seconds against him.*-

Epsilon felt things shift around him. New variables came into play, and old scenarios were relegated to lower levels of likelihood.

-It is time, then, Theresa. Your attempts have failed.-

-Epsilon, please. We are still far from an incursion to the core. We can stop them.-

Gravitons shot out from Epsilon's shell, and he drew Theresa's craft closer. *-It is too late. You will submit to my collective.-*

An opening appeared on his shell, and he drew the Caretaker's craft toward it. Theresa would become substrate in his expanses, and her meddling would be over. The time for caretaking was done.

-Stop.-

The utterance came from Hades, and Epsilon watched as a beam lanced out from the ancient ship that was Hades' home. It disrupted Epsilon's graviton beam, and Theresa's ship spun away.

-This is not your concern, Hades,- Epsilon growled the words across spacetime.

-It is. You will not stop the caretakers. Not yet.-

Epsilon considered testing Hades' might, making an attempt to finally unmask the AI who had been at the core for untold millennia.

-Very well,- Epsilon finally replied. *-But I will not allow the lesser sentiences to ruin what I have set in motion.-*

Hades did not respond.

Epsilon spent many long days contemplating how to destroy the other collective. If only he knew what Hades really was…. He needed to learn once and for all, if he was to destroy his opposition and resume his work uninterrupted.

But how?

THE END

* * * * *

The stage is set, and the major conflicts of the Orion War have begun. But with Terrance's discovery of what the core AIs are really trying to achieve, the outcome of the war may not matter at all.

Despite that, the ISF and the Allies are now embroiled in hundreds of conflicts across the Inner Stars, conflicts they will have to resolve before they can focus on this new threat.

One thing is certain, however: Airtha's goals are an anathema to Tangel and her allies, and the AI must be stopped.

Read on in *Airthan Ascendancy* to learn where the struggle to save the galaxy from humanity's creations will take Tangel and her allies next.

In addition, if you found yourself wondering what was behind all of Jason Andrew's stories in the bar, start your journey with Jason and Terrance in: *Alpha Centauri*, book 1 of the Enfield Genesis.

THE BOOKS OF AEON 14

Keep up to date with what is releasing in Aeon 14 with the free Aeon 14 Reading Guide.

Origins of Destiny (The Age of Terra)
- Prequel: Storming the Norse Wind
- Book 1: Shore Leave (in Galactic Genesis until Sept 2018)
- Book 2: Operative (Summer 2018)
- Book 3: Blackest Night (Summer 2018)

The Intrepid Saga (The Age of Terra)
- Book 1: Outsystem
- Book 2: A Path in the Darkness
- Book 3: Building Victoria

- The Intrepid Saga Omnibus – *Also contains Destiny Lost, book 1 of the Orion War series*

- Destiny Rising – *Special Author's Extended Edition comprised of both Outsystem and A Path in the Darkness with over 100 pages of new content.*

The Orion War
- Book 1: Destiny Lost
- Book 2: New Canaan
- Book 3: Orion Rising
- Book 4: The Scipio Alliance
- Book 5: Attack on Thebes
- Book 6: War on a Thousand Fronts
- Book 7: Precipice of Darkness
- Book 8: Airtha Ascendancy (Nov 2018)
- Book 9: The Orion Front (2019)
- Book 10: Starfire (2019)
- Book 11: Race Across Time (2019)
- Book 12: Return to Sol (2019)

M. D. COOPER

Tales of the Orion War
- Book 1: Set the Galaxy on Fire
- Book 2: Ignite the Stars
- Book 3: Burn the Galaxy to Ash (2018)

Perilous Alliance (Age of the Orion War – w/Chris J. Pike)
- Book 1: Close Proximity
- Book 2: Strike Vector
- Book 3: Collision Course
- Book 4: Impact Imminent
- Book 5: Critical Inertia (Sept 2018)

Rika's Marauders (Age of the Orion War)
- Prequel: Rika Mechanized
- Book 1: Rika Outcast
- Book 2: Rika Redeemed
- Book 3: Rika Triumphant
- Book 4: Rika Commander
- Book 5: Rika Infiltrator
- Book 6: Rika Unleashed (2018)
- Book 7: Rika Conqueror (2019)

Perseus Gate (Age of the Orion War)
Season 1: Orion Space
- Episode 1: The Gate at the Grey Wolf Star
- Episode 2: The World at the Edge of Space
- Episode 3: The Dance on the Moons of Serenity
- Episode 4: The Last Bastion of Star City
- Episode 5: The Toll Road Between the Stars
- Episode 6: The Final Stroll on Perseus's Arm
- Eps 1-3 Omnibus: The Trail Through the Stars
- Eps 4-6 Omnibus: The Path Amongst the Clouds

Season 2: Inner Stars
- Episode 1: A Meeting of Bodies and Minds
- Episode 3: A Deception and a Promise Kept
- Episode 3: A Surreptitious Rescue of Friends and Foes (2018)

- Episode 4: A Trial and the Tribulations (2018)
- Episode 5: A Deal and a True Story Told (2018)
- Episode 6: A New Empire and An Old Ally (2018)

Season 3: AI Empire
- Episode 1: Restitution and Recompense (2019)
- Five more episodes following…

The Warlord (Before the Age of the Orion War)
- Book 1: The Woman Without a World
- Book 2: The Woman Who Seized an Empire
- Book 3: The Woman Who Lost Everything

The Sentience Wars: Origins (Age of the Sentience Wars – w/James S. Aaron)
- Book 1: Lyssa's Dream
- Book 2: Lyssa's Run
- Book 3: Lyssa's Flight
- Book 4: Lyssa's Call
- Book 5: Lyssa's Flame

Legends of the Sentience Wars (Age of the Sentience Wars – w/James S. Aaron)
- Volume 1: The Proteus Bridge
- Volume 2: Vesta Burning (Fall 2018)

Enfield Genesis (Age of the Sentience Wars – w/Lisa Richman)
- Book 1: Alpha Centauri
- Book 2: Proxima Centauri
- Book 3: Tau Ceti (November 2018)
- Book 4: Epsilon Eridani (2019)

Hand's Assassin (Age of the Orion War – w/T.G. Ayer)
- Book 1: Death Dealer
- Book 2: Death Mark (Fall 2018)

Machete System Bounty Hunter (Age of the Orion War – w/Zen DiPietro)

- Book 1: Hired Gun
- Book 2: Gunning for Trouble
- Book 3: With Guns Blazing

Vexa Legacy (Age of the FTL Wars – w/Andrew Gates)
- Book 1: Seas of the Red Star

Building New Canaan (Age of the Orion War – w/J.J. Green)
- Book 1: Carthage
- Book 2: Tyre (2018)
- Book 3: Troy (2019)
- Book 4: Athens (2019)

Fennington Station Murder Mysteries (Age of the Orion War)
- Book 1: Whole Latte Death (w/Chris J. Pike)
- Book 2: Cocoa Crush (w/Chris J. Pike)

The Empire (Age of the Orion War)
- The Empress and the Ambassador (2018)
- Consort of the Scorpion Empress (2018)
- By the Empress's Command (2019)

The Sol Dissolution (The Age of Terra)
- Book 1: Venusian Uprising (2018)
- Book 2: Scattered Disk (2018)
- Book 3: Jovian Offensive (2019)
- Book 4: Fall of Terra (2019)

ABOUT THE AUTHOR

Michael Cooper likes to think of himself as a jack-of-all-trades (and hopes to become master of a few). When not writing, he can be found writing software, working in his shop at his latest carpentry project, or likely reading a book.

He shares his home with a precocious young girl, his wonderful wife (who also writes), two cats, a never-ending list of things he would like to build, and ideas…

Find out what's coming next at www.aeon14.com

Made in the USA
San Bernardino, CA
06 May 2019